*W*hen Bone Melts

Elise Keitz Harlow

Copyright © 2024 by Elise Keitz Harlow
No part of this book may be reproduced or transmitted in any form
or by means, electronic or mechanical, including photocopying,
recording, or by any information storage and retrieval system,
without the written permission of the copyright owner, except
where permitted by law.

Part 1

January 1893
Suna, Piedmont, Italy

1
Pasquale

"One of?" My brothers chorused.
"You have daughters? How many?" I asked our father.
"Two still living," Pim answered. He had accidentally revealed that today was the anniversary of his daughter's passing.

He rarely talked about the life he abandoned in Smolnek; when he did, it was mostly in allusions. Marinovas governed Smolnek since the rise of the Romanov dynasty. Waiting for his stories to emerge was the only way to hear them; there were no formulaic triggers. He might look at the spine of a book I read and explain his not-so-distant relation to the author. He connected people to cities, battles, and whole eras in foreign lands. His world held history and complexities but no unknowns.

After the night Pim displaced me as his eldest child, my brothers and I constantly searched for opportunities to learn about our half-sisters and his ex-wife, Varvara. If we managed to bend the conversation at dinner to his first family, Mother would leave the room. Our questions had to be strategically rationed. Any information obtained became part of a carefully excavated collection. Varvara was a second cousin of Maria Feodorovna, wife of Tsar Paul I. Pim left Varvara for an American singer pregnant with his lovechild, cloaked in disgrace. Pim took Mother to live in northern Italy to build a family in a warmer clime on Lake Maggiore. We learned that the divorce took years to conclude. This took months to learn. We still did not know our half-sisters' names.

In the final weeks of autumn, Pim received a letter from Varvara sharing the first family's tumultuous past year. Varvara had been bedridden with cancer of the stomach for ten months. Their older daughter, Tatiana, married a year ago, and only last month did she give birth to her own daughter. The younger daughter's fiancé died at some point during the year, and the girl's mourning put off potential suitors. As Tatiana was preoccupied with wifedom, motherhood, and caretaking for an ailing mother-in-law besides Varvara, there was no one to champion their younger daughter's future. She was not living the life of a princess of the House of Marinova. Varvara wrote that by receiving Anastasia, Pim could reignite that which was currently dimming.

The letter sat on his desk for a few days.

※

"Mary!" Pim called inside when the enclosed, worn-down carriage was swaying in more ways than left to right up the gravel driveway. Mother emerged from the villa.

When the carriage came to a stop, my brothers and I straightened our spines as Pim walked up to open the door. As he reached for the handle, the door burst open for the back of a heeled foot, searching for the narrow step. Pim's hand hovered at her back without touching her.

When she turned, I realized I had imagined that she would resemble my brothers. But instead, she was beautiful, unparalleled. She wore a black cossack hat with a thick fur trim, though the rest of her clothes were the red of cascading pinot noir before it built and darkened in the glass. Under the hat, she had tousled long, reddish-brown hair. Her round, swan-feather pale face held a petite feminine nose, not resembling the Marinova nose at all. Her large brown eyes made me feel close to her already. They sang of a perceptive intelligence and a warm approachability.

Pim must have experienced a similar shock because he kissed her winter-pink cheek after a moment of staring.

"Anastasia."

Then he hugged her tightly. She looked younger in his grip. He spoke in Russian to her. I could make out only part of his words, *I've wanted to meet you*, though my translation must be mistaken as they had met before. Her large eyes became teary.

"This is your family," he said in English as he turned toward us. "My wife, Signora Mary Marinova." Mother nodded without any attempt to embrace Anastasia. Anastasia reached for Mother's stiff hands, which were offered reluctantly.

"It is a pleasure to meet you. Thank you for welcoming me," Anastasia said in English. Pim must have written to inform her that English was our home's primary language, a longstanding rule to accommodate my mother.

Mother tilted her head a few degrees as if she had agreed to invite Anastasia.

"This is my son, your brother, Pasquale," Pim gestured. Anastasia smiled cordially. I kissed her cheek lightly. Is that how one greets their sister?

"And these are your brothers, Enzo, and our youngest, Luca." They both followed my lead and kissed her on the cheek. Enzo looked at her skeptically. Luca, only thirteen, beamed.

"Thank you for welcoming me," she repeated.

"You speak English well," Pim complimented her.

"Thank you. My brother-by-marriage works at the British consulate. We practice English for dinner."

"I can speak a little Russian if you would prefer," I offered to show her I was connected to my heritage.

"I appreciate that," she responded kindly.

The steam from her breath, compounded by her crimson coat, gave an impression of innate heat. She was leisurely in the cold while even Pim shifted like he would prefer to transition the party inside.

Anastasia took a few steps back to Mother. "What should I call you, Signora Mary?"

"Signora Mary is fine. What should we call you? Do you have a nickname?"

"No, you may call me what you like."

Our father smiled and moved to bring her trunks to her bedroom. Enzo and Luca leaped to assist him. I felt rooted to serve as the guardian of this interaction.

"I will call you Ana, for short," Mother said once Pim was out of earshot.

Anastasia smiled from the heart. My jaw buckled. Enzo and Luca, preoccupied with each taking a leather handle of the same trunk, failed to notice Mother's pronunciation.

"We'll give you a tour, Anastasia!" Luca offered over his shoulder.

Anastasia followed them inside as Mother smirked at me, knowing that she pronounced Ana too closely to *ano*, which, in Italian, means anus.

2
Enzo

After exhausting my knowledge of various furniture and art pieces' origins in addition to the architectural details of the house for Anastasia, Mother volunteered me to show Anastasia her bedroom. Pasquale returned to his studio. Pim had discontinued the tour at his study to remain there. The guest room was not as large as ours but had a washroom and one large window overlooking the lake. The room held a cherrywood armoire, a double bed, a small bedside table, and two antique brittle chairs. The quilt, pillow covers, and drapes were blue, so we called it the Blue Room.

"Wow," she said as she swept the drapes and light sheer aside.

Her trunks were neatly on the floor, smallest to largest. They were not expensive nor well worn.

"How long do you intend to stay with us?"

"I don't know. Did Papa not say?" She sat in one of the two small woven chairs and gestured for me to sit in the other.

"Pim only told us a few weeks ago that you were coming."

"You call him 'Pim.' Is that American for Papa?"

"No, it's his initials P.I.M., Petyr Ivanov Marinova. It was Pasquale's first word and what he called him. It stuck."

"Do you have any interests, Enzo?"

"I study classical texts. I am studying the correspondence between Saint Jerome and Pope Damasus I. I study language through translations. Most of my time outside the library is spent in museums or churches in neighboring towns and Milano and Torino."

Her posture wilted with the day's drain, though her attention was locked on me. It was a natural charm I had seen Pasquale expertly wield. I found it unnerving.

"Luca is a budding outdoorsman. He swims, fishes, bikes. His favorite pastime is shooting. He's an excellent shot. Luca's been shooting since he was six when Pim gave him a Winchester M1887. The second-floor terrace is his outpost."

"Maybe I could watch him shoot one day."

She stood up, tipped over the enormous trunk with her foot, and started unpacking.

"It's all red!"

"Yes," she laughed, pulling items from the trunk and laying them on the bed. "Red is my favorite color."

"Isn't it a little…" I wanted to say *provocative*, but that was unsuitable language in a woman's company. "Aggressive?"

"Only sometimes. Red is the Russian color. It is a feeling as much as a color."

The red dress she held undulated with her gestures.

"And it goes best with my hair," she laughed.

"Well, I will leave you to unpack. Dinner is at eight o'clock in the dining room."

In my room, I lay on top of the bed, with my socks and leather shoes still laced, and stared at the rosette ceiling molding, musing on how far I could translate the concept of red.

3
Luca

At some point in the afternoon, I fell into a deep, paralyzing nap. I woke to Mama calling me to dinner from the hallway. I threw on a clean dress shirt, tucked it into my brown pants, and leaped down the curved staircase, only glancing at four of the stairs on the way. Everyone was already seated. I slid into the empty seat between Enzo and Mama. The crystal chandelier's twinkling candles gave the ceiling a fluid, underwater likeness.

"My apologies."

Pim grabbed a large bread roll and spooned the ragù Bolognese onto his plate. Each table member followed suit, except Pasquale, who had a special vegetarian version of the sauce already placed at his seat by Mrs. Figlia.

"Enzo said that you have extraordinary gardens here," Anastasia said, her gaze gliding around from Pim to each of us and landing on Pasquale.

"Yes," Pasquale answered. "This is the worst time of year for it, but you'll enjoy it in a few months. There has been more frost this winter than usual."

"Is frost bad for the plants?"

"Not necessarily; it depends on the species," Pasquale answered. "Some blooms have abnormalities and emerge discolored. Peonies may come out orange. Grapes will look a little bluish and produce sweeter wine. Those kinds of things. If there is too much frost, though, then some vines may die."

"I don't know the terms for different flowers," Anastasia smiled. "I'll have to see them to learn."

"I will show you every type of flower, citrus fruit, and tree on the property when they renew with life," Pasquale promised her.

Mama forcibly handed me the bowl of potatoes. She took forgetting the food for conversation as an insult, whether she was the one who cooked it or not. I willed myself to remember to tell Anastasia later that in Italian culture, people begin eating once the food is served so as not to let it go cold.

"I will tour you around the gardens myself, Anastasia," Pim said as he soaked his bread in the sauce. "We have more than 1,100 plant species on the estate with 8,300 plant varieties, so I am not sure showing every single one is feasible. It took thirteen years of work with landscapers and botanists specializing in Italian agriculture, exotic species, and hybrid seed experimentation. It has been a huge success. Travelers come from all over the world to see the garden. Taking the time to construct the gardens carefully was the key."

"Hard work is the noblest road to achievement."

"Thank you, Anastasia." Pim nodded, accepting her compliment.

"Pim had to cut down hundreds of trees on the property to make space for the endeavor." Enzo shared.

She nodded politely before glancing at Pasquale's plate.

"Pasquale doesn't eat meat!" Enzo admonished Anastasia. He did not intend to embarrass her, but she couldn't yet know that Enzo bluntly verbalized his observations.

"Everything in moderation," Pim repeated this line every time the subject of Pasquale's vegetarianism emerged. Pasquale's refusal to eat meat often exposed him to criticism or debate.

"Moderation is boring," Anastasia whispered to Pasquale.

"Pim, would you open the Barolo?" Mama asked.

"You are a sculptor." She said to Pasquale. Not a question; a confirmation.

"Yes, since I was young. But only recently have I had steady work."

"That's very impressive. Do you do full sculptures or busts?"

"Both. Still life busts are where I've dedicated most of my time lately. I apprenticed at the Brera Academy in Milan."

"Pasquale is a true wonder," Mama said, looking fondly at him. "Leo Tolstoy commissioned Pasq. I'm sure you know him. He had two plaster sculptures purchased by the National Gallery of Modern Art in Rome. Pasq also spent a month in Athens last summer, creating a bust of Queen Sofia of Greece. Queen Sofia personally sent Pim and me a letter saying how pleased she was with the result, how it is a fixture in her husband's office and complimented by everyone who sees it."

Anastasia lengthened her nods at each name in proportion to Mama's emphasis.

"Mostly, I get paid by minor royalty and rich foreigners to fill their large homes."

"But you're only nineteen!" Anastasia exclaimed.

"I have been fortunate to apprentice under two very talented sculptors."

"Don't believe him," Pim contradicted Pasquale. "It's natural-born talent. He hated his studies. I arranged for him to learn from Barcaglia, and he complained for months in his letters that he was spending most of his time as an observer. He only lasted five months before I moved him to his second apprenticeship. He found the pace inadequate there and returned to Suna. However, after Bazzaro, you improved significantly. That time ironed out the folds in your work no matter how bored you were. He works out of his studio here now."

"I'll show you my workroom tomorrow, Anastasia."

"Fantastic!"

"Anastasia," I started, horrified to hear my voice crack on the final vowel. "When the weather improves, I can take you on our rowboat to Pallanza for gelato."

"I look forward to that, Luca."

"Can I call you Stasi?" I asked.

"Yes, of course," she said earnestly. "That fits my new Italian life."

"I will continue calling you Ana," Mama added as she took her last bite. Pasquale shot a brief look at her.

"I will use your full name." Pim declared. "Anastasia was my favorite grandmother's name. It is an important name in our family."

At that moment, the wooden legs of Mama's chair screeched on the hardwood floor as it forcibly slid a few inches past the rug.

"I'm quite tired, as I'm sure Ana is too," Mama said. "I think it's time we all retire." She looked directly at me. "Come, Luca. Walk me up the stairs. Goodnight, everyone."

I held in my urge to resist her command. *Why me?* I nodded goodnight to the table. As I reached the hallway, I heard Pasquale say, "Tomorrow, Stasi."

4
Pasquale

I dressed in the near-dark as the periwinkle sky adjusted to dawn. The mountains to the east detained the light from touching the lake; the light only kissed the shores of our home in Suna once it rose high over the eastern mountains.

Looking at myself in the mirror above the washbasin, I smoothed my blondish-brown hair. I had been whisking it from my amber eyes for days now. The length distracted from my long nose, though it would have to be cut before the next time someone sat for me. My studio clothing consisted of black pants and a white long-sleeved shirt tailored to be loose.

Luca fires his M1887 from our shared terrace at exactly eight every morning. This morning, the sound of the piercing blast prompted a terrified scream that echoed through the house. The cold air and marble floors permitted the sound to travel without obstruction.

"Are you alright?" I called in against Stasi's bedroom door. She opened the door in her red nightgown.

"Did Luca wake you?" I took a step back from the wide doorway.

"Yes, sorry to be loud," Stasi said in the stupor of one deep in sleep seconds ago. "I hope I did not wake you."

"I was already awake. Luca does this every morning, I'm afraid. Mother decreed that he couldn't shoot any earlier than 8 a.m. Thus, he fires a shot at exactly then every morning. It has become the family wake-up call."

She nodded, dazed. Her loose curls fell to her waist. Her eyes rested on me before they flickered to take in the moment. Her hands softly touched her clavicle as she reached for a proper robe in the armoire, which quickly enveloped her body without obscuring her shape.

"Breakfast is in the dining room." I fumbled, stepping backward into the hallway even further. "I'll show you my workroom this morning if you would still like to see it."

"Yes, that would be great. I will join you soon," she said, climbing back into bed. I leaned in to close the door.

The staircase wrapped the wall of the grand foyer in a crescent-moon shape. A small, circular stained-glass window sat high above the villa entry, portraying a ship braving jagged waves. The little artistic window was never brightly illuminated because it faced the mountain. Our dining room table was perpendicular to the large window, so each head of the table had a view of the lake. At breakfast, I took Pim's dinner seat. Pim's custom was to skip breakfast and walk through the gardens in any weather. Then he began the day from his office, where our cook, Mrs. Figlia, brought him a tray.

Enzo was already seated and filling up, the member of the family who most delighted in the morning meal. Though he was precisely mannered, his chewing in the morning was without pause, as his gaze was invariably consumed in some book, scribbling notes in the margins, his coffee splashing on the pages, and crumbs sinking into the page folds. He never greets me.

Mrs. Figlia sets out a five-part spread, tea, coffee, and an in-season juice every weekday morning. Today was pear juice. *Il Sole* was folded neatly beside my monogrammed napkin. I perused the headlines and ate half of a cinnamon pastry with blackberry jam. There was a small basket of fresh kiwi beside the half dozen pastries. Kiwi was sold by the crate in the winter months. I read half of one article and skimmed part of another. Luca scrambled in and made a brisk circle around the table, placing an apple in the crook of his elbow, putting an entire quiche in his mouth, and then squeezing two pastries in one hand. He nodded to me and left for school.

I put the paper aside and cut four kiwis in half. Holding a half in my domed fingers, I slip my little coffee-stirring spoon under the scratchy skin and along the fruit's flesh until I can slide the skin loose and eat the fruit in two bites. The iterative process keeps my hands busy as I stare over the lake. This morning, the low cloud cover gave the lake the illusion of extending forever into the abyss.

I started to remember all the facets of the mess in my studio. It was mostly full of mistaken works I could not sell. The only completed novelties I kept there were unorganized sketches, which were unimpressive. It was too late to clean now. Stasi could be down at any moment, and I could not make her wait or lead her to suspect I had forgotten her.

Enzo's eyes swept the lines of his book, racing his hand, wedging in a bookmark horizontally from the book's center. He slammed the book shut and left the dining room without a word.

I found myself subject to the schedule of another, with kiwi juice streaming down my hand to my wrist. Not typically an idle person, I felt uncomfortable watching the little motions of the room breathing: the swaying golden chime of the seven-foot grandfather clock, steam rising without interruption from the teapot's spout, the changeling clouds revealing Stresa across the lake. I read and reread newspaper passages. My tongue was scraped raw from the kiwi seeds.

Then – the sound of delicate footfalls descending the stairs. I adjust my posture and lock my gaze on the newspaper. She wore a long, bright red dress that fell slightly above the floor. It cut at her decolletage like three sides of a box. Her hair was half-up, lifted, and pinned at the level of her cheekbones.

"Hello again," she smiled. Her thick crimson coat was draped over her arm. When I looked at it, she said unsurely, "Your studio is outside the house, yes?"

"It is." I nodded three times. "But would you like to have breakfast first?"

"I don't think so," she eyed the kiwi skeptically.

"At least take a cup of tea. Mrs. Figlia won't have lunch ready for hours."

A single nod. She took her seat from last night while I went to the kitchen to request Mrs. Figlia prepare something for Anastasia to eat mid-morning. Mrs. Figlia, usually quite kind, neither assented to nor declined the request. Mother must have whimpered to her.

Stasi was staring at the ceiling when I returned, tracing the moldings with her eyes.

"Let's go to your studio. I'm eager to see it."

I helped Stasi into her overcoat. It was as heavy as it looked. She fastened the buttons and pulled on her red gloves as she followed me out the side hallway, past Pim's office.

"The gardens are off over there." I gestured with my right arm to the arched entryway, the most accessible entry point from the villa, as we walked up the mountain that hid the property from the main road.

"In two months, everything will start to come alive again. You'll see. In three months, you will feel like Diana, reveling in the untamed woodland." I smiled, but she stayed quiet, watching her steps along the uneven path. I worried she may not understand the reference. "Do you know the Greek goddess Diana?"

"Yes, my – our – sister is obsessed with mythology. She's shared many of the stories with me. She likes Egyptian mythology best. Though I don't think I quite identify with Diana."

"Really? Which goddess would you be?"

"Which one do you think I would be?"

"I've only known you a day. My guess would be superficial."

"I've known you for a day, and it's obvious. Apollo. You are the golden sun, adored your whole life, and this is all for you." Stasi made a sweeping gesture to the villa and lake behind us, over the gardens. Her tone was kind, but she may have stopped herself from continuing: *all for you, at the expense of....*

The studio key stuck in the rusting knob as my cold fingers unsteadily jerked for the click of the lock. Like yesterday afternoon, she was unbothered by the cold.

"What does that mean?"

"What does what mean?" I turned to look at her. She pointed to the engraved stone at the foot of the door. It read: *Enter into the Eye.*

"Oh, it's English."

"Yes," she caught her laugh. "I know what it says. I'm asking what it means."

"Well...." I hit the door with my shoulder, and it swung open. I gestured for her to enter ahead of me. She picked up the dank stone and brought it with her.

The studio was a large, rectangular room with high windows spanning the entire wall that faced Lake Maggiore, overlooking the gardens and villa through the trees below. There were opened gifts ungratefully still surrounded by their wrappings, as if someone could reenact how they had been opened, on the counter and the unswept floor. The winter light was uninspiring. Everything looked half-abandoned rather than half-accomplished. I went to start a fire for us at the modest fireplace on the wall opposite the door. A faded green rug covered the bulk of the space. Dust pooled in sand dune-esque patterns on the uncovered cement floor beyond the rug's reach. The right side of the room bore long wooden shelves. The dozens of books I failed to shelve properly were piled unintelligibly. The wood for the shelves came from one of the larches cut down to make room for the studio. Pim was conflicted about removing several larches since they were nineteen meters tall and natural to the land; they must have been two hundred years old. The builder insisted that this was the only plausible spot for a level foundation; anywhere else on the hill would have required dynamite. I was eager to complete my first commission, a small perching fox, so Pim consented to felling the larches. Luca, only six then, suggested we incorporate the tree carcasses into my studio as homage.

She looked at everything but touched and said nothing. The shelves were jammed with unbound sketches, leather-bound journals that were used and new, a few flawed busts, paints, chisels, and covered with sparkling blue and violet agate stones. The first time I saw one as a child, I was convinced it was a crystallized form of the lake. It was irresistible to a tactile child. My desk was humble, an antique Pim purchased in Switzerland on a trip over the border. It stood free, floating in the room. Discarded newspapers created a perimeter around the sides of the desk. In the back corner, sixteen imperfect busts were lined up, four by four—originals with unsalvageable mistakes. I kept them with the faith that I would divine an alternative purpose for them later. Closer to the door, there was one bust in progress with the underwiring crudely showing. It sat on a column carved from the rock of the neighboring Dolomite Mountains and custom-measured to bring full-size busts to my eye level. It was the same Piedmont region dolostone used for the *Duomo di Milano*.

Once the fire caught from the sacrifice of two long matches, I moved the desk chair to the hearth and offered her its cushioned seat. She walked over, sat, placed the stone on her lap with the words face-up and the dirt-caked side against her dress, and removed her gloves. I brought over the stool from the workstation.

"Why paint the walls gray?" She asked.

"Only light gray," I shrugged. "White walls drive me crazy, and I couldn't decide between colors."

She nodded and turned the stone in her hands. "And this? Why these words?"

"When I started sculpting in Milan, I had talent but much to learn. I was a teenager, and each time I made a mistake, maybe a lip was too small or eyes too harsh, I would torment myself over how I had taken perfect marble or set plaster and ruined it. I felt like I had a gift for uglifying. Then, one of my creations was purchased. It was a small owl that I had a low opinion of, though the feathers were decent. And, not to be crass, it was purchased for a fair sum. My peers were shocked. When we told our master, who was a quiet man, he looked out into the distance and said, 'Symmetry is objective. Appeal is in the eye of the beholder.'

"Since then, when I make a slight mistake or something doesn't meet my standard, the thought of allure being subjective gives me comfort. Other meanings of 'the eye' emerged and seemed to follow me—all kinds of references. There's one part of the Bible when Jesus says it is easier for a camel to pass through the eye of a needle than for a rich man to enter heaven. I've spent entire nights in here sculpting, not sculpting. Chiseling can flow through me or paralyze me and make me terrified to begin.

"Ultimately..." I rambled but, upon looking at her, felt stupid. "Never mind."

"No, go on, tell me."

"This studio is my safe haven. Where I can see beyond myself. It's the eye of the storm. Whenever I'm here, I have entered into the eye."

"That's a lovely feeling."

We sat in silence for a long minute. When she finally spoke, it was to the fire.

"I don't know if I've ever felt that way about a place. I don't have a haven."

"You can share mine," I smiled at her.

5
Franca Rossi

"Franca, that wasn't the first time we met."

I looked at Luca, confused.

"I was four," he continued. "My brothers and I were eating chocolate cannoli outside the sweets shop in Pallanza. We were with our cook. I ate the cream and chocolate flakes but not the crust. We were outside, though it was going to rain. The lake disappeared beneath the clouds. There was thunder, and then the rain fell in straight sheets. We were soaked in seconds. Mrs. Figlia pulled Enzo and me into the narrow shop, following Pasquale. She went to the counter to purchase more desserts for us. Pasquale was trying to take the last *cannolo* Enzo saved from the downpour.

"I was dripping wet and looked out the window – it was streaming water like we were under a waterfall – to see your mom in a drenched black coat running to carefully land her heels on the slick stones without falling. Your mom was running while carrying a baby girl in a soaked pink coat while three little girls rushed behind her. All of you were wearing matching pink coats and had your arms extended like wings, water streaming from the sleeves like strands of beads to balance your heels from slipping out beneath you. It looked like a bevy of pink swans. A mother leading her babies away."

"The first time you saw me doesn't count as the first time we met! We met at school. I remember Professoressa Garibaldi being cruel to you because you couldn't stop fidgeting."

"And because my Italian was so bad," he chuckled.

Truthfully, at that time, he came off as slow-witted. He preferred to sit quietly, hoping to be unnoticed, but the teacher called on him more than anyone else. He stuttered so badly during oral exams that I could only watch my fingers twitch in my lap. I had a distinct thought that I should be nice to him. We each sat on the edge of the aisle that split the room into the girls' and boys' sides. I remember staring at him for a minute, and I was not a girl who stared.

It was not unusual for northern Italians to have blonde hair like him, but he was unmistakably foreign. He was a little chubby in the cheeks and had brown eyes that narrowed on the playground but were empty cups in the schoolroom.

My mother and father knew decades of my classmates' family history; they even remember the days some were born. Before I ever passed through the thick double doors of the school, I had played with our classmates in my home and theirs. Every child in the classroom had that benefit except for Luca Marinova. Mama said Luca's mother was bent proud by her husband's wealth. She came off aloof. Maybe for that reason, Luca's only friend before the first year of school was Mario Guilatti, whose grandparents owned Café del Gallo. Though he played football with several of our classmates most afternoons, it took time for Luca's Italian to become effortless.

In grade three, Valentina Rula told me that Luca said I was the prettiest girl in class in my new yellow dress, with a white-collared blouse, white enamel buttons, and a white sash tied around the middle. She asked if I had a message for him; I did not.

Then he began to talk to me a little. He would ask how I was in the formal *come sta*, not the informal *come stai*, which I found endearing. I usually didn't answer. The first time I did it was after school, and I said I was well and kept walking. He leaped up from the curb where older girls were watching him, praying his handsome brother Pasquale might come to meet him. He asked why I was well. I expected he might walk me down the street and leave me at the corner, but he walked me all the way to my building, enthusiastically carrying our conversation up the steeping incline of my neighborhood. While Mama would have been pleased to prepare us *merenda* and learn more about the Marinova family, I did not invite him inside. I left him on the steps of my building and said curtly, "See you at school."

From then on, he would walk me home even though it added an extra forty minutes to his walk home. We talked about school and our classmates. It felt nice to have him around, and I came to miss him after he would part or on the days when he couldn't walk me home. On days when Arabella went to school, which wasn't very often as she didn't enjoy it, Luca would join my sister and me on our walk home. My sisters teased me when Mama talked about how much the foreign boy must like me. I always yelled back that he was born in Suna, which made him an Italian, but then Papa would say that it didn't matter where he was born or if he had an Italian first name. Our blood was one hundred percent

Italian, while Luca's was Russian and American, and who knew what else?

One afternoon near the end of the school year, Mama sat waiting for us on the steps outside of the building, playing with Imma.

"Luca Marinova," she sighed kindly and stood from the steps. Little Imma hugged me. "I saw your mother on Via Ruga today and asked her if you could stay for dinner tonight. She said yes." It was presented kindly. To allow the seat of her beautiful, three-quarters-length paisley dress to rest on the dirty steps meant that she didn't trust me to deliver the invitation.

"Thank you, Signora Rossi." Luca was surprised but excited. I was terrified.

Mama sat Luca next to Papa and me at the other end of the table, placing my three sisters between us. Only days ago, I had turned ten but felt much older having a boy come for dinner, especially before Arabella. Papa told Luca about the day I was born. The doctor had left Mama and the newborn to speak to Papa in the living room. In front of my uncles and grandparents, the doctor congratulated Papa on having "a little fighter" and walked out. Papa proclaimed that his first son was born, and the room erupted excitedly. He declared the boy would be named after him, Franco Rossi. When he entered the bedroom to meet his second daughter a minute later, he decided I would be called Franca instead. I had heard the family story many times, and Luca seemed amused.

We passed around eggplant and tomato bruschetta, followed by linguine. I kept pulling apart the soft bread rolls Mama made. Arabella discussed her plans to play at the sliver of beach on the lake's edge in Intra every day this summer. Gianna, the third of the Rossi girls and my open nemesis, asked Luca probing questions about his family: *Your family is very rich, right? Are you in love with Franca – why else would you walk with her every day?*

I pleaded with my eyes for Mama to stop her, but she could not resist her curiosity for the answers. Papa mercifully sent Gianna the sternest of warning looks. Dessert was a *marron glace* cake, which was far more extravagant than my birthday cake last week.

After dessert, Papa glanced at Luca and flatly told him it was time to go. Luca looked at each of my sisters, thanked Mama for inviting him, and promptly left. I cleaned off the table with

Gianna. It would be days until I could know what he thought of dinner. Tomorrow was a Saturday.

※

Three years later, he was still walking me home.

It was February, and the *tsarevna*, Luca had taught me the Russian word for princess, had been in Suna for a month. To break up the cold walk home, Luca and I were sitting on the floor of the grocer's office. Mama became the grocery bookkeeper at the base of our neighborhood when she married Papa. Papa was a fisherman on a boat he would never own. The night before my parents' wedding, my Nonna Illari told Mama not to marry Papa. She cried that her only daughter would destitute herself and her future children, forced to move up the mountain where the apartments cost less. *See the vulgar children running around town? Your children won't even be their filthy pack leaders.* Luckily, my Nonno liked Papa; his blessing was stronger than Nonna's concerns. Still, Mama couldn't forget the image described by her mother. Mama and Papa lived in his parents' home up the mountain for their first year of marriage. The grocer is Papa's godfather and first hired Mama as a favor, though he came to rely on her. If my grandmothers were unavailable during one of her six work days, Mama would leave her baby girls with one of our neighbors. Arabella said women in our building call Mama unnurturing and an embarrassment to her husband. There is a worse rumor that the grocer has emotions for Mama.

Mama countered the whispers with an obsession over our presentation. She believed no insult could truly etch itself to her family when her daughters were polite, exquisitely dressed, and adored. The clothes in our shared dresser and closet were always vibrant and stylish, velvet by winter and cotton by summer. Mama makes or mends dresses, shirts, skirts, nightgowns, mittens, socks, and scarves. She only purchased our stockings and Arabella's coats. For as long as I can remember, Nonna Illari has received compliments on her beautiful granddaughters, the best-dressed children in Pallanza.

This frigid afternoon, Mama helped the grocer arrange produce in the aisles as she reiterated the neighborhood credits she felt were relatively high. When Luca's Russian half-sister came to live in Suna, I was shocked to discover Luca's father had left a marriage and family. The prince was the only person I knew to be divorced.

"How does your mother feel about Stasi being here?" I asked Luca.

"She is happy to have her here," he responded, glancing around the grocer's office.

"You are a confabulator."

"What's that?" His eyebrows tightened.

"Someone who believes they are telling the truth, but the person's perception is not reality."

"So I'm a liar?"

"No. You don't know you're lying."

"What?"

"You can't believe your mother is happy to have her husband's daughter from his first marriage here! You want your mother to be happy. But it has to be difficult for her."

"Yeah. I guess you're right." He relaxed against the wall.

When he described how his family members handled the arrival of Anastasia, it became clear to me that people were kinder in Luca's world. It was a testament to his honesty that he viewed others as equally transparent. He simplified what was complicated.

"She and Pasq have become terrific friends. He and I are still the closest, but they think similarly. Stasi spends plenty of time visiting him in his studio, and he's started returning to the house for lunch. It must have been lonely for him during the days, working in his studio while I went to school and Enzo studied."

"She is very pretty," I said, examining my tights. There was a run on the left shin that I must conceal from Mama for as long as possible. I was flying through pairs of tights this winter. "I saw her shopping on Via Ruga."

"Yes, Stasi's beautiful. She is also inquisitive and cares to know us."

"Have you told her about me?" I looked up from my tights. He was sitting across from me in the tiny, windowless office. His brown eyes were calm and big. His eyebrows wilted outward.

"Of course."

"What did you say?"

Luca crawled on all four haunches around the cluttered floor, closing the few feet between us. He had grown taller over the last two months. We were sitting at the base of the door. We would be the first thing anyone who opened the door would see. He bent his right leg and planted his foot against the base of the door. The left side of his body leaned against me, and he looked me in my eyes, his whole gaze alternating between them.

"I tell her that I love you."

I could hear my heart pounding in my ears. My thoughts became vapors. I looked away to keep him from seeing me struggle to contain my dawning smile.

"Can I kiss you?"

I nodded, though I still faced my legs. As I turned my neck, it felt like the bravest act I had ever done. I lifted my face as he leaned in, and his lips met mine for the first time. We held there for a moment and then parted. He smiled and released a held breath.

"Go back across the room now," was all I could say.

6
Pasquale

It bloomed subtly, beginning with the *ano* comment. If Stasi entered a room, Mother would leave it. If Stasi spoke during dinner, Mother's eyes appeared to be elsewhere. If Pim were not joining us for a meal, Mother would not set a place for Stasi at the table. Mother did not recommend Italian food to try, where best to sit in the gardens, stores she must shop in Pallanza or Intra. She never offered the Italian word for anything, as Enzo, Luca, and I always did to help Stasi learn the language.

When she had to speak to Stasi, it was cutting. She was challenging Stasi to respond impolitely, but Stasi never did. Her pale face would take on confusion before crediting the situation to a language or cultural misunderstanding. Mother would say that she was headed out to make a visit and then remark how it must be terrible for Stasi not to have anyone to meet. She made incessant comments about how Pim felt bad for Stasi. If Stasi were overheard speaking in a self-deprecating way, Mother would twist the self-criticism: *Really? Your hair is your best feature. It's your short neck I'd be concerned about.*

It took Stasi weeks to share how powerless she felt to respond. After I was christened Stasi's confidant, I felt Mother's sins expand, as if her hate were directed at me. Stasi began to avoid being alone with Mother. My brothers and I had never lived with feminine tension, and no one except Pim could ignore it. Sometimes, I tried to defend Stasi, but Mother's attacks were always quick jabs. My momentary shock allowed her the time to flee. If I tried to pull Mother aside, she deflected by saying I was too sensitive.

I recounted her actions to Pim several times, but he would only look off into the corner of the room or over the lake, sigh, and say something about Mother being entitled to her reaction to Stasi being here and that she would adjust in her own time. He claimed that there was nothing he could say if she remained civilized.

April

7
Enzo

There was only one time when I felt Pasquale, Luca, and I were equidistant to Stasi. My brothers were more similar to each other than either was to me; this is natural with odd numbers. They seemed at ease with one another and unafraid to say farcical things. I considered and chose my words. Conversation is an uncertainty.

Since Stasi arrived, Pasquale had become her breathing shadow. One might have assumed that Luca and I would have become closer in response, but that was not so. Luca was their first and only choice for elaborate plans that required a third person. Otherwise, Luca happily flitted around town with his schoolmates and Franca Rossi. My interests filled my time enough.

During lunchtime one sparkling spring day, I noticed Stasi from the dining room window walking along the property's large rocks perforating the lake from the land. She was barefoot and alone. She made quick, deliberate leaps led by a poised front foot. The calculated arcs happened in a moment. She paused after each landing to regain an upright balance and choose the next rock. Her expression was focused, given seriousness by the slow-moving light reflected from the water. When the stones were angled too sharply for her to jump, the *tsarevna* used her hands to crawl down the shoreline. Balancing on a smaller rock, she lifted her long dress with one hand and took a wide step, but the rock shifted under her weight, causing her to slip and fall. Stasi landed forcefully on her elbows and lower back. She remained lying on her back and cradled her right elbow to her chest. I dropped my sandwich and rushed out the backdoor.

I removed my shoes as fast as possible and traversed the rocks. She had not moved. My steps were noiseless, but the shifting stones alerted her to my approach. She dabbed at her eyes before turning her head. We looked at each other without knowing what to say. I sat beside her and gently held her left hand as I reached under her shoulder blades to help her sit up. Her hair was fraying from her side braid.

"Stasi!" Pasquale called out dramatically from the side of the villa. He must have rushed from his workshop. His long coat billowed around him as he frantically ran to her, to us.

"I was being childish," she said to me.

"It's more slippery than it appears. It happens to all of us."

"I don't think I've bruised myself playing outdoors in a decade. I'm becoming like Luca." The enormous pink scrape on her elbow would undoubtedly morph into a bruise.

"Me neither," I admitted. "I haven't been on the rocks in years."

Pasquale moved dexterously toward us with his shoes still on. I maintained my hold on Stasi. He landed squarely in front of her, squatting on the rock between her and the lake. He took one of her ankles in his hands. The edges of his coat soaked in the lapping water.

"Thanks for meeting me here, you two," Pasquale joked, breathless.

"*Ciao!*" Luca called from beside us, oblivious to the fall. "*Cosa state facendo?*"

"We are giving Stasi a swimming lesson!" Pasquale answered confidently. "But Enzo would rather we all sun on the rocks."

Luca came over without looking where he stepped. He spread out to lounge comfortably on the other side of Stasi.

"Great fun! You have surely swum before?" Luca asked her.

"No!" She said adamantly with her fists. "And I do not plan to learn today… or ever!"

"Truly Stasi?" I asked. "You should learn, not necessarily today—"

"Why not today? We could teach you." Luca began rolling his pant legs up teasingly. He heel-toed his shoes off at the water's edge.

"The water is freezing!" She protested.

"How can you be so sure, safe on these rocks?" Pasquale took his coat off and started rolling his pant legs up. "Or unsafe on these rocks."

"You both are joking," she said falteringly, betraying a hint of fear.

"Let's see..." Pasquale slipped a pale foot into the water. "Warmer than bathwater!"

Luca waded knee-high into the lake. He turned toward the group and grimaced from the cold, trying to summon his strength. "Yes, it's so warm. Don't you want to try, Stasi? How about you, Enzo?"

Pasquale laughed loudly as if I would never. But he was wrong. The sun had warmed me quite sufficiently. I stood, rolled my pants up, and took my shirt off. Both brothers stopped laughing.

I looked at Stasi. "I'll test the water for you."

None of them made a sound as I sidestepped into the chilled water. It was about three weeks too early for swimming. I glided in slowly, watching for rocks, and paused thigh-deep to turn toward them. Only the dancing ripples of reflected sun moved across their unblinking faces. I saluted them with my right hand, held my nose in my left, squeezed my eyes shut, and let myself fall backward.

My whole body convulsed beneath the cold, and I bounced back to the surface, trying to swallow the shiver from my chest to speak.

"See – see? It's f-fine."

They all clapped and roared, laughing. I swam around for effect. The sharpness of the water's temperature abated. Luca shrugged at Pasquale and waded fully into the water, too. We mockingly and sloppily performed synchronized water dances and stretches. Pasquale reached his hand out to Stasi and hoisted her to her feet. Then they walked into the water hand-in-hand, she leaning on him and yelling out at each step until they were both waist-deep beside Luca and me, where they slid their shoulders under together.

"It's not a full swimming lesson unless you go all the way under," Pasquale told her before he slipped under, holding her hand below the water's surface. When he reemerged, he smoothed his dark blonde hair back.

"Then help me."

Luca held her right arm, and I took her left, placing a hand on her back to keep a firm hold of her. Pasquale continued holding her hand in his. She closed her eyes and trusted us to lower her head under the crystalline water. She squeezed her face as she braced the cold, and her shoulders tensed reflexively. After a moment, we lifted her. Shimmering droplets clung to her eyelashes and eyebrows as the lake streamed down the sides of her face. Her skin revealed a blue undertone, and her lips turned a pellucid purple.

"Should we begin the initiation chant?" Pasq jokingly asked.

We all stood close in the water for a minute, shaking and smiling, the boys dripping from our Marinova noses. Stasi sparkled, newly christened. When we heard Mother yelling from the lawn, we helped each other out of the water. Soaked, we grabbed our dry coats, shirts, and shoes. We followed Luca's wet footprints and climbed back over the rocks. Though each step up the lawn was heavy, I felt lighter than ever.

8
Luca

Pasq and Stasi were lying side-by-side with their stomachs on the sitting room floor, writing in the same notebook. She scribbled on the left page, and he wrote on the right. Both right-handed, it reminded me of a rowing team's synchronous strokes.

"What are you two working on?"

"A play! And we have a special part for you." Stasi beamed.

"Acting isn't really for me."

"You will play the neighboring shopkeeper. He's comical. It's about a brother and sister who own a photography shop that is also a gallery and exhibition space."

"The central conflict," Pasquale began. However, he kept writing as if the inspiration could dissipate at any moment, as even I knew it ultimately would, "is that the sister is the photographer and the brother is the business-savvy one, though the pictures sell better when everyone thinks the brother is the photographer. They try to keep the secret."

"Does everyone find out in the end?"

"No. When the sister dies, the brother claims that he has retired out of grief," Stasi said.

"That's a dark turn!"

"Life can be dark," Pasquale educated me. "The sister's photographs become famous and highly valuable as they are limited." He turned toward her. "We should arrange the stage so the back of each photograph faces the audience. That way, they can imagine the pictures based on the actors' faces."

"Brilliant, Pasq!"

"So, where are you going to show this play?"

"It's called *Still Lifes*. We'll start slow, a local showing in Pallanza for a season or two. Then take it to Milan. Realistically, though, who knows? It's difficult to plan for success."

They worked in symmetry. When one was ready to turn the page, so was the other. She wrote the dialogue with occasional input from him while he concentrated on the production: lighting, props, creative staging, and the movement of the actors. I shuffled off to the back patio to play cards by myself. I knew better than to ask them to start a game as they sprinted to finish before their interest burned off. I lost track of time playing, but sure enough, in the early afternoon, they drifted outside to take a break.

"Would you like to play?"

"Not now," Stasi answered.

"Stasi," Pasq drawled, his head leaning over the back of his chair, "tell us about the Marinova relatives we've never met."

"The Marinovas are unpleasant, mostly. Each of the women had a rude comment at Tati's wedding. It was too grand and not grand enough. They are all second cousins, of course. My real cousins are on my mother's side."

"We don't know if we have any cousins on our mother's side." Pasquale mused out loud.

"I thought Mary Mari was an only child."

"In a way…" he began slowly. He wished he had not said it. "Mother's parents were never married. Her father was married to someone else."

"I'm sorry… I don't mean to smile." Stasi covered her mouth with her hand. After months of Mama's comments, she tried to straighten her mouth when she said: "That's awful."

Pasquale was not watching her. His shoulders faced the lake. He was the most sensitive about Mama's origin. How unlike him that he would even tell Stasi. It was not a secret, but it was never discussed. It didn't bother me. It didn't matter. We had never met Mama's parents or her father's family, and we never would.

Stasi regained her composure and must have felt bad about her reaction because she reached over and touched Pasquale's arm to console him. He came back to the moment.

"*Still Lifes* is going to be a tremendous hit," Pasq said excitedly.

"If only Pim's brother had survived to grow up with him. He could have had this kind of fun, too." Stasi responded sadly.

"What do you mean?" I asked.

She looked confused.

"What do you mean by "his brother"?"

"I'm referring to Papa's little brother Ivan."

Pasq swung forward in his chair, as did I. Pim said he was an only child. She appeared caught on the back foot.

"What happened to the little brother?" Pasq asked.

"He died."

"How?"

"He became very sick."

"Stasi, come on. Tell us."

"Yeah, go on," I added.

She dropped to a whisper. Her whisper voice held more accent than when she spoke at normal volume. "Papa was about six, and his brother Ivan was three. Papa got sick. Babu thought it was only a head cold. Ivan caught it, too. Papa recovered… and then Ivan's cold became pneumonia, and it took his little soul. Our grandfather blamed Papa, as did everyone. Babu said it wasn't Papa's fault—"

"Of course not!" I chimed in Pim's defense. "It was an act of God."

"Yes, illness is blind and unjust." Pasquale dismissed with a short sweep of his hand.

"Yes, but… that wasn't exactly Babu's argument. She blamed our grandfather. This was the fourth consecutive Marinova generation but the sixth time in total, then that is – to have the second-born die young. Babu had been warned that the House of Marinova was cursed.

"Our grandfather was the firstborn, and the sister who came right after him drowned in a frozen lake. Older, bigger children were playing all about, yet the ice broke beneath her, and she fell right in. They couldn't find her body until the ice thawed months later. They say the corpse was swollen though fairly preserved. Our great-grandfather's little sister was pushed out of a window by the man she was betrothed to. She landed on her neck. We still don't speak to that family, the Sokolovs – horrible people! The generation before that, Babu said that one Marinova brother killed his older brother, and that's what started the curse."

Pasq and I met each other's eyes with skepticism.

"Accidents happen, Stasi. Coincidences of tragedy befalling the secondborn do not prove anything occult," Pasq dismissed the superstition, unwilling to play along. He shook his head and muttered flippantly, "Enzo made it to adulthood."

"Enzo is not Papa's second child!" Stasi shouted, her eyes incendiary. "I'll remind you that his second child, Elena, *my sister*, died as an infant! Papa didn't believe in the curse until Elena died. That is when he became melancholy and began… questioning."

"He always questioned his life there."

"Not until Elena died! If she had lived, he never would have left."

"You can't believe that. You're too smart to dwell on false reassurances fed to you."

"No one fed me that thought, it's mine!"

Stasi stood and picked up the *Still Lifes* notebook. Holding it with her thumb on top and her index and middle fingers below, she flicked it off of the terrace, slicing the air. Several of the abandoned cards flew off the table from the force. It landed on the rocks below with a thud that felt louder than it sounded. She looked at Pasq with fury before storming off, her red hair swishing violently behind her.

We heard her bedroom door slam shut through the open window above the terrace. The window stayed open. We knew better than to remark on the last few minutes. After another few minutes, Pasq took a deep, pained inhale, retrieved Still Lifes from the lawn, and carried it back into the villa.

I left the mess of cards and took one of the canoes out on the lake. I could pick up the cards later. The window was still open.

9
Anastasia

I wade into the gardens to take in the scents, attempting to note the strength and mixture and name the qualities of the new smells. I imagine perfumes I could create. I brush, lift, and hold many blooms, though Papa's signs request visitors not to touch. Papa sees his flowers as collectibles, as if they lived by the same rules as Pasquale's sculptures. When my palms turn green, I trudge back to the villa. My pale skin ripens to a sensitive pink faster than a healthy brown.

I wonder if Mary Mari ever met her half-siblings. It seems an unusual similarity between us that we could have bonded over. Perhaps her father is alive somewhere. Maybe she wishes she could have spent time in his home. While all of my grandparents have passed, I tend to forget others still have them. There are more older people in Suna, Pallanza, and Intra than I ever saw in Smolnek. These people are not on the younger side of "old," where they discover their limitations, but very old when fragility has succumbed to frailty. When a short walk could extinguish the day's allotted energy, Pasquale muttered about them: "Gravity always wins." We uncovered that Pasqulae is scared of relying on others. He is fearful of the day he won't be able to sculpt. I reminded him that orchestra conductors work into their eighties. He doesn't have to worry about that for a long time, and maybe by then, he'll be less interested and ready to be finished. He responded crossly that he is not "interested" in sculpting; he is one with it. I let the conversation go. I like the idea of being old. Papa says we will be happy in old age in proportion to the childlike wonder we have left.

"Stasi."

Pasquale is sitting in a rickety chair at the entrance to the garden side door. The way he hastily stands betrays that he was waiting for me. He looks at a letter in his hands. Then his eyes move to my face as he holds the letter out to me. I had been so untethered, elsewhere, and distracted. It felt like I had fallen as far as the noose stretched.

The letter was from Tatiana. It was too thin.

It has happened: Mama is dead. My eyes burn, and tears spill over. I retreat to my bedroom with the letter between both of my hands. The tiny square felt like a deadweight to hold. The only thing I want right now is not to see Mary Mari. Unable to see where I'm going through the onslaught of tears, the layout of the house and its furniture are muscle memory. Rounding the corner of the sitting room too widely, I spare myself from bumping into the wooden frame of the couch or rebruising my right thigh on the tall end table. Pasquale follows me. I'm unsure if I want to be alone, but then that word, *odinochestvo*, reverberates.

Pasquale closes my bedroom door behind him. Something in him knows not to come closer. I stand at the window and let out a soft wail – a sound that has been lying dormant within me since Tatiana shared how sick Mama was. It was the sound of a buried breath.

"Stasi, I'm so sorry. This is terrible."

Did she feel pain? Was she relieved I was not there to witness, or did she wish I were by her side? This tiny note from Tatiana would convey nothing more than the facts. That was her way, especially since she feared Papa coming into possession of the letters she sent me. She did not want him to have any information that he didn't ask her.

I've always carried an inherited sorrow for the events in my mother's life. It seemed like she always had one terrible thing happen in the middle of another drawn-out, worse thing happening. Growing up, she saw three of her older siblings die. She does not know how many children her mother had, at least thirteen. There were four babies born after her who did not live longer than a month, and they never spoke of a sibling after they died. Her father, a prince of Tilsit and a losing general of the Fourth Coalition in the Napoleonic wars, beat her brothers. He would single out the son he felt was somehow conspicuous-looking at that moment and then command the other children to leave the room. Once, my uncle Desya stole a pillow from one of the tsar's summer houses, the new Alexander Palace, when their mother wished to visit her cousin, Empress Maria Feodorovna. When my grandfather found out, none of the children revealed who had placed the imperial pillow on the sitting room couch, and he beat them all, boys and girls.

Mama, having three daughters, was unlucky. She said of the experience of losing Elena: "The sun still rises." Her only regret was not having one more child. "Genders come in threes," she said. Her next child would have been a Marinova prince, surely. She never considered that Papa would leave. It wasn't done. Marriage is the spine of every other institution. It was survival, succession of status, and protection of wealth. It had the power to mend fractured communities and nations in the most sacred way. A member of royalty abandoning a wife meant betraying your family, her family, and the peace assured to the people by the union. It was unfathomable.

When I arrived in Suna, the natural wintertime beauty left me thinking: *of course, he ran here.* Who wouldn't yearn to retire in warm, dazzling splendor and shed the piled duties of blood and conscription? Mama did not have an easy life, but she never abandoned her post.

I sit on the bed and open the letter. Tears rise before old ones can be blinked out, so I must keep wiping at them and my running nose. Pasquale moves to the chair beside the bed and watches, unsure how to comfort me. The letter is one small page, folded in half. The stationery bears Tatiana's married initials in red ink.

Dear Anastasia,

I truly hope you are doing well in Italy. I have failed to write you as often as I would like. Do you remember my dear friend, Ivvona? She is newly expecting, and I have lunch with her most days. Nothing has changed with me. All is well. Katrina is healthy and growing quickly. Mama says hello and reminds you to stay out of the sun.

I've enjoyed the postcards you sent Mama, and I wish Dmitri and I had a postcard from Italy, too.

With Sisterly Love,
Your sister T

A captive breath escapes my body. The tension in my chest uncoils. The white-hot tears stop. I drop the letter on the bed, where it falls open with a sigh. Mama has not died.

I shuffle to the bathroom sink to rinse and pat my face until the color is even again. My decolletage has become a web of bright red splotches. I feel the fear slipping back into my chest again. The ax will fall another day.

Pasq reads the letter. Her penmanship is exquisite and simple to translate. This letter is Pasq's first interaction with Tatiana, and I wonder what she would have written if she had thought about that. These could be the only thoughts she had ever passed to her half-brother, and she wasted them by sharing nothing.

He cycles through monosyllabic sounds, 'ahh, wow, huh, mmm' and hangs his head in his hands, relieved as well, though how could he be?

"Well." Pasquale finally breaks the silence. "I think this calls for a walk."

I nod and follow.

We refrain from speaking as we walk toward Pallanza along Via di Lago Maggiore, the long main road stretching the east side of the lake. The lake mirrors the blemishless sky. I'm unsure if Pasq is leading us somewhere or if we are wandering, but I don't feel the need to ask. After the sharpness of the moment had passed, I became aware of something formerly unacknowledged within me now exposed. I won't be at her side as she dies. I won't return to Smolnek to bury Mama in the same cemetery yards from Petyr Mikhailov.

Despite my mother's admonishment, Tatiana passed along, I am not wearing a hat beneath the beating sun. Each step I take churns my fury over her letter. Partially for what I thought it meant, mostly for its emptiness. Tatiana is nothing but bland observations and feigned interest. Once, at an anniversary party, a friend of my uncle's told me theories about how birth order shapes personalities. He presumed that a family of two sisters could be a hostile environment, for two girls were destined to become complete opposites. One would be in pursuit of the parents' attention; one would openly concede the competition. One sister would be a rule follower and the other a rule breaker. He asked which one I was, but at that moment, Tatiana appeared and demanded that I introduce myself to one of her friends with a formal tone and shoulders posture forming a perfect T. The man chuckled before I was swept away.

Tatiana always kept me at arm's length. She thinks she has more right than me to suffer from Papa leaving. And yes, she was older with more of a relationship and a concrete image to lose. But she also has an arsenal of memories that she rationed to me in pieces. She knew I wouldn't ask Mama for stories about Papa. It was ever a one-sided conversation. From an early age, I could see these memories were skeletons made of facts devoid of the emotions that transpired, motives, or complex implications. Her retellings answered so few questions that eventually, I stopped begging for stories from her.

In Pallanza, everyone is leisurely enjoying the day: taking a coffee, shopping, eating, closing their eyes, and giving their faces to the sun. Pasquale, the town's favorite son, totes the foreign girl in red up the hill of Via Ruga to the circle. I follow Pasq into the small newspaper store, a hole in the wall between Café del Gallo and the *farmacia*. Is Pasquale buying cigarettes? Papa had *La Nazionale* and *La Republica* delivered to the villa every morning. The entire left wall was cluttered and disorganized. There were dozens of publications in sloping stacks on the bottom shelf and ill-rowed books on the higher shelves. It was so much I considered that it might be designed to incite an urgency in buyers. At the counter, Pasquale motions to a little wooden stand on the counter labeled '*Cartoline*.' There were four postcards, all featuring a distinct angle of the lake.

"Pick one," he says.

I chose the picture that painted the scene as a fairytale with Isola Madre in the foreground and Intra in the background. Pasquale purchases it along with a stamp. Then he takes me by the other hand and pulls me to the *gelateria*. Pasq directs me to sit at a small circular wooden table, and I, an obliging catatonic, obey. A minute later, he returned with two gelato cones: a raspberry cone for me and a pistachio cone for him. Then he pulls a pen out of his pocket like a magic trick and places it next to the postcard and stamp.

"What?" I shrug between licks.

"You're going to write a postcard to Tatiana. She said she wanted one."

"I have nothing to say to her."

"Write that."

"No, that's mean!"

"Meaner than you not responding at all?"

I shrug again, exhausted. I'm not convinced she is owed the consideration of what would cause her the least suffering.

"C'mon," he pointed to the pen. "You can write: 'Now I've written you,' 'Have a nice day,' or 'I'm not interested in how you're doing either.'"

I laugh at each of these scenarios. When I finally knew what to write, I handed him my drippy cone, which he finished.

Dearest Tatiana,

This is a postcard from Italy.

With Sisterly Love,
Your Sister Anastasia

Pasq smoothes the stamp flush onto the card, and we rush to the post office like bandits, laughing, skipping, and leaning into each other.

10
Pasquale

After a long night in the studio, I was content to spend the day in a warm sleep. I was too exhausted to be disconcerted by Luca's morning shotfire, so I turned my back to the blinding western mountains; the tilt of the terrain reflected the sun directly into my eyes. With my face buried in the pillow, I was pulled awake again minutes later by sweet knocks, soft in their arrhythmia.

"Come in," I mumble. I wrap my arms around the cool pillow, refusing to commit to waking up fully. Stasi tips her tousled head in the open door.

"Did I wake you?" She comes in without an answer.

Stasi sits on the oversized brown chair in the corner by the window. There are gentle sweeping creases of sleeplessness under her eyes. Her legs fold upward so that her heels are on the seat, and she is hugging her shins, making her appear small. Her chin rests in the ravine between her knees.

"Do you sleep on the left side of your face?"

"Yes," her hands flew to cover her cheeks. "How do you know that?"

"The crease at the edge of your left eye looks deeper. Wait—don't catch me out! You have beautiful skin. It must bounce back into place before breakfast every morning."

"I'll have to start sleeping on my back from now on," she said sensitively. The girl could not bear even a shadow of criticism.

"Don't worry, you will be exquisitely gorgeous for at least... four more years." She threw the chair pillow at me. "Your prime may be behind you..." She whipped the basalt pen on the side table at me, and I lifted my bed cover to deflect the impact and yelled, "But you are still young enough to exfoliate the worry from your face each night!"

She looked away to conceal her smile. I yawned and resumed lounging.

"You are quite lazy this morning."

"I was in my studio until three in the morning."

"In English, when does the night become the morning?"

"I don't know. Maybe it should be night until the sun comes up?"

"No, I think it should be three at night and four in the morning."

"Thus it is decreed! Anastasia Marinova has spoken. Inform History of her decision."

She smiled and turned to stare out the window quietly. She had something to tell me, but she wanted me to dive for it. I rolled over and propped a few pillows to face her without sacrificing comfort. I considered not asking her anything and remaining like this all day.

"Why did you wake me up?"

"I'm not sure. It's nothing, really. It's only a very strange, very vivid dream."

"What happened in the dream?"

"Have you ever woken yourself up crying? That happened to me this morning. I was woken by my tears streaming and soaking my pillow. It was so ethereal and yet felt so real. In the dream, I was before a large crowd of angels. At least, I assume they were angels. All were dressed in white, but each had distinctive features and glowed in their unique shade. I knelt in front of them, asking for help. I was humbled… I mean… emptied, no, exposed. My hands were cupped together and overflowing with marbles I laid on the ground before them in a crescent. No two marbles were the same, not even all round or crystalline.

"A kind woman leaned forward and examined all of my sorrows—because that's what they were, the marbles were every breathing trouble I have. She picked up an opaque black one with thin spikes. When she picked it up, I instantly knew it represented… " Her bold eyes flickered, expelled from her trance.

"Which trouble was the spiked one?" I asked, not allowing her to choose when to be secretive.

"Pim and me."

"What did the angel do with it?"

"She held it at eye level and examined it. Her intent to help me made me feel hopeful and elated. She wanted to understand and advise me. For the first time, I could see a glimmer of time when that suffering was behind me. Her mouth opened, and she began to speak. I would give anything to hear her explanation. Except – I couldn't hear her! Her lips were moving, but there was no sound. I strained and cried, literally cried, repeating 'I can't hear you' over and over. She paused and started again but stopped when I shook my head. This went on a couple of times. Two gentlemen-angels moved their lips, looking at me curiously, trying to share their wisdom about another marble between them. But I still couldn't hear.

"Finally, I thanked them and started stockpiling my marbles again. They didn't dissolve exactly, but their glow dulled. And I remained there, kneeling on the ground, holding all of the marbles carefully to safeguard them from rolling away, sobbing and unable to wipe my eyes. They were so heavy. And I was alone, weeping because I am deaf to the frequencies of angels. Unable to hear those who wish to help me."

Stasi's eyes shine as she continues muttering how real it felt. She used her hands to tell the story; she was becoming Italian that way, but then her hands gripped her feet, making herself small again. We never discuss her relationship with Pim.

"Come to The Eye this afternoon. You can read as I plaster."

She nods, still in a pensive daze. She stands to leave. I surrender my eyes, strained by the light, to what will hopefully be a return to dreamless sleep.

"Is that a birthmark?" She stops as she passes.

"Yes," my hand goes right to the spot on the back of my neck. "It used to be bright red."

The weight of the bed shifts as she sits, and the soft pad of a finger touches my birthmark. She traces the faded mark my mother once called God's fingerprint.

"I have a similar one," she whispers in wonder.

I roll over to face her. Her dark brown eyes are wide and excited. She lifts her nightgown to show me a seashell-shaped birthmark on her left thigh, inches below her hip. It's the exact same faded pink as mine and, at one point, must have been cherry red. I reach out to touch it, but she stands up and strides out of the room. It happens so quickly that the mattress still bears her impression for a moment. My hand is still perched several inches above the sheet.

11
Anastasia

Mary Mari has swept her sons off to the family tailor in Baveno, a town directly south of charming Stresa. It's impossible to distinguish the lights at night between the two towns. Pasq forewarned that a trip to Baveno to measure the three would take all day. He feigned the whole thing was an inconvenience, but I could tell he wanted to refresh his wardrobe and might even enjoy the day out. Luca said his favorite restaurant on the lake is in Baveno. His mouth began watering when describing *pizza melanzane*.

I intentionally lingered in my bedroom until I heard the door close behind them. After washing my hair with pure Castile soap over the sink, I cut off a few inches of hair and discarded the remnants in the small waste basket. I had intended to cut it for weeks and already had the scissors beneath the little oval mirror. I moved one of the room's chairs beside the open window to dry my hair by the sun. I propped my feet on the other chair. Minutes passed. I sat in my red nightgown, intent on remaining in my room all day.

My indulgent self-pity was punctuated by the sounds of Papa taking his tea on the patio below. Papa usually had tea alone in his study. I changed into a looser day dress and stepped out into the hallway. Partway down the stairs, I changed my mind about the chrysanthemum shoes I had on and returned to my room for the darker pair. What if he did not invite me to join him? Or if he said he would prefer to be alone? I returned to my room for a shield in the form of a book Enzo recommended that I hadn't yet opened.

Papa was framed by the double doors with the shining lake and forested mountains across the water for his backdrop.

A light breeze off the lake caught one of the doors, and the dry hinges exhaled to swing the door inward. Papa turned at the gentle sound to see me standing in the doorway.

"Anastasia," he relaxed, "come join me."

I beamed and skipped to the seat on his right, which put me at the head of the patio table with the lake to my right.

"Thank you," I murmured as he poured tea for me. I stirred in a few drops of milk, watching the milk curl and cloud.

"I like that you prefer black tea. The boys do not."

"I did not prefer it as a child."

He looked out over the waterscape. It was difficult to tell if he was at pause or finished speaking. He began reading his newspaper again. The sparkling view of Pallanza and Intra north of us was plenty in the silence. My doubt evaporated. I opened Enzo's book and looked at the first page.

"Growing up, did you ride horses?" He asked in Russian.

"Only a little," I responded in our language.

"Tatiana loved the horses," he reminisced. "When she was little, she would sit in front of me in the saddle. She watched me break them from the fence. Every time I landed a jump, she cheered."

I nodded politely and looked at the lake.

"Did they continue to breed horses?"

"No." I turned the page of my book with false focus.

"Are the horses still there?"

"No."

"What happened?"

"A little after," *you left*, "one of the horses kicked the stable boy in the head. The boy survived the accident but never spoke sensibly again. His head was damaged; it was even dented. He was eight. Tatiana became in charge of the horses. She was never afraid of their power. That winter, three of the horses caught equine flu and died. They were able to save the other three, but that summer, or at least a few months later, I think, the last mare was stolen in the middle of the night – Tatiana's favorite, Dobrota, the black and white one you used to train the foals. Tatiana had felt she and Dobrota were connected. Mama reported the theft, but Dobrota was never returned or found. Then there were the two brothers left: Prochnost and Uporstvo. Not even a year later, Prochnost had been foaming at the mouth for a few days when I, by chance, looked out my window to see Uncle Desya shoot him. A year or more after that, a neighbor reported that he had seen Dobrota's frozen body on the side of a road. She had been starved, abused, and finally abandoned."

"And Uporstvo?"

"Still there. He spends his days alone in the field. Tatiana doesn't have anything to do with him, especially now."

"What was the name of the stable boy?"

"Pasha Orlov."

"I knew his father and uncles. They are hard-working people. Their father worked in the Marinova stables his whole life, except when he was gone with my father fighting the wars in Caucasia. When he returned, we would coax him into telling us everything. He was the first person I knew who enjoyed traveling. Whenever I set out for somewhere new, I would think of him. Daniil never measured up to him. It was clear early on that he never would. Does he have any other sons?"

"Pasha is Daniil's only son. There are four daughters in that family, all of whom work. His wife Lia takes care of Pasha. He is an eternal toddler but strong and can be aggressive. Mama used to have the whole family for dinner once a year. She would have me sit next to him. Daniil always caught Pasha before his fist could land on me, but he had a grasp on my hair once. That's why Lia keeps her hair so short."

He folded his newspaper and placed it on the table.

"As I grow older, Anastasia, I see how each decision a person makes is the making of ten more decisions we do not yet see."

A breeze taunted the paper and sent a chill from where my hair was still damp on my neck. Shadows on the mountain ridges in the distance shifted with the clouds, like muscles flexing on the mountains.

"Is having me here difficult for you?"

"In some ways," he answered honestly. "Is being here difficult for you?"

I opened my mouth to answer with a light lie, but when my eyes met his, they filled, and I couldn't speak without blubbering. I took a deep breath to settle the slight shaking between my lungs. I opened my mouth to hear my voice break in my throat again. Covering my face from him with my hands, my book slid from my lap onto the floor with a smack.

"Anastasia, what is wrong?" He rotated in his seat to lean forward squarely in front of me.

"Did you decide…" I began, but I was incapable of releasing the question. Where tears spotted my dress, the red became sanguine. "You left."

"My life in Smolnek was forced. I didn't forge it for myself."

All I could hear was: My, I, myself. That's who came first to him, then and always. I, his child, was, at best, an afterthought.

"I left your mother plenty of money to keep you three comfortable."

I stammered with my hands. This moment had gone terribly wrong. It felt wholly lost to me. How could I tell him how little a sum mattered, especially given that Mama treated every tomorrow as the day we would finally become beggars? I could feel hundreds of small collapsings in my chest, tiny bridges the size of pomegranate seeds crumbling.

"You left me. And Tati. My whole life has been watching Mama's unravel. There was always something to remind us of how alone we were. The lesson of my life is that I am my only layer of defense against this world."

He had no idea how to soothe a crying girl. Would he apologize? Did he even know how? My residence here was likely as significant a concession as he was capable of.

"You are so fragile, my sweet daughter. Everyone has hardships they must bear. You had a fine childhood."

How could he know? I let out a long breath.

"Go rest, Anastasia," Papa dismissed me in English.

"I'm sorry," I nodded and mumbled an apology for what I was unsure of.

My eyes were slow to adjust to the reduced light inside, and I could only see vague outlines of the furniture. I could barely see the stairs, so I wrapped my right arm around the railing and bent over to feel each step guiding my body up them. Feeling unsteady when I reached the top, I crawled from the top of the landing to my bedroom, sliding my tear-wet palms on the floor. My knees wiped the floor behind me with my dress.

I shut the door with my foot and hoisted myself onto the bed to sob with my whole body, fully surrendering to the overwhelming rawness of how disregarded I was by him. He may have been a shade of remorseful, but he was not regretful. I thought I already knew this. How could he not take me in his arms? It would be unlike him to apologize, but I hoped I might receive an acknowledgement. If I didn't receive a concession this afternoon, it was never coming.

He should have taught me how to ride a horse.

We should have spent weeks anticipating exchanging gifts at Christmas each year.

We should have danced together at Tatiana and Dmitri's wedding.

He should know what I don't find funny.

I should have an inkling as to why he feels foreign to those who share his upbringing.

He should know why I only wear red.

I should have piles of reasons for resenting him and still not succumb because I have a treasury of reasons to adore him.

Staring at the ceiling, an unmistakably clear thought emerges: I am mourning a relationship I never had. It is a beautiful fabrication, a lovely story, but ultimately unreal. This is not the relationship I have with him. Those nonexistent memories and the closeness I desired were never within the capacity of the one father I was given. That is not the relationship Enzo, Luca, or even Pasquale have with him.

My attention has been on what was theoretically lost to me, not what was actually lost. I have been consumed by daydreams built on the assumption that only his presence was required. The reality is that he is not the god I have spent years molding in my mind. From this moment, I will only mourn real things.

12
Pasquale

"How do you intend to spend your lonely, empty, meaningless days as a spinster?"

"How do you plan to spend your days once your patrons forsake you for a rising star more talented than you ever were?" Stasi retorted.

"But really, jests aside, how would you like to spend your time?"

"You'll mock me if I tell you."

"I won't mock you *for* telling me."

"I want to design women's hats." We sat beneath my favorite pergola for a mid-afternoon picnic. Her fingers combed the grass into straight lines.

"Magnificent. The best of the best. Your hats will be iconic."

"Do you think so?" Stasi lit up. "I imagine huge hats that are heavy to wear but uncomplicated and chic, that curve and dip." She mimed a wave in front of her face.

"Let's extract these visions from your mind. How many sheets of paper do you have hidden in your skirt?"

After we went to my studio and found an empty sketch pad, we walked far into the northwest corner of the garden, passing where we had left our picnic setup. We chose an alcove where she could perch on the bench as I sat with an open page at her feet.

"I'm imagining a hat with a seven-inch brim; the front has a slight dip to conceal one eye. Black, with a short black ribbon that ties into a bow in the back."

"What's the material?" I furiously drew.

"I don't know…but it is meant for the springtime."

"Black in the spring?"

"Black all year. Another idea I have is a sort of metal crown without jewels. To be worn for evening drinks."

"Evening drinks is referred to as *aperitivo* in Italian." She repeated the word a few times.

I took artistic liberty to add an opulent flair to each design, staying within the essence. I drew three versions of the black one: one with a black ribbon precisely as she described, one with a long red ribbon and no dip that would evenly frame the face and reveal both eyes and a third version with a wider brim and Dalmatian-print ribbon—our afternoon continued in that fashion. She would describe the bones of an idea, and I would contribute the flesh. We made a small black felt hat with a short brim adorned with green and blue peacock feathers. There were many colorful satin cloth headbands and wrought ones with arranged precious stones, preferred by Stasi to fine jewels, as they were not daywear; on one side, several headbands had glamorous netting gathered over the eyes.

"I dream about going to Paris and commissioning an artisan to make these," she said as I drew. "But where would I find the funds to manufacture? Eventually, they would fund themselves completely with plenty of profit."

Stasi's eyes shone with uncontainable glee as she examined each completed drawing, holding it delicately and tilting her head in each direction rather than the paper. She pleaded that we make this a proper project. Around lunchtime, she would borrow me from my studio, and I could conjure her words into pictures. Her goal was an extensive portfolio of styles and options to build in Paris.

The ambitious sculptor in me deceptively hoped that her entrepreneurial vigor would fizzle out. I presumed we would meet twice more or so, and then her interest would fizzle out. However, she arrived at The Eye the next day, at exactly one in the afternoon, with sandwiches and fruit from Mrs. Figlia. The following day, she was there again, glowing and fluttering about our progress the day before; she called the batch of sketches "yieldings." My work started suffering, for just as I became fully immersed in what I was doing, there would be a knock on the door. Years ago, I aggressively guarded my time in The Eye, threatening Pim and Mother that they were derailing me with their visits. But I found myself unable to turn her eager face away. One rainy day, she resolved to clear my desk, and I let her, but the sight of mixing categories of piles gnawed at me.

A few weeks later, Stasi arrived as I was absorbed in my twentieth sketch attempt of a bust of a mother holding her infant daughter over her shoulder. I wanted the baby's eyes to match her mother's calm wariness. I asked Stasi to return later. Instead, she chose to wait in the chair and stared straight ahead for minutes. I suggested that she could begin eating or start writing down her hat ideas, but she declined and insisted she would wait... then went on staring. I was unable to obscure her from my peripheral vision. Each minute she stared at nothing was infuriating. It became a battle of who would be the first to concede. After an entire turn of my thirty-minute hourglass, I finally accepted that it would be better to postpone my sketch for the sake of quality deliberation rather than redo half-conceived work later. I became increasingly enraged that she didn't care that my work was suffering for her illusion of advancement.

Out in the garden, her animation returned, and she became as talkative as usual. My mind attacked each of her words, finding them frivolous or stupid. It felt like there was a fire inside my throat, ready to leap forth and lick the ends of her unruly hair. I declined today's sandwich and made quiet assenting noises as she continued. To distract myself, I started drawing her face.

"What are you doing?" She interrupted her monologue to ask.

"What does it look like?" I responded with a bite.

"Are you drawing me?"

I made a sarcastic bow of my head.

"Stop that!" She snapped. *I was annoying her!*

"I'm going to draw the hat-of-the-day on you as a model."

"These are meant to be professional."

"It will help your non-existent buyers visualize how the yet-to-be-created hat will look."

"You are sour today!"

"I'm sour because I should be working right now. My work is vital. I earn my wages by honoring my commitments and answering inquiries. No one does my work for me."

"Do you think I like asking you for help?" She screamed each overly emphasized word, breaking the silence of the garden. If there were tourists, they would hear her. "You are selfish with your talent!"

I shook my head and continued to shade one of her cheeks. She lurched over, grabbed the paper from the middle, squeezed it into a ball, and tore it out of the large notepad.

She stood straight over me, those dark brown eyes ignited and pointed with the fist that held her crumpled portrait.

"I'm no one's muse."

She left me to sit alone in the garden. I ate both of the sandwiches. I didn't want her to be mad at me, yet I returned to

The Eye. That evening, I cut a white rose from the garden and placed it outside her bedroom door as a peacemaking gesture. At dinner, she sat next to me and smiled. All was forgiven, but the hat drawing stopped.

13
Franca Rossi

Luca spent far more time with my family than I spent with the Marinovas. Luca no longer felt like a guest at the celebrations Mama loved organizing. His absence became more noticeable than his presence. Imma referred to him as her future husband. My father offered Luca ferry rides if he ever felt like going to Stresa or the lake's islands for an afternoon.

The family's affection for Luca surged after Mama invited Arabella's suitor for dinner. Paolo Terracci was an Intra boy who was twenty-eight years old, twelve years my sister's senior. His facial hair made his expression challenging to gauge. Sometimes, I thought he was smirking at me. Luca said Paolo was just nervous, and if I wasn't sure, then I couldn't be insulted. Paolo's light brown eyes were droopy, like his plump belly. Mama sat him apart from Luca to thwart any unfavorable comparisons. Luca's skin and hair were kissed by the summer sun. I wanted to kiss him again very badly. How could Arabella want to kiss Paolo?

Gianna and I were equally repulsed when Mama told us who our guest would be. It was the first opinion Gianna and I ever admitted we shared and our first secret from Ara, whom each of us was closer to.

"You are unkind, girls! You must support your sister!" Mama yelled at us.

"Resenting this courtship is supporting her!" Gianna yelled back. "I will drive away every disgusting man I have to!"

Mama turned from where she stood in front of the stove, and with a downward arc, she hit Gianna in the thigh with the wooden spatula she was holding. Gianna howled on impact and stepped back.

"You'll probably wed me to a dog!" Gianna yelled over her shoulder as she limped off.

"Go away!" Mama snapped at me.

I sat next to Gianna on our bed. She grimaced from the pain, but the tears were for fury for failing to prevent the dinner. There was a fire within her that took very little to stoke. This was the first time I admired it as bravery. She must have regarded Luca favorably because she never limped when he came around.

48

Mama sat us next to each other, intending that I would temper Gianna with a glare or a pinch under the table. But for the first time, I wanted to be like Gianna. Her wild hair matched her outspoken personality, while my flatter curls seemed to externalize my amiable nature. Luca was the first one onto his second helping when Gianna leaned toward Paolo as if she were waiting for the moment when everyone else was chewing to unleash an incendiary remark, but Mama broke in, almost screeching:

"Paolo! Your grandmother says that you like sailing on the lake?"

"Yes, yes," he said. "I enjoy it very much. My cousins and I share a small boat."

Arabella inclined her head toward him in a gesture that made me cringe. The eagerness with which she listened to Paolo was uncomfortable to watch.

"Luca has several boats," Gianna said. "He can fit all of us on one of them."

"That's kind of him," Paolo responded, not appreciative of being compared to a fourteen-year-old with wealthy foreign parents.

"Is it true that your cousin Gino—" Gianna began.

"Dessert!" Mama shrieked like she saw a mouse named Dessert.

"—stole money from Signor Bonnali, the butcher, when he fired him?"

"Gianna! Do not insult Paolo with rumors!" Papa shouted, horrified. "I apologize for my daughter."

"It's not a rumor! It's true! Isn't it, Paolo?"

"Signor Bonnali refused to pay him for his last two days of work." Paolo shrugged.

"Because he had already stolen that amount and then some!"

Papa snapped to his full height and looked at Gianna with undiluted rage. He pointed to our bedroom. Beneath the table, I could feel Gianna's knees shaking inches from mine, not from fear. She remained determined to appear unrushed, unintimidated, unapologetic. She dabbed her lips with her napkin while Papa held his arm firmly. Gianna stood up slowly and tucked her chair into the table before walking to our bedroom with her head high.

Everyone was still. Papa reclined in his seat and moved his hand through his hair. Luca had unfinished food on his plate, an unmanned fork lying on the table, and his hands in his lap.

Mama put her chocolate and *marron glace* cake in the middle of the table. It was the same recipe served at Luca's first dinner with us, but it tasted like a flavorless mass of obligation.

Gianna slept soundly that night. I nuzzled into Imma, pinned between her and Gianna, to give Arabella the second bed to herself. Arabella cried herself to sleep. Paolo returned a few days later with a bouquet of cyclamen for Mama and a necklace for Ara. He stayed for another dinner.

December

14

Pasquale

Assuming Mother would only have Christmas gifts for her sons, I purchased a leather notebook, a children's book in French, a French dictionary, and a small brooch adorned with creamy pearls for Stasi. And yet, Stasi ended up with the most gifts of all. Mother gave her a pair of shoes (black, not red). Pim purchased her a miniature painting of wild horses. With my focus on Stasi's first Christmas with us, I was pleased to open stationery embossed with my monogram from her, an armwatch to tell the time anywhere from Pim, and refreshed studio supplies from Mother, Enzo, and Luca, as was their tradition. Stasi retreated to her room to rest when our large breakfast gave way to early afternoon grazing and lounging. Once she left the sitting room, I slumped on the couch, feeling unsuccessful in consoling her for being away from Varvara and Tatiana, whose daughter was now old enough to speak. I brought the new supplies to The Eye and spent the evening and night there.

I worked all night to complete my non-commissioned bust of Homer, trying to capture a blind gaze with a burning vision framed by deeply custodial creases. After finishing, I poured myself a celebratory glass of Barolo. For a few times a year, I can sit back, behold a completed work, and feel accomplished for molding matter to deliver an idea into its physical form. It is a moment of arriving when the difficulties that arose during the process feel small and fade away. It is one of the few sensations worth living for.

❋

A team of thirty-six attendants worked three days to prepare Villa Oro, the summer palace of the Count and Countess of Poitiers, for their annual New Year's Eve affair. It was an uninhibited display of spectacular wealth. Invitations were sent in September to thwart the thought of any competing events. As the daylight hours waned, wives became anxious about whether the jewelry they would receive for Christmas or Hanukkah would measure up to that of their rival socialites. This was the only New

Year's event that mattered in all twenty-two towns encircling Lake Maggiore. I never looked forward to it.

It was always the same. The daughters of the esteemed patrons were singularly marriage minded. In the whole of the attendee list, I was the only sculptor. They had looked down on my artist status for years until I did Tolstoy's bust, and then, suddenly, I was marketable. The menopausal matrons always wanted my ear to share their artistic hobbies. As the women passed me around, I indulged them and suggested to their husbands that there could be monetary potential to their wives' "work." Pim counseled that I endure the party to establish and rekindle connections that could lead to buxom commissions. This meant I always set the tone for the upcoming year to work above play.

Stasi was ecstatic about the soiree, ignoring my not-so-hinting hints about how boring the night inevitably was. She started getting ready after breakfast. My preparation included bathing, liberally applying Eau de Cologne, and slicking back my hair.

I knocked on Stasi's door, and she said, "Come in."

She stood in front of the mirror in her room. Her luminescent skin contrasted with her dark eyes and slight pout. Stasi's reddish hair, darker in the lamplight, was softly interwoven, pinned with delicate pearl pins, and crafted to perch a small diamond tiara. The tiara was dazzling, but my eye was hypnotically drawn to the base of her neck, where an exquisite ruby teardrop necklace inlaid with a halo of pinprick diamonds rested.

"You look… very nice." I stammered like a complete amateur. "Where have you been hiding that jewelry?"

"Is it too much?" Her hand hovered above the sparkling necklace without touching it.

"No. It's fitting. Fitting for a *tsarevna*."

"I was nervous to be more… to dress…" she began.

"Less than wholesome?"

"No. I meant I was nervous to dress more extravagantly than your mother."

"I think you are on a collision course with the inevitable."

"And I don't want to be described as wholesome!"

※

Luca was granted amnesty to miss the event. Instead, he would spend the evening at his sweetheart Franca's house as her family was having a party for their family and neighbors. Enzo's request to stay behind was firmly denied by Mother, who said that Luca was asking to be with someone else, whereas Enzo would have been alone.

Stasi and I were the first downstairs in the sitting room, ready. I poured us a drink as we waited. The thought of other men ogling at her also made me wish to abstain from attending. I heard Pim's slow and heavy footsteps behind his office door, but we were silent on the other side, and he didn't expect us there when he opened it. Upon seeing Stasi, his expression moved through a rapid series of emotions of which I caught surprise, dread, awe, and paternal pride. He kissed her on the cheek, and I handed him a small glass of brandy.

Mother's heels smacked the marble floor as she descended the stairs, holding a huffy Enzo by his elbow. She was wearing a royal blue dress that bunched around her waist flatteringly. Her curled, graying-blonde hair was also held high by many small, yellowish pearl pins, though she did not own a tiara. Upon seeing Stasi, Mother and I must have sampled from the same speculation: if Varvara's younger daughter shimmered like a chandelier, then Varvara could presumably be mistaken for an empress.

"We should be on our way." Mother said while pulling on her long gloves. "Enzo and I can skip drinks. I want to arrive by nine."

Pim finished his drink in one swig.

"LUCA!" Mother yelled up the stairs. "Happy New Year! Wear a hat and scarf!"

✻

When we arrived, there were already plenty of people there. Pim took Mother's hand in his. I offered Stasi my arm, and she took it. Our heavy coats were taken in the grand entryway. Five servers greeted us, each bearing a silver tray and holding a glass of champagne. Villa Oro's golden ballroom was packed with guests. Floor-to-ceiling windows overlooked the glistening nighttime lake on the far side of the room.

"We are going to greet the count and countess," Pim said over his shoulder as he and Mother waded into the crowd.

"Come, Stasi, I will show you around."

Her expression remained imperially still as she blinked her eyelashes in assent. To my discomfiture, she signaled for Enzo to follow us to the drawing room.

We cut through the thickets in conversation, bees roving to extract the scent of every flower. I nodded at guests I recognized as we passed by, but they only watched Stasi glide with her gaze fixed ahead. Ladies weighted down by more diamonds than Stasi were curious about this newcomer. Upon looking at her, young men found the limits of their confidence.

"This is my favorite room," I told Stasi. "Two summers ago, the count invited Pim and me to Villa Oro for luncheon. We had such a delightful time that we ended up staying for dinner. The count told us that his late mother, Countess Estelle, designed the ceiling molding of this room unbeknownst to her. After she died, they found stockpiles of her notebooks. There were crates and crates of them; he spoke of one little red book at the bottom of a crate so long the cover had taken the imprint of the crate's diamond squares.

"The count is her only surviving son, and they were very close, but he never realized the volume of her writing. Anyway, interspersed in the notebooks, there were all types of things. She drew, wrote poems, scribbled lists. The notebooks had no cohesion of topics, but all had this same design drawn into the margin of a page, an earmarked corner, or on the inside cover. It was this geometric design on the ceiling now. The molders complimented her symmetry and thoughtfulness. This is his ode to her."

Stasi admired the vaguely Persian pattern and, with the assistance of her half-finished drink, released a smile. Enzo examined the untraditional design as if he were asked to measure it.

"What is so moving about that story to me," I continued, "is the ability to give someone's life further texture posthumously. To think that one could be known for something after death that was never part of their identity in life."

"But it was a part of her identity," Stasi said. "At least privately. I think the beautiful part of the story is that the son finally sees his mother's talent."

"The geometrics embody the characteristics of Islamic mosaics," Enzo began. "Countess Estelle must have studied Islamic architecture."

"Enzo—" I responded to his exclamation, "Studying is not living. Maybe she visited mosques."

"Be agreeable, Pasq," Stasi tugged my arm. "Tell me more about this villa."

"Let me show you the bookshelves where her journals live now."

"I will go inspect the art," Enzo said dejectedly.

I felt terrible for anyone destined to confuse him for someone they would enjoy speaking with. Stasi's expression returned to its dignified elegance as I led us toward the library.

"Pasquale Marinova!"

Signor Albertini, the exuberant owner of the ferries that take locals and tourists around the islands of Lake Maggiore, hailed me. I attended French classes with one of his sons, Gino, who once told me that sculpting is a dying art form and is "a waste of an occupation for a gentleman of means." Gino's family had only been 'of means' for the lifespan of a barn cat. My insecurities felt insurmountable then, and criticism bruised me like a peach. I never forgot what he said. I felt better after his sister told me Gino had failed miserably at painting. And then I felt even better after I fucked her.

"Signor Albertini!" I matched his volume and greeted him with a handshake, my hand tightly enclosed in his, as my head swiveled to see if his daughter was nearby. "This is my sister, Tsarevna Anastasia Petrinova Marinova."

The large man made a slow forty-five-degree bow. He kissed the flat of her hand and beamed.

"*La principessa bella!* I am thrilled to make your friend. Lady Marinova said you are in Suna a year now. I refuse that you are here so long and not meet my sons. They are here now. Tonight, you meet them!"

"Anastasia loves to dance. Your sons should be sure to ask her after the midnight toast." She shot me a locked smile, eyes fuming with anger.

"*Si, si,* I must introduce them now..." As he turned, I could see his daughter Lorena huddled with two other girls, glaring at Stasi as they spoke to each other. The condemnatory looks on their faces fit their plain dresses and flat hair.

"If you wouldn't mind excusing us," I interrupted him. "Anastasia will have to meet them later; we were just heading to the count's library to meet a friend." I didn't know whether the Albertini brothers knew about my rendezvous with their sister. Signor Albertini happened to be Luca's girlfriend's father's boss. It would be best for the Albertini brothers not to connect me to Franco Rossi.

"*Certo, certo,*" he kissed her hand again. "You meet them later, *è una promessa*."

As I spun Stasi toward the library, she leaned in and said, "You are parading me around trying to sell me to the highest bidder!"

"Pim offered a commission to the brother who closes the sale."

Our posture broke with our laughter.

"Anyway, that would be an unfortunate strategy for Pim, as I would be the highest bidder to save you."

"I know you would."

"Pasquale!"

It was our hostess, Countess Josephine. She was encircled by a handful of stern women summoning crowd members for questioning.

"Pasquale," she purred as I lightly kissed her gloved hand. "You remember Lago Maggiore's most notable sculptor, Pasquale Marinova? He completed a piece for the count years ago of a girl holding three wagtails. It is in Paris. It was too magnificent to leave here. Pasquale is international now. I daresay commissioning you today would cost tenfold."

"It is still one of the dearest works of my career, Countess Josephine," I recited. "I have the pleasure of introducing my sister, Tsarevna Anastasia Petrinova Marinova."

Stasi curtsied and smiled with enough teeth for me to suspect she was somewhere past tipsy.

"Tsarevna Anastasia, welcome," the countess said. The women, held tall by stiff backs unrounded by age, nodded in Stasi's direction.

"Thank you, Countess. I admire your home very much. Pasquale told me all about the molding in the dining room."

"Yes," the countess rolled her eyes. "My mother-in-law haunts me from the grave. The molding doesn't look like much of anything to me. Did I tell you, Pasquale, that Lady Melanie is engaged to Viscount Le Norough?"

"Congratulations to you and your daughter. My mother informed us all when she received our family's invitation to the wedding."

"We are quite in the throes of planning. The wedding will happen here in Stresa in June but at the Grand Hotel des Iles Borromées. I couldn't handle the stress of hosting it at Villa Oro! The Count closely monitors our spending, but I tell him your only child only gets married once. I know your father is quite easy-going about you boys marrying, but my advice is not to wait too long."

"I will take your wisdom to heart, Countess Josephine. I am eager to show my sister the library and congratulate Lady Melanie. Do you know where she may be?"

"She would be pleased to see you. She was near the east sitting room the last I saw."

I bowed and led Stasi away.

"Were those Mary-Mari's friends?"

"No, they are too high-brow for Mother."

"How could they know?" Stasi whispered, referring to Mother's unsuitable origins.

"You, of all people, should know that the more time you spend with Mother, the more evident it becomes. At first, she is perceived as shy for not speaking about her upbringing, but once she tells a story about her days as a singer, it becomes clear that humility can be a mask."

A tall waiter passed by, and I replaced our empty glasses. When we finally made it to the library, there was such a large crowd that we decided to return to the ballroom. As we gazed at the crowd, I saw Enzo speaking with one of Lorena Abertini's stale friends.

"Enzo seems to be enjoying himself a little more."

"Where is he?" She looked around.

"By the dour brunette in light purple."

"That is exactly the kind of girl I imagine him with."

"Really? I can't envision him with anyone."

"You need to be nicer to him. Boys need their brothers like girls need their sisters."

"I don't see you very attached to your sister. And, anyway, that's why we have Luca as our buffer brother."

"I was attached to Tati when I was little. Not being close to her now makes me realize how much I wish we were closer. You shouldn't be an obstacle for Enzo."

"I'll be nicer to him next year."

"Looks like that is about to take effect in a few minutes." She nodded toward the orchestra as it stopped playing, and the count and countess took their place in front of the musicians.

"*Felice anno nuovo!*" The crowd hushed for the count's annual New Year's address. "*Bonne année!* Thank you for coming. Each year, Countess Josephine and I cherish sharing these moments with our dearest friends. These moments hold a mystical serenity—a pause to reflect on what has happened in the past twelve months. A spring, summer, and autumn have risen and set. And we are still here. This moment invites us to remember the loved ones not here with us – whether they are elsewhere this evening or were lost to us this year or in years past. I recall my late mother, whose soul passed seven years ago but whose thoughts and deeds are etched in the memories of all who knew her.

"In these quiet moments, in the ether between what has happened and what will happen, one is called to question oneself about how the year 1894 will be different. As I age, I see how time only grants us a small window to accomplish important work. The way I have come to see it, we all have two missions in this life…. Maybe you have more than two, and may God bless you if that's your prerogative… Our first purpose is to leverage our talents and fortunate positions to enhance this world where each of us sees the greatest need. The depth of the role you play in lifting up this greatest need is up to you; whether you are a creator, a visionary thinker, a financier, a guide, or a supporter – you must find your own way to contribute to the betterment of others and your own satisfaction. The collective influence of this room inspires me.

"Secondly, our simple calling is to love each other. When it comes to love, never hesitate; your life will not be spent wondering. The risk of disappointment rarely outweighs the risk of regret. Hold your loved ones closely and allow yourself the joy of a full cup.

"I drone on as the new year approaches…. A year in which my daughter Melanie will marry Viscount Le Norough." The room clapped and turned toward the kind face of Lady Melanie and the stiff, militaristic viscount. Melanie could have anything yet asked for nothing. Of anyone I have ever met, she is the most capable of achieving happiness. "I am very much looking forward to the wedding, where I can again give a lengthy speech. Now it is time, I am being signaled, for us all to count down to the new year."

The count lifted his glass. A couple of hundred glasses rose to mirror his. "To 1893, all it bestowed upon us and all it takes with it. And to 1894, may we give more than we seize. To 1894!"

"To 1894!" The crowd cried out before taking a final sip, swig, or gulp of 1893. Then the crowd began, increasingly riotous: "Ten, nine, eight, seven, six–" Stasi and I shared one more smile before we joined in, "–five, four, three, two, one!"

At "one," she wrapped her arms around me, and I lifted her off the ground. I thoughtlessly released the drink in my grip, and it spilled down the back of her dress. The glass tumbled to shatter on the marble floor. No one noticed, not even Stasi. She was concerned with her drink slopping over my tailcoat's back. We turned to the strangers within reach and hugged or shook hands with them, all well-wishes, blurred faces, and smiles.

Then, I felt a hard thump on my back. It was Pim, equipped with a brandy. His eyes were foggy but jovial and lit up his face.

"My son!" He held me tight as if I were a little boy. I couldn't match his strength, having been surprised and lacking the capacity. "Happy New Year!"

"My beautiful daughter!" Stasi beamed and bounced into his tight hold.

Mother and Enzo unfurled behind Pim. I kissed Mother on the cheek; she squeezed my arms lovingly. Stasi cordially did the same, her composure resurrected in Mother's presence. Tilting up from Mother, Stasi stumbled, which made Pim laugh, and he put his arm around her. I reached out my hand to Enzo, and as we began to shake hands, Stasi said my name admonishingly. I clasped Enzo's hand and pulled him into a hug. He soberly pushed me away after a few seconds. I patted him on the back.

"What wonderful brothers!" Stasi called.

"If only Luca were here as well," Mother said sentimentally.

"He's where he wants to be," Pim said. "I swear that boy has been a man his whole life."

"Have you enjoyed the party?" Stasi asked Mother.

"Yes, thank you," Mother responded coolly; she didn't look at Stasi when she replied. Mother caught my eye and then faced

Stasi. "It has been a lovely evening. How about you? Have you met anyone interesting?"

"A few people, mostly Pasq, have been telling me all about this house."

"It's remarkable."

"The word 'remarkable,'" Stasi hiccupped, "fascinates me. While it means extraordinary, it also makes me think that when someone calls something remarkable, the subject is worth remarking about. But what exactly are you saying by saying remarkable? Does that make sense? Or is it clear to mother tongues?"

I saw Mother laugh for the first time with Stasi in the same room.

"I fear I'm not making sense." Stasi laughed as well.

"No, no, I am laughing because you made an interesting observation."

"Well, my children, or my grown children," Pim began, "I have enjoyed myself too much and am ready to retire."

"No!" I yelled, my feelings becoming words faster than thoughts. "The dancing is starting. We should stay."

"Yes, let's stay!" Stasi pleaded, swiveling from under his arm to look at him desperately.

"I think you've all had enough to drink," Mother said. "My mother always said nothing good happens after one in the morning."

"That's still an hour away!" I exclaimed.

"Let's leave," Enzo whined. "I'm exhausted."

"You all leave, Stasi, and I will stay," I declared with a swish of my hand. Stasi folded her hands in mock prayer, begging alongside me to continue the night.

"I'll ask the Borgognis if you can ride home with them. They are always the last to leave."

The *tsarevna* clapped with exaggerated glee. We thanked Pim profusely. I turned to reach for passing cocktails, but Mother put her hand on my arm to stop me. Her look reiterated that we had had enough. I could wait until she left.

"Well, good night all. Dancing has begun," I stated in a brazen effort to dismiss them.

"I barely see anyone dancing," Enzo observed rigidly.

"Then we must be off to start it!" I grabbed Stasi by the hand and pulled her away.

When we were across the room beside the orchestra, there was a renewed opportunity to clutch two glasses containing a pinkish liquor being circulated.

"Can you believe it? We are alone." I clinked my glass against hers and sipped, unable to taste the liquor's bite. "Well, not alone, but you know what I mean."

The first dance was between sweet Melanie and the viscount. They dutifully performed a waltz. I felt an overwhelming sensation that their entire lives had been choreographed; even the crowd's delicate awe seemed arranged.

I whispered in Stasi's ear: "They are getting married, and we are getting tipsy."

As I watched Stasi stifle her laughter and rise to full height, Mario Gismondi asked her to dance, and she accepted in a hummingbird's wing beat. She handed me her drink, and I took it, unsure where I had found the wherewithal to do so. I should have been grateful she didn't throw her drink's contents at me.

"Ciao Pasquale, this is the first chance I've had to talk to you all night." I turned to see Alessi, one of my grade-school friends.

"Alessi, good to see you," I finished my drink in one large take and placed the glass on a side table to free my hand to shake his.

"The Russian princess is your half-sister? She is the most striking woman here. I am very eager to dance with her after Leonardo."

"She's dancing with Mario," I slurred at him. He pivoted me by the shoulders toward the dancefloor to show she was, in fact, now dancing with Leonardo Siuso. As he spun her, Stasi caught my gaze and mouthed, 'Save me.' I spent a moment questioning whether I had imagined it, but my desire to intervene was without doubt. I finished the other cocktail I was still holding and forced the glass into Alessi's open hand. In three strides, I was beside them, and for a moment, Leonardo looked like he would not surrender the *tsarevna*, but he registered the absence of humor in my face and reluctantly kissed her hand before dissolving away.

I hold her, leading our movements, while she keeps us upright and makes me look better than I am. Her hair has lost a bit of its taut curl and seems more welcoming. I inhale the subtle floral scent deeply, willing my memory to remember this.

When the viola player lingers on for a final few solo pieces, I peel myself from Stasi to see her makeup has started to smear. Her brown eyes have become dark and smokey.

I let her go to wipe my forehead with the back of my hand and loosen my collar. A man I've never seen before is offering to have her at his home for dinner. A possessiveness moves from my stomach to my chest and tightens, twisting like many screws. Reaching for her hand in mid-extension toward this man, I rip her from him without explanation or apology and pull her toward our coats and the Borgognis, the elderly couple who will bring us to Casa Bianca.

Signora Borgogni greets Stasi with care. Stasi assures her that she is all right and that I am okay, too. I attempt a confirming nod because I actually feel nauseous and would rather not speak. I crawl into the carriage first (very ungentlemanly), hoisting myself from the floor onto the seat with Stasi's assistance. Stasi continues polite conversation, but because the Borgognis do not speak English well, she sloppily overcompensates with gestures.

"Go to sleep, Pasq; I'll wake you when we are home."

Like an instant spell – I plant my face against the side of the door. The swaying carriage sashays me to sleep.

The carriage makes a right-hand turn, and I wake up knowing we have arrived at our pebbled driveway. Preferring the consistency of darkness, I keep my eyes closed and listen to Signora Borgogni's steady sleeping breath. Stasi's left hip is sidled against my right one.

The carriage stops. The door opens. Stasi softly asks me to wake up, her voice dry and quiet. I open my eyes and sit up obediently. I thank Signor Borgogni and follow Stasi out of the carriage, stumbling but feeling better than when we left Villa Oro.

I follow Stasi through the door and into the black foyer. The rug catches my foot, and I trip on the first step. My hands and right knee slam on the marble floor, and I announce the pain with yelling but instantly know I have made a mistake as it echoes through the house. Stasi helps me stand again. She kicks her shoes to the side of the staircase without letting go of my hands in hers and guides me up the stairs, whispering. "Take a step up now... step up again... five more... last one."

She leads us to her bedroom, the closest to the stairs. When she finally lets go of my hands, she lights the weeping candles in front of the mirror, and then there is a double, quadruple light. I sit in the chair beside the bed. In the corner of the room where I first saw her this evening, she removed her necklace and looked completely different. The *tsarevna* laboriously untangles the tiara that has become affixed to her hair.

"Your hands were so cold," my throat hollowed with the sound of my voice.

"My fingers are never warm. Maybe my blood runs cold."

"What time is it?"

"Late. I couldn't see the clock downstairs."

"Who was that man who invited you for dinner?"

"A man I will not be having dinner with."

"A well-crafted non-answer."

"Look who can articulate again. I don't know if you know, but your expression becomes gentler when you look at Lady Melanie."

"I think she is the purest soul in the world. She came to the house once. I kissed her in the garden. But she isn't for me."

"You could be happy with a simple girl." She finally liberated the tiara from her head. Her long hair was voluminously teased at the roots. Stasi placed the sparkling tiara at the base of one of the candles.

"All of the evidence points to me being a devotee of the complicated."

Stasi lies on top of the bed, emits a long yawn, and rests her head on the pillows still in her dress.

"And you accept yourself for that?"

"I must if I intend to go on cohabitating with my demons."

"That may not work out for you." She closes her eyes and exhales. I should go to my room, but I feel leaden in this chair, and my eyes can't fight the heavy pull. The candles appear like one source of continuous light with an elastic flicker. As I drift under, Stasi's whole body suddenly shudders with cold. It startled me, and I looked on, wondering how the movement didn't wake her. She shudders again. I look around the room for a blanket, but there are none.

I walk over to the other side of the bed and climb on it. Slowly, I lie beside her, terrified to breathe, wondering if she'll snap awake. There is a third shudder. I reach for her hand on her middle to take it in mine. The long bones are cold beneath the skin.

    Slowly, I shift to compress my body against hers, which is a little too upright. I place my head against her arm and settle there. The shudders cease. I worry she is too still. As she finds new breath, I release the one I am holding. I lift my arm and wrap it around her middle.

    I notice her tiny imperfections for the first time. Though her ears are the same size, one is higher on her head than the other, if only by centimeters. Her eyes are marginally asymmetrical in shape; the right eye is a little bit more of a coin than an almond, but each of her eyebrows is primmed to diminish the difference. The light dims as the flames fall beneath the mirror's frame. I am left contemplating how perfect she is until I finally slip under the surface of consciousness.

15
Enzo

Despite the wool socks, my toes ached with the morning cold. It was still dark outside. The contents of my head felt singular and heavy. My neck was tight from sleeping with my chin extended from my clavicle; each vertebra felt drily stacked upon the other. I climbed out of bed on the right side, as I do each day, combed my hair to the right, and put on a house robe and slippers in search of sustenance and reading material.

Stasi's heels were feet apart and tipped over sideways at the bottom of the steps. Her bedroom door was ajar, though I dared not look inside. I moved her heels to the foyer closet to prevent Mother from becoming flustered and regressing on the progress the women had made last night. Out the kitchen window, the azure sky blossomed. The definition of Stresa's church-spire skyline was evident over the water. The colder the air, the more precise the view.

I stacked all of the food I could carry in the hook of my elbow: an entire ciabatta bread loaf, blueberry jam, a small plate of gorgonzola, a glass bottle of milk (which was easier to carry than a full, sloshing glass), an apple, candied citrus fruit peels, and a knife. My feet could no longer remain on the unapologetically glacial marble floor. The sky's emerging light blue glow lit the stairs enough to make balancing my loot a fair undertaking. A tiredness resurged, calling me to my warm bed.

Stasi's peaking open door, emitting the bluish sky into the dark grand foyer, was also calling me – to close it and insulate her room from the foyer's air. As I reached the door, without intending to, I glanced inside the room and nearly dropped everything. The waxing daylight betrayed Pasquale sleeping against Stasi. She lay on her back like an enchanted fairytale princess, her red hair spread to her right side and trailing off the bed. Pasquale slept at her left with no space between them; his face rested on her shoulder. The sight resembled children who fell deeply, innocently asleep exactly where they were after an exhaustive playtime. And yet, the image was striking.

I stood there, rooted. *Close the door.* I could not stand here, staring on, until I made sense of it. My outreached hand hovered above the doorknob as if all consciousness had left that hand.

Below, Mrs. Figlia enters through the kitchen door. Someone might see me here. I turn and bolt my bedroom door latch.

16
Pasquale

"PASQUALE!"

I snapped awake faster than I could realize where I was, half-beside, half-against Stasi on the bed in the blue room. Mother was shrieking in the hallway, pulling in breath between screams to strengthen them.

I sat up quickly, but as my head swung above my body, my head was shrouded in a sheet of pain. The sunlight from the lake overwhelmed my soporific eyes before they could properly adjust. But the piling symptoms of excess didn't feel as demanding when compared with the asphyxiating terror of my mother screaming my name over and over, overcoming her echoes. Stasi, newly awoken as well, looked at me with dread.

A gunshot thundered from Luca's deck, and our bodies leaped at the sound.

"Stay here," I said, rubbing sight into my eyes. I closed Stasi's door behind me to protect her from whatever might be said.

Mother stood at the bottom of the stairs, fuming in her robe. Upon seeing me leaving the blue room, still in the same clothes as last night, she turned, fists clenched and shoulders high, and walked into the dining room. If I only cared for myself, I would head to my room and fall asleep until midnight. It would be sufficient for Mother to know we were separated. But for Stasi's sake, Mother's rage needed to be diffused, so I patted my hair down as I descended the stairs.

As I turned into the dining room, Mother stood, facing me with her back to the window. Fine lines dashed her face all over. Beside her, Pim sat at the table with his breakfast. Strangely, he was in my dinner seat. His broad face was one grim expression.

"I'm sorry." Quick to apologize. "We arrived home very late. I was tired and had had too much to drink. I just fell asleep."

"It is extremely..." Mother swallows, "Immoral, Pasquale. I am... disgusted."

"It was an accident, Mar–Mother. It was inappropriate but not... sinister! I just fell asleep! She is my sister. It couldn't have been even four hours."

"Four hours too many. You need to reign yourself in. You are forgetting yourself."

"Mary," Pim interrupted, his voice hoarse and his hand lifted to slow Mother down. "He said it was a mistake."

"This is revolting, Petyr! Utterly RE-VOL-TING. Inexcusable. How have I raised such delinquents?"

"Luca only fell asleep at Franca's when it became too late to walk home. He was home by seven. The Rossis are good people." Pim told Mother in the same flat tone.

"Pasquale," Mother shook her head. "This can never happen again. Do you understand?"

I nodded.

"So help me, God, Pasquale, I will send her away."

We both knew the decision to send Stasi away lay with Pim solely. But I nodded again.

"I don't like it." She concluded with a flick of her wrist to dismiss me.

I took a chocolate *fagottino* from the tray in the middle of the table and made the trek to my bed as the headache sunk its claws in. In my bed, I positioned the pillows to my right and wrapped myself around them, remembering how her breath rolled slowly into her lungs like a building wave before crashing.

April 1894

17
Anastasia

I trudged up the stone steps, hoping to find him on a break or at a point where I could convince him to take one. I knocked at the door of The Eye, but when I heard his nearing footsteps call back, I leaped into the pile of old leaves around the corner of the studio. When the door opened, I imagined Pasquale looking around, confused and wondering whether he fabricated the sound. A giggle escaped me, and my hands flew to cover my mouth; I held my breath. His face peered around the corner of the little structure, and I screamed and ran the other way. Crunchy leaves announced each landing of my foot as I ducked and pushed stray branches. I stopped to see if he was following me, but then I heard him chasing me from the left, and I ran back up the hill, laughing and yelling. I let out a scream as his arms wrapped around my middle.

I let my limbs droop, and my body turned heavy. Even so, he hauled me inside and positioned me in the chair that had been moved beside the window. Once seated, he stood over me, took a breath, smoothed his hair down, and said in faux seriousness, "You knocked?"

"I'm restless today. Every idea I have is more boring than the last."

"Mrs. Figlia used to say that if you're bored, you're stupid."

I contorted my face into feigned outrage.

"She would call me stupid regardless."

"So, how do you plan to protect your immaculate reputation as an intelligent woman?"

"That's why I've come to you. You have to help me!"

"So then... how shall we channel all this?" He waved both of his palms at me unevenly. "I usually start writing letters, walk through the gardens, sketch, swim, but it's too cold right now, tidy up the studio, run an errand into town… any of this sound appealing?"

I shook my head.

"We could go on the boat? I could row us around until I tire."

"We wouldn't get far at all," I jab. "Were you working? I don't mean to commandeer your day—"

"You know exactly that's what you are doing."

"I don't want to take the rowboat out. That feels like a whole ordeal... walking down to the shed, putting it in the water—"

"Which you would watch me do."

"Taking my shoes off—"

"How strenuous for you."

"And then rowing to Fondotoce—"

"As you take in the sights."

"Exactly." I sighed. "A complete ordeal."

"We could dance?"

He looked around. There were plenty of loose papers accumulating under the desk and lining the base of the bookshelves, but the floor was mostly clear by the fireplace.

"Let me clean up. Then I will spin you until you are too dizzy to worry about boredom."

I twirled to the window and theatrically flung the curtain aside to let in more light. I pirouetted to each window to adjust the curtains. Pasquale swept papers into one large pile with his feet and then lifted the pile into the fireplace.

"What are you doing? Are those important?"

"I don't remember."

"The correct answer was that dancing with me is more important."

"I work hard not to appear desperate."

After minutes of tidying, the studio seemed larger. I opened the windows to invite the air and light in. There were latches at the top and bottom, and once pulled, the windows swung lengthwise inward, elated, as if these windows had been born to be doors. I stood in the open doorway and closed my eyes.

At the smell of smoke, I turned to see a fire nipping his newspapers, notes, receipts, and letters. The smoke was not the rich smell of a slow, labored fire but the sharp bite of something burning too quickly.

Pasq reached out for my hand. He spun me three times before we danced around the room without music. He curled me into him, and we swayed there.

"I never open these windows."

"I would keep them open all of the time."

"What were you thinking before, at the window?"

"I was trying to memorize the mountain's contours and the lake's reflection."

"And you closed your eyes for that?"

I nodded. He shortened his reach. He smelled like the garden. When I opened my eyes, Pasq looked at me bare, without reserve. His eyes were locked on my face and hair and moving into my eyes.

He lifted my hand, wrapped in his, closer to our faces; now my face was in the nape of his neck. I could feel his breath on my ear.

"I want to be able to draw your fingerprint from memory," he whispered. His hold on me tightened without sacrificing our rhythm. "I want to name the constellations of your freckles."

I lifted my head. His light brown eyes met mine. He leaned in and kissed me.

The moment felt fragile, like water in cupped hands. I kissed him back. We stood, our legs no longer swaying, our lips embracing softly.

His hands moved fluidly from the back of my head down my arms and lower back. But then his grip lingered at the back of my neck and tightened around my arm, and I could feel him leveraging his body weight to lower us to the floor. I pushed him away. He released his hands from my body and closed them around my face, tipped my lips upward, and tried to kiss me again. But the moment was gone. I pushed him again, this time hard, and he took one wavering step backward.

"Stasi."

I shook my head. I wiped the sides of my mouth with the back of my right hand. Now was not the time to speak. Swallowed in a daze, I stepped out of the nearest open window and walked down the hill through the woods, forgetting the path, chanting in my head: *don't think, don't feel, don't think, don't feel, don't think, don't feel, don't think, don't feel.*

18
Pasquale

Hours later, Stasi's dinner seat was empty due to a supposed thick migraine.

I never had the chance to knock on her door as Pim insisted I play a few chess games in his office over his newly imported vodka.

"Why did you turn down Baron Lutzvendorff's commission?" Pim asked.

"I don't want to go to Vienna right now." As he spoke, I relived kissing her. I shifted in the chair to hide the reflexive twitching of my hands, recalling their part this afternoon.

"You've refused how many, seven commissions, this spring?"

"About so."

He checkmated me with less effort than usual, comfortably maneuvering his queen to my first row, where my king sat trapped by his pawns. He gestured for me to reset the board.

"Baron Lutzvendorff is a friend. It's important to them they have the companion piece of his daughter-in-law to the bust of his son you made in '91. You've said before that Vienna inspires you." I shrugged, and he continued. "It seems you are producing more letters of declination than sculptures. That's not how one stays relevant."

"I'm having an off night," I gestured to the board. I gripped the chair to suppress the resurfacing physical memory of Stasi's skin. He poured me another drink and gave me a cigar. I started talking, unable to remain inside my treacherous head.

"It's time I enter a new phase in my career. I want a priceless collection in a museum, an intact body of work, not a diaspora of pieces hawked to private bidders. These past few months, I have been considering a new project." He reclined in his seat. "The project would be to capture flowers from our gardens. Arresting the movement of their emergence, rise to full bloom. The moment of wilting. An ambitious collection that I forge in private from my studio."

A light flickered in his eyes. His gleam was not merely a reflection of the embers on the tip of his cigar. And this project was not purely designed around my professional aspirations.

✺

After losing sleep scrutinizing yesterday's events, I stood outside Stasi's door in the late morning. There was no sound from behind it. Was she sequestering herself, or had she fluttered elsewhere?

I took a breath before entering the dining room. As I stepped forward, Pim knocked me beelining for the front door. He had on a thin jacket and his black top hat.

"Good morning, son." He sidestepped and proceeded toward the door. "Your mother and brothers went for a coffee at Café Sublime. And I'm off!"

I wave a lackluster swipe, which he doesn't see. The house is quiet, open, and cavernous. She is somewhere here.

China shatters on the veranda tile, followed by a darling curse word. I sit on the bottom-most step, my knees bent high like a tree frog. The third hand of the dining room clock intones each hollow moment. I could take asylum in The Eye.

Yesterday may not have been what she intended, but the instance was tame compared to what I wanted. I need to know if she feels the same. If she does, we will move from there, in the dark of a new moon, without leaving a note.

I pulled myself upright and did three star jumps to dissipate the nervousness, alert her to my presence, and give her the courtesy to ready herself or flee. Stasi is looking through the open door frame in my direction before she can see me. When I take that final step outside, her lips are parted like she might speak. I try to begin. My prepared defense of yesterday begins to boil and I forget what to say. I stride to the railing, take a breath overlooking the water, and tilt my head to look at her again. Her watchful eyes swell with a soft receptivity for me I wasn't expecting. I want to hear her honey voice consent and command. I can't hold my ground – hold back – any longer. I close the space between us.

Holding the back of her head, I kiss her, pushing my tongue into her mouth, and she welcomes it. She has us like this by my neck, but I pull out of her hold. I kneel beside her and use one hand to pull up her dress while my other hand glides underneath and tenderly moves up the inside of her thighs. With my index and middle finger, I find her and begin slow, diamond-shaped strokes. She looks into my eyes as she sharply inhales. My other hand glides up her stomach, over her clothing, brushes her left breast, and stops to stroke her collarbone. She tips her head back in the chair and emits a moan.

    Beneath the dress, my rhythm moves from slow, wide halos to tighter and faster knots. Her chest swells. I wrap my fingers around her cascading hair and roll my thumb up and down her neck. Her breath shortens, and her cries become completely reactionary. I move faster and smaller until her entire body is reduced to one spot.

    Then, with one hand entwined in her lush hair and the other under her dress, Pim steps out onto the veranda.

19
Pasquale

The moment cracked like an egg: shell in a million pieces and contents released formlessly and irreparably.

"Go to your room, Anastasia."

My head whipped back to her, only knowing that she would refuse. She must protest and proclaim that she would leave with me. But she did as he said. Her eyes fixed on the floor. She shuffled to a standing position around my hand that remained between her legs, avoiding my eyes. I wasn't keeping my arm there on purpose. I couldn't feel it. It felt like my entire fucking arm did not belong to me. I had to shove my shoulder with my other hand to rotate the languid arm to the side. My *tsarevna* exited with her head down, shamed by the man she respected more than me.

Pim stood at full height, towering over me, still on my knees.

"Leave." He spat.

There was no resistance in me. I mechanically walked down the terrace steps, disappeared into the gardens, and departed through the north gate along Via di Lago Maggiore.

I walked until the sun went down, retracing my path at times, and then wandered some more. I walked past families in the afternoon and lovers in the evening and steadily became the sole loiterer of the streets. If I kept moving, I could keep the cold air from saturating my bones. I spotted several strands of her long brown hair on my sweater and left them there, where they radiated heat.

What was she thinking right now? I envisioned her whirring in her room. We could never stay here now. We will go somewhere where our relation is not known and live on my earnings. Pim could never forgive this, but he would never expose us. Back at the villa, what reason did Pim give for my absence at dinner? Was Stasi at the table? Did he tell Mother the whole, a slice, a crumb? Mother had intuited the threat of this in her marrow.

After hours and miles, my feet grew tired, though I was too roused to sleep. I chose a wooden lakeside bench to lie on; the stone benches felt like ice blocks. Staring at the stars and occasionally the horizon of lights stretching across the water from Stresa, Baveno, and Arona, I formulated our next move.

The eastern corner of the sky eventually became light blue. The stars winked *au revoir*. I heard the myriad sounds of footsteps, the piazza cafés opening, and bike tires humming. The church bells play at six, and when the last ring subsides, an inner chime tells me it is time to walk again. How quickly the sun rises behind the mountains to kiss Stresa with light. At the Intra library, I recline in one of the lawn chairs facing the lake. From the bow of the land's curvature, our white stucco villa can be seen floating on the edge of the lake in the far distance. I will leave that house today. Conceivably forever. The treasures and tools in my studio will have to be left behind. Two proud swans glide along the lake's reeds.

A single gunshot sings over the lake and reverberates until the hills absorb it. Luca is provoking the day.

I return exactly how I departed, a mounting constriction in my chest, and sit at the northern edge of the gardens to think. I will walk straight into her room and convince her to leave.

It was quiet inside the house. My neck pivoted for threat. Mother passed me in the hallway, humming with a gloating smile.

"Oh, Pasquale–," she said. "Where have you been?"

"Where is Stasi?"

Her eyes grew large, and she reached out to me. I dodged her touch.

"Oh my dear... she is gone. She just left."

"For a coffee? To Via Ruga?"

"No, for Paris. She's gone." Her smile returned. I could have struck her for oozing such victory. But there was no time to hit my mother. I ran up the stairs to the blue room, threw the door open, and – the room was emptied.

Enzo was on the daybed reading in the sitting room, his feet casually crossed at the ankles. My exhaustion abated with my soaring disbelief. My words became as disjointed as my thoughts.

"Where is Stasi?"

"She left by carriage an hour or so ago for the train. Papa announced she was leaving last night. Where were you?"

"Train? Enzo, look up. What time does it leave?"

He was annoyed to be interrupted while reading and said without looking up from his page: "Now she is gone, you want to talk to me?"

I lunged at him and grabbed him by his ears before he could register the assault. I shook him by the ears and bellowed from my chest: "TELL. ME. You pompous piece of shit!"

"It departs–" he tried to loosen my grip on his ears, "–in twenty-five minutes!"

I didn't make it to the train on time. I didn't even see it pull away. It was gone before I made it to Fondotoce.

I bought a ticket for the next train leaving at the same time tomorrow. I walked the seven kilometers home, estimating I had walked over twenty kilometers. I sweated through these clothes and walked them dry thrice over. It was noon when I stood in the center of my bedroom, unsure where to start. I realized I hadn't eaten for a day, marched down to the kitchen, and danced around Mrs. Figlia to grab a jar of blueberry jam, a loaf of bread, and the entire bag of apples.

"Can you make several sandwiches for my journey tomorrow?" I requested.

Upstairs, I threw my leather Portmanteau trunk on top of the bed. Forgetting to bring a knife for the jam, I tore the loaf into pieces and soaked each one in the jar before devouring it.

Mother burst through the door and found me sitting on top of the bed, surrounded by my things and licking the blueberry residue off my hands and wrists.

"Where are you going?" Her voice was low, bent in fear for the answer she already knew.

"To Paris."

"You can't."

"I am." I shrugged, unprovokable.

"Why not go in a few months once she is settled?"

"No. It has to be now."

"You don't even know how to contact her."

"Once I do, I'll be on hand."

She cried to me for an entire hour, raving about how she always knew "that girl" would be the destruction of our family. She kept grabbing at my arms to slow down my packing. As she cycled through strained reasonability and despondent crying, all I could think was that I still hadn't washed my hands since yesterday.

Finally, Mother's stamina curdled. She demanded that I tell Pim my plan, and while I made her dragging me by the elbow difficult, I wanted to be done with this unavoidable encounter.

He was in his office surveying the lake as if he owned it, sipping his *aperitivo*.

"Pasquale is going to Paris tomorrow."

Pim did not turn around. "Let him go, Mary."

Thoroughly defeated and exhausted from the day's emotions, she fled the room in unseeing tears, bumping into furniture on her way out.

Pim turned to face me. His glare held disgust, as though I were something other than his child, other than human even. His bottom eyelids twitched. The look was uninhibited as if I could see his soul. And this uninhibited soul flatly said the words that will echo in my head forever: "You are the greatest disappointment of my life."

Paris, France

20
Pasquale

The train journey consisted of two days of staring out the smudged window with the newspaper neglected on my lap. After I settled into Hôtel de Luxe, I explored the neighborhood. A week later, I had my bearings on the surrounding streets and two neighboring arrondissements. I began the search for the hat shop where Varvara had shopped on her honeymoon with Pim. Stasi had not taken the hat sketches out of sentimentality. I was not sleeping and unable to recall the shop's name. All I knew for sure was that the hats came in cream satin boxes with pink lids that Stasi played with in her mother's closet as a girl. The hotel concierge produced the names and addresses of all the milliners in the city.

With more persistence than luck, I located Les Chapeaux de Marie. The store had a pastel-blue door and a small window with matching trim. The tired seamstress who told me about it warned that the shop was très petit and could be easily missed. A single hat of each style was displayed neatly in a line at the profile view.

The owner greeted me from behind the counter. I was too spent to be insecure about my terrible French.

"*Bonjour.*" I rubbed the back of my head.

"*Bonjour Monsieur. Qui est* the woman *chanceuse pour laquelle vous magasinez* today?"

"*Monsieur, parle anglais?*" He nodded sideways to signal that he could try. "Thank you. *Merci.* I have an unusual situation. My sister and I were separated on the train. It seems she got off at the wrong stop by accident, and I wasn't alerted until I reached the platform in Paris."

My eyes darted between his beady eyes, shrouded by a furled browline.

"We – that is, she – has original hat designs and has always admired your shop." I continued. "I believe she made it to Paris safely. And once she is settled, I think she will come here. I am concerned for her safety and would like to request that you contact me when she comes here. I am staying at the Hôtel de Luxe. Her name is Anastasia Marinova and I am Pasquale Marinova."

"The lady does not know Hôtel de Luxe? Would she not go there?"

"The plan was, uh…" I fumbled unconvicted, "to find a suitable place once we arrived. We did not have a prior reservation. Please… *monsieur*, don't reduce me to waiting outside your shop like a beggar."

"I will take your information. If the lady comes here, I will give it to her so she can contact you."

Fair enough.

✳

Beneath the late-morning outcast sky, I sipped my *café au lait* and wrote letters to pending clients to announce that I would not be keeping my appointments for the rest of the spring. I anticipated more disappointment than rage since I had not yet taken money for these ventures. I reached out to a few contacts in Paris. One of them could assist me in finding a suitable apartment with an acceptable temporary workspace. I felt a pang of longing for The Eye. I wrote to my Jewish banker in Pallanza to send some of my savings. I could live on what I have for a few years without any new commissions. For good measure, I penned Luca to write to me immediately if Stasi sent her new address.

Days passed in which I admired the polished trees lining the streets and flower beds of yellow irises, unable to hold their petals high, and daffodils with slender stems. Paris was a fascinating destination for someone who appreciated botany. The plant life was stewarded to feel gloriously bare yet lush and worth the effort. There is a harmony between nature's living colors and the stone streets and buildings.

A friend of a friend offered to tour apartments with me in the Montmartre district. I am hesitant to settle in one place before I find her, though I want to save us from living in hotels. The more significant part of my reluctance lay in that Stasi may criticize any choice that was not hers. When I returned to the hotel, the concierge told me I had a visitor. He gives me a suggestive look behind his wire glasses as he says, "Visitor." My heart holds mid-beat. The millions of cogs in my mind start whirring. He slides a slip of paper to me: *A. Marinova* above an address. I read it four times at the counter as if he might take it back. I step away in a stupor, realizing on the stairs to my room that I forgot to thank him.

After bathing, I can't begin to choose what to wear. Do I look like I have been busy or well-rested? Both would be lies. I combed my hair. Then it seemed too flat, and I ran my fingers throughout, but then it looked too greasy. I shook it out and combed lightly again. My cologne will wane by the time I arrive. I changed my shirt again. I leave around five in the evening, intending to catch her too early to be away at dinner.

The twilit orange sky shone above the tops of the buildings and between the streets. It had rained for about thirty minutes this afternoon, and the air felt washed. The streetlamps lined the way in a soft yellow-white light.

Her building was four stories high—a residence, not a hotel. Before I could ring the bell, I was let in by a gentleman entering, who I followed to the second floor and continued ascending. I gripped the railing to stabilize my shaking knees. On the top floor, I walked toward apartment 3E with heavy feet. Her apartment was facing the street. I had practiced the knock in my head and hoped it came off confidently.

Steps approaching... not a woman's. The man who opened the door was not French.

"I apologize," I stammered, "I have made a mistake."

I must have knocked on the wrong door. I looked at the address again in my hand. Am I on the correct floor? Could I have come into the wrong building? Perhaps I had misread 3E.

"Who is it?" Stasi called out in her most airy, carefree voice in English.

"Pasquale!" I called out, projecting far too loudly before this motherfucker could utter anything. He was in a cheapish brown day suit and surveyed me through his square jawline. He stood in the doorway. He had a compact, muscular build. Stasi's silhouette appeared at the end of the apartment's entrance hallway, shrouded in light from the windows behind her. She was in a long jewel-tone blue dress. I had never seen her in blue before; it was a gorgeous color on her, making her more slender. Her long hair was parted down the middle, making it more brown than red.

"Pasquale, how wonderful to see you! Come in!" I moved past him and hugged her closely. "John, this is my brother—one of the brothers from Italy!"

"Can we speak privately, Stasi?" I said directly to her, unable to look at him.

"Of course, Pasq. I'm thrilled you are here. What an exciting thing that you would visit Paris! John was about to leave. Let's go to dinner."

Stasi approached the large fireplace framed by an elegant white marble mantelpiece. The apartment was large, with high ceilings and five long windows spanning the open, already-furnished sitting room. Perhaps some decorative accents needed to be added, but she had more than the essentials. The sketches were not in sight. In the center of the spacious room, two doors opened to a small onyx balustrade. It framed the aesthetic mastery of Paris, giving the room grandeur and texture. The windows faced east, something Stasi had always desired, while managing to avoid a view of the gauche *La Tour Eiffel*. I presumed the kitchen, washroom, and bedrooms were down the left side of the hall. I was too off-kilter to request a tour. Six pairs of shoes were lined up neatly in the basin of the otherwise clean fireplace, and she bent to buckle the pair she had slipped on.

He walked over beside her, past me, and said in English—American English—"What time works for you tomorrow?"

"Lunchtime, darling." She mimicked his bodiless American accent. When she stood to full height, he pecked her on the cheek, turned to grab his hat off the chaise lounge, and departed.

The door shut completely with a thud. We were alone. She constantly pivoted to keep me in her sightline while she busied herself with finding her purse, reapplying her lipstick (pinker, less red), and locating her keys. The last time we were together was on the patio. It hadn't yet been a month. Doubts whispered through my chest in my stomach and circled there.

"I'm ready, darling." She finally said. Why use the same term for me as her pet American?

"Do you have a favorite restaurant I can take you to?"

"I have many favorite restaurants here. There's one around the corner with terrific plates for vegetarians."

The pivot dance continued as she locked the door and gestured for me to walk ahead of her down the stairs.

"How was your trip here?" I tried to bestir our former ease.

"Pleasant. Everything went very well. I only spent four nights in a hotel before finding this apartment."

"You've been able to rent and furnish an apartment that well in a few weeks?"

"I'm not renting; I purchased it! I wanted to settle in quickly. Glorious find, no? That is why it took me a little while to get to Les Chapeaux de Marie, where you accurately predicted I would go." She said this last note with a sour upturn.

"I left for Paris the day after you."

"Is that so?" She looked both ways before crossing the street. Her long hair, darkening with the night, swished side-to-side. "Do you have sculpting business in Paris?"

"No...Stasi... you know I came to see you." Speaking at a level volume was difficult as I dropped behind her single file to accommodate each passerby on the crowded sidewalk.

"That's kind, but you should have let me get settled, and then I would have written."

"Did you write me? You look settled now."

She did not answer.

I followed her down the stairs into the sublevel restaurant. She didn't speak with me as she used to. My heart pounded in my stomach. I was annoying her. We took our seats. I kept rereading the same options, unable to make sense of the French on the one-faced menu. I started to feel sick. I unbuttoned an upper button of my shirt, feeling suffocated in this brick-walled, dimly-lit basement.

"Can we speak openly?"

"Let's order first."

I put down the menu and wiped my forehead with the back of my hand, where there was now a trail of pearled droplets. Her eyes stayed on the menu. I was unable to bear the patience she was requiring of me.

When she ordered, I told the waiter I would have the same, but I was unsure what I would receive. I leaned in across the small table and caught her eyes. I pushed back the urge to reach for her hand, which rested from her wrist on the table beside her plate.

"The last time I saw you..." I began, looking her in the face as her gaze fluttered around the room, "I regretted letting you leave. It makes me sick that I left the house that afternoon. That was a mistake." I felt a momentum in my chest and continued. "You are the person I feel closest to in the whole world. It's like we can be one mind sometimes. The thought of living separately from you causes me physical pain. As long as you are in Paris, I will stay in Paris."

"I intend to live here for a long time."

"I think it was divinely arranged that you would come to Suna. You made me see that I was building a lonely destiny. I am powerless over my days and even my focus… I can't keep my thoughts away from you. The only time I feel at peace is when we are together."

She sighed and leaned back.

"Pasquale, I appreciate how strong your affection for me is. This is all very heartfelt, but what happened on the patio and in your studio… those were the mistakes. We can never be anything more than siblings."

"You don't believe that. You can't deny how close we are! I felt alone before I met you. We honor each other's visions and dreams. Our situation is not ideal, but we're in Paris now. We can be together here. No one will know."

"We have the same last name!"

"People will think you're my wife."

"The world is shrinking. The truth would come out, and then we would be pariahs. You would not be able to find work, and I would never succeed with the hats. That is not honoring each other's dreams. We could never have children. Our family would never speak to us again."

She closed her eyes, and a shudder ran from her shoulders through her body.

"None of that matters to me more than being with you. I'll be an anonymous sculptor and still make enough money."

"It matters to me. That's not the life I want. And that's not the life I want for you."

My eyes swelled with rising white-hot tears. My throat clenched in embarrassment, and I couldn't speak the word I wanted her to hear: *please*.

The food arrived: braised chicken with gruyere. If I had been able to read the menu, I would have ordered something vegetarian, but my stomach felt too high in my rib cage to chew anyway. She picked at her meal.

"Pasq," she began, seeing the pain in my face. Now she looked at my face as I looked at the dirty cement between the bricks on the wall. "One day, you could be revered as one of the greatest sculptors of our time. You are already renowned. I don't think you are thinking about how much you have to lose. In Suna, I was unsure where I belonged. You were lacking a connection in your life with someone like-minded. I'm not sure when other interests started developing, but that was wrong."

"What if it's less wrong than being apart?" I said too emphatically. "You are shutting this down for your desire for notoriety. Your greed is suffocating your happiness. We love each other. We can laugh and play, be serious and fight–" I gestured from her to me.

"Like brother and sister!" She interjected. "We have to untangle this and move on with our lives."

My soul and body were drained. She took a bite and pushed her food around. She was the one thing charm, money, talent, or hard work could not give me.

"You don't want to be together?"

She took a few moments to dab her lips, minding the lipstick.

"Pasq, you are my best friend. You will always be in my life. I want to see you regularly for visits, meals, and walks. We can explore Paris while you are here. When you go home, we will write letters. I intend to see you at all the stages of your life. I want to see you marry a brilliant woman who complements you. I want to see your work in museums across the continent and evolve with your perspective of the world. When I introduce myself using the Marinova name, I want to hear your name. I'll read about how terrible you think old age is, yet how pleased you are with how your life unfolded. There is so much more that you owe this world, Pasq. And none of that can happen with me romantically."

"Is there even a chance for you to be that woman?"

"There is no chance. I do not feel that way. I know that is hurtful to you, but it is honest. A new chapter has begun, and our ships must be righted."

"I can't go back there. Pim will never forgive me."

"It would all find a way. I am going to visit the washroom."

I found myself unable to rise as she stood. Shock weighed my whole body down. I could not persuade her to vindicate my ruin.

"Why did you order the chicken only to waste it?" Stasi said when she returned.

"Maybe it's time for me to take the bill," I said absentmindedly, turning to beckon the waiter.

"I've already paid," she said nonchalantly. "We can leave."

I walked her home. I tried to keep pace with her on the sidewalk. She wished me goodnight outside of her building. We did not make plans to see each other again. I stood at the door to hear the heavy bolt lock clunk *adieu*.

I stayed in my hotel room for the next few days, thinking over our meeting. I decided to rent a studio apartment near Stasi's. I could operate from Paris for a time. To leave would be to sabotage a miracle.

Part 2

1
Franca Rossi

It was a difficult spring for both of us. Luca's oldest brother and Anastasia had left Suna. Luca said it was as if six people were gone for all of the excitement those two brought to the villa. He swore he could hear phantom laughs coming from the garden. The family had known that this had been something she wanted, yet the golden brother's departure changed the Marinova household. His parents withdrew from each other. One day, when Luca grumbled over his tutor, Mary threw her hands up and proclaimed that she was done hearing his complaints and negotiating with him and that they were finished with it. His unexpected win weighed more like a pit of guilt for several days, but he was relieved to have the extra two afternoons each week to shoot squirrels in the hills, row on the lake, and be with me.

Enzo became quieter. He moved through the house only for a change of scenery while writing his poems and short stories. Luca never read any of Enzo's work. He frequently made submissions to publications and was published several times, but even with the prince's connections, he seemed unable to launch a lucrative career as a writer. Pasquale once told Luca that Enzo blended English, Latin, and Italian in his poems too much to be followed clearly and that his fiction was not relatable. I told Mama about Enzo living at the villa without a profession or income, and she remarked that she had only ever seen "the pale Marinova boy" a few times. Mama said Luca was the best of his brothers, the most Italian. She bore a grudge on my behalf against Mary because I had still not been invited to their home for dinner after years of Luca holding a place in the clockwork of our family. I had been over to row on the lake with Luca or have lunch with him on the patio and in the gardens but was never invited for anything by the family.

It only mattered when I thought about it. Otherwise, I spent evenings reading about anatomy and maladies as I contemplated becoming trained as a nurse or midwife. When our neighbor, three doors down the hallway, went into labor with her sixth child, her oldest was sent to alert the midwife, who lived down the street in a neighboring building. Giacomo rushed out the door, panicked. He tripped on the rug and slammed his forehead on the hallway floor tile. My mother was arriving home from an errand with Imma in time to witness his fall. Mama said the boy stayed down exactly as he fell for a full second, and she, often saying that feelings came to her in words first, was struck: *he's dead.* As she bent over him, nudging aside his three younger sisters, wearing clothes handed down from Imma, he pressed his palms into the floor to lift his chest and stand. Mama brushed some dust off his chest and told him to wait a moment, but he swatted her hand away and took off down the stairs. She motioned for the Esposito girls to come to our home, gave them biscotti and milk, and offered to make a cake with them. They were several years younger than Imma, who was in Giacomo's year, and Imma reveled in hostessing for them.

"We'll keep the girls with us until the Esposito baby is born," Mama told her older daughters. "Ara and Gia," Gianna went by her new self-proclaimed moniker now, "watch over the four girls at the table. Franca, why don't you come with me to Eleonora's? Her young boy is there too; she'll need someone to watch over him."

Despite the labor, we could hear Signora Esposito shouting at the littlest child from the hallway. Mama knocked before entering. She was not especially close with Signora Esposito.

"Eleonora," Mama called and let herself in, "it's Isabella and Franca. Your girls are with mine. I offered to make a cake with them while we waited for the baby to come. I figured I'd visit with you until your husband and the midwife arrive."

"Take a seat! My husband is oblivious. Or possibly far smarter than he seems. He's never been here for one of my births." Signora Eleonora Esposito joked. "I think this one will be a boy. During my pregnancies with the girls, I had sharp, insatiable needs for sour citrus fruit, especially pomelo, but the smell of coffee was intolerable! With Giacomo and Leonardo," the flailing toddler on my lap, my arms incapable of holding his tiny body still as he leveraged its weight against me, "my cravings were indistinct, much less."

I couldn't remember Mama ever remarking on her pregnancies. I enjoyed listening to Signora Eleonora's humorous tales about the discomforts of womanhood. I felt special to be here, not with the other girls.

By the time the midwife arrived, Signora Eleonora's "soft labor" was becoming something else. She started to interrupt her monologue by contorting her face. Mama offered to bring Leonardo to our home, but she became more concerned with Giacomo, who returned with an emerging circular bruise above the center of his eyebrows. He ducked from Mama's reach and wouldn't let her touch his head but conceded that he had a headache. When it was time for "hard labor," Mama brought the Esposito boys to our apartment and made Giacomo lie on her bed to rest. The boy's will was becoming pliable; he lacked the energy to resist her. That is when I began to osmose Mama's concern.

Mama and Arabella baked with the younger two girls while Imma told stories to the oldest at the table, and I played with Leonardo in the living room. I left the toddler to check on Giacomo. He was sleeping, breathing evenly in the dark. The living room light exposed the morphing bruise on his forehead. The circle's boundaries had broken; it was now the shapelessness of fear.

"Mama," I was a teenager and nearly her height, and still, I tugged at the draped fabric of her blouse tucked into her mid-length wool skirt like a child.

"You look flushed, Franca. Sit down."

"Something is wrong with Giacomo."

I didn't have to say anything more. She wiped her hands on her expensive skirt, having sheathed two girls in both of her aprons and walked straight to the bedroom.

"Franca!" Mama called me, knowing I did not intend to go back in there.

"Get Doctore Lombardo." Without looking at me, she said, "Tell Arabella to take Gia, Imma, the girls, and Leonardo to Nonna Rossi's. Don't tell the other girls."

I trailed behind the stampeding footsteps of all the girls, with Ara holding Leo, descending the stairs. I followed the girls' laughter a couple of buildings over, where my grandmother and Doctore Lombardo lived. I wished I were going with them. As they approached her apartment in a pack led by Gia, Arabella gave me a lamenting look before she carried Leonardo over the threshold. I continued two stories higher to knock on the doctor's door.

"Doctore, I am Franca Rossi, Giuseppina Rossi's granddaughter; my father is Franco Rossi—"

"Yes, yes. What do you want?"

"My neighbor, he's nine years old, fell and hit his head this afternoon. He has a huge bruise. He is sleeping now, but my mama told me to get him. We're concerned for him."

He grunted and nodded. Then he closed the door, leaving me in the hallway. I looked from side to side to see if I was alone in the hallway. I was. I looked at the grout between the tiles on the floor until the doctor opened the door again, ready to leave.

Minutes later, I sat on the chair in Mama's bedroom, watching Mama alternate between pacing and holding the boy's hand while the doctor examined him. The space between each boy's breaths lengthened as he fell asleep. Doctore Lombardo said the boy had sustained a catastrophic hematoma, an aggressive brain bleed. When Papa came home, Mama sent me to tell him what was happening. He hugged me and said that I could stay in the living room, that it was too late for me to walk to Nonna's alone, and that I did not have to be in the bedroom with Mama. But I couldn't leave her now and decided to return to sit in the chair.

Mama whispered questions to the doctor that I did not hear. Strands of dark brown hair fell from her bun. She was touching her neck without thinking, with one hand at a time or both simultaneously, and blotches appeared. Papa wrapped a quilt around me and tucked it in the chair, which he hadn't done since I was little. As the doctor prepared an injection of morphine, Giacomo passed away. The doctor, Mama, Papa, and I stopped to look at his chest, willing it to move. The doctor pronounced him deceased at 10:47, but the clock in my parent's room was two minutes slow.

The doctor's composure drained me. I expected more empathy and assistance with what to do now because he was Nonna Rossi's neighbor. Signora Eleonora had to be informed. Had she given birth yet?

"We should have tried to find Signor Esposito. Do you think he is with his wife?" Mama asked.

"No. I know exactly where I would have looked for him first." Papa often said that Signor Esposito was not a "family man."

"Stop. Please. I can't hear about that. You've done well today, Franca. Thank you for helping." I had never seen her more stripped of spirit.

"I only followed your directions," I began to sob. A boy only Imma's age, dead. The doctor even took two minutes from him. Papa pulled me into a hug and then walked me to the couch. "I didn't do anything."

"I'll go with you to tell Eleonora," Papa said to Mama.

"No." Mama dabbed the corners of her eyes. "Let it be mother to mother. And Franca shouldn't be alone. You–" Mama pointed to me, "go to sleep. By the morning, we will know how they want to move the body, and we will fetch the girls and the Esposito children."

Papa hugged her one more time before she walked out the door. I sat on the couch, afraid to hear Signora Eleonora scream from down the hallway. Papa cleaned up the living room and the kitchen, which had been destroyed by the children playing and baking earlier. After an hour of inspecting my fingernails, Mama had not returned.

"I don't think we should wait for Mama to return."

That night, I slept in the bed Gia and I shared, and Papa slept in the bed Arabella and Imma shared. He left the bedroom door open in case Mama came home in the middle of the night. His snoring woke me up in the night, but I was grateful to be reminded that I was not alone.

✳

Giacomo Esposito's funeral was held three days later. Signora Eleonora requested our family to sit in the church pew directly across the aisle from her family, which was customarily intended for grandparents, aunts, uncles, and cousins. Mama reduced her weekly hours at the grocery store, cooked for the two families, helped plan the church service, and made the three Esposito girls and her own four daughters dresses for the Catholic funeral. Arabella, Gia, and I received new long velvet dresses with beading detail along the top line of the collarbone. Imma and the three girls, Sofia, Chiara, and Elisa, wore short cotton black dresses with thick sashes around the middle and tied into large bows at the back. The girls came over to have my mother do their hair. The doors of our two apartments began to stay propped open; the mothers and daughters moved fluidly between the two homes.

    My sisters cried more than me during the funeral service. Giacomo had been three months older than Imma, and she now felt called to be an older sister to Sofia, Chiara, and Elisa. I only fell to tears when I imagined Signora Eleonora's suffering. It was easier with Luca sitting next to me. I told him he did not have to accompany us as he had no relationship with the Esposito family, but he told me that my relations were also his. We could only hold hands when allowed by the motions of the mass.

2
Anastasia

Tati will be here in a few days. She will not bring Katrina or Dmitri, as she has expressly written that this is a rescue mission, not a holiday. The thought of her parachuting in to tell me how to live my life ignites an old fury. After all, I am doing quite well. The owner of Les Chapeaux de Marie has agreed that he would provide the manufacturing costs for the exclusive rights to produce and sell my designs, for which I will receive twenty percent of the profit. The best part is that I have had the opportunity to discuss my forthcoming hats with several of his most loyal patronesses. Sharing the sketches and inspiration behind some designs felt like being on a cloud.

I am seeing John, the former Brown collegiate rower. He is an entirely new specimen of man to me. John is well-traveled for an American. He has become part of a close community of foreign correspondents, which he calls his occupation. However, he makes his living through his talent for poker, which he plays once or twice a week. He makes comments that he has stayed in Paris for too long. I am unsure whether he will stay for months to come or finish lunch one day and depart that very afternoon. His sense of freedom mystifies and inspires me. And yet, I have not decided whether or not to introduce Tatiana to him.

Tatiana writes in harsh tones, demanding I come home to Smolnek and settle down. She accuses me of living provocatively, and I repudiate her, but I am frustrated that some attuned part of her has predicted my relationship with John. Tatiana seems incapable of accepting that I have choices. I will welcome her, show her the best, and listen to her, but I have already decided to send her away unsuccessful. Our mother's suffering has endured, unbroken. She is perpetually dying, and yet I feel that I cannot abandon forging ahead with my own life. I wish Tatiana were bringing my niece; it would have been nice to see her after so long.

Unfortunately, Tatiana's visit does not trouble me as much as the thorn Pasquale has become. For a time, we kept a weekly dinner appointment. Offering him a scheduled time kept him in plain sight. When I moved here, I anticipated the Parisians would have tightly-knit groups more inclined toward exclusion, but instead, I found an insatiable social hunger in the city for *new*. There is a competitive rush to recruit notables into certain circles. Pasq and I are each currently *nouveau*. He is an artistic phenomenon to the Modern Style fanatics here and has made friends who are gallery curators, architects, painters, and poets. They interpret his inactivity as an intellectual hiatus. Our acquaintances are overlapping, which I suspect is not a coincidence. I uneasily enter every restaurant, gallery, and home salon, suspecting he could be there too.

    Last week, I carelessly let Pasquale wait inside my living room as I finished preparing dinner. He saw Tatiana's letter on my desk. With his half-beard and the yellow light of the summer sunset making his hair appear darker in contrast, he looked eerily like a very thin Papa.

    "I would like to meet her," he said.

    "Meeting you would overwhelm her."

    "It's my right to meet my other half-sister."

    I felt protective of Tatiana and said coldly: "You will probably never meet her, and you can credit Papa for that, not me!"

    "Why are you cutting me out of your life so wholly? You're vicious. Why can't you see that a small meeting could be nice?"

    "Tatiana is not your entertainment!"

    "I am not the one who treats others like entertainment, Stasi. You don't even really like her. She mistreats you. It is very "little sister" of you to keep crawling back for more of her disapproval."

    "Look who's talking! Why are you even here in Paris? I don't want to see you anymore. If I see you a mile near Tatiana, I will scream."

    "You would never," he brushed off my threat. "You're more socially minded than me. I'm the one who would share our love with the world."

    "WE DO NOT HAVE LOVE! I am with John! You've lost your mind! I refuse to see you anymore and indulge in your fantasies. I will not play this part any longer." At that moment, I started gathering my things and headed toward the door.

    "Where are you going?" His voice wavered.

    "I'm going to John's. I do not trust you are sane. You should return to Suna and salvage your accomplished life." Saying I was going to John's place hurt him; his face fell, and his eyes held all of the disbelief in the world. But I had to break his persistence.

He followed me out of the building without saying anything, which I was thankful for. I walked to John's at an urgent pace.

That was several weeks ago, and while I haven't seen him since then, I suspect he will lurk around Hotel Esmée to try to see Tatiana. I couldn't write to her to switch hotels because I thought that would alarm her. Nor could I ask John to escort us because I was not planning on introducing Tatiana to him.

"Anastasia." Tatiana began gravely over tea in the hotel's dining room. "I have to tell you why I have come."

Because Papa told Mama I had an illicit interaction with one of our half-brothers?

"I had a dream... and in it... you died." She paused and stared at me to let gravity settle the thought. "I couldn't save you because you drowned somewhere else, and while it was only a dream, it felt so real. I woke up weeping. It felt like you were lost to me."

"What a troubling dream. You traveled far for something that could have been shared by letter."

"Anastasia, don't play the fool. I'm here to bring you home to your family. Let's restore you to your path. You should have been married years ago. Don't you want to spend time with your niece? Mama could use your happy energy."

"I certainly wish you had brought Katrina with you now, but I have engagements and commitments in Paris. My hat designs are being made as we speak. I have orders for more. Also, I meet more eligible men here than I ever would in Smolnek."

"These introductions can't lead anywhere virtuous without your family being respectably involved. A woman should not live alone. I can't imagine how you convinced anyone to let you come here to live alone."

"Would you like to talk about Papa?" I wanted to disarm her.

"No..." she said, taken aback. "I am here to talk about you, not to talk about him."

"Really? Because it seems like we are dancing around the assumption that he was an inadequate chaperone. And you would be right."

"How do you mean?" She leaned in and whispered, concerned I meant what I said.

"I mean, I had relations with a man. It happened under Papa's watch, so he finally allowed me to leave for Paris. In his eyes, my virtue was already compromised. My chance for the life you have died with Petyr Mikhailov. I have other pursuits now."

"Anastasia." Tatiana took a breath. Her shoulders kept their rigidness, but her face, thinner than mine, tilted softly. "Despite anything you've done, in my dream–" I rolled my eyes, "–no, listen, in my dream, it was an accepted fact that you were going to die. It was destined. I'm hearing now that you believe you can't have a quality life based on one tragic experience. You are keeping empty relations to avoid hurting again."

Her eyes glossed over in a moment of rare vulnerability.

"You are my only sibling. When Mama goes, you will be the only anchor I have left. I have my husband and daughter, but you are a Marinova and the only person who understands my suffering. If something happened to you, I would lose my refuge."

"You can't save me to save yourself."

That's when I saw him out of the corner of my eye. We were sitting at the end table in a line of small and pristinely set tables, and he was sitting alone against the wall to my back right.

"But I would like to start anew with you," I mumbled. "We should be less serious. Shall we go shopping?" She nodded, looking defeated. I placed francs on the table.

"What a glorious day it is," I rambled gaily, even though it felt like there would be rain in the afternoon. "Why don't you wait outside and watch the people go by while I use the ladies' room?"

She agreed absentmindedly, dazed. I waited for her to leave the dining room, staying seated myself. He slid into the seat across from me.

"I was serious when I said I didn't want to see you anymore, Pasquale."

"You know that I needed to see her. This is the best compromise: I see her, but we won't meet."

I stared at him with fire in my eyes.

"I think that now I know what your mother looks like." He mused out loud. "Tatiana looks more like Marinova than you; she is taller, and her expressions are similar to Pim's when he disagrees. Haughtily composed, wouldn't you say? You are clearly more beautiful. I've finally seen what your mother must look like." He repeated himself. "The shape of your face and coloring must come from her side. Tatiana may even look more Marinova than Luca, Enzo, and me. Oddly, she looks closer to how I imagined you would look before we met. The bone structure of your face—"

"Stop looking at my bone structure! Stop following me! You are rogue!" I stood up firmly and not-so-calmly. I pulled on my midnight-blue gloves and said with exaggerated clarity: "I do not want to see you for a month. Do not come near me. Do not approach Tatiana."

I walked away, leaving him forlorn. The time for feeling bad for him had passed.

Outside, Tatiana was sitting diligently on the bench, hands folded in her lap, her head turning at the speed of passersby as if she were observing a tennis match. When I walked over to her, she stood, bent over, and brushed her long chocolate brown skirt straight. As she leaned up to a standing position, a man accidentally bumped into her right arm without knocking her posture off kilter.

"*Excusez moi*," Pasquale said, with poor pronunciation, though Tatiana couldn't tell the difference.

Tatiana nodded curtly before turning her attention to me and asking, "Where can I buy gloves like yours?"

3
Franca Rossi

Arabella was planning for one hundred guests in less than two months. Whenever Gia saw Arabella, since she had become engaged to Paolo, she began crying. Every time. We thought it would pass, but Gia was mourning. Arabella tried ignoring Gia, yelling at her, throwing anything within reach, and asking Mama to command Gia to be happy for her. No one could make Gia do anything, and her sister's wedding was no exception. Gia refused to stand for her bridesmaid's dress fitting, but her resistance was moot since Mama knew our measurements within a quarter inch. I was tasked with ensuring Gia's attendance and participation on the wedding day.

Mama asked me early in the planning stages if the Marinovas would lend their gardens for Arabella's reception. I felt a surging rage that she and Arabella were conspiring to steal my rightful wedding. Hot tears came to my eyes. *"No! The Marinovas are foreigners without a shred of generosity!"* Mama did not ask again. While I knew her suggestion would ease the financial burden, I woke up infuriated for days. When I told Gia and my friends about it, they did not see why it was an offensive notion.

I did not loathe Paolo like Gia did, but I found myself searching for the merits that had won my sister over. Papa mostly cared that the Terraccis had enough to provide for Arabella. They were comfortable and lived in a four-story house in the city center of Intra, which was more urban and two kilometers north of Pallanza. The bottom floor was the family's stationery store, which was the only one on this side of Lago Maggiore. Arabella would have cafés and shops steps away in every direction. Intra's three piazzas at the lake's edge were where merchants sold all a person could want during the day, and bands played for festivals. Parades marched there on saints' days and holidays. Pallanza mainly had Via Ruga for shopping and was otherwise more composed of apartment buildings, churches, restaurants, and two schools. Arabella was eager to move into the Terracci home and begin her "city life." I did not have any complaints about spending more time in Intra, but Mama warned me that things change after a woman gets married and that I would need to give Arabella space to become a wife. The thought of my relationship with my only older sister changing physically hurt. I tried not to think about it.

In the weeks leading up to the wedding day, there became a natural divide of Mama, Arabella, and Imma leaving for errands while I remained home with Gia. On one of these occasions, only six days from the wedding, Gia and I sat at the kitchen table eating tuna, tomato, and lettuce sandwiches when she started crying. For Gia, crying was anger overspilling; she rarely reached sadness for that required acceptance.

"He's terrible, Franca," she cried. "His cousins follow me around town. They are trying to intimidate me because he told them I know about the theft."

"Everyone knows about that, though. They have nothing to fear from you. The butcher hasn't reported it, so maybe we don't know the full story."

"The full story is that Gino is now intimidating Signor Bonnali after taking fistfuls of *lire*. His daughter is in the year above me, and I overheard her telling one of her friends about it. Gino wanted to continue working there after that, but the butcher paid him more money not to return. That agreement has been honored for now, but who knows how long it will last? It's been a year, and the Bonnalis still live in fear. The Terraccis are bad people! We are giving Ara to bad people!"

"Gia, if that were true, why wouldn't Signor Bonnali report Gino?"

"Because he threatened him! Because the butcher knows he is capable of following through with his threat. You're so stupid, Franca!"

"You're the one being stupid! You're sitting here churning your stomach rather than being happy for Ara. She is not marrying Gino; she's marrying Paolo. The Terraccis will be our family this time next week. It's done. If Gino is a true wolf, Arabella will need us, and you are turning your back on her."

"I hate that I can't stop this," she swallowed, her eyes filled with tears again. "I don't see why everyone doesn't feel the same way. I sometimes wonder if you are indifferent to Arabella's choice because you already have a perfect love story. Maybe you don't care what her life will look like because you know what yours will."

It felt like she cracked my heart open in my chest. "That is… so mean. I love Arabella… I would never want anything less than perfect for her."

"But you are allowing it! You smile and prance about helping it happen!" Gia yelled.

"You are a bitch, Gia! I can't tell her who to love!"

We both sat at the table crying into our palms over our crumb-riddled plates.

※

The long sleeves of Arabella's dress were sheer for the early autumn weather. Mama had made it for her, piece by piece, late at night when everyone was asleep. She said the silence helped her focus. Ara never gave her any instructions for the dress and trusted Mama entirely with the vision of it. The sleepless months took their toll on our mother's appearance. Strands of gray hair emerged. Lines on her neck remained whether she was sitting or standing. Nonna Illari purchased Arabella's veil; it was far longer than the dress train, fine as spun air.

On the wedding day, Gia quietly followed the schedule Mama set for us. She sat still for me to do her hair and dressed when she was told. Gia, nearly fifteen, was by far the prettiest of us. She had inherited the best features of Mama and Papa, holding onto Mama's large green eyes and Papa's narrow face. Her body had developed the shape of a woman's, an hourglass shape that Arabella and I used our clothes and corsets to replicate. Gia's gaze was fastened on the opposite wall as I applied the lipstick we passed around. Mama was working on Arabella's hair, which was within arm's reach of us in the living room, which was rearranged to be our beauty room. Meanwhile, Imma was giddily talking through the next few hours. None of Imma's reasons for why she was excited included the groom.

"You're perfect," I said to Gia, the words pushing past a notched throat. I held our great-grandmother's handheld mirror for her to admire herself, but she swatted it away. She stood and took Arabella's hand in hers. Ara looked up with her eyes so as not to disrupt Mama's brushing and pinning, and Gia smiled, which brought tears to Mama's eyes that she couldn't wipe for the task at hand.

Once we were ready, the Rossi women walked to the church together. Papa was to meet us with our grandparents in the adoration chapel built beneath the church in 1672. It was the only part of the church that had never been renovated. Four brick walls and three pews faced an altar bearing only a golden solar monstrance holding the Eucharist and a burning red candle on a white tablecloth. Luca would be waiting inside the church with the rest of the guests.

The bridesmaids wore floor-length crystal blue chiffon dresses and short veils that covered our faces. Blue was a traditional color in Pallanza weddings, serving as an ode to Lago Maggiore. Mama wore a dark blue dress and borrowed pearl earrings from her mother, though Nonna made her swear to return them as she desired to bequeath them to my uncle's wife, Aunt Nuncia, upon her death. I had failed to break my new shoes in before the wedding day, and on the downhill walk to St. Catherine of Siena, the tightness around my baby toes and the bend of where my ankle bone pressed against the shoes set my feet to suffering.

I held Arabella's bouquet as well as mine and walked beside Imma as she carried Arabella's veil. Gia walked beside Mama a few feet ahead of the bride. The autumn breeze drifted off the lake. The sun sparkled on the water in the distance between the stucco houses and at the turn of every street corner. None of us spoke. I still did not know how to feel about Paolo Terracci. But I felt so bodily thankful for these women in front of me, to be one of them and to have them as part of me.

4
Anastasia

John escalated the night from casual drinks to recklessness. He generously supplied the alcohol, which was blue. The women of the party kept up with their dates in drink count but fell far behind in sobriety. I barely remember the burlesque show, only how the dim lights around the perimeter of the sublevel room did not illuminate the performer very well. She seemed like more of a dark shadow than a person, making the whole endeavor less seductive. She took off all of her clothes to reveal heavy silver tassels attached to her nipples. John recounted it all quite well. Then I remember we were drinking on the streets; I held hands with my girlfriends for balance and then fell into my man's arms for more stability. One of John's friends mimicked the burlesque dancing on a park bench in the Tuileries Garden on our way to an intimate bar beside a hotel I had never heard of before.

After another two rounds of drinks, we stumbled about fifteen minutes from the tiny bar, twisting through narrow, winding residential streets to the fourth-floor residence of a psychic that Ines had visited. My feet ached. John told me that I had declared anyone too afraid to spend five minutes discussing potentials with a stranger "an un-fucking-worthy coward."

When we arrived, I was surprised to see the woman dressed in an ordinary light pink dress with short white ruffles at her collar and wrists. She was a letdown to the dramatized shawls-and-beads gypsy image in my mind. Her living room was crammed with assorted seating and designed to accommodate groups twice our size. There were almost too many places to sit between the couches, floating sundry dining room chairs, and poufs on the floor.

Ines went into one of the backrooms first, and Chloe accompanied her to observe. The woman said we should make ourselves comfortable but requested we stay quiet as her children were asleep down the hall. I distinctly started to feel more awake. When Ines returned, the group turned inward to choose our next sacrifice.

"I'll go." I stood up and declared.
"Could I sit in?" Chloe asked.
"Yes."

"Can I accompany you too?" John asked, moving to stand up.

"No," I said without even considering.

I followed Chloe and the woman into the backroom, which only had four chairs pushed in around a small round table covered by a light green cloth. The walls were bare, but there were layers of colorful and pallid paintings on the floor leaning against each other, shrinking the room and drawing the eye to the floor.

"Sometimes I am paid in art." She said, seeing my eyes flitting around the floor.

"Maybe Anastasia will also pay you in art; her brother is a famous sculptor!" Chloe exclaimed.

I smiled gently but was apprehensive about speaking lest I give this woman advantages. She motioned for my palm. She asked if I would prefer to talk in French or English; she would be more limited in her English, but I may understand French less. I chose English, and she began to narrate from the lines on my palm.

"You are a journeyer—thrill seeker. You are a foreigner here but do not treat yourself like a foreigner. A dreamer and pursuer of dreams. You have a sister, but you are not close with her… you have had one sibling die; was this her?"

"No, actually, my mother had another daughter die young. I have one living sister, and you are right that we are not close."

"Your older sister has a clear place in this world… a defined role she either created for herself or a mantle she was destined to pick up."

"She's married with a child. She was always the good one."

"There are no bad ones. People commit wrong because they haven't found another way to address the wrong inflicted upon them. Judgment belongs more to the corporeal state than the soul. But you feel you do not have a defined place in the world. Your soul is unsure which role it should play; you likely try out many."

I didn't speak.

"You need to watch out for dementia in old age," she continued. "You are on your mother's line; they suffer from this. Did your grandfather die in his nineties?"

"My mother's father died in his sixties, and my father's father died younger. I'm not exactly sure how old he was."

"It seems that you attract difficult situations. When one problem falls from your mind, three more draw breath. You have a current struggle that is weighing on you."

I suddenly regretted that Chloe was there. "A man follows me around. I'm not sure how to get rid of him. His behavior is erratic."

"You feel responsible?"

"Yes."

"Has your response to his interests also been erratic? His hopes cannot die while your responses are inconsistent."

"They have been consistent as of late."

"Do you have a question for me?"

"Does my father love me?"

"If you are asking, you have already measured."

Back in the waiting room, I told John I was tired and wanted to go home. He consented, relieved. The next day, I pretended not to remember the night.

5
Franca Rossi

"Do you have a dog?" I asked, peering into the house. A pampered pet dog was something I expected of the Marinovas. They had the money to feed one. My first dinner with the Marinovas was held on their patio five years after Luca had become a regular at our family dinners. I wore a jacket over my brown dress on this crisp, late October night.

"No, Pim doesn't like dogs," Luca answered while shuffling the unruly card deck. Luca and I played at the table as Mary bustled around with Signora Figlia, who I knew from my neighborhood. We had not yet been introduced in this context. "I think he grew up with them. He says they would be havoc in the gardens. I would love to have a dog someday."

"Are there any cats?"

"There is one that Enzo started feeding, and now it lives in the garden. Pim doesn't mind because it keeps the mice away. We call him–" Luca switched to English for the name, "Garden Cat. He's a big-boned tabby and keeps other cats away, too. He killed another cat! I mean, no one saw him do it, but a grey cat was found dead with claw and bite marks at the base of the tree with the hornworts."

He seemed in awe of the little beast.

"I would also like to have a dog someday."

"We will. Once you finish your training," he said as he dealt us each seven cards.

After we graduated from secondary school, I decided to go to Gallarate, a town between Lago Maggiore and Milano, to train as a nurse for the next three months. I would live in a dormitory with forty or so other trainees for the duration of the course and report directly to a doctor at Gallarate's hospital. Our teacher, Professoressa Mila, had arranged it all. She had many friends in the Milano area and set up various schooling and work opportunities for all her students.

"And you'll be in Baveno making all types of boats."

Luca wanted to spend his days making row boats. He did not need to work for money. He wanted to live in his family home for the rest of his life, even if Enzo did too. Prof. Mila introduced Luca to a boatmaker in Baveno for whom he could apprentice before embarking on his own. From Casa Bianca's edge, Luca could row to and from the boat maker's small warehouse in Baveno in less time than it would take to walk there.

"Baveno isn't the same as Gallarate; it's simpler training."

"Gallarate?" Mary Marinova walked out onto the terrace, carrying a glass holding its last swish of wine. "Is that for nursing school, Franca?"

"Yes, Signora Marinova."

Luca swept up the cards as Signora Figlia brought out dinner.

"Your father won't be joining us," Mary told Luca. "He would prefer to eat in his office tonight." She turned her head and screamed, *"ENZO!"* causing the cook to jolt. "Franca, why would you go to Gallarate? You won't actually be a nurse. You don't need to work. And there are plenty of doctors in the Pallanza-Intra hospital."

"Mama, Franca wants to help sick people. She wants to work."

She looked at me with eyes that strained to be piercing. Enzo strode onto the terrace with a bottle of wine and three glasses for us. He did not greet me, though we had met often before.

"Pim won't be joining us," Enzo announced as he took the head of the table.

"We know," Luca said, taking the crystal glasses from him and positioning them at our table settings. I shuffled to adjust my plate and utensils to their original perfection.

"But, Franca," Signora Marinova continued as Enzo poured the Barolo I could smell as it tumbled into my glass, "why are you leaving for Gallarate – that cultureless waste of all places – to become a nurse?" She spoke too quickly for my English, but her tone said no answer I could give would be correct.

"If you leave next week, when will you and Luca be married? Next year?"

"Mama…." Luca groaned.

"Really, Luca. I'm asking. I have three sons of marrying age, and not one is married. It's curious. I am just inquiring about your plan."

Enzo passed me the roasted potatoes. We hadn't even started eating yet. I did not need Mary's love, but I would have appreciated an effort to make me feel comfortable in her home. I did what my mother expressly forbade us from doing and drank from my glass in pursuit of reprieve.

"Franca will go to Gallarate, and when she returns, we'll make a plan."

"Fine. Franca, you've barely put anything on your plate. Here–" she heaped a chicken breast and a few creamed basil leaves onto my plate, landing it directly on the side dish servings. My father, a proud Italian man, would never allow foods to touch on a plate for disgust of destroying the integrity of each taste. I was watching my figure this week, but now I had to eat all of this to avoid insulting Signora Figlia. Gia wouldn't have eaten it. I nodded with gratitude.

"We already have one vegetarian too many. My oldest, Pasquale, is currently in Paris working on his sculpting project...." Mary carried on. She spoke of Pasquale's time in Paris, using one hand to gesture and the other to hold her wine glass in orbit a few inches from her face. Luca told me Pasquale had written only four letters in six months. I felt a pit in my stomach at the thought of future years' worth of dinners with her.

"What exactly is Pasquale working on there?" Enzo asked, too innocently for me to look directly at him or Signora Marinova.

"Various commissions, I'm sure. We have quite a network in Paris."

I chewed my food slowly, nervous she would fill my plate again if it became scant. Yet I was unafraid of Enzo refilling my glass for the third time.

The tension I felt was releasing, but Luca's embarrassment rose as his mother spoke. He sagged over his food and stayed silent. I wanted to reach across the table and take hold of his hand. I kicked my foot toward him, but it wasn't the delicate touch I had intended; instead, the point of my shoe made sharp contact with his shin bone. Luca yelled, spitting shreds of his food.

"I'm sorry! It was an accident!" I sloshed my wine on the table as I gestured upward for God's forgiveness.

"It's ok," Luca said as he rubbed his shin.

"Luca, are you alright?" She attempted to rub his shin, too, but Luca swatted her hand away. "How did that happen?"

"*No lo so*," I tried to say apologetically, but I hiccuped on the third syllable. Luca started to laugh. Signora Marinova did not. Enzo might not have known how.

The rest of the dinner passed with Enzo discussing poetry he wrote in his ode to *Le Morte D'Arthur*. I tried to listen about the British Lord Tennyson, who also undertook this endeavor of passion, though it was difficult to concentrate with Mary evil-eyeing me like I might kick her too. I pushed my glass away to prevent any further sips.

Signora Figlia returned to clear the dishes when we were finished. She was one of the loyal shoppers at the same grocery store where my mother worked. Her children were older than me but younger than my parents; my mother was familiar with them, and my father had grown up as a neighbor of her son-in-law. And now she was removing my grimy plate that bore the refuse of chicken breast without meeting my eye.

"*Grazie*, Signora Figlia."

"Well, I'm off to bed." Mary left her glass on the table. "Luca, will you walk Franca home?"

"Of course I will. See you in the morning."

"Franca," her shoulders shifted to face me. It struck me that she did not know how to behave around me. "If I don't see you before you leave, I hope your training course is everything you want."

"Thank you, Signora Marinova."

She sashayed from the terrace through the open doors. Her heels chopped up the marble stairs.

Enzo stretched his arms over his head as much as his gentlemanly nature would allow. He gazed out at the lights of Stresa lining the lake and emitted a sigh like he was holding in the world's cares. I felt guilty for not knowing him nearly as well as Luca knew my sisters.

"Would you like another drink?" Enzo asked Luca. "Mrs. Figlia is bringing an espresso for me, but I might have a glass of port as well."

"What were you thinking of having? I can show Franca the cellar and grab what you'd like."

"Any bottle Pim ordered from *São João da Pesqueira* will do."

Luca placed his cloth napkin on the table and walked over to help me stand. Once I was upright, he pulled me up by my hands and held my waist with his right arm. I leaned on him for balance and because I could.

The cellar entrance was outside, around the corner of the terrace, beneath the kitchen. He went down the stairs ahead of me, and I placed my hands on his shoulders so we descended as one shimmying caterpillar.

The wine cellar was a single, square room. Two candles burned in the center of the room on the clunky standing-height wooden table. The adjoining bar stools had a thick layer of dust on the seats. Three walls were floor-to-ceiling wine racks filled with varyingly dusty bottles. I let go of Luca and took a turn around the room. The racks were labeled by location rather than white or red, dessert or *vinho verde*. After the Portuguese botanist's extended visit nearly two decades ago, the prince was still a devout patron of Portuguese wine, only ever ordering from the vineyards operated by the botanist's friend or those he recommended explicitly. He had more Italian wine than French wine, but my father would have been displeased that there were any French bottles at all.

"I feel like I'm traveling the world," I said.

"We can," he said as he strode to the Portuguese section and found Enzo's requested bottle. I could hear Enzo's chair slide against the terra cotta tile on the terrace yards from the open door of the cellar. He placed the bottle on the table and closed the space between us.

Luca had to hunch over to fully wrap his hands around my lower back and press my body to his. I held his upper arms for support but tilted my head back to look him in the face. He looked into my eyes and brushed my hair behind my right ear, but the curls kept sliding back into my face.

"It's a losing battle," I whispered.

"I'm going to miss you. A lot."

"I'll miss you too."

He held his hand along my face so the hair was finally pinned down, and his eyes returned to mine. His eyes closed, and he leaned in to kiss me. Our lips touched softly as they had only a handful of times before, but this time, our lips opened, and his tongue found mine. He kissed me slowly and deeply. Our focus was so complete that our hands were forgotten. Until they were remembered, he moved both of his hands up and down my body, shifting me to step backward until my back was flush against the wine rack, and I could feel the bottle rings molding worthy bruises into my back.

When the bottles began to rattle in their wooden perch, we separated for a moment to laugh. When we started kissing again, he grabbed the edge of my dress, squeezing the fabric in his fists and pulling me by it. He knew better than to lift it. But just the weighted brush of the back of his hands above my knees made me unsteady.

After some time, I straightened my dress and tried to smooth Luca's tousled hair.

"Go up before me. I'm going to blow these candles out."

My feet staggered. I made my way up the cellar steps into the cold night air. I took a deep breath and let it out, looking over the lake. Luca shut the cellar door behind him and took the uneven stone steps two at a time. He held the port in one hand and took my hand in the other.

He led us to where Enzo was sitting and placed the bottle on the table, which was cleared except for one espresso cup on its petite gold-fringed saucer and an empty port glass. Luca placed the bottle beside it. Enzo looked up stupefied, removed from inside his mind, without a trace of worry about how much time had passed.

"I'm going to walk Franca home."

"OK. Bye, Franca."

6
Pasquale

I wish I could say that I stood solemnly at her burial, grieving on the inside. But I wept inconsolably: mouth open, ropes of blended tears, snot, and saliva hung from my face until they broke off onto my coat. My hands shook.

Stasi's lover stared at his folded hands the whole time. Heavy tears slid clean off my nose and cheekbones. She never would have married him.

He was the one who told me she had died; he came to my studio himself. I don't know how he knew where to find me. That morning, I was in the middle of a blind insanity brought on by the clogged bathroom sink, which was causing the entire place to smell of ruminating, days-old spit. I didn't want to let him in, and he didn't want to come in.

I didn't believe it. I hadn't even known she was ill. It was pneumonia, cloaked as a fever and then suddenly terrible. He was the only one with Stasi when she died—the only one. He said she had no last words because she believed she would improve and pull through.

"She said you two were close," he tried to console me.

"What did she say?" I sobbed, slumped on the floor where I had been standing when he told me.

He looked confused.

"What exactly did she say?" I repeated louder.

"Just that. That you two were close." Then he departed.

Days pass. Here we are having this ceremony for people who didn't know Stasi to dab at their meatless tears for their loss. The priest did not know her and was recycling words that were more fitting for simpler lives. People patted my back. They said they were sorry for my loss.

Anastasia Petrinova Marinova. The chisel work on the temporary headstone was too flawed to remark on, even to the untrained eye.

7
Franca Rossi

Though only an hour and a half from Pallanza by train, I had never been to Gallarate before, and I had never been on a train, either.

The morning before I left, I visited Professoressa Mila at her home in Intra. Her husband taught at the trade school there. She told me about her friend, the doctor at the nursing school in Gallarate, and she had a gift for me to bring him. The gift was a wrapped book, and I was a little surprised by the weight of it, envisioning myself carrying it around this block for weeks until I met him. Professoressa Mila told me she had arranged for me to have dinner with his three daughters at the doctor's house. She chuckled that I was used to having dinner with three other girls at the table. This pulled at my heart more than consoling it.

"Are you excited?" she asked. Elena Mila was a tall, slender blonde of middle age, still more beautiful than most women decades younger. She and her husband had no children, but her happiness did not seem to suffer for it.

"Prof. Mila, I'm nervous."

"What is there to be nervous about?"

"I'm nervous I will get there and be an awful nurse. And that I'll eat every meal alone."

"You'll have the chance to do the work that interests you. Didn't you tell me you gave your family and neighbors impromptu health check-ups? Pallanza needs a nurse like you. And you already have one dinner invitation, so your fear of eating every meal alone is already resolved."

"It feels like my life is on the other side of this program, and I'm putting everything on hold to study in Gallarate."

"What is on hold?"

I looked at her. Unsure how to say...

"Becoming Luca Marinova's wife?"

I nodded. "And when that happens, I won't even need to work, which everyone keeps saying. It makes me feel stupid for even thinking I should make all this trouble to go to nursing school."

I could feel the heat in my chest rise and the skin becoming red and splotchy. Luca was kind when asking me about the program and where I would live, but I could tell even he didn't understand why I was doing it. Ara was confused about why anyone would wait to be married and kept saying that I was deferring my responsibilities. This was the first time I was voicing my frustration to anyone, and it felt like a smack in the face to remember that I was complaining about the opportunity to the one person who supported it enough to make it all possible.

"But I am thrilled to be going, Prof. I couldn't be more thankful. You have done so much for me, and here I am whining."

"It's not easy to leave your home, your life. You may even return to see that others have changed or that Suna, Pallanza, and Intra differ from how you remember. You will miss your family, home, and longtime boyfriend, and they will miss you. But I have no doubt you will make many friends in Gallarate. And you will cherish those friends too. You're not putting your life on hold—you're enriching it." She folded her long, slender hands with the perfect nails of an affluent academic before continuing. "The lavish lifestyle you will assume with a marriage to Luca Marinova is something few people will truly understand. Thus, you will receive unsolicited advice from those who dream of being in your position. People will try to advise you by their fantasies and not by your reality.

"Franca, you are an intelligent woman who will receive specialized training in a field that serves others in their greatest need. For someone like you, the work you get to do is a privilege. You do not need to work. It's your choice. But money cannot fill the absence of purpose in daily life. Only you can and must live your life. I support you if you can find meaning with your feet up overlooking the lake for sixty years. And if you want more from your days, then you have enough determination and intelligence not to need my, or anyone's, approval."

❈

That evening, Mama organized a large family dinner of *panzerotti* with my grandparents, Luca, and the Esposito family, including Signora Eleonora's parents. All the living room seats were given to the elderly while the children were given seats at the table, where Imma talked animatedly with Sofia and Chiara. Luca arrived late.

"Silence, please!" Paolo Terracci called out over the room. When everyone in the space looked at him, he yelled: "Arabella and I are expecting a baby!"

Mama praised God and then began crying. The news eclipsed my departure, which I didn't mind as I was happy to be present for the announcement rather than to read about it in a letter.

Paolo's parents were invited to our dinner but chose to be absent without giving a reason, which Mama took as an insult. Ara dutifully defended her in-laws. Gia stared blankly at the inches of space between Arabella and Paolo for the rest of the evening and only spoke with Luca half-heartedly. Imma, who had been so eager to discuss my upcoming months in Gallarate, swooned over the marvelous fact that she would be an aunt. Imma doted on her favorite sister, getting up throughout the meal to hug her again and again. Chiara asked Ara questions. Sofia and Elisa seemed to view pregnancy as banal and continued eating.

"I'm happy I'll be back by the time the baby is born." I hugged Arabella.

"The next time you see me, I'll be so wide."

I nodded. My heart felt heavy at the thought of being away from my family for months.

The news of a baby also distracted me from anticipating the next big family event: my wedding to Luca. He and I had yet to discuss the timing or what it would all look like, but it already felt like a fact. I found my way over to him in the living room and asked him to follow me to the hallway.

"What's happened?" I asked him, but he seemed distant.

"Stasi," he pinched the bridge of his nose. "She died. It was pneumonia... in Paris last week. We found out yesterday. Pim slept in Pasquale's studio. I can't believe it."

I hugged him. I promised him that we – he, Enzo, and I – would have a mass for her soul when I returned. The prince would never attend because of his flat rejection of religion; Mary would never attend because of who we would be grieving for.

"Why did you come tonight? You could have stayed home."

"I wanted to see you before you left in the morning."

"I could have come to you. You didn't have to come here."

"There's a party," he waved his hand. "And then they announced Arabella is pregnant, and I didn't want to take any attention. Please don't tell your family tonight."

"Are you going to be alright while I'm away?"

He shrugged. I felt even more terrible for leaving.

8
Pasquale

John hand-delivered a box of Stasi's things two days after the funeral. I knew by how he held the box that the contents were precious beyond comfort. He said he wanted to return her jewelry promptly to prevent the loss of any family artifacts. John assumed her apartment was now in my care. I told him to put it down by the fireplace and invited him to stay for coffee. Loathing him had become insignificant. I would meet the devil for lunch if he would understand what I was talking about. He declined the coffee but sat down and took his hat off. I made myself another coffee.

John was a competitive rower in university days at Brown. He talked about what that was like. His statements made him sound self-made like the nouns were laurels achieved by the verbs he mastered. He did not go so far as to claim that writing miscellaneous sports articles solely funded his roaming lifestyle. He was a child of privilege, too. He wished to coach rowing at Pembroke or one of the other great European schools.

"Will you go back to Piedmont?"

"I'm not sure. Part of me thinks I should return. I'm also considering neither staying here nor returning there… I would go to Vienna, I think. I don't trust myself with making decisions right now. I've become unpredictable to myself. One hour, I want this; the next hour, I want the opposite."

"Yeah, me too," he said. "I have this gaping sense of time now. Like time is not real, it doesn't matter. I can embark on my next step after this conversation or in five years. My sense of urgency has changed."

"It's like a veil over my eyes made me believe I belonged here, and now it's lifted. I don't belong here. After you leave, I probably won't see anyone else until I run out of food."

"I see why you and Anastasia got along so well."

"I will never…" I rolled my eyes upward as the spreading cracks in the plaster ceiling blurred away, "…find anyone else I can speak with like that."

The tears in my eyes boiled as he looked out the window.

"Anyway," he transitioned us, "I came to return the box, but I also had something I thought might bring you comfort. Anastasia kept Tatiana's address weighted beneath a heavy ring on her vanity. I don't need to know about your family politics, and I may be speaking out of turn, but I know you have never met her. Tatiana was upset that Anastasia had taken the jewelry in the box. Anyway, here it is."

I didn't reach out for the slip of paper, so he placed it on the cluttered coffee table.

"I appreciate you coming over here."

We shook hands, and he left, off to let his wound begin to scar.

9
Franca Rossi

The Gallarate Hospital nursing certification program consisted of thirty hours per week in the hospital, three classes making up about ten hours of classroom study. Then, after the first month of training, I would add another ten hours of patient home visits by assisting one of the doctors with house calls. My time in the hospital was long and grueling and mainly consisted of cleaning patients, rooms, floors, and medical tools. Yet the hospital time familiarized me with the routines. While I enjoyed the classroom study segment, it was when my exhaustion seemed to emerge mercilessly. I had difficulty tracking the conversation when it became base or uninteresting. I was slow to recall details about readings from the night before that I had been thinking about all day.

The two women who owned and operated the apartment building that housed the dormitory for my program were sisters who inherited the building from their father. The nurses-in-training were divided between two large rooms, sharing eight bathrooms. The younger sister, Maria Caterina, was a veteran nurse at the hospital where we were training, Ospedale di Gallarate. The sisters renovated the two dormitories and rented beds to training nurses by the week, which I hadn't realized until my second week when nearly a fifth of the girls departed and were replaced by eager, rested faces. I had already paid for the three months upfront, securing myself a top bunk by the window, which seemed like a good idea until I realized that I was the first victim of the cold draft that whistled in through the top of the worn wooden frame. The morning light woke me up on days I worked through the night. Certain nights of the week, the noise off the street echoed so loudly that it felt like I was one of the revelers.

The first week, I was consumed with learning the town's geography, finding where to purchase what I needed, and meeting people. I never knew whether I would see someone again, even in the dormitory, and tended to forget the right names. The training was covered by a scholarship Professoressa Mila secured on my behalf, but I was responsible for the cost of meals and any daily spending. Mama gifted me enough money for about three weeks, but the plan was for me to take work once I arrived. At the end of the first week, I met with the shrewd older sister, Maria Benedetta, and she offered me a cleaning position. I held the position for six evenings before she fired me. I was decent at tidying, but mopping the five hallways of the building took me hours.

I was folding blankets in the courtyard when Maria Benedetta called out her office window three stories above for me.

"Drop the bedspread and come see me in my office." I hesitated to react. "You can drop it on the ground, Franca. It will be just as clean there."

Maria Benedetta shared her office, formerly their father's, with her sister. She sat behind her desk, finishing a letter as I took my seat, a stern chair with a thinly cushioned seat and short back. There were two old desks about eight meters apart in the long room. The office was worn in by generations of men filling the bookshelves, scratching the surfaces, corners, and legs of the two heavy desks that ended in the hands of two spinsters operating the family estate from this room. A door in the corner of the room behind Maria Caterina's desk led to the sisters' living quarters.

"Franca, I must dispense with your services. To be plain, you are awful at cleaning."

While I knew she was not wrong, my face fell, and my shoulders lost their air.

"You will be alright. Caterina says you are a promising nurse."

"Thank you, Maria Benedetta. I am enjoying my course."

"Are you in absolute need of a position outside your training?"

"Yes." I rubbed my eyes. It had been the longest two weeks of my life, and with this disappointment, the exhaustion began to set into my muscles.

"You've received a letter," she reached over the side of her desk. And while you have no business cleaning living quarters, I have spoken to my friend, the pastry shop owner around the corner. I'm sure you have seen Il Café Gatto Bianco? She needs an employee to wipe down tables, mop the floor at the end of the day, and help behind the counter."

"Thank you, Maria Benedetta! Thank you."

"Good. You start there on Tuesday. She can accommodate your training schedule."

"Yes, Maria Benedetta, and thank you for being so kind. I really appreciate—"

"Don't speak of it," she interrupted, pointing her finger to command my silence.

I nodded and smiled, dumbfounded by my prospects' swift fall and rise.

"You're dismissed." She waved me away. The lines of her forehead and those branching from her eyes smoothed back into stone while the deep-set lines around her lips became more pronounced with her pout.

I bounced to the door and smiled at her before closing it behind me, even though she wasn't looking at me. In the hallway, I avoided the other girls' eyes, staring at the ceiling and thanking God for providing for me. It felt like the world had conspired to my benefit, validating my mission to become a nurse. I returned to the courtyard and sat at a corner table, the furthest from the fountain in the center, to read the first letter I had received in Gallarate.

It was a note of encouragement from Professoressa Mila. She estimated that it must be a difficult transition, inquired about whether I had given her gift to her doctor friend yet, and told me to contact her if I needed anything.

10
Pasquale

The slip of paper stayed in a safe place (on top of my desk), then a safer place (in the box of safe-keeping paperwork on top of the desk), until finally, I copied it three times and placed the original and three copies in separate places. No matter what I was doing, my thoughts returned to whether I should reach out to Tatiana or preserve her peace. I asked one friend for his opinion, and he tensed. It was as if I had asked him to alphabetize hieroglyphics – and he insulted my handwriting. I sometimes forget that other people have ordinary families with simpler problems.

I decided not to write to her for now. Not today, but I'll decide again tomorrow. The ultimate reason for writing would be to meet her and her daughter. I don't need a pen pal. Nothing could be gained by going back and forth over paper with Tatiana. I would have reached out for nothing if she didn't want to meet in person. What little was known to me of her did not seem encouraging. A rejection might break the little composure I still have. If she did want to meet, if I were successful… that was also a fearsome possibility. She was likely a disappointment, unable to hold a candle to Stasi's charisma. Our chemistry could never be recreated, transferred, or matched, and it would be better to carry unconfirmed suspicions than be flattened by proving my convictions about her as facts.

There was no rush to write to her. At any point, the mind can change, alternate plans can be made, commitments can be shed, and an illusion of security can be constructed. Each day without change is consenting to yesterday's decisions. One of the Marinova traits is to rake oneself over the ever-burning coals of former decisions. Every day, Pim lives with the decision to leave Varvara. My decision to not contact Tatiana could be reversed at any time, which made it the safe choice, though I risk that Tatiana could also die, or my apartment building could burn down with all of the copies of her address. The next time I leave the apartment, I should open a safety deposit box and place a copy there.

11
Franca Rossi

My dinner appointment with Professoressa Mila's friend was scheduled for my third week in Gallarate. I was eager to have a family meal outside the dormitory courtyard and shared kitchen. I ate an apple before getting dressed so I would not embarrass Prof. Mila by being ravenous at dinner. This was the first night I could reasonably wear one of the four nice dresses I had packed.

"Miss Fancy!" Tina joked as I said goodbye to the girls who were eating dinner together. Maria invited me to join a supper club with six other girls in Dormitory A. Dormitory B girls kept to themselves, and the other girls in A had declined to join the supper club for the work it took on the night of your turn. One day each week, one girl made dinner for the group. We connected over the differing cooking styles of Piedmont and Lombardia.

Doctore De Costa's home was in the middle of a row of identical stucco houses, all three stories high, with two square windows facing the street at each level; it was number 304, which made me think reassuringly of my mother's birthday: April 3. I let myself in through the front gate, and my first knock on the door was instantly met by all three daughters greeting me. The oldest, Alessia, was only two years younger than me, about Gia's age, and was eager to hear all about the nursing program.

"I intend to enroll in the program, too," Alessia said proudly. "After I graduate."

"Elena Mila was your teacher, right? Our Elena is named after her." The middle child, Giorgia, shared.

"Yes. She arranged this program for me. I'm very grateful to her." They surrounded me on the couch as we talked before dinner.

"Our Mama passed away four years ago," Elena said. "That's why we have a cook now."

"I'm very sorry. That's terrible."

"She experienced a hemorrhagic stroke at the top of the stairs and tumbled down. She was gone before the end of the fall." Alessia told me with her hands clasped in her lap.

"I was the one who found her," Giorgia added.

"That must have been terrible," was all I could say.

"It was."

Doctore De Costa came to greet me as the cook was serving dinner. He had a sterile demeanor. The girls spoke at a lesser volume.

"I met Elena Mila when I was a young man at university in Milano. I instantly admired her. It's quite a compliment to have her speak highly about you. I met Elena Mila the same night she met her husband. We were scholars together. I believe I met her first, but I stepped away to speak to a colleague, and when I came back, she was speaking with him."

The girls' silent chewing and flawless table manners made me self-conscious as I concentrated on not scraping my knife against the plate while cutting the lasagna. Giorgia and Elena watched me closely, so I maintained a neutral, pleasant expression through his stories of Prof. Mila. She must not have sat down with the doctor in years. I don't believe she would have sent me here if she had. His haunted eyes looked like he could only see half of what was before him, clinging to the images of what had been lost to him. Alessia fetched the *torta caprese*, a regional favorite dessert I served at Il Café Gatto Bianco. I chewed each bite of cake for far too long to avoid speaking.

"Do you see that ceramic vase on the mantelpiece?" He asked me, pointing to the medium-sized white and black vase. The girls' eyes followed his finger.

"Yes. It's beautiful."

"My wife's family is Roman. Her parents were born in Milano but are deeply proud of their Roman heritage. Never let us forget it. Except they seem to forget that the Romans cremated bodies into the second century. The Church changed that for burials. If Christ had been cremated, cremation would be the prevailing method today. It's not Catholic of me, but I opted to have her with us. I have seen enough cadavers. Have you seen any in your training yet?"

"Not yet."

"Well, you'll see them. I couldn't let her body become that… its soul departed, bared without shame, blue as if sunlight had never warmed it. And I couldn't put that in the ground. Covering it with dirt but knowing what would be happening under there." His left hand tented his long fingers by his temple as he made a motion of twisting his mind. "Visualizing the decomposition. My only reasonable option was to have her cremated."

I had never known anyone to be cremated, but I did not feel the judgment he was looking to arouse in me. Alessia and Elena stared at their empty plates. Giorgia watched her father without emotion. My father always said that who a man is sitting at dinner with his family is who he is in life.

"Did you know that bones do not succumb to fire?"

"I did not."

"Bones can char, but in cremation, the bone fragments are pulverized into ash."

I looked directly at him. His cheeks were gaunt, and his light brown eyes loomed. He was searching for someone to put his pain into.

"It's time I return to my dormitory. The landladies of my building lock the door at eleven." They were all caught off guard by my bluntness. So was I. Placing my cloth napkin on top of the table, I looked at the vase, then at each face, ending on the doctor. "Thank you for dinner. I'll tell Professoressa Mila how welcoming you all are."

There was a chill to the night air. I couldn't seem to get warm. The whole way home, I thought of what constitutes the dissolution of a family: death, delusion, mental disorder, estrangement, greed, illness, resentment, adultery, divorce, selfishness, rejection, disrespect, manipulation, and abuse. There are more ways for a family to fall apart than to be held together. Gia's hate for Paolo and Pasquale Marinova fleeing to Paris flashed to the front of my mind. Every family has cause for erosion. When the family is allowed to disintegrate that is when bone melts.

12
Pasquale

Though I was losing weight, my home was becoming heavy with furniture, books, papers, and unused sculpting supplies. An artist is measured by their impact on others. The worth of my talent could only ever be evaluated in the eye of another. And yet, I have not produced anything new since arriving in Paris. I updated former clients with the news of my beloved sister's death. I try to create an atmosphere of unavailable novelty by claiming I am contemplating alternative techniques. I hint that my work will return stronger, groundbreaking, and worth the anticipation. A few patrons were sufficiently hooked. I accepted a retainer from a Polish count to be the first on my list when I resume work as if it were in my control.

The mourning didn't keep me from sculpting; sculpting would have been the best release. It was my hands. They shook when I tried to sketch. They trembled as I held a pen, a cup of tea, a spoonful of soup. A single shake would cause my lines to veer or another spill on my lap. Becoming frustrated by the tremor made it worse. It was like my hands were not connected to the whole of me, no longer my agents. Somehow, they had colluded with each other to unite in unbearableness. Only by having a drink could I subjugate them into docility.

I had a cavernous absence of rest. I often lay down for hours during the day, but my mind never went quiet. Despairing thoughts streaked inside my skull like raindrops on a window, blotting the view of everything outside my mind.

13
Franca Rossi

The doctor I was assigned to support on house calls was an ancient man named Doctore Uliassi, who always called me "Infermiera Rossi." When I first met him in the sparse basement of the hospital, packed with the other nurses-in-training meeting their designated doctors, it seemed that the short straw had been drawn on my behalf. He was older than both of my nonnos. *He can't be of any help to anyone. I'll learn nothing.* Most of our time was spent walking to our visits. His pace was impossibly slow, whether we were on the way to a routine visit or an emergency awaited us. As I was in uniform and he was not, I felt sure I would be mistaken for his personal nurse.

However, during these slow walks, Doctore Uliassi explained the symptoms and stages he anticipated encountering when we finally reached the patient. He verbalized his thinking for me and considered multiple scenarios (*if this, then… but if that, then… and if somehow…*), the questions we would ask, and our possible course of action.

He always asked: "What do you think, Infermiera Rossi?"

"I don't know, I haven't seen the patient," I would say.

"No, but what could it be? What are you expecting? What has your training taught you?"

This made our lengthy walking time very valuable. I learned how to respond to more scenarios than the ones we would encounter. My mind was rewiring; he offered me a new way of thinking.

Doctore Uliassi was never alarmed by a patient's condition and was quick to recommend medicine or remedial action. I became increasingly impressed by how the events that came to pass almost always fit precisely into one of his forecasted threads. I regarded him as my most incredible medical resource and more instrumental in my training than the hospital or classroom. On the way to a patient's home, I would think about how lucky this person was to have Uliassi coming for them. I tried to remember all the questions he asked his patients so I could write them down when I returned to the dorm. I respected his advanced recall; he made his patients feel cared for and was a calming presence for the family. If we did encounter a scenario he had not considered, he approached the case with passionate curiosity. He embodied a professional humility I yearned to emulate. He answered my questions thoughtfully and prompted me to ask the patient questions. I was confident following his instructions, a luxury compared to some of my classmates' grievous experiences with their assigned doctors.

On the weekends, I thought about the week's patient visits as I worked at Il Café Gatto Bianco from six in the morning until noon. The baker arrived at four each morning, having his key. But he was deaf and a paranoid. If ever he was tapped on the shoulder unexpectedly, he jumped audibly and emitted a sound a man couldn't ever know he was making. Yet he made the best *bombolone*, *panna cotta*, and *cannoli* in Gallarate. Instead of disturbing the baker, I stood outside in the cold, waiting for the owner's son, Gino, to descend from the family apartment above the café in the morning. The owner, Maria Benedetta's lifelong neighbor and friend, referred to her son as lazy and useless. He was responsible for unlocking the door for me and waving a morning hello to the baker to alert him to my presence. Otherwise, Gino had nothing to do all day.

Working at the café allowed me to meet Gallarate natives outside of a medical context. I accepted every dinner invitation, though I made it clear that I was not interested in any eligible son or nephew and was eager to see people's homes, meet their families, and have a full meal outside the dormitory. I always brought my hosts pastries from Il Café Gatto Bianco. Every dinner since the De Costa's had been lovely and warm. These few blocks became mapped according to where my acquaintances lived. I never ate at any of the restaurants. I might have liked to, but I bought groceries for breakfast and lunch and then had dinner at the homes of my new friends or with the supper club.

After dinner, two girls in the supper club frequently went to the bar beside Il Café Gatto Bianco. I went with them a couple of times and tried vodka, which was awful and expensive. One night, my friend Maria and I were walking home after a late dinner at another nurse's apartment when we were chased by a drunkard who came charging at us from down a narrow road. He was yelling, though I was too frightened to make out what he was saying, and he was a little wobbly, but not slow. We screamed and ran in our short heels, luckily only a right turn and two blocks away, and outpaced him to the dormitory. Maria was able to unlock the door with a serenity I couldn't have achieved. His fists banged on the tall wooden front doors of the building for five minutes before voices on the street shooed him away.

In the third month, I decided to try to save enough to see Milano, Verona, and Venezia the week immediately following the end of the program. When I wrote Luca about my plan, he was not over the moon about extending our separation. He had been to these places throughout his childhood and wrote that if I could not pull the money together, then he would take me someday. It was kind of him to assure me, but I was determined to make the trip happen for myself.

"I would like to take on more hours," I said to my patroness at the café one Saturday morning while she was socializing.

"You already work more than anyone should."

"I want to go to Milano, Verona, and Venezia."

"Why would you want to do that?"

I paused. "See my country... while I'm closer to these places before I go home."

"And you would go alone? A woman? No. I won't help you. Absolutely stupid." She walked away.

The next day, after she returned from church with Gino, she yelled to me over the counter as I was gathering pastries for a gentleman sitting by the window.

"Franca, I know what to do! Gino will travel with you. He must see the country too, understand our history. I will pay for the train fare and hotels in each city, one room for him and one for you." She looked at my face. He looked at my face. "Think on it."

When I arrived at the dormitory, I searched the kitchen and dining area, her bunk, and the small sitting area outside Maria Benedetta's office. Finally, I found Maria bundled up, reading in the courtyard despite the cold.

"Maria, I've been looking all over for you."

"Why so? How was the café?"

"My patroness offered to pay for my train travel and hotels."

"Truly?"

"Only if I take Gino with me. She said she'd pay for us to have separate rooms, but I don't know if I can accept that. I can't stop thinking about what my mother would say... or Luca... and I can't imagine eating every meal for seven days with Gino. It will be the week before Christmas, and it is an insult enough to spend that time away from my family. He wouldn't hurt me or anything. It is a generous offer. It's just Gino, ugh!"

I rambled until she looked longingly at her book and then held up her palm to slow my mouth.

"You cannot go with a man alone. You already know that. It would be unfair to Luca and your dignity." She began to smile conspiratorially. "Instead, I'll join you. I'll pay for my train and share your hotel room, so there will be no cost to Gino's mother. Gino will be there to protect us, and I won't have to ask my grandparents for accommodation money. Will that work?"

14
Pasquale

All decisions felt too significant. I would stay in Paris for another year to focus on beginning my next sculpting phase. My plan of debuting an exhibition of twelve to fifteen works returned. Moving into a grander apartment would have been ideal. Relocating to Anastasia's apartment was not an option once Pim's esquire attained access and arranged its sale. I received a letter, not from Pim himself, advising me not to enter the building.

Before creating my great collection, I had to conquer the trembling, which would mean reducing alcohol. An occasional barmate reminded me that sobriety meant lying in bed for hours before falling asleep. It meant I couldn't fight the bend of my thoughts that incessantly led back to Stasi. Liquor was the only way I knew to stagger the conicular thinking. It was all ruinous.

Stasi's words played in my head as if she were standing beside me, though the sound of her voice had become watered down: "Every day, your actions reinforce the decisions you made yesterday."

15
Franca Rossi

My last week in Gallarate was scheduled to the minute. I barely slept.

Maria Benedetta invited me to her apartment for a farewell meal with Maria Caterina. We played a game of cards as our *pizze* dinner heated in the oven. They had many book recommendations for me and told me about their travels and what it was like growing up in the Risorgimento. They still felt more *Lombardi* than *Italiani*. Their father wanted them to attend university in Milano, and while Maria Benedetta did as directed, Maria Caterina felt pulled to the hospital. She had developed portions of the nursing program. Drinking wine with these remarkable women made me wish I had enjoyed them more in Gallarate. We parted that night, knowing I would not stop by the office before folding my sheets and leaving them on the bed beside the window on Saturday morning. It was better to parcel out the pain of leaving through the week than altogether on the final day.

The other significant dinner of that week was at the home of Doctore Uliassi. Saying goodbye to him was the most difficult. He had trouble writing letters, and I felt a foreboding sense that I would likely never see him again. Doctore Uliassi and his wife had five grown children, two sons and three daughters. All were present at dinner with their spouses and all twenty-two grandchildren – and one daughter and one daughter-in-law were pregnant. I could not grasp which child belonged to which couple because the aunts and uncles hugged and spoke to them the same way, kissing their heads between bites and chewing. I confused the doctor's sons with his sons-in-law but could easily distinguish the three Uliassi daughters because they all had the same heart-shaped face as their mother. The three of them were born in four years. They wore their hair the same way and had similar conversational mannerisms – quick to interrupt, contradict, or voice when they didn't understand something.

I was in the middle of an age gap, older than the oldest grandchild yet younger than the pregnant daughter-in-law. I spoke with the children as much as the Uliassi siblings. The children called me Infermiera Rossi and asked about where I was from. I told them about the lake and what Pallanza was like, and they promised to visit when they became older. They asked me what it was like being a nurse, and I said that I didn't know yet because I was graduating from the program.

"You are so lucky to have so many cousins," I told the four little girls sitting on the floor around me.

"We had a cousin named Rino, but he died," one of the girls said sadly.

"He was my baby brother, but I never met him," said Ludovica. "It was influenza."

The girls looked downtrodden momentarily as if grief was a learned facial expression.

"Why aren't you married?" Little Martina asked me after the moment had passed.

I told them about Luca, but I wished I hadn't, as after that, the girls shouted about my Russian prince fiancé for the remainder of the evening.

During the meal, the three sisters made an apparent effort to include their sisters-in-law, whom they had known through childhood. Signora Uliassi served the pasta with a spicy sausage sauce and boiled salted potatoes. Her sons carried the large, heavy ceramic dishes to the table. Everyone served themselves and one another all at once, so several people, including me, ended up with two servings on one plate. The long table fit sixteen plus squiggling children on the laps of those who adored them.

"Infermiera Rossi, I have a gift for you." Doctore Uliassi said to me over the voices of his children.

"I've already seen it," one of the daughters shrugged.

"I have too, you'll like it." Another daughter said.

Signora Uliassi fetched a brown package from their bedroom.

"Thank you," I said as she handed the bulky package to me. "Thank you for having me at your home this. Your family is—"

"Just open it, Infermiera!" The third daughter commanded.

It was a brown leather medical bag with brass studs on the bottom. It was a smaller, new version of the one Doctore Uliassi carried. I began to cry. The family reacted with laughter, applause, sighs, and sympathetic tears.

"Thank you, Doctore Uliassi. You've taught me... so much. Because of you, I will be a better servant for others."

16
Pasquale

The last dozen times I attempted to sculpt, I couldn't achieve the meditative trance I used to access freely. My focus has deteriorated. The daylight hours wilt. I haven't completed a piece since moving to Paris. The quiet absence of self I used to slip into for hours eludes me. I tried to push through the shakes but could barely work for fifteen minutes without needing a break. It's not coming back. I can't resuscitate it.

17
Franca Rossi

The three of us traveled well together, even though Gino spoke with his mouth full at every dinner. By the end of the week, I could not watch him gnash another bite. In the mornings, he slept in late; finally, he was free from his mother dictating his daily schedule. During the day, we were on our own, and if we returned for an afternoon rest, Gino would be spending the money his mother padded him with at the hotel bar, surrounded by belligerent tourists. He had a terrific holiday without entering a museum or touring a historical site.

Maria and I toured the places we had heard about all our lives, all decorated for the Christmas holiday. We attended mass at the *Duomo di Milano*. We found ourselves lost in the alleyways of Venice in pursuit of the *Basilica Cattedrale Patriarcale di San Marco*. Verona, our middle stop, was by far my favorite. It was a pocket of Roma in the north, wholly different from Milano and Venezia's tributes to the Renaissance. The partially decaying Roman amphitheater, the *Arena di Verona*, was the closest structure to the Roman Coliseum I had ever seen. The streets were wide, and the people walking them smiled. It was the only place of my travels, even Gallarate, that wrung the thought from my mind: *I could live here.*

And yet, the most saturating feeling I found was in my long conversations with Maria. We shared an education and Gallarate, but what came next looked different for each of us. I would marry a prince and live in a palatial villa on the lake. I would be a new aunt in a couple of months. I could serve my community as a nurse. I would have to broker a truce with Mary Marinova. My next year, my next decade, felt scripted.

On the other hand, Maria was orphaned by her parents and the only grandchild of the wealthy grandparents who raised her. She did not desire to return to Torino, "at least not yet." She was completely free, so much so that she felt overwhelmed by having too many choices. In Gallarate, she would be a nurse at the hospital and write poetry in her spare time. Her grandparents toured her around Piemonte, Liguria, Toscana, Umbria, and Campania during the summers. During one of those summers, she had a romance with the son of a fisherman she never kept in touch with. Their intimacy over a single month marked her, in her mind, as a woman liberated. Whether she married or not didn't seem to concern her. I had never had a friend like her before, a confidant very different from myself.

There were two trains from Venice to Pallanza. Maria, Gino, and I boarded the second train at our connection in Milano. They would take the earlier stop for Gallarate, and I would continue to Pallanza. Maria and I were physically exhausted from walking miles and miles for pleasure and weighed down every second day with our oversized suitcases, which Gino never helped us with, through our newest city. As the train approached Gallarate, I couldn't suppress the tears. I turned my face toward the window to see my trembling lips and eyebrows twitching for each other. I felt Maria touch my arm, and when I looked at her, she was also trying not to cry.

"I'm sorry," I wiped my eyes. We started to laugh at ourselves, looking ridiculous. "I am realizing it is all over – the nursing program, Gallarate, our trip...."

"I know. It feels wrong that we have to separate now. Gallarate won't be the same. I don't know why I'm bent on returning there."

"You should come visit Pallanza soon. Promise you'll come to my wedding?"

"Of course I will," her smile quivered. She must have seen my doubt because her eyes grew wide. "I swear it, Franca. I will be at your wedding. It will be beautiful."

I could see Gino, more often short of breath than short of words, unsure what to say about all of our emotions. The *controllore* came speedily down the walkway of the car announcing Gallarate as the next stop, in two minutes. Gino gathered his things and pulled his suitcase down from the straps overhead. When he moved to fetch Maria's, she told him not to worry about it and insisted she could do it herself. Gino resumed his seat.

I felt a burgeoning sense of urgency for Maria to start gathering her things. After checking back into the dormitory, she told me about how she needed to purchase new tights this afternoon. Her eyes stayed steady between her lap and me, but the sound of her voice rose and fell and peaked and broke. The signs out the window became readable over her shoulder as the train slowed.

"Maria–" I interrupted her.

Her eyes teared up, and she clutched my hands.

"You have to gather your things now." I moved to help her, but her grip tightened, and I stayed seated.

"I can't, Franca. I just can't."

"What? You have to get off here."

The train screeched to a complete stop.

"Farewell, Franca," Gino said, moving to embrace me. When he saw I was held in my seat by Maria's shaking hands, he bent over to kiss my head. As he pivoted to kiss the crown of Maria's head as well, she shook her head away, and he landed on air. He nodded to me as he placed his new hat on his head and lined up to depart the car.

"I can't, Franca. I don't want to be alone for Christmas. I'm not getting off the train."

"You must, Maria. What about –"

The train whistled for the new passengers to board. Maria closed her eyes tightly and bent her neck toward her knees as if that would make it all disappear. I let her grip my hands, looking around to see if anyone was watching, unsure how to help her when everything was moving so quickly.

She opened her eyes briefly after the train pulled away from the station. Maria smiled and released my hands to push her hair out of her face.

"Franca," she smiled at me like we were at lunch. "I'm coming to Pallanza with you for Christmas. If I like the lake, I may stay for the summer."

We laughed. She had all of her belongings. No one depended on her to return to Gallarate, though I asked her to write Maria Benedetta a letter to save her any worry. I was delighted at the thought of having my best friend with me in Pallanza. She seemed relieved to be giving herself something that was not solitude. Maria stayed at my parents' house for Christmas, in the room Gia, Imma, and I shared. In January, she rented a small room on the Pallanza side of the bridge where Pallanza bordered Intra for a convenient walk to the hospital.

18
Franca Rossi

Luca, Papa, Mama, Gia, and Imma met us at the train station. Luca's eyes teared when he saw me. He waited for my father and mother to hug me first. Mama had gained weight that showed on her face and neck. I couldn't pause to look because Luca lifted me as we hugged. I was surprised by the new beard he was growing. Luca bought a *bresole* and *mozzarella tramezzino* from the station café before we walked home in the December cold. Luca carried Maria's suitcases the whole way. I only let Papa carry one of my suitcases for me. Mama, Gia, and Imma were surprisingly quiet as Maria and I told them about our travels. Mama had left the tomato sauce simmering on the stove so we could eat lunch as soon as we arrived home. I stopped talking about my travels too much, sensing that I may have upset them by not returning home as soon as my program ended.

After a long afternoon and evening of Maria becoming acquainted with the family, everyone was exhausted. Luca promised to return the next day to take me to dinner on the lake. I fell asleep early that night.

I could have been better at writing letters to my family and Luca during my program. I attributed receiving a few letters to the fact that I only sent a few. Only the following day did I realize that silence should have been terrifying. I received only two letters from Arabella and assumed she was busy with her growing family, position in the store, and adjusting to life with Paolo's family in Intra.

Imma, who had grown a couple of inches, sat me in the living room to tell me the news: "Arabella is on bed rest until the baby comes. Arabella will not be making an appearance on Christmas. Paolo wrote saying they wouldn't come for breakfast or dinner."

"Imma! I need you to go buy bread."

"Mama, no! We have enough bread!" Imma protested.

"Just go!" Gia yelled from the kitchen table where she sat with Mama. Imma took the coins from the table and left, letting the door slam behind her with the hallway's suction.

The door was closed only a moment before Sofia Esposito opened it, and Mama yelled in the same harsh tone she used with Imma: "Go find Imma, Sofia!"

The girl quickly turned and ran away, slamming the door behind her so hard the floor shook. Gia, more beautiful than ever, put her hand on Mama's shoulder. Mama looked older than when I had left. There was gray at her temples. I had never seen Mama and Gia united before. Maria emerged from the bedroom and took a seat at the table. Gia filled the Mokka pot with water and packed the coffee in its steel bed with the back of a spoon.

"We have to tell you what's been happening," Gia said. "You don't know the turmoil we've been living with." Mama made the sign of the cross. "After dinner a few weeks ago, Arabella told Mama Paolo had hit her. It wasn't the first time, but it was the first time he had hit her-" Gia swallowed, livid, and stared at the table "in her middle. Mama advised her to be overly thoughtful and not make him angry."

"I failed her," Mama mumbled at the table.

"He's a bastard," Gia spat. Mama made the sign of the cross again. "Two days later, Paolo wrote a note to Mama saying that Arabella was feeling ill and wouldn't be coming to dinner that week. Mama asked to see her, and he said they would find another time to visit. Mama went to Intra anyway. We weren't thinking then, so Mama didn't bring Papa or our uncles. Signora Terracci refused to let Mama in the house. She said Arabella was too ill for visitors."

"I could hear Arabella call me from the window." Mama's eyes filled with tears.

"Well..." Gia continued looking sympathetically between Mama, silent Maria, and me, "Mama became... hysterical. She said she wouldn't leave until she saw Ara. She threatened to return with our uncles. The police were fetched. One of the police officers was Paolo's cousin. He did not appreciate his aunt being insulted. He ordered her to leave, said there was nothing illegal about a pregnant woman being bedridden... and when Mama refused, they arrested her."

"They arrested you?" I gasped. "But is Ara alright now? Have you seen her?"

Mama and Gia looked at each other.

"Papa saw her, let me tell you," Gia said curtly. "But no, we haven't seen her or received a letter since then. We've tried to persuade the police to go into the Terracci home to see her but haven't been successful. I stormed the Intra station and damned every officer straight to hell for taking Mama there."

"I wept the whole walk home," Mama whispered. "So many of our neighbors and friends saw me."

"But everyone in Pallanza is calling the Terracci's tyrants–" Gia added.

"I'm humiliated."

"Papa went to the Terracci's store the next day and convinced Paolo to let him see Ara for a few minutes. Papa said that Ara was lying in bed resting when he came in and insisted she was unharmed. He admitted that she cried when she saw him. He asked her if she was being treated well, and she answered yes. But obviously she said that, Franca — Paolo was standing over Papa when he asked!" Gia was infuriated by Papa's lack of fire and salt. "Now, no one has seen Ara since. That was weeks ago. And we received a letter from Paolo saying that she couldn't come for Christmas."

Gia showed me the letter. It was short. Paolo wrote that Ara was strong and as happy as ever, awaiting her child. I passed the letter to Maria, whose face had fallen, her right hand covering her throat.

"When the baby is born, we will bring Ara and her child home for good," Gia swore.

Mama shook her head and began to cry. I cried too, frightened for my big sister and without any conviction that we would be able to change the situation.

✳

More heartbroken than ever, I splashed water over my swollen eyes and readied myself for dinner with Luca. Maria would be fine with my family. Her personality fit somewhere between mine and Gia's. Mama took to her immediately.

Luca knocked on our apartment door as the sun set behind the western mountains. Luca's time with the boatmaker of Baveno changed him, as did Anastasia's death. He was more focused than before. We walked down Via Ruga with the wind whipping at our faces, and finally, when we reached the edge of the lake, we hid from the cold inside one of my favorite restaurants. Luca ordered us each a glass of Roero and olives, cheeses, and cold meats to pick over as we caught up. The breath relaxed through my body as I remembered the ease with which Luca ordered food and drink without care for money. It was the opposite of how I was raised and how I stewarded my meager finances in Gallarate. There was too much to catch up on. We only held hands across the table for a while and talked about how much we had missed each other and how happy we were to be reunited.

"I have to tell you something unpleasant I found out this morning," I began. "It's about Arabella." His face stayed the same, and his hand squeezed mine tighter. "You already know?"

"Everyone knows." He nodded. "We can talk about it if you'd like, or we can talk about everything else."

"It would be nice not to have to talk or think about it."

"Good. Then tell me about your travels. Which did you like best: Milan, Venice, and Verona?"

He had traveled to all three cities at some point in his childhood and Milano many times; he debated my rank of Verona as the best and was surprised that I was unmoved by Venezia. He said he would take me to Firenze and Roma someday, and then we would see what I thought. I told him about Doctore Uliassi, Maria Benedetta, Gino, Il Cafè Gatto Bianco, and the dinner at the De Costa's home. The restaurant began to fill around us, and we were interrupted by neighbors and former classmates who came over to say hello. I gathered that they had not seen Luca for some time. He had been keeping himself to Suna and Baveno.

Salvestro Nucci, our mouthy tableside visitor, said some of their former football teammates thought Luca had followed me to Gallarate or locked himself up in Suna for missing me. Then Sal asked if I could examine one of his fingers, broken from roughhousing with his brothers years ago, that had never truly healed and was starting to swell at the proximal interphalangeal joint. I was already feeling my wine and confirmed there was swelling. I asked whether it was painful (it was not) but could not provide a reason for why the swelling was occurring. I recommended that he not lift anything heavy with the hand for a few days and see a doctor if the swelling continued. He sauntered off, mumbling, "Thanks for the wisdom." I stared at his back and searched my mind for further advice to impress Luca with my knowledge and competency.

"Don't worry about him. He's a peacock. A few weeks ago, I sliced the side of my hand." He showed me the newly forming gruesome scar, still discolored, on his right hand that ran four inches from his pinky finger to the base of his wrist. "Did I tell Master Agostino? Or whine to his wife? Or demand a break? No. I didn't want to lose a day and be sent home. I tied a cloth around it and finished weighing and coating the oar. Then I forgot about the hand until I rowed home across the lake."

"That's not good, Luca! What if it had become infected? You could lose your hand!"

"It didn't," he laughed. "Mama and Mrs. Figlia shrieked and almost fainted when they saw the bloody cloth. Mama made Pim call his doctor, the retired one who lives on Via Garillo, to come and stitch it. Enzo couldn't look at it. He lost his appetite and skipped dinner."

"I'm sure that made Signora Figlia happy."

"She always says," he went into her accent and high voice to quote: "There is making plans, and then there is knowing Luca Marinova."

Instead of ordering another glass of wine, he ordered us the bottle.

He told me about Baveno and Master Agostino. Besides the excitement of playing and watching football, he had never felt enamored by a process the way boatmaking made him feel. He found himself content with mediocrity at school, but now he yearned to perform expertly. He found the attention to precision soothing. The physical demands of lifting, cutting, shaping, and sanding wood required a whole-body focus. Luca's eyes lit up as he told me he had never seen himself like Pasquale before, but he supposed this was how sculpting must feel.

"You should write Pasquale a letter telling him!"

"Pasquale is not speaking to the family right now."

The prince, who had recently taken a more profound interest in Luca, proclaimed he would build a boatshed on the lake for Luca. Until then, the prince had been adamant about keeping the lawn leading to the rocks pristine, and the low-tide beach made the lawn appear larger. Luca's mother protested any structure on the property line that would blot out the view from the villa. The prince arranged for construction to begin, possibly as early as February if it were a mild winter.

"Would you like to walk to the lake?" He finished his remaining quarter glass of wine in one swig. He motioned for the waiter's attention.

"If it's not too cold." I was feeling a little unsteady but wanted to see the water.

He led me by the hand from the restaurant toward the water on the other side of the piazza. There was no other person in view. I adjusted Gia's scarf to cover my neck. He slowed his pace to walk fully at my side.

I looked at his face with every other step, taking him in after so many months apart.

"What? What're you looking at?"

"Just you. I'm happy to be back."

"I wasn't sure you would be," he said honestly.

"I am."

"Do you promise?"

"Yes."

As we reached the water's edge, with the lights of Stresa dotting the land and streaking the water, Luca took both of my hands in his and turned to face me.

"Franca, I love you. I have always loved you. I want you to be my wife. I met with your father two weeks ago, and he gave me his blessing. Will you marry me?"

"Yes."

Then he kissed me.

19
Franca Rossi

On the walk back to my house that night, we conspired to have a short engagement. After Christmas, Maria and I became nurses at the hospital. Maria flourished in the hospital environment. I only worked a few days weekly at the hospital as I preferred visiting patients at home. I hesitated to commit more time to the hospital since it was thirty minutes from Luca's villa. The news that I was a certified nurse spread through our building. Knocks on our door came all day and night for me to see our neighbors. Gia started screaming in the marble hallway late at night that Infermiera Rossi was unavailable. She woke up so many neighbors that we could hear them shouting back that Franco Rossi's "daughter of fire" could leave the building if she didn't like it. From then on, I started sleeping on the flat couch in the living room so I would be the first to hear any knocking at night. I didn't mind. Helping the families I had grown up with made me feel useful and seen by them when I had formerly only been another Rossi girl or Luca Marinova's love interest. I also felt forgiving of any nightly knocks because of the fleetingness of my time left living in the building. In Suna, I would be out of reach for late-night knocks.

Luca and I disagreed about the size of our wedding. I told Mama I wanted a small wedding, especially after Arabella's. Mama insisted that I have a large wedding, saying that weddings were her right as the mother of daughters. Luca and I discussed the wedding over lunch while I was three floors above, making a bedside visit to the oldest man in the building, the great-grandfather of my former classmates, who was dying. I had never had a patient die before, and it recalled the memory of Giacomo Esposito. I was sensitive to the weight behind my eyes while completing my tasks of making the man comfortable in his small bed, usually shared with one of his great-grandchildren. I instructed the family on how to feed him as they all gathered to pray over him in his remaining hours. It was only two in the afternoon, but I came home only steps away, depleted. Mama and Luca were sitting at the table.

"Good afternoon, Franca," Luca said over his espresso.

"We've planned it all for you. You won't have to worry about a thing." Mama smiled and even clapped, the happiest I had seen her since before Gallarate. "Luca's checked with his mother, and the Marinova Gardens can host three hundred guests!"

I stood over the table, staring down at their notes.

"I don't want to get married in front of three hundred people."

"You'll be thankful on the day to have everyone there. There will be a parade. You are becoming a princess."

"You're not listening to me!" I yelled at her. I started crying, and Luca held his hands up in alarm. "You only care about impressing our family and neighbors!"

"You are ungrateful. You are rejecting the gifts life has given you. Why do you bury yourself in a hospital when you could have the finest life of anyone on the lake? What about Luca and what the Marinovas want? Will you deny your new parents their say?"

I stormed off to the girls' bedroom. I hadn't considered what Luca wanted and felt badly for not asking. I felt no expectations from him, but there was an unspoken urgency.

Paolo's mother sent one of her neighbors to inform us when the baby arrived. Arabella's baby boy, little Paolo Terracci, was born on a misty spring morning. A baby born in the morning when clouds veil the lake is fortuitous. The sky knelt to meet the child. I was more grateful for Ara's straightforward childbearing than anything; I had been losing sleep for fear that Arabella had inadequate medical support for the birth. While in Gallarate, I envisioned myself being present and supporting the birth. Without seeing Ara myself, I hoped and convinced myself that Paolo would not harm her while she was with child, which was consuming my mother's thoughts and warping her beauty. My conviction allowed me to have productive days and even smile and laugh. Gia seemed to have more energy and was out of the house with her sweetheart, a police officer at the station the day Gia rescued Mama. Mama was told that she and Papa could visit tomorrow, but there could be no further visitors.

Gia saw this limited invitation as an outrageous insult and mobilized Luca and her officer boyfriend Marcello to escort my parents to Intra. Luca agreed, without hesitation or thought, before I could counter Gia at the dinner table.

"Luca shouldn't get involved!" I protested.

"It's no problem. I'll go, Gia," he insisted. Perhaps he thought that the presence of the youngest son of the wealthiest immigrant of all three towns might keep the situation amicable.

"Then I'm going too." I declared.

"We should!" Gia agreed.

Marcello was deeply in love with my sister; he would travel to the world's edge if she commanded him to. He was proud to be included and relied on for this matter. Gia had stronger emotions for him than I had ever seen her show before, but I knew she wanted him to be at our parents' side to prove that Paolo wasn't the only one with connections to the police.

We all walked to Intra together. Imma refused to be left with the Espositos. Marcello and Gia held hands ahead of Luca and me. During my parents' visit, with the five of us standing outside against the opposing kitchen tools shop, the Terraccis agreed that Gia, Imma, and I could see Arabella and the baby, too. Above the stationery shop, the Terracci home included bedrooms on the second and third floors. The kitchen and living area on the top fourth floor had a lovely terrace overlooking the tiled Intra roofs sloping to the lake. Flanked by his stern parents, Paolo asked that we visit Arabella separately, not to overwhelm her. We were eager to see her under any condition and agreed.

"Would you girls like coffee?"

"Yes, thank you, Signora Terracci," I said nervously, afraid of Gia opening her mouth. "Gia, you visit Ara first." Gia nodded, and Paolo's father gestured for her to descend to the third floor. Imma and I sat across from each other on the small chairs in the kitchen as Signora Terracci prepared us coffee. We said nothing.

Our parents, Luca and Marcello, waited for us at the café next door. Gia was with Arabella for the better part of an hour. I'm not sure why I thought she might hurry to let me in sooner. When Gia finally emerged, I almost knocked over the porcelain cup as I let Gia take my seat with Imma.

When I saw Arabella sitting upright in her large bed, holding her precious baby boy and her long hair combed and gently cascading over her shoulders, I started to cry. I hugged her, careful of the baby between us.

"Tell me everything that has been happening since you left. Don't leave anything out."

I must have spoken more than I ever had at once. I was there twice as long as Gia. Imma was allowed to come in for a few minutes before Paolo insisted we let the new mother rest.

※

Our forced separation from Ara ended, and Mama could see Arabella and her grandson regularly. The Terracci's control seemed to shift from Arabella to her baby. I was permitted to visit the Terracci's on Sundays. Yet, with the battle over, Mama's stamina had left her; she grew tired quickly. Even cooking dinner was becoming too much for her, so she would instruct Imma or me to help her. I came to feel guilty if Luca and Maria joined our family for dinner on nights she was not well. After every meal, I cleaned the table and kitchen so Mama could go to bed. She had the most energy when Ara visited with the baby. Ara was always holding baby Paolo except for at our home. Signora Terracci berated Arabella if little Paolo cried too much or too loudly. She was protective of her son. While she seemed to have a more challenging time defending herself, she found her voice and became more assertive and argumentative with Signora Terracci regarding the baby. At first, Ara worried Paolo would be angry if she stood up to his mother, but she found that when the women argued, the men wanted no part of it.

All of this made me hesitant to plan my wedding. Not because Luca would ever strike me or that his American mother would ever abuse me, but because I felt I would be kept in a way. Arabella was in Intra, and I would be in Suna, further from our family home than she was now. My whole life, both sets of my grandparents, the Rossis and the Illaris, lived within five minutes of us and were around them regularly. Mama could visit her mother and brothers briefly before coming home from the grocery store, bringing them bread and tomatoes and hearing what was happening that day. Who could I visit on the way from the store? My children and I will live a forty-minute walk from my mother. Visits will be deliberate.

I tried to tell Luca some of this, but he didn't understand. He said I would love living on the lake, where I could swim in the summer right outside my door. I would never have to cook or clean. The gardens were the jewel of the region. It was private and away from the dust and noise of Via Ruga. As he extolled the benefits of his cold marble private home, I saw he did not belong to the community like I did. He did not understand how intertwined one's existence could be with so many others. He did not have the obligation of belonging. It was the first time I saw him as a foreigner.

I agreed to marry in July. Then, there would still be plenty of days for me to swim.

※

I visited Signora Esposito for lunch whenever Mama and Imma ran errands, and Gia was with Marcello. I craved company more and more during mealtimes. Signora Esposito was newly pregnant with her ninth.

"I've never been to the gardens. Are they spectacular?" Signora Esposito asked me as she repaired one of the older girl's sweaters. The gardens were seen mainly by the Pallanza community at a distance from a boat and primarily enjoyed by the prince's foreign relations and the Marinovas. My wedding ceremony would be the first time many of my loved ones would experience the gardens.

"Yes, they are amazing. Luca's father imports plants from Africa and South America. It is especially beautiful in the summertime."

"I can't imagine the piles of money that have gone into it. Will the wedding be costly?"

"The Marinovas have offered to pay for everything. They say I can have three hundred guests. But St. Catherine of Siena can't fit even two hundred people… and I barely know one hundred."

"Your parents and grandparents do. They'll invite everyone they bump into on the street. I would, too if one of my daughters was marrying a prince, even a Russian-American one. You'll be the princess of Pallanza."

"Of Suna, maybe," I said, and she shrugged. In the other room, we could hear two little ones arguing.

"Don't be sensitive about that. You liked Gallarate. You came back quite the traveler. This time, you will have your own space and still be close enough for meals, church, and everything you want to be present for. You'll just walk more."

"I would prefer to keep it small. I don't like the idea of so many people looking at me."

"You won't be focused on that. Why would you deny so many the memory of a *bellisima* meal in the most beautiful gardens in the world?"

"Not in the whole world—"

"In our world then. They are willing to give everyone you know a night of dancing and lavishness beside the lake. Who do you help by refusing?"

"Who am I to have such a thing? The second daughter of a steamboat worker?"

"Franca," Signora Esposito rolled her eyes. "Stop questioning whether you deserve great things. And don't deny my children, nieces, and nephews the memory of Franca Rossi's wedding to Luca Marinova. Your prosperity is our prosperity. Think of what the Terraccis will say when your wedding is far better than your sister's!"

"Signora!"

"Well, they may treat your sister more kindly, knowing her sister is rich. They are greedy climbers! If I were you, I would expect them to plot to gain from their connection to the Marinovas once they become family."

"The Marinovas won't see it like that. They won't see the Terraccis as family or give them any money. They will never even invite them for dinner."

"No. They are not like us. The Marinovas are not Italians. But you will be the Italian Marinova and come to influence them."

✺

At the dawning of summer, my mother had a heart attack in her office at the grocer's. He found her clutching her heart with her eyes closed tight in pain. He closed the store and sent his grandson, the counter boy, to fetch my father. Gia and Marcello went for Doctore Lombardo, and Sofia and Leonardo Esposito were sent to notify Arabella in Intra. No one was sent to tell me at the hospital as my shift was nearly over. I saw Sofia, Leonardo, and Arabella pushing her carriage yards ahead of me on our street as I returned home and thought *how great Ara's come to visit*. I was too tired to run and catch up with them. When I arrived home, I sensed the seriousness of the situation by how many people were crammed into our apartment. Even Luca was there before me. He was lingering by the open door, caught me, and immediately swept me back into the hallway to tell me what had happened.

"Your mama had a heart attack. She is OK and currently on bed rest. Your father and Doctore Lombardo are in the bedroom with her. They said they will let people see her soon."

I looked inside the door, and Mama's brothers, my Illari uncles, were here with my grandparents. Luca held me and cried against his chest in the hallway for a few minutes. I was displeased to have Doctore Lombardo in my home again.

"How did you find out?"

"I was on my way here for dinner." His blonde hair fell over his eyes; it had been growing longer, making him look more like Pasquale.

"They'll let me see my mother. I want to be there as a daughter, but I need to be there as a nurse."

✳

Mama's skin tone took on a gray hue. Arabella brought her the baby often. That improved her spirit for several hours but left her exhausted once they were gone. Maria came over often and cooked for the family. I found myself easily provoked. When my father, the kindest man in the world, trailed dirt on the floor of our home, I swept it up while clenching my teeth. When Gia invited Marcello for dinner without telling me ahead of time, and I had to stretch the meal, I secretly yearned to accidentally spill the food to keep any of us from eating. If Imma woke our mother up from one more nap to tell her something before she left for her new job at the grocer's, I swore I would lock her out and make her sleep in the hallway.

My leisure time became dedicated to the household. Once I had finally ceded my dreams for my wedding and accepted the Marinovas' offer for three hundred guests in the gardens, the prince moved the wedding date back to September because he said that he would still be mourning the death of his daughter for July. On July 8, the day we originally planned for the wedding, I swam with my sisters at the crowded sliver of public beach beside the small port of Intra. The wedding day was eight weeks away now. I met Mary Marinova several times each week, armed with Gia, to settle the plans.

At the end of August, Mama had a second heart attack in the kitchen. Imma and I were the ones who found her on the floor of the kitchen with Bolognese sauce burnt in the saucepan.

20
Franca Rossi

I was dressed in black at my mother's funeral when I should have been dressed in white as Luca's bride. She had taught her daughters to be intelligent and dedicated workers and showed us how to be strong and devoted mothers. Mama was the force that settled every concern and kept us all moving. In each new day without her, I couldn't find the energy to do more than keep to meal times and complete the most basic tasks. My grandmothers were now constantly at our home, Nonna Rossi focusing on Papa and Nonna Illari keeping the place she always called unimpressive to my mother clean and the three girls fed.

"Where are you going?" Nonna Rossi asked me.

"I'm meeting Luca to have a coffee."

"Is he coming for dinner?" Nonna Illari asked. Both grandmothers were resting on the couch.

"I don't think so."

"Why not? Are you disagreeing?" Nonna Illari snapped. She adored Luca.

"We might. I want to postpone the wedding."

"Absolutely not!" Nonna Illari shrieked. She swung her feet up to throw her heels toward the base of the couch for the momentum to stand.

"Franca, my dear," Nonna Rossi cooed, "you don't really want to do that, do you?"

"You'll be a spinster nurse all of your days! He will leave you! What man would tolerate this?"

"I don't want to… I just can't next week." I started to cry, feeling who I am today at vicious odds with who I have been my whole life. Nonna Rossi hugged me. Nonna Illari continued to yell.

"Nonna, stop yourself!" Gia yelled from the kitchen table. "Franca is a grown woman. Go, Franca! Or you'll be late to meet him."

I wiped my eyes and swept my bag over my shoulder. From the street, I could hear Gia and Nonna Illari screaming at each other.

I met Luca at Café Sublime on the border of Suna and Pallanza to say what I needed. I felt him trying not to meet my eyes.

He was wearing sunglasses and kept a straight mouth. He left me alone at the table while he ordered us cappuccinos at the bar.

As he sat down and placed the cup in front of me, my eyes spilled over silently as we sat outside on the lakeside café deck. I loathed that it was a perfect day. "I can't get married next week."

"I know." His eyes were unreadable behind his sunglasses. His shoulders bent to face his knees, but his head was turned toward the lake. "I knew at the funeral."

"I'm so sorry... I am too broken right now. I never want to leave the house. My grandmothers are suffocating us. Nonna Illari yelled at me. I can't leave Papa alone to take care of Gia and Imma. And I can't leave Imma only to have Gia. Arabella is no help in Intra. It's all wrong. It's all gone so wrong."

"I understand, Franca." There was a long minute as I collected myself and evened my breath. "But I must ask, do you promise you want to marry me?"

"Yes. My feelings for you will never change."

"Then I can wait." He kissed my hand.

"It won't be forever. Just until I can get the family settled."

"Then you will want the same wedding in the garden?"

"I don't know..." I dabbed my eyes with my handkerchief. They continued to stream. "I only want to be married to you. I can't even picture a wedding without my mother. And I can't stop thinking... that she would have been there if we had been married in July as planned."

"You can't think like that. It's not good." He sipped his cappuccino.

"I'm not trying to...."

"Let's go for a walk along the lake. We don't need to have everything worked out today. I'll walk you home and tell Nonna Illari not to yell at you. I have your promise."

"You have my promise."

I sniffled and smoothed out my dress, which Mama had made me. When I suddenly saw it had a frayed thread, I began to cry again.

✳

For a time, I only cared about "today." As autumn took its last breath, I came to tell myself I would be better when the warm weather returned in March or April. Until then, I only had to focus on what the day would bring.

My inconsistent schedule of home visits, many of which were false concerns that led me to suspect Signora Esposito was plotting with our neighbors to keep me busy on my off days from the hospital, prevented me from always cooking dinner for Papa, Gia, and Imma. My grandmothers took turns cleaning and cooking for us. Nonna Illari was very vocal about all the ways we would be disappointing Mama right now: me by delaying my wedding, Gia by proving unable to hold a job after talking back to the lawyer she had been a secretary for, and Imma for not caring to tame her wild hair. Nonna Rossi doted on Papa, and together, they would diffuse Nonna Illari, so Imma would beg him in the mornings to come home early each evening. I did not believe I belonged at home anymore, but I did not try to set a date for the wedding. That would have required more energy than I could piece together.

In December, Arabella announced that she was expecting her second child. My older sister felt more distant than ever. She was isolated in her grief in Intra, living among her awful in-laws and husband she had come to be repulsed by and aggressive toward. Ara carried a pang of heavy guilt that none of us could negate, knowing that something changed in Mama when her request to visit pregnant Ara was refused nearly a year ago. Ara said that all her suffering was to bring little Paolo into the world, and she loved him more than anything. She told me over lunch that she had the urge to bite Signora Terracci's hand when she reached to pull the baby from Ara's arms. Ara said she had envisioned this so often that she must be a lunatic.

"I would never act on it, Franca!" She said, seeing my face. "I only had to tell someone."

This time, I would be here for her pregnancy. I promised to come to the Terracci family dinner on Sundays for her. I could bring Papa, Imma, and Maria. Gia could join as she pleased.

Christmas day was difficult. The world stopped, and you had to look at yourself and who you were surrounded by. The day became about who was not there.

In February, Gia announced that she and Marcello were getting married in March. My first instinct was that I couldn't believe Marcello hadn't received Papa's blessing, but as it turned out, he had, but Papa didn't tell me. I felt shocked by that. I was not his wife, but Papa and I stayed at the dinner table the longest to tell each other about our days. He would tell me I was allowing my emotions to get in the way of my happiness. I would say to him that I was doing the best I could. Also, I was surprised Gia would be married before me. Luca wondered how Gia could marry Marcello when she had only known him for a little over a year, while I chose to delay us. Still, I was happy for her. When Mama died, Marcello was helpful, kind, and forgiving. He gave her space when she asked for it; Gia was never shy about sending him away. If Gia were ever to swallow an opinion rather than say it, she might explode. And yet, Marcello always returned the next day delighted to see her.

"How do you feel about Mama not being at your wedding?" I asked her.

"I haven't thought about that. Why are you growing problems in your head?"

"Perhaps because I had the option."

I told Luca I wanted to marry in May, six weeks after Gia.

Gia did not ask for my help planning her wedding, nor did I ask for her help planning mine. Instead, we both went to Arabella, who had quickly swollen to be very large. Arabella seemed happy to be heavily involved with our weddings and very much looked forward to both days. I complained about Mary Marinova's heavy hand in my wedding and her offer for me to call her "Mother." Gia would be moving to Intra, too, which she and Ara talked about without end. That part did make me feel left out more than Signora Esposito said it should. Signora Esposito prated on how lazy I aspired to be if I was so frightened by an hour's walk to my sisters' homes.

Gia's wedding was spectacular. Not because it was expensive, because it was not, but for the atmosphere of love that surrounded all who could be with the joyous and triumphant couple. I missed Mama with all of my heart. The thought of her absence brought tears to my eyes. However, despite our void, this was the first night the Rossi family was happy. All forty people in attendance in the chapel of St. Catherine of Siena took pride in being in the presence of this high love. It was inspiring. Luca's eyes were locked on mine throughout the night, whether we were dancing or steps away. He was trying to read whether experiencing a wedding without my mother would push me further from him.

However, for the first time in a long time, I couldn't wait to marry him, couldn't wait for my body to be loved by his, and couldn't wait to begin my life in Suna with him.

When Gia and Marcello returned from their four-night honeymoon on Lake Orta, Gia was the happiest I had ever seen her. She never stopped smiling. Even though Arabella had already married, and I was Gia's older sister, it seemed a part of me needed someone else to trailblaze what a wedding could look like without Mama. Gia painted the perfect picture for me.

21
Franca Rossi Marinova

On May 3, 1896, in the attendance of two hundred and twenty-two of the Rossi, Illari, and Marinova families' acquaintances, I married Luca Giovanni Marinova.

The gardens were radiant with the blooms of spring. We had the ceremony in the center of the groves. The aisle was the main walkway that divided the exotic regions of the world from the tame. Arabella's wedding dress was far more detailed than mine, but my bohemian-style dress, chosen by Mary Marinova, encapsulated the modest uniting with the extravagant. My veil fell all the way to kiss the ground and was fastened to a small silver crown Mary purchased that was clasped over my loose hair. I carried a bouquet representing our families' nationalities. (This was the only part of the wedding where the prince demanded to be consulted.) The bouquet held giant white lilies for Italy, baby white camomile flowers for Russia, and little blue American forget-me-nots with plenty of filler greens from the gardens. Gia applied my make-up. Papa walked me down the aisle, beaming and sweating slightly, concentrating on not misstepping as if he had never done this before. I saw the faces of everyone I had ever known except my mother, Pasquale Marinova, and my dear acquaintances in Gallarate. Luca was under the vine-covered pergola at the end of the long walk. The moment felt unreal. I felt like a princess by birth. I wanted to look at him thoroughly but was nervous about not tripping over my dress. As I stood and knelt through the ceremony, every time I dared to glance at Luca, he was framed by the shining sapphire lake. When I repeated the priest's vows, I imagined I also promised myself to the lake.

The priest only agreed to have the wedding outdoors because of the donation the Marinovas made to St. Catherine of Siena and because we held a small ceremony the day before in the church. Nonna Illari denounced me for being the first woman in the history of our family not to marry in a church fully, but I did not care. Finally, the priest pronounced us man and wife and said we could kiss. We kissed to rowdy and eager applause from the Pallanza locals. The applause rang in my ears, taking my thoughts away as his mouth met mine momentarily. It was better than a dream.

Luca and I went into the villa's large living room to collect ourselves as the guests descended to a lower level of the garden to begin the merriment. We kissed in private, releasing the nervous energy steaming within me. Mary Marinova's heels stopped on the granite floor when she found us locked together on the oversized blue velvet couch. Our lips parted at the sound of her, but Luca did not let up his grip and kept me held to his chest, so I had to swivel my neck to see her out of the corner of my right eye.

"You two will need to come down in five minutes. Most of the guests are settled now."

"We will," Luca responded. I heard her heels turn and rattle off.

"You have to be considerate of her," I felt compelled to say.

"She should be considerate of us. We are married now."

We kissed more, and when we were ready, we joined the celebration in the garden. Arabella was not due for another six months but had difficulty carrying around little Paolo. Two members of the band, the singer and the cellist, were my mother's cousins, and they were delighted when Nonna Illari asked if they would play for my wedding. Unsurprisingly, Gia and Marcello were the first ones dancing. The sun was warm, but there was plenty of refuge beneath the canopies tied between the different types of palm trees; this corner of the garden was called Palm Landing. Small maps were made to guide guests if they chose to explore the gardens.

The prince, Mary, and Enzo sat on Luca's side at the head table that faced the lake and the revelry. My father, Imma, and Maria sat on mine. Arabella, Gia, and their husbands and in-laws would have imbalanced our table, so they sat at the nearest two tables. I could feel the disdain steaming from the prince. He was fuming, considering how much he was paying to entertain illiterates. Around town, he only made eye contact when he had to with the riff-raff he was serving a four-course dinner to today. The prince feared I might open a passage for the locals to come and go from the villa and gardens he built. Tomorrow, he may discover that the teenagers in attendance had defiled parts of the gardens. Another explanation for his sulky posture was Pasquale. We did not receive an answer to his invitation. Pasquale's indifference broke the heart of their small family, not to mention all of the mothers of unwed daughters at my wedding who were now eyeing Enzo zealously. But as my mother used to say, this is not my tragedy. My happiness made me impervious today.

    Luca and I danced with each other and my family. I did not eat much of the food, only what Maria put on the plate in front of me, which was the equivalent of one or two bites of several items. A few critical neighbors informed me that the chicken was better than the grilled pike and octopus, and the pesto pasta was better than the sun-dried tomato pasta. I was terrified children might smear candied hands on my dress, but I didn't mind that the bottom inches were browning from the Marinova dirt.

    Hours after the sunset over the mountains behind Stresa, candles were lit, and the last songs were danced to. Luca and I boarded an open carriage to more applause. The carriage brought us down the Marinova driveway and through the only road connecting Suna to Pallanza. Via di Lago Maggiore cleaved to the lakeside so that we could see all of the lights across the water and down the water's edge to Intra. Our wedding guests escorted the carriage to our hotel in Pallanza. Over two hundred people walked beside and behind our carriage. The band members carried their instruments and played them as they walked. Those who could not hear the music sang drunken songs together. I looked for my sisters and father in the crowd to no avail. The parade ended with a final cheer when Luca helped me dismount from the carriage, and we entered the Victorian Lakeside Hotel di Pallanza.

    The concierge was poised at the entrance, expecting us, and led us straight to the Empress Suite while nervously sharing a memorized account of the room's history. It was named for Napoleon's wife, Joséphine de Beauharnais, who spent a few nights here waiting for Napoleon to arrive and take her to Isola Bella. The room was as large as my family's apartment and grander than the Marinova villa. There was a four-poster bed, expansive and lush, a French walnut dining table with two intricately carved chairs, and an ovoid balcony that gave the lake view in every direction visible from Pallanza. The cobalt carpet held faint yellow diamond lines. There were a dozen electric lamps, tall and proud. Our suitcases were already positioned on luggage racks against the wall. We were packed to leave for our train to Switzerland for our honeymoon in the morning.

Luca thanked the gentleman for welcoming us and led him to the door. He may have given him money. My focus narrowed to my heartbeat, thinking about what came next. After seven years of kissing in secret, years of speaking love, or seeing it with presence and smiles, it would now be made real.

The door closed, and he turned to me.

"I'm nervous," I confessed.

He shook his head and walked toward me.

"Can we turn off the lights?"

He shook his head and took his final steps to me.

When we kissed, it was all lips, gentle and slow. He turned me around and began the labor of unbuttoning my dress. He was slow. My breathing shortened as I tightened my stomach, starting to feel insecure. When the buttons were undone, he turned me back toward him and kissed me again. I wrapped my arms around his neck to prolong the familiar. He pushed us apart softly and then wrapped his thumbs under the sleeves of my dress held in place by my shoulders. I nodded, and he slid the dress down my arms, and the silk fell to the ground in a small pile.

"You are perfect," he said.

Then I set a held breath free.

My grandmothers, Arabella, Gia, Maria, Signora Esposito, and even Mary Marinova, had all warned me at some point in the planning that something would go wrong on my wedding day: people could fail me in their duties, the weather might surprise us, the night would be unpleasant. But they were all wrong. It was perfect.

November 1899

22
Luca

It was a beautiful day for an explosion. The air was weightless and cold. Mama cracked open the kitchen windows as dinner cooked. Wafts of garlic could be smelled from the yard. Pasquale and I sat on the enormous rocks at the lake's edge. The visibility of this evening was unmatched. I could make out the church spires of the Stresa skyline. The shadows behind Bella Isola and Isola di Pescatore grew over the water and exaggerated the size of the island houses.

"How's work?"

Pasquale shrugged.

Mama had been sending him money for months. I had been expecting him to ask me for money at some point during his visit. He had savings but could be cheap, and I wasn't under the pretense that he was working. I didn't press him on why.

"How's Paris?"

"It's Paris."

I nodded as if I knew what that meant.

"How's Franca?" He asked.

"She's good. Busy at the hospital most days. She's been at her sister's all day. Her sister, Ara, is in labor. I'm not sure Franca will make it in time for dinner."

He nodded.

"Mama was happy to hear you were coming to visit."

"And Pim?" It was rhetorical but not sarcastic. He knew his status in this house. Whatever happened between Pim and Pasq was still present here. Pim couldn't look at Pasq head-on. Pasq didn't expect me to respond, and I had nothing to say to comfort him.

Instead, I pretended to be engrossed in watching the lake mirror the changing clouds from white to pink to orange-red back to a final pink. Pasquale looked ten years older than he was. The lines in his forehead were so deep it looked like he etched them there himself with his dullest chisel. He had a trimmed beard, not because he tended to it but because a full beard had always been out of his grasp. His posture was that of a war veteran – a war that veteran lost. Sitting beside him in silence, I wonder if this is the closest he's been to another human in weeks.

"Pronto!" Mrs. Figlia called to us from the kitchen window when dinner was ready.

I followed him as he crossed the rocks. His balance was off, long out of practice, and I thought he would fall a couple of times, which reminded me of when Stasi slipped on the lopsided rock. What shook me most about losing her was that we also lost the spontaneity and the lightheartedness she brought out in Pasquale. They magnified each other. Their energy made you feel like you were seeing something so absorbing it must have been choreographed. It was unlike anything else. If the loss of that dynamism saddens me, only an observer, then I can't imagine how Pasq, a principal of it, can even carry himself into the villa now.

23
Pasquale

The table was set perfectly. Mother had selected red cyclamens from the garden as the modestly elegant centerpiece. The table runner, a handcrafted Italian crimson piece with silver brocade, was a gift from Pim on one of Mother's birthdays and was dotted with fresh pine cones and holly. When I sat down, I regretted agreeing to this one family meal together for the holidays. Mother's only request was a family dinner when she sent the money for my travel here. The sixth chair I last saw used by Stasi five years ago was removed from the dining room entirely. Franca generally used my chair. Perhaps Mother hoped our first family dinner since I moved would prove civility could pave the way for reconciliation. I didn't share her hope that Pim and I could rebuild that conditional bond, but I was here on a mission to evaluate whether I could, now or ever, return to Suna, The Eye, and life on the lake.

Despite the beauty of the table and the chandelier's shimmering light on the ceiling, here sat a bitter snake coiled to strike. In Pim's eyes, Stasi's death did not absolve me. The tension felt like a wire in the center of my chest screwed tautly into Pim's chest. There were other slackened lines of tension from me to Mother, from Mother to Pim, and then maybe between Enzo and Luca as they hypothesized that Stasi's death or the degradation of my profile and failure to produce new work was the core of Pim's blistering disdain for me.

Pim cut the lasagna into four large pieces and passed it to Enzo, sitting alone on the broad side of the table. The others took their walloping servings, skipping me, as Mrs. Figlia had made me vegetarian lasagna and had already served the steaming dish directly on my plate. The advance consideration was touching. Even so, looking at the heaping portion of focaccia bread, okra, and peas and speculating about dessert, I couldn't eat it all. I did a weak job of feeding myself regularly in Paris, and my stomach would suffer from the richness of tonight's meal.

"Luca," Mother began, "have you decided on a name for the new rowboat? Pasq, Luca finished making another row boat. I saw you move the white paint near the lakeside shed."

"I have ideas, but I'm not sure. I just moved the paint beside the shed because that's where it should be stored." Luca was twenty now, but he still ate hunched over his plate and spoke while chewing. The steam of the lasagna escaped from his half-open mouth.

"Creativity is more of Pasq's expertise," Enzo quipped. He was probably trying to be conversational, but his delivery was brusque as ever, though Luca wasn't the sensitive one. "Pasquale, do you have any suggestions for the dinghy's name?"

I shrugged. Of course, I didn't. I barely felt in communication with my motor skills; my creativity was long out of reach. "The Mary? Maggiore's Minore Boat? Charon of Lago Maggiore?"

"What's Charon?" Mother asked.

"He's the ferryman of the dead over the rivers Acheron and Styx to hell," Enzo said. He was helpless against his desire for his intelligence to be recognized.

"That's quite dark, Pasq," Mother forced her loud laugh, which I associated with cruelty toward Stasi. The heat of my body rushed into my face, and the muscles of my lips tensed tightly to keep from screaming: *You cackle like a bitch!*

"Life is dark," I muttered.

"That's enough," Pim said quietly but with command. I felt the tension click tighter between us. I couldn't let that go unacknowledged.

"Oh," I said mock-playfully, "are you talking to me?"

Pim simultaneously rolled his eyes and narrowed them in aggression.

"Enzo, what have you been working on? Another short story?" Mother asked.

"Yes, I am in a terrific mood each morning, working on it as the sun rises. I find that my mind is clearest then. Pasquale, you are most productive sculpting at night, indeed?"

As I was mid-nod to confirm that I have always found magic in working while others are asleep, Pim said bitterly without looking up from his plate, "He doesn't work at any time of the day."

I let it slide.

But I watched his controlled gaze on his food, his beard rippling with his jaw muscles clenching, making his chewing laborious and slow. He was livid. The hate oozing inside him was directed at me, and I felt a rising tide of reflected loathing. In his eyes, my "fall" nullified the hurt he caused others. His desire to have a son cost him his honor. And for what? He put me in the public eye, leveraging the influence his name had left, and held me up so high that everyone could see me break. That wasn't my fault.

"This is not my fault," I said. "I will not accept that this is my fault," I repeated.

"What are you talking about, Pasquale?" Mother said nervously.

"You were supposed to be great," Pim said without emotion. "Everyone who met you saw greatness. People would say: 'Pasquale's work will live in museums for the rest of time. As long as people appreciate art, there will be the name Pasquale Marinova.' And now you've allowed yourself to become this tainted disgrace. You can't even hold your fork right! How could someone from my flesh cause my skin to crawl?"

My eyes stung, searing with tears — a man in his late twenties on the brink of crying!

"I can't even sit in the same room as you!" He spat and whipped his monogrammed napkin on the table with such force it made a slapping sound that caused Mother to jolt. She lifted her hands slowly in each direction as if she could stop this.

"And this is my fault? You wear your guilt around your neck for all of us to see, day and night. It's like *we* should pity *you*. When you are the one who created all of this chaos, and we're the ones who have to live with it! You are exhausted from living with the decisions you've made? Well, so is everyone else! You ruin everyone around you. Stasi's death can be traced straight back to your fucking abandonment. You never even wrote her letters. It would have been better if you had died. You were not meant to be a father, you selfish piece of shit!"

"You take no responsibility for your actions? Because I'm *i tuoi* father, I played a part in *voi* deviance? You bend reason to live with yourself. I can't communicate with you."

"Yes, I take responsibility for my actions. I take responsibility for my unconsummated intentions, too. I live with the outcome of it every goddamn day."

"Good, I'm glad for your suffering. I'm pleased there is divine justice for your illicit relations. I can't begin to think how long it had been going on, but I'm glad it was ended for you."

Mother was crying, covering her eyes with both hands to shut us out and trying to cover her ears in defiance, but it was too late. "What... are you... saying?" she cried, but no one answered her.

"Do you think this is what I had planned for my life? Christ!" I yelled. "And it was only ever that one time!"

Then he looked me fully in the face. His brown eyes, lightening with age, were large with surprise and... pity. But then his mouth and beard lifted into a frozen, open smile – like there was a joke here.

"She asked me to meet her on the veranda that morning."

I shook my head. All I could say was, unconfidently, "That's not... that's not true."

"I feel truly sorry for you. You are a pawn in a dead girl's futile game."

"That's not true."

"It is. I have been thinking she had wanted to end it and couldn't quite ask for assistance and thus devised an intervening, but now–"

"IT'S NOT TRUE."

"She is a devil!" Mother sobbed with understanding. "I never should have let that demon in my home! She's destroyed my family. She's destroyed my family."

"BUT NOW–" Pim yelled over Mother. Enzo and Luca sat there, unsure whether they could even breathe this air. "I see that she has used you. You were a stepping stone to accelerate her ambitions. You're pathetic. You were not an equal partner in committing this wrong. You were only collateral damage. She set you up to be discovered, no matter the cost. You're a casualty, not a co-conspirator. How could someone remotely intelligent fall for this? How could someone of substance, beloved and supported, have allowed himself to be deceived from his path? You never had the strength of character I accredited to you. You're nothing but an allegory for children."

He stood up slowly and departed in the direction of his study. Luca stared at him. Enzo stared at his nearly full plate, head hanging. Even he didn't want to witness this. Mother sobbed unabashedly, her whole body rocking in her chair, repeating without end: "She destroyed my family."

May 1900
Paris, France

24
Pasquale

She lives in the moments between sleep and wakefulness. Pillows are soft and willing accomplices as I imagine she is next to me, stroking my arm, stretching beneath me, her mouth gaping like a fish when I enter her.

※

Her cherrywood hair is the last I see of her before she slips entirely under the covers. The sight is like glimpsing the perfect seashell before disappearing beneath a wave. Only then.

Only then to feel the force of that wave hit me as I was distracted.

Only then to feel it again.

※

Prostitutes have never interested me. The drinking companions I've made at my local Bar Enchantee, who are there for me in a revolving-door fashion, believe I should take up one or several prostitutes. My hesitation is that I'm not confident my imagination could transcend the transactional nature of it; it seemed squalid, not delicious. My companions' ultimate point, and one I can't disagree with, is that a man of my age requires someone to have sex with on a reliable basis within one's budgetary restrictions. Enter Simone.

I was short on my bill by a few francs at my regular café. Luckily, I was sitting outside, so I put all my money on the table and slithered away, conscious of being perceived as walking at an average pace, determined to return once I had time to go to the bank. But then it never felt quite right to return to pay my tab, so I tried somewhere new for my breakfast tartine.

Sitting outside despite the cold, overcast morning, Simone was my waitress. I barely looked at her when I ordered a cappuccino. Only when she turned and walked inside did I notice how shapely she was for a French girl. Her underfed waist and bony shoulders emphasized her generous backside. When she returned to the table, I studied her face. Her blonde hair was pulled into a low bun, though loose strands swung around her gray eyes, more unkempt than sexy. Her large arctic-sea eyes were a fortunate distraction from her overgrown eyebrows and thin lips. Maybe because she was unused to someone looking at her, she gave me an uncomfortable smile that, sadly, revealed a slanted jumble of teeth. She was no trophy to parade.

We spoke in French about how the café was unusually empty. I said that I was lucky to have her all to myself. She nearly swooned. I shamelessly told her about the Tolstoy bust. After a while, when she needed to attend to other customers, I stood up, left a moderate tip on the small table, and bowed to her from a distance.

The next time I saw her, we walked east from Café Liberte. We walked far and talked about me. My work and travels sounded grand with minimal romantic spin. Though I had omitted any details about Stasi, I realized my feet had subconsciously led us to Père Lachaise Cemetery. I must have had a visceral reaction because Simone took my arm.

"Are you feeling alright?"

My oily words faltered. I said yes, though my head reflexively shook no.

She didn't understand and suggested I return home to lie down. That would be needed, but I couldn't be this close without paying homage. The thought of bypassing Stasi's resting place arm-in-arm with another woman, even one like Simone, made my stomach flip. The tsarevna would loathe the disrespect—it was wholly inexcusable and unforgivable. She would absolutely hate it. I had to touch her unfit headstone.

"I know someone buried here."

"That is terrible. How very sad." I may have underestimated Simone's intuition because she hesitantly asked: "Was the person your wife?"

"My sister."

Simone sighed.

I requested she stand outside the gate as I said a few quick words. I stood hunched beside the patch of green grass at her plot – how could it be so green! – and began crying, servile to my grief. Simone came up behind me and placed her hand on my shoulder. Seeing me suffer and believing that she understood it seduced her into a deep illusion of intimacy. An illusion that could rationalize my indifference toward her as merely a strong exterior of someone who has experienced tragedy. From that moment, my future cruel behavior came with the caveat of irreparable foundational damage.

Six weeks later, I married her. It was small. I invited none of the guests. It was a lengthy procedure followed by a dragging reception at her brother's home. She was not better than nothing, only a change of pace. *Truly, my dear Stasi,* she was the opposite of what I wanted: simple, ignoble, transparent, but within reach.

May 1901

25
Pasquale

    Simone wanted a child; she wanted many, but she only pressed me for one. She fantasized about the perfect family with her invented magnanimous image of me at the head of our family dinner table – a long table this studio could never accommodate. Her smoking desperation leaked into every verbal exchange we had. Every single fucking thing we talked about was really about a baby.
    Simone didn't work at the café anymore, which had put me in the straining position to either insist she stay for the menial wages and thus reveal our true financial stature or work myself to preserve her illusion. She became interested in analyzing her dreams and discussing them ad nauseam. The recurring dream of hers that I could never escape hearing about was of her with her daughter, a four-year-old blonde with ringlet curls and cherub lips. The girl liked wearing navy exclusively with pink or red ribbons. I heard about how sweet this girl "is" and the bright red birthmark under her neck. Her name was Therese, and she adored me like no one ever had. When Simone said that, I just nodded from behind the newspaper, unsure why any daughter of mine would love me: every day, I was becoming more and more of a nobody. While my savings, supplemented by amounts sent from Mother and Luca, kept us above the waterline, I used a loan from Mother to prepay this year's rent to thwart the temptation to spend it. Adding a child to the equation would exacerbate our finances. Unless my hands could stop shaking, I wouldn't be able to move us from this studio. To sculpt again, I needed rest and to afford my small comforts like having a daily coffee, newspapers to read, and interval luxuries, like days to the countryside and a trip to the theater. Thus, no baby.
    Unfortunately for Simone, I know some games women play to get what they want. Without an older brother, I was forced to gather information independently and have never been shy about asking older men about their experiences. I've never uncovered a refusal to answer or a response of "I don't know." Every man claims to be the expert. Once these veins of conversation are opened, these pioneers boil to tell you more. It was during one of these bar conversations that I was explicitly warned that if a woman

wants a child and you're fucking her, she's going to win. This drunken companion, whose name I did not know, said that if I was serious about not having a baby, I had two options. Either I could abstain from my wife – to which I responded, "Then why have a wife at all?" – or I had to be diligent to never finish inside her. His weathered, hollow eyes were slow with drink and grave when he repeated that my body would resist this, but I had to be committed to my mission.

Several hours after that insightful conversation, I came home after losing the week's budget in a card game. I drank until the tide of my anger ebbed. Simone was making us dinner. I had no clue what she did all day while I was out. I could imagine her thin and increasingly anxious form standing at the window, plotting her conception, waiting to see me turn the corner so she could get up and pretend to have been occupied.

She greeted me with a dry peck on the cheek. I brushed her hips with my hands. When she turned away to stir the sauce, a tired sauce that she constantly added ingredients to stretch further, I kept my hands on her hips and let her guide me to the stovetop. I kissed her neck and tightened my grip to hold her body against mine.

"Choose a bottle for us," I whispered in her ear.

"I think you've already had enough wine." She veiled the refusal with a teasing tone.

"I've had enough liquor," I corrected her and nuzzled my face in her faintly geranium-scented hair.

"My husband and his indulgences."

I sashayed to the small, café-sized table and took my worn seat. The surface had not been cleaned off: it still had two plates with the crumbs and residue of dried jam sitting out all day from Simone's breakfast, which was perhaps the only thing she had eaten until now. She brought over the Chablis I had been saving, and I knew she knew I had been saving. I had the instinct to command her to bring me another bottle, but I figured, why not allow myself one luxury today? I removed the cork messily, chipping it with the corkscrew; my left hand slipped and hit the table hard. Finally, I managed to pour myself a high glass. Simone brought dinner to the table: roasted potatoes and vegetables in that *velouté* sauce we had five times a week.

"You didn't pour me a glass," she said.

"I haven't decided if you can have any yet."

"How unkind of you," she laughed one hollow 'huh' sound. This is precisely what was wrong with her. Simone took every comment I made with humor. She lived insulated within her naivete, blinded by her love for who she thought I was.

I poured another glass, and more than a few drops splashed onto the table. Now, her second-rate doll face soured.

"You're having a second glass before even trying the food?"

I nodded. The first glass had set in, and I couldn't taste this one.

"I'd rather eat later."

"It will be cold then. You won't like it."

"I'd rather do something else."

We had been married for months, and she remained modest in the bedroom. I wanted to rip that reserve from her. I got up from the table and pulled her from her chair. Her fork clanged weakly as it hit the floor. She moved to turn the light switch off, but I clasped her by the shoulders to stop her. The dark would impair my poor coordination.

I had to do all the work, undressing each of us just enough. She didn't push me away, but her body seemed to contract inward in an attempt to fold in on itself. She kept her eyes closed, which was fine by me. Until it wasn't. Then I turned her onto her stomach and knees and entered her from behind. I pulled out of her and finished myself with my hands beside the listless slump that stayed face down into the pillow.

When I woke up, before I even opened my eyes, there was a gruesome headache prowling behind my eyes. I felt trapped inside my stale mouth. As the ungentlemanly events of last night came to me, my stomach moved. I slowly lifted myself to a sitting position and opened my eyes. Simone was sitting at the table, in my seat, facing me and the bed as she read a book.

"I don't think I've ever seen you read." My French came out croaky. My mouth was odorless and unmercifully dry. The bright window illuminated her.

"You see my books on the shelf and around the studio," she responded without looking up from the page.

"You collect plenty of books. I don't think I've ever seen you sitting and reading one."

"My mother used to say, 'Never let your husband see you at leisure.'"

I stood, paused, and felt my head grow heavier. My stomach was empty and roaring. Suddenly, my mouth drained of what little moisture it had. I vomited yellow chunks and thick bile. My body dry heaved in pursuit of yesterday's lunch. I washed my face. There is always an overwhelming sense of self-pity that comes with throwing up that makes me shed tears. I trekked to our kitchenette for water. I drank the glass in four gulps.

"Concealing your leisure time from me forever would have been challenging."

Then my stomach turned over, and I returned to my privy worship. Simone did not help me or ask if I was all right. Though I didn't expect her to.

When I exited the bathroom, after rewashing my face, I said plainly, "I think I'm going to live." A verbal lob to see if she would play.

"Ever since I was a child, whenever anyone speaks to me while I am reading, I feel a surge of frustration," Simone said, letting her open book lean against the table. "I'm not sure if reading appears to be an interruptible activity, but it is not."

"Well, now I know. I'm going to sleep a little more."

"No. I don't think you do know. You've disrupted my concentration because you are selfish and unkind. Silence distresses you because you are disappointed in yourself. You are sick by your own doing, Pasquale Marinova. I hope you vomit ten more times today."

My head was pounding, and my body was sweating and shaky. I knew it had been all wrong last night. She didn't enjoy herself, and neither did I.

"I'm sorry I was rough with you, Simone. I had been drinking all day and was riled up." I sat on our bed, staring at her even though it hurt to keep my gaze on the light blaring behind her from the open windows. All of the curtains were open.

"Do you promise it will never happen again?" Her eyes glossed over, but her voice was flat.

"I promise. It was a mistake. I will not do that again." I looked at the pronounced veins in my hands.

She turned down the corner of her page, closed her book, and closed all four curtains. The apartment instantly felt forgiving of my broken state. She came to the bed and hugged me. Her right arm stretched across my torso as she held my head to her bony clavicle. She felt more warm than soft. There was a faint thumbprint bruise on her arm. All at once, I was overcome with loathing for myself. How have I become this? I used to have my choice of women, and now I have to fuck my wife against her will?

I sobbed like a child. And it hurt. My eyes relinquished the little hydration my body had. My headache did not subside for crying. The pain in my chest became sharp, as if it were trying to puncture me. All of this was overshadowed by my sloshing stomach, debating whether it had finished purging. I was defenseless in my physical vulnerability and seized by a heavy mourning for who I was, who I am, and who I would never become. Simone kissed my head and held me the whole time.

September 1901

26
Pasquale

Varvara Marinova died six months ago.
 Luca was the only one who thought about telling me. One of Pim's cousins, not Tatiana, wrote to him, breaking decades of silence between them. A brood of cold bitches, that first family. Luca's letter was not even so much about Varvara's death as it was about how Pim has become highly irritable and depressed. At the moment when his current marriage of nearly thirty years is legitimized, and he should be free, he clings to his guilt more.

At the moment this apparition has dissolved, and the threat of meeting her by accident, the fear of her declaring that I defiled her daughter, the possibility of Pim returning to her, or any number of overly-thought, spun-out scenarios that have played through in my mind ever since I found out about her existence, her death is somehow empty of finality. While inevitable and anticipated, it does not feel real.

Luca wrote that Pim shuts himself away in his study for days, and Mrs. Figlia delivers his meals directly there. Mother, now the only Mrs. Petyr Marinova, is silently horrified at this grieving and unsure how to handle his reaction, which she talks about with Franca. Mother threatens to visit me here, but Simone serves as my shield.

I have been hurting Simone regularly. I try not to, but her mouse-sized presence derails my sanity. She knows this. While she formerly spent her dull days in the apartment, she is now out the whole day and typically still gone when I return home. Apparently, shopping for dinner's seven ingredients can take nine hours. Only this week has the air begun to turn cold, and I have seen her choose to return with purplish lips rather than come home before the sun dips below the skyline.

Some of my friends will still meet me, though I mostly only hear from acquaintances visiting Paris who haven't seen me in years. The friends and acquaintances of my life, even my Parisian life, were established when I was Pasquale Marinova, the conversationalist, sculptor, and first son in a long line of Russian-Lithuanian princes. That Pasquale Marinova had money. These people like to pair three wines with seven courses for dinner. Conversation circles around the last time each person spent too much money. Each day, my relevance or interesting factoids drift further into the past; I draw from a diminishing well. This Pasquale Marinova sits in cafés too long trying to estimate when his wife will return home so he can arrive after her to prevent himself from sitting in the studio alone staring at the box of Varvara's jewelry and Stasi's other personal items gathering dust on the bottom shelf of the bookshelf and thinking about people who he is, at best, estranged from and who are, at worst, dead.

December 1901

27
Pasquale

In the morning, Simone was gone. It doesn't take a genius to surmise where she went. Sad Simone only had one place to go. After I passed through the morning symptoms of last night's drink, I prepared myself to bring back what was mine.

When I arrived at her brother's rowhouse, I marched right up to the front door, propped open by another neighbor, climbed the short flight to the second floor, and knocked on his door.

Silence.

Would they pretend no one was home? Cowards, beware – I won't shy from a scene. As I started considering how much force I would have to use to kick in the door and whether I would be more likely to succeed on a full stomach later, footsteps approached, and the heavy latch pulled back. The door opened and closed faster than my reflexes could register as Clément, my brother-in-law, pulled me down the half flight of stairs by my arm to the small landing at the entrance.

"Don't ever come here again," he said quickly. I took a step back.

"What do you mean, brother?"

"I saw the bruises. She needed four stitches along her jawline, you poisoned fuck. It's unsightly. She won't be able to leave the house for weeks. If my father were still alive…." He shook his head, jaw buckled, and wrung his hands.

"Listen, listen," I croaked. "Let me tell her I'm sorry. It was an unforgivable mistake–"

"It was many mistakes, over and over–"

"It was the alcohol. I'm sick. I'm very sick. She has to come back. I… I don't know how to be…" *without her* wasn't the correct conclusion, but something along those lines, "…alone."

The corners of his eyes sloped downwards. For a moment, I believed he had been persuaded. But then his skin tightened around his mouth, and after a long sigh, he chose to act primally.

"Being alone is what you deserve. You have earned a lonely life. Listen, Pasquale. I may not have my prince-daddy's money to care for Simone, but I don't have the self-restraint to send her back with you. I'm not afraid of the jailhouse. If you ever come back here again—"

"Clément, —"

He pushed me out of the building, quickly tossing my withering figure, standing at disequilibrium. I fell back and fumbled a few steps until I barely caught myself with both sliding hands on the stoop's foot-wide cement railing.

"You don't fool me anymore. You and Simone are getting divorced. She's left you. Do not come back here, you bastard's bastard."

He slammed the building door shut.

The colors of the world drained for fury. Simone told him about my mother's birth? I careen into a bar somewhere between Clément's home and the Seine, I think. Actually, I don't know where I am. I can't see or hear outside my blaring rage.

I have four drinks. I try to tell a pair of old men about my predicament, but they say they can't understand me, and I realize I'm speaking in Italian, possibly thinking in Italian, too. My attempt to switch to French is bleak; my pronunciation is pathetic, always has been, and they won't hear past my slurring. They aren't even trying to understand me. I have another drink. I start to tell a boy younger than me, or possibly he is my age, but I look fifteen years older than I am, — "How old are you?" — but he doesn't have a wife to hit accidentally and can't empathize with me.

No one is listening to me. No one wants to look at me. I realize I haven't eaten today, and it's getting dark outside. I order dinner from the bartender, but he says he must be paid for the seven drinks I've had first. The pockets in this coat only have about a quarter of the money I owe him, and he demands I leave. He is suddenly at my side and furious. I am thrown from a door for the second time today, but this time, I hit the pavement. Hard. The right side of my head lies on the ground. *Am I still alive?* There is an instant pain enveloping my left eye. The bartender's shadow pauses over me, perhaps regretful for the level of strength used. When I decide I can lift my head, there is no blood on the sidewalk. I unleash profanities upon him, though I can't confidently determine my volume and the door shuts. Even without his shadow, I curse him.

People are staring at me as they walk around my slouching body. I cradle my head intermittently; the entirety is heavy, and the right side is pounding. Passersby are careful not to come too close, like I am vermin.

"I have… conquered… obscurity!" I scream at all of these people who live boring, insignificant lives.

I decide I can stand. Men pull their women away from me with their gloved hands—mothers mutter warnings to their bundled children. I can't be on this side of the street any longer.

I step off the curb into the stone street and instantly feel the impact of an automobile hitting the length of my left side body. I am thrown a few yards, where I land on my back and am seized, body and spirit, by a powerful, illuminating sobriety.

The sharp, cold air coils around every centimeter of exposed skin at my ankles, my slack hands, my weakly bearded neck, and my scraped face. The air hadn't felt as frigid before. Without being able to move my neck to see, I feel the cold air frame my warm blood as it emerges on my hands and how it mists from my open mouth onto my cheeks. When I take a breath, it feels as if there are a million tiny, fractured, jagged crystals in my chest, and the microcrystals rip me apart at each cubic millimeter. Every second holds a million acute pricks of agony.

Part 3

The Life of Luca Marinova
Franca Rossi Marinova

1

Luca is with a prospective customer in the boathouse when I return from spending the night at Gia's house, located on the northernmost hill of Intra. From where her house is perched, she can see our villa in Suna jut out onto the lake when there is no fog. It is a large house for a police officer's family, but its position high on the mountain and far from the center of Intra made it affordable for them. Gia had her second daughter two weeks ago, and I decided to spend a couple of nights on and off at her place helping with her older daughter, Lucia. Lucia did not sleep through the night for her mother, and she did not for me either. She was a tyrant and undoubtedly Gia's child at nearly one-year-old.

It is challenging to leave Gia's whirling home for my silent one. Though our homes were relatively equal distances to our father's building and the journey to Gia's included a steep incline, Papa still chose to visit Gia more than me. It wasn't the distance. It's because he saw his granddaughters at her house and his three grandsons at Arabella's, and he could only see glimpses of Marinova melodrama at mine. Gia's home was a place of love and belonging, and my home was a cold, albeit gorgeous, museum collection of foreign objects. If I had a child, he would make the trip to see me without me begging him and offering to arrange a carriage for his return. After my wedding, I became attached to the private thought that Papa would come live with me eventually. I was his namesake child. There was plenty of space here. But he was becoming closer to Gia and particularly enjoyed her in-laws, who were proud Italians like himself but more of the working class, unlike the Terraccis.

I would say "Good morning" in English to Mary at the breakfast table every morning. I was nervous about disrupting her contemplations and being snapped at. On the other hand, some days, she required a confidante to listen to every thought she had as a pure listener unobstructed by obligations or time. As Mary told me how she would have liked Luca to have been born a girl, I thought about how she had failed to see an opportunity to have a mother-daughter relationship with me. She had known me since childhood, and I could have used motherly encouragement. I always visited Signora Esposito when I visited Papa, but she had eight grown children. It would have been nice to speak about my presumed infertility or essential cooking tips for the nights when I cooked for us in the absence of Signora Figlia, whose ill health was slowly eroding her work schedule. I thanked God daily for my sisters, but they were experiencing much of life alongside me, or, at times, it felt beyond me.

When Pasquale visited for a short time from Paris three years ago, I barely interacted with him. He was not the handsome icon I remembered, but someone who looked like he went out of his way to be filthy. I assumed that was for the benefit of the prince, but the only time they were together was when I was with Gia. Luca told me that the source of the chasm between Pasquale and the prince was something unsanctified that had happened between Pasquale and Anastasia. Luca shared many things but did not tell me he was sending Pasquale our money. I discovered that in a letter while tidying our room.

For a couple of days, I was furious. It smelled like a betrayal to my hard work and hours spent walking to and from the hospital and my old neighborhood for nursing visits that they served to fund the Marinova heir's Parisian hedonism. I was unsure how to confront Luca, and after speaking with Maria, I decided not to. I chose to allow Luca his secret generosity. After all, I was not contributing to the lifestyle the prince was providing us. This was once Pasquale's home, but it would forever be mine. Would I not give my last *lire* to any of my sisters? Pasquale and Enzo were my brothers, too, and I could find it in my heart to help them even if I disagreed with their choices.

※

"You refer to Pim as the prince and call Mama Mary," Luca whispered. I was facing the ceiling, trained by my mother to sleep on my back to avoid creasing my face. He was on his side facing me, level with my bare shoulder. I could feel the heat of his breath on my skin.

"I hadn't noticed."

"It's like you have more respect for him than her."

"I think I do respect him more."

He stayed quiet and still.

"I'm sorry," I said, nervous that his concern could have been prompted by a conversation between him and his mother. "What would you like me to call her?"

"I'm not sure. Maybe you could call him Pim?"

"I can do that."

He kissed my shoulder and then fell asleep with his lips pressed there.

2

When Pasquale died, Luca's family fell apart. Not immediately, but piece by piece.

It began with Enzo, who surprised us all at dinner one night with the announcement that he would be moving to London to write poetry collections and work in publishing. I had expected he would be a permanent intellectual fixture of the villa; he would be our children's brilliant but disconnected live-in uncle. He was kind to me and unknowingly interrupted the tension between Mary and me. The prince and Mary were shocked at Enzo's announcement. It stunned Luca, whose mind now associated Pasquale's quick decision to move to Paris with his self-demise. But Enzo was not Pasquale. He would not have decided from emotion alone. If anything, grief catalyzed a dream he had held for a long time.

The morning Enzo left, we had a short conversation. He looked much older than Luca.

"Will you come back?" I asked him, craning my neck to look him in the face. Even when Mary was around, he spoke in Italian to me.

"I don't expect so," he said bluntly, his voice having only one volume.

"So this is goodbye?"

"I expect it is."

"And your family?" My eyes began to stream. This singular individual had been in the periphery of my entire life. I'm not sure I ever truly understood him or what aspirations he had beyond the page he was reading or writing in.

"I can't protect them from themselves."

"Will you come back if I have a baby? To meet your niece or nephew?"

"The answer is the same. I have lived here for nearly thirty years and am finished."

I started crying. Enzo put his bags down and hugged me. He held me tightly, and I wept on his immaculate wool traveling coat.

"A child is not the solution to everything. Nothing is missing from your life."

"My mother is missing. And you're leaving forever."

"And yet you are whole."

Luca opened the front door and saw me, whole and weeping, in his brother's arms.

"Good luck. I hope to see you soon."

"Goodbye, Franca." Enzo released me.

The prince, who had to be fetched from his study, and Mary, who had to be pried from her bed, went with Luca and Enzo to the train station. I requested to stay.

I was young, and yet it felt like I was becoming more and more alone. I was powerless to grow my family. I yearned for my body to let me fill the villa with children and infuse these rooms with love. Married for six years, but no child. In the beginning, I expected to be heavy with the child within months. I even dreaded it. I attributed all sounds, pains, and movements of my body to pregnancy. When I would roll over in my sleep, I'd wake myself up thinking that I couldn't lie on my stomach because it would be bad for the baby. I promised God that I would be happy with just one. I don't care whether it is a boy or a girl. It felt unfathomable that a love like Luca's and mine could not bring a child into the world. Children are born from loveless unions all the time, and yet we can't have one? Arabella can only bear a polite respect for Paolo, and they have three boys. Luca and I have love. We have plenty of money and space. And we only have his parents to care for.

3

Once it happened, the shock was momentary; weeks after, no one could say they were shocked.

Sitting at the table while Mary and the prince were late to dinner, Luca and I held hands over the table as I told him about the hospital that day. We would not dare begin eating without them, and tardiness happened from time to time. We overheard their raised voices from upstairs. Fighting occurred from time to time, too. Then the prince swept into the dining room alone, breathing heavily, and took his seat. He served himself first and then passed the dishes to Luca, who served me and then himself. The prince ate quickly. We could hear Mary screaming from her room. It was terrible to carry on as if we couldn't hear her. The prince dabbed at his mouth and beard with his monogrammed napkin. I put my fork down, sensing he wanted our attention. Luca kept eating.

"Son."

Luca looked up. Commanded into the moment, his brow took on the weight. He wiped his mouth and motioned with the fork in his right hand, *go on then*.

"I am leaving Suna. Tomorrow morning, I will check myself into Hotel di Pallanza. I will stay there until my finances are in order. Then I intend to move to France."

Luca was dumbfounded. His mouth moved, but there were no words. His eyes searched the room.

"You and Mama are going to France?"

"No. Your mother will stay here."

"You are moving to France alone?" Luca asked, confused.

"No," the prince exhaled, annoyed as Luca was about to ask another question. "I will be taking Claudia and making her my wife."

"Who is Claudia?"

"Claudia Bruno."

"Claudia Bruno? What are you talking about?" Luca gaped.

"Your mother will stay here and keep the house. You and Enzo will inherit it when she dies. Though you will share the inheritance with any more children I may have."

"What about your gardens, Pim?" I blurted out, not knowing what to say.

"I have spent my best years in those gardens. But I can not take them with me. I must cultivate a new life. It would be dishonorable to deprive you and Mary of this home, so I must leave."

"Dishonorable... are you leaving us an endowment to take care of the property?" Luca said, dazed and unarmed, still searching the table and the room.

"Well, no. Given my age—"

"Sixty-eight. You are sixty-eight!"

"—I would impoverish myself if I left funds to operate—"

"So, instead, you'll impoverish us?"

"If the gardens were opened for admission, the incomes could fund the maintenance and upkeep required."

"You figured out that you can no longer afford your lifestyle and are abandoning us to liquidate your possessions? You'll leave all your books? All of Pasquale's remaining sculptures? What are you talking about? That girl will bleed you of your remaining money. She doesn't love you. You can't be in love! Claudia Bruno? She—"

"Luca! That's enough." The prince pounded his fists on the table. "You are a child. You and Franca will figure it out. I will leave you no money, but I will not leave you with any debts and am generously bestowing you my furnishings and assets – that I could choose to take. My choices are not for you to question. I don't regard the judgments of the dimwit Marinova."

Luca scoffed but could not hide his hurt.

"Luca is not a dimwit," was all I could manage to say, looking at my husband.

"Fine," Luca finally said with a bitter shrug. His hands clasping each other to grip his fury. "Go then. Mama doesn't deserve this, yet she should have known this would happen. Maybe you are right. I must be the dumbest person in the world not to have seen this coming. I should have known that you will always obey what is destructive inside you. You passed that to Pasquale, too. Leave. Take your sickness with you. Franca and I will finish our dinner."

"You are ungrateful." The prince threw his napkin on the table. "You have allowed your life to amount to nothing."

Luca leaned forward to look the prince in the eye. Their expressions of hate mirrored each other, and loathing twisted their faces similarly.

"*You* have allowed your life to amount to nothing," Luca repeated.

The prince ripped himself from their locked gaze to grab his empty porcelain plate and smashed it against the table. I covered my face but felt the jagged shards hit my hands and arms. Then Luca began yelling, and the prince was screaming back, They were like uncaged beasts. When the prince reached for his wine glass, I slid to the floor and curled into a seated ball under the table. The backs of my hands were bleeding from the lacerations made by the plate, but I held my hands over my face all the same. They raged above me, yelling and breaking. I could hear Luca reach for the prince, and the prince pushed him back into the cabinet on the wall, shaking the dinner china. Luca started throwing the dinnerware stored there at his father, who grunted at the landings but kept struggling to grab Luca.

I was terrified of what this would escalate to once everything that could be broken was. Luca threw himself at his father, and both of their husky bodies hit the table above me, at which moment I finally screamed. Debris flew off the table's surface all around me. I dared not look up. I could feel which body was Luca's. Both men panted hard until Luca pinned the prince on his back, and the prince finally growled: "That's enough."

He had not struck him, but that was no longer an impossibility. Father and son heaved apart at the end of the table, and each stood there for a moment, wrestling his breath. Then, the prince stumbled out of the dining room toward his office. Fragments of glassware fell from his housecoat and sang as they met the marble floor.

Luca reached for my hand and pulled me out from under the table. My husband tried to hug me, though I leaned away from his broad chest, where there were still jagged pieces. We were both shaking.

"I'll clean this up," I mumbled.

"Mrs. Figlia can clean it in the morning." He sighed, still reaching for me.

"I'd prefer we not leave this scene for her. There will be enough rumors already."

4

"Do you think the prince met Claudia at your wedding?" Gia asked me in her kitchen.

"I do not know. He never said. He sulked the whole wedding day; I didn't see him talking to people."

"He was looking around. And Claudia Bruno is beautiful, no matter how mean she is. Do you remember how she used to make fun of Imma for how she dressed? She used to say the Rossi girls thought that they were too good for the neighborhood."

"Do you keep a list of the people who have wronged you and your family somewhere?" I laughed because I had not remembered. "I only remember Nonno Illari talking about how the four Bruno brothers he grew up with were always rotating in and out of jail. I don't know if they met at the wedding, but the prince has been going to Luigi's for dinner over the past few months."

"And Claudia is a waitress there? It's so far, she must boat to Arona?"

"Yes, and so was he for a while. I should have known."

"You should have known. Signor Esposito is the only husband I know who does not bring his wife to dinner outings."

✻

It took about three weeks for the prince to close his affairs in Pallanza. Despite what he told us at dinner, he did arrange two accounts, one for Mary and the other for Luca and me, that were "entrusted to uphold the splendor of the Marinova villa and gardens." However, there would be no trustee, and we would be free to determine how the funds were used. The accounts cooled Luca's rage into silent resentment. By how he spoke, the accounts were the fair price for abandonment, and we had no further quarrel with Pim. It was better that he felt that way. Mary and I knew that the accounts were the leverage to obtain Mary's agreement to a divorce.

My mind became flooded with instructions in my mother's voice, louder and louder. From her years of bookkeeping for the grocer, I picked up a basic financial understanding that one needed more money coming in than leaving. I tried to broach a conversation around money over dinner several times, but my questions fell on carefree ears. Luca seemed to count the combined value of the accounts rather than only what was in our name. While the combined value was enough to maintain our current comforts without selling a part of the estate, it made us dependent on Mary remaining here. Mary acted as if she was above speaking about money to hide that she had no idea whether her settlement was generous, enough, or limiting. And yet, she would not even receive her portion until the divorce was official, which would be months from now. I said we needed to ask the prince about the wages of Signora Figlia and the gardeners, but Luca and Mary refused to speak with him, and they both refused to ask the workers directly to avoid awkwardness. They said I worried too much. The mother and son could not fathom insolvency. The two were in denial of the reality of their financial situation.

When the prince lived here, I mostly only encountered him at dinner. The man was never a source of solace or discomfort for me. Yet now that he was gone, I heard phantom sounds of a book closing or a tired sigh come from his office, which no one entered now. His departure was present on Mary's face. She aged in weeks, reminding me how my mother's worry for Arabella took her beauty. I became tender toward her. I found myself lingering around in case she needed someone to speak to or a chore done. Not even Signora Figlia, Mary's decades-long ally, knew how to talk to Mary anymore. Signora Figlia's Catholic repudiation of divorce made Mary no longer relatable. She implored Mary to seek an annulment, and the moral intrusion tore their bond. Mary's meal directions became more curt and formal.

I invited Papa, Gia, and her family over for lunch to try filling the house with love, but Mary didn't budge from her chair and gave clipped responses when they spoke to her. She was disinterested in Gia's daughters. She didn't enjoy them or see them as relatives.

Luca asked me one night why I was waiting on her.
"Because she's shattered."
"And you think you can fix her?" He asked genuinely.
"I don't think anyone can fix another person."
"Said by a nurse."
"If there's one thing I learned from Doctore Uliassi, it's that a person needs to want to get better. The will and the body are all connected. The spirit takes more time to heal than the body."
"I don't think she sees herself as ill."

"That's what scares me. It's why she needs me to help her."

He kissed my left temple, rolled over, and whispered, "Thank you for caring about her."

5

The villa and land were too much for one family: the heavily wooded land up the east hill with the artist's studio, the slight stretch of grass and rocks to the lake with Luca's protruding boathouse, the far-reaching gardens to the north. I could stare at the swirling patterns of soft gray and white streaks on the marble floors for hours, but it was cold under my feet, even in the summer. The rooms were covered in twenty-by-thirty-foot handcrafted cotton and silk blended Persian rugs. Mary and Luca were comforted by the elegance, but I could only see that selling small boats and being a hospital nurse could not sustain this luxury.

My life changed when we had to cease the services of the maid who visited three days a week, and the cleaning fell on me. Luca's day changed when we discontinued the services of the second gardener and reduced the first gardener's schedule to one visit a week – to which he, Signor Garibaldi, protested and, with tears in his eyes, declared that the garden he had worked on for decades would fall into immediate and unsalvageable disorder. He demanded that he volunteer his time two more days a week. We accepted but decided to provide him breakfast and lunch on those three days, which was the least we could do. But Mary declared that she would not eat with Signor Garibaldi and insisted that she eat in her bedroom on those days. Signora Figlia, whose cousin was married to Signor Garibaldi's sister, did not take this well, and her coldness toward Mary multiplied. Despite her attitude toward Mary, Signora Figlia became extra helpful to Luca and me; our meals became more complex as she suspected we might intend to dismiss her next.

I worked to give Mary and the house my attention while keeping my nursing schedule to four days a week, split between home visits and the hospital. The hospital became a place where I came to feel that I was building something. I could see Maria, who was newly married to Professoressa Mila's great-nephew Lorenzo Mila, and my fellow nurse friends. It was a relief to be at work.

While I poured my attention into the Marinova estate and its orbiters, I had a crueler inner eye turned on myself. It had been seven years since Luca and I were married. I was now twenty-six and had not conceived a child. My former neighbors gave me looks mixed with kindness and remorse. Children always asked me why I didn't have a baby. The mounting fear over the years that I couldn't have children was now molting into a fact. I felt strangled by it. I didn't know how to discuss it with Luca. How could I tell a man who had lost so much that the most important people in his life were already present?

    I entered a time of constantly inviting my family, friends, and acquaintances to the villa. I wanted to flood this gorgeous but cavernous home with life. I tried to invite ease back into my life. I wanted to fill the time I wasn't working with laughter, storytelling, good food, and sunshine. I figured I could make an event of Signor Garibaldi eating lunch with us three times a week. As the weather improved, my loved ones seemed more willing to walk the distance from Pallanza or Intra.

    When Signora Figlia complained about the labor required for a meal of more than six people, I invited her family to join us for the night. The fragile old woman started crying. She was usually stern with me, generally seeing me as her Pallanza-originated equal.

    "In my thirty-two years of working here, I have never been invited to dine with the Marinovas."

    "You are always welcome to join us for dinner," I told her. "If the weather is ever awful, you can spend the night in one of the guest rooms, too."

    "Thank you, Signora Marinova," she sniffled. I hugged her; that was the first time she called me by my married name. "Go. Go now. I have work to do."

    Professoressa Mila came for dinner about once every three weeks. It was a long walk for her from Intra. I always sat her next to me. Maria and her husband Lorenzo would visit on the weekends and bring groceries. Signora Esposito and her unmarried teenagers, still living at home, brought Papa over every week. He had been living alone since Imma married Enzo Fanelli, a first cousin of Claudia Bruno. We didn't tell Mary that. Imma and Enzo lived in Pallanza near Papa. My sisters, their husbands, and my five nieces and nephews called the villa, which I finally claimed as my home, their happiest place. They came as often as they could and invited their friends and neighbors. They could swim and sun on the rocks, take one of Luca's boats out on the lake or eat and play games on the terrace. Little Paolo was nine years old and planted himself as the authority over his brothers. Gia's oldest, Lucia, was very special to me. Gia let me keep her for nights at a time, and I enjoyed having her company on my errands. For the first time, Papa spent a night at the villa. He boasted about it in the neighborhood for months as better than any hotel, though he had never stayed in one. I sometimes felt exhausted by the amount of engagements we had on top of my nursing schedule or the extra hours of cleaning it all required, but it helped fill the cracks in time with joy.

But the barrier of distraction I insulated myself with crumbled. On a September night at my dining room table over a beautiful *caponata,* pumpkin ravioli, and chicken stew dinner, Arabella announced to the entire Rossi family that she was pregnant with her fourth child. I froze, fully and wholly seized in every part of my body. My wine glass remained inches from my lips. My face must have fallen because Gia, holding toddler Ginevra, nudged me gently under the table. I smiled and said congratulations. It took all of the strength I had.

I sent Signora Figlia home early so I could clean the table and kitchen to avoid hearing Paolo Terracci, the increasingly heavyset dud of a man, husband, and father, tell my family how much he hoped for a fourth son. It made me sick that Luca was in there with them. I wanted to scream at all of them to leave.

While Ara's boys and Lucia played in the prince's old office, Gia found me at the small two-seat kitchen table. I couldn't look at her without burning tears in my eyes. She was airing out her sweater, which had been spilled on. I tried to speak, and my lips trembled. She motioned not to say anything for the echoes. I put one hand on my stomach and gestured with the other answerless palm up to God before both hands flew over my mouth to stifle a sob. One word was repeating in all forms in my head: *broken. Something inside me is broken. Luca married a broken woman.* Gia hugged me, even though her shirt leaked onto my blouse.

6

A month later, I dragged myself to dinner at Arabella's house. A sorrow had knit itself across the tops of my lungs, which meant I could not breathe at full capacity. I wore my favorite blue dress and spent more time preparing than usual. My curly brown hair looked kempt for the first time in a long time, loosely gathered in the back by one of Mary's silver clips. My skin glowed from the idling summer sun. My complexion was bright and clean. After a bit of rouge, I felt confident.

When I descended the stairs, Luca was whittling in the sitting room. Earlier in the day, he had said that he would prefer not to go to Intra tonight in favor of fishing in the evening.

"Franca," he looked at me without blinking. "You look beautiful."

"Thank you. If dinner runs a little late and I do not feel like walking back, I may spend the night at Gia's."

"Of course." I bent toward him and kissed him goodbye on the cheek. As I leaned away, he grabbed me by the wrist and pulled me back to him for a real kiss. I wrapped my arms around his neck. It helped.

"Never mind fishing, I'm coming with you. Can you give me ten minutes?"

The walk to Arabella's was about forty minutes. I smiled much of the way, looking at the clouds folding the colors of the sky when the sun fell behind the mountains of Stresa. Luca held my hand most of the way. *Everything is good.* After a long week, I needed an evening not about me. The sorrow in my chest could only slacken if I allowed myself to be engaged in Gia and Imma's vibrant stories, play cards with the children, and sit beside my father to hear about his week.

"Zia!" Lucia yelled happily from the second-story window of her cousin's bedroom. Her tiny frame danced around me and pulled me to the top floor of the Terracci home, where all my sisters gathered in the kitchen and the men in the living room. "Papa, Zia Franca is here!"

Marcello poured glasses of wine for Luca and me as soon as we walked in. Luca held one hand to my back until I walked away to sneak up behind Ginevra and lift her into a sweeping hug. I walked into the kitchen where my sisters were talking and helping with dinner as Signora Terracci fretted about the stove.

"What an amazing dress, Franca!" Imma complimented me. "Why haven't I seen you in weeks?"

"There is so much to clean at home; I've been exhausted," I responded. Gia eyed me.

"Is Luca here?" Arabella said as she kissed my cheeks.

"Yes, he's with all of the men."

"Wonderful!" To Arabella, Luca's presence meant the Terraccis would put their best face forward for the evening. The rumor around town was when the prince ran away with Claudia Bruno to France, Luca inherited his land, possessions, and money. People thought Claudia Bruno made Luca Marinova the wealthiest man for miles.

"And did you see the boys?" Arabella asked me, somewhat aggressively. A bit of her natural kindness had been scooped out and replaced with several qualities of Signora Terracci.

"Of course. I heard them in their room as Lucia led us up here."

"Good. Well, take a seat and start peeling apples with Imma."

"Goodness, Arabella! You are like a general!" Gia yelled from her stool in the corner. "Let Franca relax."

I had only a few sips of my wine before Imma refilled it. I didn't mind peeling apples. I enjoyed the challenge of trying to achieve a single serpentine peel. Once I turned the apples over to her, Imma sliced them while Arabella told us about the daily discomforts of pregnancy. I kept my face in a sweet smile. I had anticipated this topic of conversation. Today was not about me.

"Were you sick this often when you carried any of the boys?" Imma asked Arabella.

"Not this much," Arabella said as she stirred the sauce, and bubbles popped onto her apron.

"You were!" Signora Terracci interjected as she whipped whatever she was baking. "You have been ill during all of your pregnancies. You want to think you are having a girl, but really, you only have a short memory."

"No one asked you," Arabella snapped without looking at her mother-in-law. None of us said anything in Signora Terracci's defense. "And I might really be having a girl this time. It's not fair that Gia gets all of the daughters."

"My girls make me feel like Mama," Gia beamed at us. She and I looked the same age now. She was still effortlessly stunning but had seen many sleepless nights. I wished Mama could see her now. Mama spent years of her life fighting with Gianna. Mama never got to see love soften her. Perhaps, from her place in heaven, she had helped Gia find this path. Maybe she would help me now.

Imma refilled my glass with a wink.

"But you are not suffering?" Imma pressed, stuck on Arabella's pain.

"No, Imma," Arabella conceded. "It all feels more inconvenient than painful. It's nothing I can't handle."

"Why are you so persistent, Imma?" Gia patted Ginevra on her back to go to the living room.

"Well…"

Imma stopped slicing the apples and put down her knife. She wiped her hands on her dress slowly, theatrically.

"I am pregnant, too. I intended to tell the family last week at dinner, but when you announced, Enzo and I decided to wait."

Arabella flung her arms around Imma and began to cry. My eyes filled with tears, too. Gia looked at me with eyes wide in shock. Signora Terracci clapped her hands over her mouth and thanked God while performing the sign of the cross. I hugged Imma when it was my turn and returned to peel and slice the apples while Imma told us how she suspected a month ago. There had been no sickness, and she could not be sure until the second time her period did not come.

"Why didn't you come to me?" Arabella scolded her.

"I almost went to Gia," Imma laughed, "but by then, I knew it to be true and thought it would be best to tell everyone together."

"God has blessed you, Imma, God has blessed you. And may God bless your little one." Signora Terracci chanted *God bless* between every sentence my sisters completed.

I felt invisible. The only evidence of my presence was the mountain of apple slices in the ceramic blue bowl and the disappearing wine from my glass. For thirty minutes, no one looked at me as they spoke.

"Franca," Arabella interrupted Imma, "are you ok? Is something wrong?"

"Let her be!" Gia shouted from only feet away.

"Why aren't you excited? What's wrong with you?"

I opened my mouth to give Arabella hell... but found my eyes filling with tears more quickly than my mouth could fill with words.

"I can't..." I dropped the knife and covered my eyes to keep from seeing them. My shoulders heaved, and the tears flowed. "I can't... after years... and years... it doesn't happen!"

"You are too tense! This is why–" Signora Terracci began to lecture me before –

"GET OUT!" Gia screamed at the old woman. "GET OUT!"

"Leave!" Arabella snatched the bowl she was stirring and turned her mother-in-law by the shoulders toward the living room.

"GET! OUT!" Gia shrieked again.

The woman, who had no daughters of her own, left her kitchen in a huff.

Arabella knelt on the floor and tried to hold my hands as I cried uncontrollably, murmuring words I couldn't hear. Gia stood behind me and placed her hand on my shoulder. Shocked at the sudden loss of attention, Imma sat across the small table, pouting.

"You still have plenty of time, Franca!"

"It won't happen. I know it won't."

"You can't know that! It's stress. You work too hard. And your womb can hear bad thoughts. What if you take some time away from the hospital to relax?"

"My home is stressful too! We have no money!"

"That's not true. Luca will figure it out. There's no need to stress over that."

"Franca," Gia began softly behind me, "have you lost while carrying? That happened to me last year. I didn't even realize I had been late."

"You never said anything to me," Imma said to Gia.

"No," I shook my head, my hair everywhere now. "I have never carried for a minute."

There were footsteps in the hallway, and Marcello's voice called, "Ladies, is everything okay?"

"We're fine!" Gia called back to her husband. The steps receded. We paused until the sound had faded.

"I'm sorry. I'm drunk," I mumbled and wiped my eyes. "I need to go home. I don't want anyone to see me like this. Your mother-in-law is going to tell everyone that Luca Marinova's wife is a barren drunk."

"She might," Arabella conceded. "But you never know. Late pregnancies happen."

"Don't give up yet. I know it's not the same, but you can see Lucia and Ginevra any time."

"If Mama were here, she would tell you not to worry so much. You had a wonderful summer. Now, you should have an easy winter. Don't wait for it. Let it surprise you."

I nodded.

"I was completely surprised when I found out!" Imma exclaimed.

Arabella and Gia cut her off with only their eyes.

"Imma!" Enzo Fanelli called us. Signora Terracci had likely told the entire party she was driven from her kitchen because I was having a breakdown.

"I'm all right, darling! Can you ask Luca to come up here?"

We all looked at Imma. She was dismissing me. I dabbed my eyes and patted my face.

"You can always talk to me," Arabella kissed me on the head, leaning over so that her pregnant belly was inches from my face.

"Me too," Imma cooed. "*Allora*. Arabella, let's get this dinner back on track!"

"I love you. Everything will be okay. Luca—Franca is not feeling well and needs to go home," Gia directed my husband to my side. I stood up, and the room tilted. I was very drunk. I wrapped my shawl around my shoulders with control. I mumbled my *adieu*, and they chorused their farewell.

Luca told everyone that we were going home. They lamented that we hadn't eaten yet, but no one held us up. I hated the Terraccis, who looked at me angrily. I loathed that Papa and Marcello played nice with them. I felt ambivalent toward Enzo Fanelli… he was nice, but even after a year, he shuffled around the room for belonging. I nodded at the group and followed Luca out of their home.

He kept asking me if I was alright. I felt sorry that he had walked to Arabella's house only to leave with an empty stomach. I vomited over the side when we reached the bridge between Pallanza and Intra.

"My sisters vomit because they are carrying. I vomit because I drink myself sick."

"You do not drink yourself sick. You only did this evening. Do you want to sit down? Are you all right to keep walking?"

"Yes, I'm fine."

"What's wrong?"

"Nothing."

"It's not nothing."

"I'm upset."

"Clearly. I'm trying to figure out why."

We were passing the hospital where I worked, and I was becoming aware of people seeing me with a streak of vomit on my favorite dress.

"I miss my mother," I said.

He tried to put an arm around me, but I clumsily stepped out of his reach.

"She would tell me how to carry on… you know, what to do now."

"What do you mean? What to do about what?"

"Luca, I know you know. I haven't given us a child, and I'm not confident I ever will."

He looked to the ground and sighed.

"Are you very sad?" I asked, wiping my face.

I moved about on the side of the street as necessary to let people pass, using my peripheral vision of their bodies and trying not to take in their faces.

"Kind of, I guess," he said. "I think I've known for a while. But I don't think there is no hope. It could happen. There is still plenty of time."

"Maybe."

"Is it difficult for you to see Arabella pregnant again?"

I nodded.

"Imma's with child too. She told us just now."

He grabbed my hand, and I let him hold it even though our arms flopped at different paces. I used the back of my other hand to wipe the tears away.

"We could be very involved in our roles as aunt and uncle?"

"It's not the same," I said from instinct.

"It could be close."

I nodded and shrugged.

"We'll do more with Arabella's boys too. Lucia, and eventually Ginevra, can visit more frequently. And Imma will want your help soon. Meanwhile, we can still hope for ourselves."

※

On my thirtieth birthday, when I had become the very involved aunt to four nieces and five nephews, Luca bought me a *Bracco Italiano* puppy and a matching calico kitten. He put both of them in my arms and said: "We have everything we need."

1919

7

There was a nineteen-month period during the Great War when Luca was training with the 2nd and 3rd Armies. He fought in six of the twelve Isonzo campaigns. His last was the Ninth Battle in 1916, one of the four Italian victories. A shell exploded yards from him, shrapnel cutting and embedding in his arms as he crawled from the blast. The Slovenia terrain was mountainous, and Luca pulled himself behind a tree, unable to hold the weight of his shotgun. He had had that gun since childhood. His comrades used military-issued or borrowed firearms. It gave him confidence in the other battles, but it felt decorative at that moment. He couldn't lift his arms or form a fist. He sat there for three days as the Italian front moved through the Soča Valley without him. He was given food periodically by his countrymen who passed, but he looked terrible, dried blood smudged on his face, arms soaked enough to cause him to shiver in the daytime. Passing medical personnel gave him water and said that they would return for him but did not, perhaps assuming his chances for survival were less than the others around him.

Beneath the tree, dehydrated and no longer calling out to those who passed him, one soldier asked if he was dying. Luca replied: "That's up to you." The young soldier was from Arona, a small town on the northwestern side of Lago Maggiore. The water of the same lake ran in both of their veins. The young man painfully clenched and unclenched Luca's fists, asking if Luca could feel them. There would be scars. He was discharged from the army and sent home. Recovery took weeks of me waiting on him as wife and nurse.

The Italian triumph was not the end of the battles or the war. His absence from the final three Isonzo battles likely saved his life. A brutal and decisive loss in the Battle of Caporetto at the hands of the Austro-Hungarians' German reinforcements and poison gas finished the Italian part in the war. My husband felt the loss of the war as if he had been there, as if he were King Vittorio Emanuele III, as if his absence condemned his countrymen. For the first time, he proved he could grow a beard like the prince; only Luca's was blonde. His time in the boathouse was more therapeutic than practical, which was difficult on his hands but healing for his spirit.

"What do you think about when you're working on the boats?"

"Nothing," he replied. "It's the only time when I think about absolutely nothing."

1921

8

    Fourteen years before Mary was born, her father had lost a warehouse in New York City to the Great Fire of 1835. She intended to tell me about his soaring financial recovery, but I asked what constituted a great fire. The fire happened in an unusually frigid December. An accidental burst of a coal stove pipe sparked a fire that spread seventeen city blocks and destroyed more than five hundred buildings. The fire could be seen from Philadelphia. Strong winds whipped the fire west to east. Firefighters drilled into the frozen rivers beside the city for water, but the pipes iced over and froze the water. Finally, the military demolished buildings to deprive the fire of further satiation.

    She wanted to resume reading, but I insisted she let me make her more tea and continue storytelling. When I returned to the living room with her second tea, she told me about the third Great Fire of New York City in 1845. This time, it started in the building of a whale oil merchant in the middle of a summer night. The memory of the fire of ten years earlier galvanized the city. Retired firefighters and even firefighters from surrounding cities rushed to assist. Once ordered to evacuate a saltpeter building, one firefighter had no choice but to escape by climbing onto neighboring rooftops. As he leaped between rooftops, the building exploded and leveled six other buildings. The explosion could be heard from New Jersey, which Mary said was further than Suna to Stresa. A second explosion in the same building killed another firefighter, whose body was never found. There was speculation the explosions were caused by contraband gunpowder being stored by the saltpeter in the warehouse.

    This time, there was city water infrastructure that meant the firefighters did not have to rely on the rivers. The fire was put out within twelve hours, though it consumed more than three hundred and thirty buildings.

    "It's unbelievable," I said.

    "Yes, it was all too fast for thinking, my mother said. Everyone feared the fire's damage in 1835 would happen again, and it nearly did. Thirty people died. The wreckage was unimaginable. Reconstruction continued into my early years. My father's company lost nothing in that third Great Fire, the first being in 1776. Of course, there was also the looting of businesses and stealing from homes in the chaos. It was an unnerving time."

※

Mary told me stories about her life. Her father was from a wealthy Dutch family with four children with his wife. Mary's mother was a maid in the Harrison home, and she bore Anthony's fifth child. Mary never met any of her half-siblings. Anthony Harrison provided Mary's mother enough money to offer Mary opportunities the other children in her neighborhood did not have. Mary was given singing lessons and learned to read music young. She attended Doane Academy in New Jersey, where she honed the piano and violin. There was a nineteen-year age difference between Mary and her mother, Florence, and the two were very close. Mary was eleven when the American Civil War began, and they made games of rationing food—on the referral of Anthony Harrison, Florence always had work. Florence's dreams of her daughter becoming a renowned singer were shared by Mary herself.

Mary was devastated when Florence died of smallpox at the age of thirty-eight. She was utterly alone. She reached out to Anthony Harrison, and they met for the first and only time. He supplied her with a small fund to last a decade. Since she would receive no inheritance from him, she admitted she was comfortable accepting the amount. She became a music teacher for a year before traveling to Europe to be a student of opera. She traveled across France, Germany, Switzerland, and Austria before finding herself in Italy and meeting Prince Petyr Marinova, who was there surveying churches.

Mary felt that we were bonded as the bloodless Marinovas. She used the words "bloodless Marinovas" as if we were offshoot species to them. For years, her trust in me fluctuated from minute to minute to hour. I understood the majority of her English and found I was interested in her stories. My nephews and nieces were not. I could see the polite, quiet ones doze off, confused or exhausting themselves to understand her while their active bodies twitched to play games or return outside.

"My sons had the finest childhood boys could have." She said this often, and it became her creed.

9

When the prince left, he sentenced the garden to ruin. We could not afford a gardener, and when our beloved Signor Garibaldi died, his last words were a plea that we not let his life's work fall to pieces. It took only weeks for the paths to become impassable. Mary pretended the garden wasn't there. I proposed to Luca that we attempt to prune parts ourselves, but he seemed content to watch his father's work bury itself.

Their indifference toward the land felt wasteful to me. It was a portion of our inheritance. As a new bride, I wished I lived near the city center, close to my sisters, but as I grew older, I found comfort in the distance and the property. When walking to the hospital for a shift or when I sat with my father in our old apartment he refused to leave, I daydreamed about what could be done with the garden. I wondered if we should hire a proper set of gardeners and open the garden to the public for a small admission fee—an idea considered by the Marinovas for years—or plant fruit and vegetables. I certainly visited the lemon trees throughout the year. I felt an urgency to decide; I was running against time if I hoped to make anything of the prince's toil.

I chose a garden section closest to the house to plant produce. My nephews complained as they cleared the land, but I gave them plenty of food and coffee throughout the days it took. For all of his apparent indifference, it pained Luca to see us tear up the roots.

"Those might be worth something," he would mutter as Paolo and Giacomo tossed the dirt-crested roots of low-growing plants into the discard pile.

"It's only worth something if you know how to sell it." I retorted. "Otherwise, the space it takes is more valuable to me."

I wasn't taking even an eighth of the gardens for my purposes, but Luca could no longer watch. He went to row on the lake with our second dog, Nemo.

I beamed at the thought of all of the small citrus trees, herbs, and vegetables we would grow: tomatoes, romaine, iceberg lettuce, onions, parsley, basil, mint, limes, more lemons, oranges, grapefruit, nectarines, strawberries, olives, zucchini, asparagus, eggplant, pumpkin, peas, carrots, and beets. The six olive trees would be very little work; I would not need to worry about watering them, but they would not bear olives for the first five years. I would not try grapes, as I did not want to make our wine. The cellar still had plenty of fine wine to last us into our twilight years. I had been warned that spinach required too much space to grow for the yield it shrunk to once cooked. I asked the boys to excavate a shady area for a chicken coop. I only needed to shop for bread, salt, beef, pork, butter, chocolate, and olive oil.

    The labor of tending the garden was mild for how rewarding it felt. When Luca squeezed a lemon into his water, I felt responsible for providing that comfort. It took months for the garden to thrive. I had many discouragements, including the garden's gruesome first winter, but when fruit emerged from the branches, I felt capable of enduring a thousand winters.

10

Mary described the problematic pregnancy with Luca as "feeling the moving waters of the sea" thrashing in her body. The doctor ordered her to bed rest, where she lay for the remaining four months, hearing the wind on the lake strengthen and watching the daylight wane until he was born two weeks late on January 20, 1880.

There was a light snow on the ground. During her labor, Mary heard the echoes of Pasquale and Enzo playing outside and was seized by a sharp vision of them stepping onto the lake's featherweight ice. Despite her orders to the nurses in residence, they were too fearful to abandon their roles assigned to them by the prince to leave Mary's side and call the boys indoors. They did not even look outside the window to confirm they were playing safely or appropriately dressed for the cold.

The doctor predicted Luca would be a difficult baby, but on the contrary, he was the easiest of all of the boys. Luca quickly fell asleep and woke up early. He ate consistently and ran as soon as he could stand. Luca was never the one to bring an illness into the home; he usually caught a running nose or fever from Pasquale or Enzo. While all her children were school-age, Mary became aware of the unique relationship between a mother and her last child. She spoke about it in poor Italian with older women, though they argued with her when she would say that Luca was her later as she was only thirty-four. Mary thought that if Luca had been a girl, "Anastasia's destructive influence on my home would have been barren." (She spat and misappropriated the word *barren*.) According to her, Pasquale would not have spiraled out, and her marriage would have withstood.

Luca fell more to his mother's charge, her love stretching beyond the firstborn. She would chase him around the gardens for hours. When she grew tired of pivoting and lurching for the fast boy, she would lie down, close her eyes, and feel him near her. More than once, she dozed off, he vanished, and she would scour the gardens shouting his name. Eventually, when she would turn toward the house in defeat and near to tears, Luca would be squatting behind a bush with both hands pressed to his mouth to stifle his amusement. He thought part of the game was to cause her panic.

At one time, the Marinovas had a Portuguese botanist living with them. Ferdinand Cavaco was a decade Prince Petyr's senior. The two spent hours discussing the gardens, breaking only for leisurely lunches. The prince filled notebooks with what Cavaco taught him. Cavaco had traveled to the Amazon rainforest in Brazil as part of a mission to explore the whole of the Portuguese empire, and he became an expert in creating environments that could sustain the biodiversity of alternate climates. The prince felt he had been sent a gift, and Mary shared his excitement about their guest at the beginning. For the first few weeks, Mary would feed the boys early, put them to sleep, and then eat dinner with Cavaco and the prince, passing hours in conversation. Cavaco was well-traveled, but Mary loved hearing him describe his Lisbon home.

Still, the pleasures of long-term hostessing are few. Mary rebuffed Cavaco's efforts for helpfulness. But when he stopped, she grew resentful of his lack of gratitude. Mary missed her dinners alone with the prince. Even before Pasquale was born, it was their evening ritual: their time of day set aside to return to each other. But the prince and Cavaco were lit from within by the same passion and working toward the same dream. He stayed for ten months.

Mary began to spend her mornings at Café del Gallo with the boys to avoid breakfast at home with the two enthusiasts. As the boys scribbled on pieces of newspaper – Mary would say that Enzo and Luca scrawled as Pasquale drew – she would speak to older women who were drinking white wine at nine in the morning, the old men playing cards and chess, or anyone more curious about the young mother than apprehensive of the language barrier. Petyr asked why she insisted on the dingy Café del Gallo. It was windowless, no one respectable would recommend it, and the atmosphere was stagnant. Why not one of the grandiose bars beside the lake or the small, lovable *pasticcerie* in the center of Pallanza with towering displays of delectable gourmet pastries and sweets? She argued that bringing children into a place where older folks lingered to speak with them, who lived with their grandchildren, was necessary exposure for them since they did not have any grandparents. Also, the presence of the children attracted adults to speak with her. If a boy threw something at one another, the patrons would compliment their spirit. It was an honest place where people didn't have to speak to one another but chose to.

Long after Cavaco departed for his next great adventure, Mary continued to take the boys there.

When Pasquale and Enzo eventually went to primary school, Luca was the only child at Café del Gallo besides Mario Guilatti, the owner's grandson. Mario's mother, Giorgia, came to the bar daily to bring her father a treat but never stayed longer than the minutes it took to order an espresso, which she did not pay for. Giorgia was kind to Mary and occasionally asked her about her husband and origin, but she did not try to befriend or invite her. Mario and Luca would run inside in those short minutes, knocking over chairs and crashing into the other morning regulars. Luca was always eager to see the owner's messy back office. Luca could be a little reserved, but Mario did not have a single shy hair. Mario was a curly brunette with improbably straight baby teeth and a broad smile to share them.

Mario motivated Luca to speak Italian. Giorgia brought small picture books for Luca and corrected him harshly. By the time Luca began *scuola primaria*, he had one best friend in the class.

Now Mario works at Café del Gallo. Luca goes there to visit Mario occasionally. I like that the bar is dear to my husband, but I loathe that place, unchanged from the dirty hovel it was when Mary began going there. Mary can't return there now alone.

Mary refused the offer of her husband to hire help to watch the boys. It reminded her too much of her mother's position as hired help for other people's children. My sisters agreed that Mary likely never wanted a governess in the home for fear the prince might be tempted. It seemed her life had revolved around infidelity. Her mother had been the maid in her father's marital home. When they met, the prince had been married to another woman in another country. My mother never divulged the adulterous affairs of the neighborhood, but occasionally, she would shake her head and tell her daughters: "How you get them is how you lose them."

11

"I received a letter from Pim," Luca said as Mary and I served ourselves at dinner. We looked at him. Pim sent about one letter each year. "He and Claudia have had a child, a son."

Mary, bones lightening with age, did not have the strength to leave the dining room table without my assistance. Her food was untouched and still steaming. Poor Mary wept as I walked her up the stairs before letting her finish her walk to her bedroom alone. I started shaking, humiliated for Mary, upset with Luca for telling us this way, and furious that Petyr Marinova had a seventh child when Luca and I did not have one. I watched Mary stagger to her bed before returning to the dining room to scream at my husband for his lack of tact.

"That delivery was cruel! Did you think that perhaps you should have shared this with me first? How is she supposed to feel about her former husband having a child with the woman he left her for?"

"She had to know. There's no good way to say it."

"There were plenty of better ways! Did you even consider another one?"

"Did you think about what this means to me? I can't stop thinking about how I have a brother forty-one years younger than me. It's something I've never heard of. Pim invited you and me to meet the baby, but I can't even respond to the letter. He is the one who put me in this position. I could have told her or not told her. Both ways, I lose. What am I supposed to do?"

I threw my hands up and yelled, "THEN LOSE WELL!"

Luca smiled slowly and began laughing. His face scrunched in all of my favorite places.

"I'll do better the next time Pim has a baby."

I could hit him for butchering something so delicate, but I sat in disbelief.

"I would appreciate that," I said as I helped myself to our cold dinner.

12

More often than was necessary, Mary spoke of how she would have made such a tremendous grandmother. She was disappointed none of her sons had children. She wished she could have met Pasquale's widow, who informed the family of his passing and secured the return of trunks of his possessions from Paris. We received so many trunks and a shipment paid for by the prince that I wondered if Simone had kept anything of her husband's.

Signora Figlia wanted us to hire her daughter as her replacement. Still, Luca and I had already decided we could not afford to and that once Signora Figlia's walk to Suna became insufferable, I would be responsible for cooking. Surprisingly, as Signora Figlia came to the villa less and less, Mary took on the cooking. When this shift happened, Mary's playful spirit revealed itself more and more. Luca and I pretended to be astounded by the dinners she made for us because she seemed so proud. She had found something that made her feel accomplished. She began singing in the living room. Mary's waist slowly expanded with what she declared "happy weight."

"I think about returning to America sometimes," Mary said between sips of wine as we finished slices of her cake. It was good enough to bring the leftovers to Imma and her four children in Pallanza on my way to the hospital tomorrow, along with the garden's bounty.

"Would you return to New York?" I asked. Luca barely looked up from his food.

"No. I would live with Enzo and his writer wife in Virginia."

"*Che bello!* How long have you been thinking about this?"

"Since they were married. It was like I was being called back. When you reach my age, you think about where you want to die, where your body will be laid to rest."

"Mama..." Luca interrupted; she held up her hand to stop him.

"It's a fact, Luca. I'm not just getting older; I am old. At one point in my life, it might have been romantic to be interred with my foreign husband in a foreign land. But now it feels odd to be buried alone in the garden he left. I haven't been to America in fifty years. I miss my home and my language."

"Have you decided then?" Luca asked her.
"No. I just wanted to feel the thought on my tongue."

13

Luca and I were born after the region's unification to one nation of Italy. His parents moved to Suna after the revolutions, the wars of independence, and the unification. My parents raised us to be loyal to the monarch and to feel a deep pride for being Italian, and yet we were never to forget that our blood is Piemontese. Luca grew up seeing himself as an authentic Italian. One day, Luca emerged from the boatshed, with Nemo in tow, to share that he was interested in becoming involved in local politics.

Suna is a small, remote town near the Swiss border. Our politics were irrelevant to Torino, Milano, and Roma—all far away. I wasn't sure what to say and didn't understand what he thought he could contribute to Italian politics. He would be shocked if I told him that they would mock him and call him Russian or American; he never built the skin for being insulted, and now he wanted to throw himself at the mercy of ridicule.

Luca felt an urge to become more involved when others faced difficulties from which we were relatively insulated. No one locally could afford one of Luca's rowboats. Only foreigners visiting for the summer might purchase a boat and receive a complimentary guided tour of the wild Marinova gardens. The children of my friends and sisters had difficulty finding jobs when there wasn't enough work within family operations. Young Paolo worked at the Terracci stationery shop that Arabella has primarily operated since Signora Terracci died. Marcello's little brother lost his position as a waiter at a local hotel, and his family of four came to live with Gia and her daughters. Enzo, Imma, and their four children moved into our childhood home with Papa. Both of them worked at the grocery store. Imma held my mother's former position, and Enzo worked as the cashier. Maria and I still had the same schedules at the hospital, but my home visits decreased to only the families I knew well, who were bold enough to ask for my time on credit. Signora Esposito's sons and sons-in-law held various roles around Pallanza. Luca, Mary, and I ate mostly from the garden and provided my sisters with produce each week.

Meanwhile, our country was in turmoil. The Risorgimento had failed to provide for the common worker. Those coming into power were born after the 1861 unification or shortly before it. This generation of leaders would be the first true Italians. Luca read the newspapers every day. I barely read them. The politicians were journalists themselves. Torino was the capital of Piemonte, the beacon of my heritage. Luca and I had only been there once for our twelfth anniversary holiday. Torino was the nation's intellectual and industrial capital. When the factory workers of Torino went on strike and called themselves revolutionaries, the disquiet spread to Milano, where workers' councils were formed. There were violent brawls on the street. Farm workers striked as well, and those not benefiting from our garden felt the impact of interrupted labor. Every week, there seemed to be a story of an inconceivably demoniac murder – in ways I could not have invented. I became terrified of the *fasces* the revolutionaries carried in photos. I was grateful nothing like that had come to Lago Maggiore. And then Mary would say, "yet."

The May 1921 election determined the prime minister's race and each party's seats in parliament. Coalitions were formed and broken many times over. The Socialist Party won most seats despite the separation from the Communist Party. Ivanoe Bonomi was elected as the first Socialist Prime Minister. The coalition of the Fascists in the National Blocs Party, led by the current prime minister, Giovanni Giolitti, came in a close third place. This united the Italian Liberal Party, Italian Fasci of Combat, Italian Nationalist Association, and the Social Democratic Party, the last of which Luca and I belonged. It was an unbelievable union of liberalism, fascism, and nationalism.

Mary read the newspapers but could not vote. Luca asked what he could do in these times for others, whereas his mother sought only to analyze the current disturbing events in Italy and across Europe. She could make observations one can only make when they believe the subject matter does not apply to them. At night, she brought Leona, my sweet dog, into her bedroom to protect her in the event an intruder broke in to rob or murder us. I suggested that we all might be safer if Leona was on the ground floor of the villa and able to roam, but she said that someone would shoot the sweet dog, and then Luca would choose to protect me and abandon her to the murderous bandits. Nothing like that had happened in my life in Intra, Pallanza, or Suna, but she insisted that the large Suna homes were in the most danger with the least social defense. Mary said those hungry for power would take advantage of those wishing for their suffering to be heard. Soon, there would be a blind tide rolling in to displace the wealthy.

Between them, my home became filled with rhetoric of fear, conjecture, and uncertainty. Mary repeated what she read with a stiffer view of the Italians.

"Italy only half-adopted an industrial spirit and at such a delay. They are far behind the United States, Britain, and Germany." Mary lectured us over breakfast. Italians don't want to work—except you, Franca. You're the only Italian who likes to work. Everyone else takes up what his father did."

I cut an apple into slices for Luca as he perused the newspaper, half-listening.

"If an Italian can't find a job, it's someone else's fault. Look at your nephews. It would never be that way in America. I fear for the millions of Italians who immigrated to the United States in the last twenty years. They will come home as soon as they can afford to."

I pointed out that "just as many have immigrated to South America or through Europe as the United States."

She waved her hand. "No matter. Everywhere works harder than in Italy. They will be called to work as they never had before. Most will be unsuccessful and return as soon as possible."

December 1921 was particularly snowy. For weeks, my nieces and nephews barely left their homes. I invited them to be stuck in the villa. I held a small party for Lucia, Ginevra, Paolo, Giacomo, Franco Terracci, Antonio, Franco Fanelli, and the youngest one here today, Imma's son Niccolo, the gimp. I laid down an old sheet so they could paint in the living room as they shared stories about work and their friends in common. As they painted, I curled up beside my husband on the oversized couch and watched them. Luca wanted to tell them about the founding of the Nationalist Fascist Party the month before, but they seemed uninterested in ideology and only vaguely intrigued by the political celebrities. Franco, Arabella's thirdborn, joked to his uncle that he did not care what happened in Roma. They only wanted to discuss the brawls. On her way to the kitchen, Mary descended from her room and harshly critiqued their artwork. She told Giacomo, my sweet, fumbling nephew who had inherited Arabella's nascent kindness and Paolo's unclever mind, that he was more suited to paint the rug than whatever he was attempting to paint. They had grown up frightened by her and stood silently until she left the room. Paolo broke the sad silence: "Maybe we should provide commentary on her cooking at dinner?"

The kids laughed, though they were not all kids anymore. When I was Ginerva's and Lucia's age, I was married and had completed the nursing program inspired by the late Professoressa Mila. But they were growing up in a more complicated time. Most of the families they knew had lost sons in the Great War. Lucia told me privately that the intelligent and bold men her age considered themselves revolutionaries and made plans for Torino or Milano to contribute to the new Italy. My nieces were used to seeing widows working endlessly. We all saw fatherless children roaming the streets. Because of that, they lacked a strong vision for what their future would look like.

14

The winter of 1922 held the usual bluish fog over the lake in the mornings, low clouds, and ice on the waterbanks. With the garden captured by frost, I wrapped myself in this natural wintry slough, only wanting to be home at peace with Luca and Leona.

If I weren't working in the morning, I would make a coffee and rest in the chaise longue by the window in our bedroom, waiting for the pair of swans to glide across my view. Luca had stopped shooting from the balcony after returning from the war. Water moved under the thin ice like a moving picture, darkening and lightening the ice with a rhythm I couldn't detect. When the sun finally rose over the eastern mountains, the light lingered in the branches of the winter-stripped trees.

Outside of our idyllic home, our country was suffering. There were reports of working women starving to death in Milano. Their rigor-mortis bodies were found reaching out or serenely in a way that reminded me of the human relics in Pompeii. First founded seven years ago as the Fascist Revolutionary Party, the party had been renamed to The National Fascist Party and surged in popularity over the past few months. It told the working class that they are the foundation our regions' economies were built on, yet they were victims of wage injustice. Fascism promised to fulfill the Risorgimento through order and discipline. It was an invitation to a hierarchy not achieved through birth or education but accomplished simply by being born Italian. It was a revolution to restore us to the greatness of the times of the Roman Empire and the Renaissance. We were the Third Rome. The founder of the National Fascist Party, Benito Mussolini, modeled himself after Julius Caesar or Augustus. He was born in Emilia-Romagna, a province I had never been to. There was an energy about him that scared me. People adored him and quoted him about town. I respected that he was born to working parents, but the rising tide lifting him in status had not brought me with it. I felt far beyond recognizable shores.

My sisters were less current on politics and more concerned with our father's health. Papa could no longer take the stairs in his building without assistance. His eyesight had failed. I performed the eye exam myself. He couldn't see me crying through it.

Imma took care of Papa along with her four children. I never succeeded in pulling my father to live with me in Suna. Papa could hold a bowl beneath his chin, spoon himself the contents, and, praise God, still feel his way around the small bathroom after one of the children guided him to it to assist himself. In March, Maria's husband, one of the doctors I worked with closely at the hospital, diagnosed him with cancer of the pancreas.

It was hard to determine how lucid he was in the last weeks of his life. Imma moved him between his bed and a chair in the living room. Arabella and Gia tried to help as much as possible, but Imma was increasingly short-tempered with them for bringing more mouths for her to feed. As a nurse bringing no mouths to feed, I was welcome.

One night, Imma's boys and girls helped move Papa to bed as they usually did, in a full troop. They left me alone with him.

"Papa, why didn't you come live with me?" I asked him as I shifted his legs beneath the blanket in his bed. Inviting me to rest, there was the old chair I sat in when young Giacomo Esposito lay in the same place, dying. "It must be so loud here."

"I like noise."

"I don't believe you. Did you want to stay because this was your home with Mama?"

He moaned assent. His eyes were partly closed, unseeing.

"Did you not want to live with me because the Marinovas are not Italian?"

He made another dragging moan.

"Not because you didn't want to live with me?"

He shook his head.

"But you approve of Luca?"

"He was my first son."

I told Luca my father said this after the funeral in June.

Though the weather around me warmed and brightened, I found joy in swimming in the lake again, and I was in a season of my own. I had a strong urge to travel now, a few years since the war, to see the scorched earth and where it had healed. I wanted to be somewhere else. Not forever, but for a time. I thought Luca and I could drive through Switzerland and Germany, curve over into Belgium, and then visit coastal towns of France and see where Pasquale was buried in Paris. We did not have the money to disappear for months and months. Our day-to-day expenses were low, but Luca didn't spare when it came to his materials. Master Agostino had taught him that you cannot forge the pristine through weak tools, cheap wood, and fast methods. The quality had to be present in pieces first.

I started looking for our escape money. I considered working more at the hospital, selling our garden surplus, or helping Luca sell more of his boats. However, our most valuable assets were the collectibles rotting in the prince's unused office, on the dusty floor of Pasquale's studio, our tall bookshelves, and hanging on our walls. We did not need any of it. The villa had seen its days of high entertaining. Luca and I had no one to impress, nor was there someone to pass it on to. This inheritance would end with us.

Late at night, we were lying in bed with the balcony door open to the breeze. I watched the vast, sparkling starscape.

"Are you awake?" I whispered. My bare back was to him.

"*Sì.*"

"I want us to travel. I want to leave the lake for a little while."

"Why?"

"For a change. To experience different days."

"Are you unhappy with your days?"

"I feel stale. My work feels more routine than important. One of the children I have been attending died after his appendectomy today. His parents, neighbors of my Rossi cousins, gave their savings to provide him with surgery that he didn't survive. He was eight years old, and I did not even cry."

"Why does that make you want to leave our home? Won't you miss your sisters and *nepoti*?"

"Yes, but we wouldn't be away too long. I need a change. I've been thinking we could travel through Switzerland or Austria to Germany and see where your brother rests in Paris. Maybe he will find his wife and meet her. Then we could find a little house on the coast of France and have a holiday for a while."

"What about Leona?"

"Leona would stay here. Gia and Marcello could move into the villa while we are gone. They would enjoy the space. And I think the girls would be happy tending the garden."

"I'm not sure." I turned to him, and he looked at me with concern.

"You want change, but the world is changing right now. It feels like Suna is the only safe place. The last time I left, for those two years of war, I missed you and our home. There is nothing better than this."

"That was different. I haven't been away from Suna in years. I hear about the world changing around Suna and would like to see it."

"How would we afford months away?"

"I think we should sell some items in the villa."

"Sell what?" He threw up his hands and sat up. "I can't hawk my father's property! It belongs to the estate."

"He abandoned the estate! The villa is ours. And I feel buried alive in this house! I don't care about what people gave him or what he collected."

"I won't talk about this!" Luca yelled. Then, fuming, he stormed out of our bedroom, slamming the door behind him. I heard footsteps down the hall to the blue guest room, and the door opened and shut. He had never done that before.

❋

I spent hours in the garden, considering whether I had gone too far. He spent three sleepless nights in the blue room before returning to our bed. He told me that he could not be responsible for dismantling his father's home. He may resent him, but everything here belonged to Enzo and the younger half-brother as much as him. With suffering in his tired eyes, he said it would be like prying strips of wood from a perfect boat. He suggested we take a trip to Vienna for a couple of weeks. I accepted his compromise to have our harmony back.

I did not know if the youngest child of Petyr Marinova would ever come demanding his share, but I certainly knew Enzo would not return for any piece of his inheritance. He would not even pursue the books lining the living room and three walls of the prince's office. There were about two thousand books between those two rooms. Several tall, old book spines had eroded so much that I was afraid to lift them off the shelf. The books I did open were in Russian, English, Italian, French, Latin, and Greek. The Greek and Russian looked similar to me. No matter what Mary says, I don't believe that the prince, Enzo, or Pasquale read all these books between them. Several of the books had bad limericks penned by Enzo buried inside of them or the prince's multi-lingual annotations in the margins. Mary's books occupied a shelf, too. Her influence was captured in how they were arranged alphabetically by title, whereas the other shelves were divided by subject, then language, and then alphabetically by author. Many bore dog-eared corners, oil stains left by fingers, and even coffee and food smudges. The books connected us to the departed reader.

I questioned my husband's reverence for our inheritance, increasing with age. Every piece of decor, art, furniture, and carpeting in the villa had an inflated story behind who made it, how far the prince had traveled to find it, the legend of the great friend who gifted it, and always the journey it made to be here today. If I tried to rearrange the surface of the dining room console, Luca would say that he preferred it the usual way and the items "where they belong." When I suggested we bring in appraisers to estimate the value of these items, simply so that we could know, he asked, "Why would we pay someone to do that?"

"Should we clear out Pasquale's studio and rent the space to a tenant? We never go in there, but it is spacious enough for someone to enjoy."

"The Eye was my brother's workspace." He sputtered, appalled. "Everything in it should be in a museum. It is not fit for living. Never suggest that to Mama."

I did not. It was confirmed that the studio was difficult to access from the villa and could barely be seen, given the overgrowth of the property's mountainside and several storms that had fallen trees in its path. When I climbed up there, I found the doorknob had rusted. I used my shirt to grip it and force the latch back. A rock beside the door with an etching read "Into the Eye." It felt like a bad omen. There was more dust than I had ever seen. Inches of dust. I covered my mouth and took significant steps that seemed like I was stepping on dirt that yearned to be cloud. The spines of journals were faded in vertical stripes on the shelves like water lines where the setting sun found them each day. I left feeling called to find a purpose for the studio. Its vacancy weighed on me.

15

The summer had been marked by intense violence in the *Biennio Rosso*, as these years were referred to immediately following the Great War. Conflicts between the left-wing and right-wing militias rose throughout the country. Fascism spread through the regions and was answered with an urgent call to assume or retaliate. Prime Minister Luigi Facta felt the threat of Mussolini's militia more than King Vittorio Emanuele III, who appeared to accept the sweeping sentiments and yet hoped that they would fade away. Facta was from Pinerolo, a small town outside of Torino. On the night of Friday, October 27, 1922, Mussolini and thirty thousand of his Blackshirts marched on Roma. Mussolini demanded a new Fascist government and the resignation of Facta. Facta brought King Vittorio a martial law decree, but the king refused to sign it. Our king could have chosen to fight them. It may not even have come to that; the commander of the Blackshirts told Mussolini that he would not act against the monarchy. But the following morning, King Vittorio refused to grant martial law. The king did not want violence in the streets of the capital and to further divide his conservative establishment from the Fascist or Fascist-leaning industrial and agrarian elites. Facta resigned. King Vittorio offered the position to Mussolini, who engaged in the talks from Milano. On Monday, October 30, Benito Mussolini was appointed Prime Minister without former office experience and a minor party holding of Fascist parliament seats.

In the latter part of that week, Mary declared over dinner that she could no longer remain in this country.

"I like Queen Elena. She and I have much in common. She attended the Institute for Young Ladies in St. Petersburg. She is an artist. Her monument design for her uncle Prince Danilo I of Montenegro was a lovely ode. But I can no longer stay in the country; her husband—the king—is running into the fine dirt of this land!"

"You're more Italian than American by now." Luca's smile dropped, and he believed his mother was serious this time.

"I wouldn't agree with that."

"You've been in Italy longer than you lived in New York."

"America is still where I'm from, Luca. You can't change where you're from."

"You're going to take a ship to America?"

"That's how it's done." Her shrug pulled my stomach high to my heart.

"But it's dangerous. What if it sinks? And disease is rampant on those things, and… you're old."

"I'm young enough to do it once more. I've done it before, and I have the money for a private stateroom this time. It will be like a holiday."

"And then what? You'll live in New York alone for the rest of your life?"

"No, I'll go to Virginia and live with Enzo. We've been exchanging letters, and it is all right with him. His wife is quite interesting, you know. She publishes articles in national newspapers and hosts dinners at her family home for famous politicians, writers, and southern aristocrats. Her godfather was Robert E. Lee. I still remember being a young girl when the men went off to battle in the South, and now I'll go live outside of Richmond. It's unbelievable."

As she spoke, I nodded with a pressed mouth and furrowed brow. I wondered how this sister-in-law of mine would take care of Mary for the remainder of her days. Mary always spoke of Enzo's wife with esteem, though there were many comments about how her sons were better at making women into wives than mothers.

Luca had a tough time with his mother's preparations. There was no room for him to negotiate with her. She only had eyes for her plan. She told him she would grant us one last Christmas with her before disembarking from Napoli on December 31. The ship would go from Napoli to Sicilia and then on to New York City, where she would take a ship to Baltimore and be retrieved by Enzo to journey to Keswick, Virginia. No one said this was the last time they would see each other. No one could say that he would never visit her or that she would never return.

On Christmas morning, Luca stared out the window onto the lake.

"It's hard for you to let her go," I said from the bed.

"She is all that's left of my family."

"That's not true. You can write her letters, which means we can keep in better touch with Enzo. We can visit your father. He's not too far away." He shot a glare that was a firm *nein*. Maybe you can go to America and visit them someday?"

"Would you go with me?"

"I don't know. I'm afraid to be on a boat that can't see land."

"Me too. I might be able to stomach it once, but it would have to be there and then back."

"Do you want to ask her to stay?" The question gulped. I could feel my face contort into a forced smile.

"You despise her."

"I don't! We are not very close after all these years, but I want her to be happy. And I want you to be happy. Why don't you ask her?"

"Could we ask her together?"

I nodded.

We walked the long hallway to Mary's room. I hadn't been in her room for a long time and felt nervous approaching the large door, hand-in-hand with my husband of over twenty years. Luca knocked and asked if we could come in. She assented.

Mary was sitting up at a stiff angle on the left side of the four-poster bed. She was still in her long nightgown. Leona was lying at Mary's feet on the covers, her front paws crossed. Christmas mornings were usually our own, during which time Mary would read luxuriously, Luca would hunt in the woods or work on a little boat, and I made the three of us lunch. After a slow lunch, I would start getting ready for an evening party when my sisters came over with their families. Mary only had dinner with my family for a short time before retiring. This year, Luca asked if we could keep the festivities between the three of us and play party games with Mary, while I had agreed that they would all be going to our old home for Imma to host the night. Yet, now I felt that we all could have used the distraction of an event.

"Merry Christmas, children." We each kissed her powdered cheek. Luca carried two sitting chairs from the window to her bedside. I sat in the second, slightly further from her.

He gripped her hand. Her mouth remained tight.

"Mama, I want you to stay. Franca does, too. Don't go live with Enzo in America."

"Luca," she started, "when I was married to a foreign prince, entertaining his guests, and the mother to three individualistic boys, I felt the most fulfilled by this home. We had many wonderful years here. Then she came, and they left for Paris. I knew that the long period of contentment was over. I lost my son. I was discarded for a girl my children knew in grade school. I've been divorced and humiliated. My time to leave came years ago. I'm finally going home. I belong with people who speak my language, who find my story interesting rather than foreign."

Luca gripped the bridge of his nose between his thumb and pointer finger, and tears still managed to come. I put my right hand on his trembling back.

Tears filled my own eyes, not for Mary but at the thought of pleading with my mother not to leave me. What I would give to have her back, even after nearly twenty-four years. I could never carry her bags, guide her to a ship, kiss her goodbye, and watch her leave my life. How could Mary, who lost her mother early in life, put my husband in this position when every other member of the family had already left him behind?

"You have a lovely life here. You both will go on being very happy without me."

"You should stay. You don't even know Enzo's wife. What if you hate her?"

"That's a chance I am comfortable taking." Her face was lined from age, not concern. "It won't be that different. I'm like the house cat. Right, Franca? You see me, but you don't need me." I nodded, but I adored our cat, Theia.

"That's not true." Luca tipped his face into the covers at her side. I leaned over to preserve my touch on his back.

"Someone is so sentimental." She threaded her fingers through his thinning hair as he mumbled into the mattress.

"I'll leave you two and start lunch." Neither of them said anything as I stood.

I looked at Leona. Her brown, lucid eyes could see my aversion to the whole scene. As I turned to the bedroom door, I heard Leona's delicate nails glance at the floor, front legs first, and I left the door ajar for her to follow me without looking back at them. Neither of us had to be a part of my husband's heartbreak or his mother's indifference.

✶

I couldn't sleep the nights leading up to Mary's departure. Neither could Luca. We each knew the other was awake but did not speak. Luca would be gone for five nights ferrying Mary to Napoli safely, securing her on her ship, and then making the return journey. Lucia would spend those nights with me in the villa. We would go to Gia's for New Year's Eve and then to Arabella's for lunch on New Year's Day. I was looking forward to thinking, going on light hikes, and relaxing with my niece. But that was all on the other side of Mary leaving, and a doubting voice in my head said she would not go.

When the sky was indigo, he sat up, placed his feet on the floor, and I put my hand flat against his lower back for the moment he sat there. This would be Mary's last image of me, so I chose to put on more than a robe over my frilly nightgown. Yesterday, Gia gifted me a handmade long, red dress for Christmas, which felt fitting for this solemn morning. As I brushed my long, curly hair down my side, I was shaking with the chill of winter and from dread of how our last minutes would unfold. After knowing her for the course of my life, sleeping down the hall from her for decades, and sharing thousands of meals, there was ground between us that would remain forever unbridged. I wondered if she might use her final words to express regret or assign blame.

I glimpsed the sparse table of pastries, apples, and tea and fetched more bread, jam, and the winter kiwi always gifted in crates for us by the Barbagaletti family from their mountainside home on Cavandone. Then, I sat at the breakfast table and held my husband's hand as the cloud-streaked sky emerged from the darkness. He sipped at his tea and ate two of everything. Their train was at eight o'clock, which, before the war, was his time to fire a single shot off of the balcony.

Her bedroom door opened and closed. As did Leona's trailing pitter-patter, slow, deliberate steps echoed toward us. As she entered the dining room, she caught her son's gaze and slid to me and my dress.

There was a flash of ire at her mouth, and she took a deep breath to say, "I'm ready. I'm not hungry."

Our hands released. We stood. I knew better than to try to persuade her to eat. I walked over to her; tears flooded my eyes. Luca grabbed her two leather suitcases monogrammed with her husband's initials and his single large haversack; they would walk the distance to the train station.

Mary opened her arms to indicate that I may hug her.

"Have a very safe journey," emerged from my voice, raspy with exhaustion. "Please write to us all of the time. Tell us all about America and Enzo."

She nodded, and I released my hold on her. I prayed to God, *please protect her.*

"Keep out of the sun, Franca."

Mary Marinova walked out the open door and down the gravel driveway to the gate, head high. I kissed Luca goodbye on the front step and closed the door behind me to keep the cold out.

✻

Minutes after they left, I realized I should have walked them to the train station only to be sure they were off. I was nervous she might return, having changed her mind. I left the food on the table and sat on the couch in the dark, petting Leona and watching the door for two hours. When enough time had passed, I finally moved around the villa freely. I used the bathroom beside the prince's office with the door open. Leona looked at me curiously for a moment, but when she could smell my urine, she quickly turned away.

I washed my hands and walked straight up to the main bedroom. Luca suggested we move into this room now, but sleeping in the same bed as his parents was unfortuitous. We had plenty of space in our room. By the look of the room, Mary took little with her. The bed was made. The collection of perfume bottles on the vanity were untouched. Not surprising that she would leave it to me to battle with Luca over disposing of a hundred of his mother's precious items. Only in the closet was it clear that items were missing. There were only four items still hanging and some dilapidated trunks underneath sagging boxes. The bottom right-hand corner of one of those trunks read "P. P. Marinova."

Late in the afternoon, Lucia arrived and we had tea in the living room beside the fire to warm her toes after her walk from Intra.

"I went into Mary's bedroom after they left."

"Zia Franca!"

"It finally felt like I could. I've never been in there without her watching me closely."

"I've never seen it. Will you and Zio Luca move into that room? I'm sure it's grand."

"It is. I'll show you. We won't move in there, I don't think. In the next couple of days, I'd like your help disposing of Mary's personal effects. If we don't do it now, Luca will never let me touch that room again."

"He is the family archivist." Lucia shrugged with a genial smile.

"Yes. And there's more… earlier today in Mary's closet, I saw a few boxes and trunks belonging to Luca's oldest brother."

"The handsome sculptor? Did Mary ever open them?"

"I can't tell. I don't know if Luca knows about them."

Lucia's eyes lit up with excitement, and she tilted her neck in the direction of the stairs.

We lifted the boxes and carried the trunks together from the closet to spread them out across the wide floor. For a moment we looked only at the four boxes and two trunks themselves. None of them had been opened in years. Perhaps the last person to know what was inside was his French widow who packed them. Lucia fetched a knife from downstairs to open the first box. The box was convexed from the weight of the ones above and below it. Inside, there were hundreds of papers: photographs, sketches, faded Parisian newspapers including the obituary of Anastasia Marinova, and notes. The contents were not packed well. There was a small, brown picture of Pasquale and Simone on their wedding day. Neither smiled in the picture, but there was exhilaration in her eyes. Buried separately in the careless pile, there were two copies of the same address for Tatiana Marinova in Smolnek.

Lucia and I examined and passed every item for the other to see. The clothes were packed as poorly as the papers. Maybe it was too painful for Simone to pack each item with care. I organized a small pile of books in the corner of Mary's room for Luca to see.

"Zia…"

Lucia stared into a shoe box she had pulled from underneath a large photograph of the villa in one of the trunks. Inside the shoe box, wrapped in a scarf were sparkling jewel necklaces, rings, bracelets, and a silver tiara. Lucia's light brown eyes widened.

"Mary must not have known about this," I breathed. It was all I could think to say.

"Simone must have just packed the shoe box without looking inside."

"Is it Anastasia's? Luca once told me that the first wife was the one who inherited all of the Marinova jewels. Mary was always bitter about it. And yet…"

"Why would the Princess Anastasia give this all to Pasquale?"

"She passed away in Paris. She must have given these to him before then." I lifted the weighty ruby and diamond necklace with cupped hands.

"Will you wear these now?"

Lucia picked up one long emerald bracelet.

"Only when I'm gardening," I replied and she laughed.

We placed the shoebox on top of a pillow on Mary's bed and closed the door behind us.

September 1943

16

My sisters, their husbands, children, and grandchildren were gathered to hear about the armistice between Italy and the Allies and what it meant for us. Should we play music and recall laughter from the past? Should we flee south? The many Espositos, my old neighbors from Pallanza, and former schoolmates gathered in front of the portico made of pink granite from Baveno at the Town Hall of Verbania. In 1939, the union of twelve localities, including Intra, Pallanza, and Suna, became one town: Verbania. All twelve were here this morning to hear what would happen next. The treaty had been signed on September 3 but was announced this morning, five days later, by the Allies. Was the war over for us? Why did neither our monarch nor government dare announce their secret agreement to the people?

Over the summer, King Vittorio had appointed Pietro Badoglio Prime Minister behind closed doors. The infamous Pietro Badoglio, a Piemontese man born in Grazzano outside of Asti, was as ruthless a politician as a militant. Seven years ago, as Commander-in-Chief of the Royal Army, Badoglio conquered Ethiopia using mustard gas and phosgene. Then he marched our army to the Ethiopian capital of Addis Ababa without resistance in the three-hundred-and-twenty kilometer March of the Iron Will. The newspapers were filled with "Badoglio" and "Victory." The Third Roman Empire was strong. If you stood in the way of our empire, you would be defeated.

The king needed a lion to defeat a wolf.

Badoglio arrested Benito Mussolini. No one knew where Mussolini was or whether he was alive. As Badoglio reassured the Third Reich of Italy's loyalty, he removed Mussolini's fascist cabinet and dissolved the National Fascist Party. With Mussolini's fate unknown, the Germans had been trying to arrange a meeting between King Vittorio and Adolf Hitler.

A crowd of over three hundred gathered in front of our Town Hall to hear whether we should pack everything and head south or if the time to consider that had passed. Were the British and Americans on their way to protect us? We would be the first to experience the German invasion only forty kilometers from the

Swiss border. Sweating as they faced the crowd, our local communal council members announced they did not know more than the newspapers. Each one went down a line on the front steps, repeating fragments of what they could confirm. The crowd booed each one. The regional council in Torino had not given any instruction except that we should go home and be with our families.

"Gia, will you come stay with us? The house is big enough for you, Marcello, and the girls. We have a radio. If there is an invasion, I want you with me," I asked her in the scramble of the crowd disassembling. Luca held my elbow gently to keep us from being separated.

"What about Arabella and Imma?" Gia looked frantically for them. Arabella was holding the tiny hands of two of her granddaughters.

"We'll invite them too, of course." We waved our family to the lakeside, many hands redirecting many elbows. With all five of Arabella's sons deployed across the continent with Italian forces, she was the matriarch taking care of her five daughters-in-law and seventeen grandchildren.

"The Terraccis will be staying in Intra. We'll be in touch." She yelled to Gia and me. Arabella turned away, and nearly two dozen people followed like a school of synchronous fish.

"I won't come either," Imma declared. Her married daughters moved into the new building beside the one we grew up in, where Imma and Enzo still lived. Of Imma's two sons, younger Niccolo had been deemed medically unfit for service due to a break in his leg as a child that healed improperly and left him with a significant limp. Imma had three of her four children near home, with her Franco off in France. "We want to stay near our children and the little ones."

"Well, you can change your mind and join us."

"Franca," Imma looked from me to Luca nervously, "maybe you should consider coming to live with us in Pallanza? Or going to Gia's safe up the mountain. Have you considered that the villa is on the main road? Any troops who cross the border and march south will pass it. The forest may keep a clear view of the house from the street, but anyone can see the property over the lake from the bends in the road. It could be a target."

"Abandoning our home would ensure that fate," Luca responded.

"Think about it," Imma insisted. "My offer always stands. You could have the second bedroom. You could even bring that terrible dog."

"We'll think about it." I held her wrist tightly as I spoke. "And as long as things stay the same, we will still see you for dinner on Friday."

"Yes, yes. I'm making *panzotti*." I hugged Imma. Luca and Enzo nodded to each other before the couple parted. The piazza was clearing away. Shopkeepers were off to hurriedly reopen as people sought to purchase everything they may need to stay in their homes.

"Franca, Imma has a point." Gia said. "The villa is too grand not to be a target. I'm not sure the girls or Ginevra's children should be there. If we vacate our home, it could be vulnerable...."

"We all have the same problem there," Marcello interjected. "But I would agree that your home is particularly... visible. We'll have to think about going there. We'll discuss it with the girls and tell you our decision on Friday."

Luca and I nodded, with skin too old and age-spotted to be this pale. I hugged them as tightly as the joints in my left shoulder would allow, and Luca and I made the walk home. We held hands the whole way. Children walking along the road would call me *"Ciao, Infermiera Marinova!"* I would wave, try to smile, and wipe away slow tears so the children wouldn't see them.

✳

Imma's words took root in my heart and mind. Luca cleaned his guns.

We kept Anastasia's jewelry in the tender shoe box Pasquale or Anastasia had used in the back of our closet. I never wore any of it; it felt cursed. Fine jewelry moves between women through suffering. I showed my sisters and their daughters when they were curious, but the looks of desire that came over their faces when they tried on different pieces proved to me that it was corruptive to the soul.

"I want to bury Anastasia's jewelry," I told Luca between spoonfuls of our cannellini soup.

"Why?"

"I don't want anyone to find anything valuable here. I want to hide it in case we need it later."

"Will you also bury the paintings and the rugs? What about Pasquale's sculptures?"

"If you would help me dig, I would bury everything except the dinnerware we need by day. Our home is the largest in Suna, with the most lakeside property in Verbania. We need to take precautions."

"I will shoot anyone who steps on our property uninvited."

"Luca, you can't fight them. You will lose, and I will lose my husband."

"We're not Jews – they don't want us." He chewed for a moment. "Bury the jewelry only. I'll move Pasquale's sculptures and framed sketches to his studio tomorrow. The paintings we should leave up. If someone comes, they must think they've found all there is to find."

He closed his eyes and pinched the bridge of his nose. His face wrinkled, and he took one long, difficult breath that failed to diffuse his trembling stress.

"I feel helpless," he whispered. "I can't protect you or my family's home. Earlier today, I could barely lift her," he lovingly referred to his shotgun, "off of the wall or clean her barrel."

"We will make it through this."

"Last time I fought for my country, I helped keep the Huns away. I'm huddled at home this time, waiting for the enemy to pull me from my bed."

"It won't be like that. If they do march over the border, if they see we aren't hiding anyone, and if they take what they want without a struggle, they won't harm us."

"You might be right."

In the evening, I lifted the dusty box from its place behind my lavender satin-heeled shoes, which I had worn only once to Lucia's wedding. They felt lighter than I remembered.

The dog, Buffo, a six-year-old shepherd mix, followed me into the front yard. Leona was long buried in the garden at the edge of the clearing where Luca and I were married, joined by my little calico cat, Theia. The two of them were so dear to my heart. In the days before losing them, Luca began populating the home with more and more pets. In the time since Leona passed, which was the hardest pet loss to bear, we buried another two dogs, energetic brothers from Domodossola (one tied to Luca's side for eleven years and the other a roamer without much interest in people, only his brother), and three cats who, unlike Theia, found more creative ways to die than from old age. Now we had two cats, Nera and Anco, short for "Bianco," that saunter around the property. Anco circled to neighboring properties, hunting squirrels in the woods and little creatures of the garden. Buffo was a dog neither Luca nor I had built a bond with over time. The poor mut was constantly breaking something, tracking dirt into the house, getting scratched by Anco, and jumping on my sisters. I let him follow me but didn't want to speak to him the way I had to Leona. Buffo was always in the way.

 I carried the shoe box, wrapped in a small burlap bag, to the third tree from the gate, slightly in the forest but close enough to the road and easy for me to access if we needed to leave quickly. I considered dividing the jewelry into two packages and burying them separately. Still, I was more concerned that I would lose track of where the multiple stashes were, increase the likelihood of portions being found, and ultimately, that pieces would be lost. I would be shortchanging those I preferred to inherit it all: Lucia and Ginevra.

 It was a warm summer night, and though my knees were used to the weight of my body leaning and digging in the garden, I sweat profusely as I scooped dirt into a pile with my small gardener's trowel. It was not entirely dark yet. I dug by the dimming light. At about twenty inches down, I felt comfortable. Buffo circled me as I worked. I was nervous he would bark. In recent years, homes bordering our property on the south side had been built. Anyone could be on the other side of the gate yards away, walking along the highway.

 I replaced the dirt firmly around the box and packed it around, praying the earth would not swallow it. After a good rain, the slight mound would disappear. At the very least, I felt relieved to have the Marinova treasure out of my house.

✻

The next day, the Germans invaded Italy.

 After arresting Mussolini, Pietro Badoglio sent Giuseppe Castellano, a friend of Mussolini's son-in-law, to Madrid to contact the Allies for an Italian surrender. A Brit redirected Castellano to

Lisbon to contract an armistice with Winston Churchill. Castellano signed the armistice on behalf of Badoglio in Cassible, Sicily, on September 3.

    Badoglio ordered the Italian Army back to Roma. He delayed the announcement of the surrender for five days. He thought that might be enough time for the Allies to envelop the peninsula and bring our men home. It seemed plausible the Allies could cross the country quickly. With Mussolini's arrest two months ago and the king's refusal to meet with Hitler, the Germans already suspected the alliance had become false. They made a counterplan for an imminent Italian defection. The radio broadcast by Badoglio on September 8 was met the same day by German attacks on the Italian Army, who had not been informed of the surrender or warned how to respond in the event of meeting German forces in the field. The majority of our troops, in transit to Roma, were unprepared, overpowered, and, in the best of cases, dispersed upon German encounter.

    King Vittorio, Prime Minister Badoglio, and other diplomats fled Roma early on September 9. They moved the government to the south in Brindisi, where they would be safe behind Allied lines. On the same day, three battleships pulled away from the harbor in La Spezia. Of those three, the *Roma* was attacked in Sardinia and sunk in the Mediterranean, killing 1,400 men. Captains unable to get their ships underway from La Spezia scuttled them. For this, they were executed.

    Three days after the armistice was announced, the Germans held Roma.

✳

    Before the sun had risen on September 9, German Panzers and soldiers marched down the highway in front of our home that stretched from Locarno, Switzerland, and fed two directions: east to Milano and west to Torino. Some insisted we blast the road, but there was no time. We were not organized.

    The 1st SS Panzer Division Leibstandarte was stationed to remain in Lago Maggiore, mainly on the western side in Stresa and Arona. Still, Verbania was crawling with those ordered to patrol and protect the highway, Via di Lago Maggiore—the road of our wedding procession. The Germans were tasked with disarming and arresting any division of the Italian Army that managed to make it to the Swiss-Italian border. This was unlikely. If any band of men survived unanticipated combat against German troops, they would be smart enough not to return by strutting down the central road. No, the truth was that the boys of the Leibstandarte were overdue for a vacation.

Marcello and Gia, braver than Luca and me, walked to Suna six days after the occupation began. We did not know they were coming, and my heart swelled in terror at hearing the calling and knocking from the gate. The motley dog fled into the house at the sound.

"Luca, it's Marcello and Gia. We're alone."

Luca slid the iron gate that allowed them to enter sideways, Gia first, before shutting and locking the gate behind them. Gia wore a brown scarf around her head. We all hugged. It had been a week since the invasion. I had not seen anyone other than Luca. It felt as if the Germans had been prowling our streets for months. Marcello signaled for us not to speak here.

Once inside the villa, I put on a kettle for tea and made coffee for us. Luca lit a fire in the hearth. Since the march down the highway, we emitted less light from the house at night and kept the radio low. From the lake or the road, it would appear the home had little happening inside: it was not attention-drawing, it was not abandoned, and there was nothing to hide.

"How have you been since Badoglio's announcement?" Gia asked, only to override her question with more. "Did the soldiers march right past your door? Did you see them? I've been worried about you, but you look as good as anyone."

"We watched them from the window in Enzo's old room upstairs. It was... unreal. My heart is heavy for the men on the front. Have you heard anything about Ara's boys?"

Gia wiped her eyes a few times in harmony with her mouth opening and closing – stopping before starting.

"No one knows anything for sure," Marcello began, touching his wife's knee. "But I am especially nervous for Niccolo, Antonio, and Roberto since they were somewhere in Yugoslavia when they were called back to Roma. Paolo was near Austria with the Second Army, but I think he was close to the border when the announcement was made. I don't know where Luigi is. His ship was stationed in Taranto when I last heard from him."

"Luigi was always the one who sought to be different from the pack," Luca said mid-sip of tea; he wiped a small dribble with the back of his liver-spotted hand. "It may have saved him. The Regia Marina might have a better fate than the army."

"I met with two of my friends in the Intra police yesterday, Massimo Carozza and Patrizio Di Ferrari–" Marcello started.

"Patrizio grew up in Nonna Illari's building, remember Franca? His mother was quiet."

"I remember him. And I used to see Massimo and his wife in the hospital; their daughter had a series of ear infections."

"Anyway," Marcello continued, "I accidentally met them at the bar waiting for an espresso. I may have retired but still have some influence with the force. And we came here tonight because I wanted to share what they know with you."

Luca and I shifted on the couch across from Marcello and Gia. He sat back to better take in the news while I leaned forward to absorb it quicker.

"The Leibstandarte began as a small regiment of Hitler's bodyguard and served the office, home, and at the personal whim of the Führer. This regiment was administrative in the '20s but came to wear the colors of the army, received a tank, and grew to the size of a full division. This group has been involved in all major German invasions: Poland, France, and the Soviet Union. They have been positioned in Verbania, Arona, and Stresa to disarm the Italian Army and have orders not to tolerate disobedience. There is word that the Italian Fourth Army is regrouping in southern Piemonte, and the Leibstandarte will meet them if it is true. Right now, they occupy many of the hotels along the lake; in Verbania, they are in Hotel di Pallanza."

I imagined these soldiers in our wedding night's magnificent stateroom.

"They are rounding up any Jews on the lake or living in the region. The Leibstandarte sent Jews from all over Europe to the work camps. In Stresa, they currently hold over fifty Italian, Greek, and Turkish Jews in Hotel Meina. They haven't been allowed to come out for days. There are women and children in there. I think they are deciding what to do with them. And if they do not have the instructions or ability to deliver them to a camp, then…"

"How can this be happening?" I was overwhelmed by evil, and nothing could stop it. I'd heard of the camps but never thought that could happen in Piemonte.

"It is happening," Luca said flatly in a soldier's tone. But what can we do about it? I'm an old man, and you're an old man, Marcello. The Americans and the Soviets will save us."

"Hopefully your heritage nations are coming, Luca." Marcello sighed heavily. His brown eyes glanced at the rug before looking between Luca and me for several moments. He swallowed. "There is a group in Lago Maggiore… a group committed to fighting the Nazi hold on our home and undercutting them at every turn. There are not many here, though there are similar groups around the region. I don't want to tell you more than you need to know. Mostly, I've come because we need your help."

Luca finally leaned forward. He looked awake for the first time in weeks.

"Italy can't beat the Third Reich, but we can make things difficult. I need you to write out shooting instructions and advice. You're an expert shot and a veteran. Many of us were not eligible for the army or never held a gun before. Anyone who would have made a halfway decent cadet is off fighting or captured by now. Next, we need guns and ammunition – everything and anything you can spare. Your guns will be better off in the hands of those who can use them than mounted on your walls and piled in the corners of rooms. Third, this is the most important: I must establish safe places to hide around the lake if our people find themselves in a predicament."

Buffo barked at the window, and we all jumped. Luca grabbed his shotgun. He and Marcello strode to the window.

"It's a pair of squirrels," Luca breathed. Gia clutched her chest, eyes closed, and inhaled with her whole frame. When Buffo kept barking, Luca grabbed him by the scruff of the back of his neck and dragged him to the hearth. "Sit."

Our husbands sat back down, gripping their knees to brace the weight shifting.

"I will write out instructions and train them on long-range, which is what you'll want. The first shots should be the only shots. Tell me where to be, and send three who can train the others."

"Thank you," Marcello said, his head bowed slightly.

"I'll be more helpful for ammunition than guns. I only have nine. Four rifles, one is a Carcano M1938 carbine and the other three Carcano M1891 Moschetto da Cavalleria used by my brothers and me for hunting. I can give you the two old M1891s, two handguns, a Glisenti Model 1910, and one of my Beretta Modello 1935. For ammunition, I have at least one hundred cartridges for the M1891s, and I think another… ninety or so cartridges I can offer between the other three models. Used well, it could be an effective supply."

"Thank you, brother."

"Taking that last action is also Franca's choice to make… there's considerable risk. I would have to create safe spots around the property. We would never bring someone into the house, but they could hide in the forest… Franca?"

I looked at Marcello and Gia.

"I'm not sure we should be involved further than providing supplies. What if they send us to the camps? Or they would save the trouble and kill us."

"I know I'm asking you to do something we won't be doing ourselves," Marcello began. We have to assume that the consequence of getting caught will be death. But I only ask because it could save the life of someone trying to tip the scales against the Reich in Verbania."

"If they use dogs to search?" Luca asked.

"Then they would find who they are looking for. But if we do nothing, what happens? They kill as they please. These young peacocks take and discard foreign women as they please. We have to make it difficult for them. I don't want them to have a single moment of peace. Even if they are standing on top of the world, a vulture will circle their heads above, and they will be terrified of when it will strike."

"At the cost of your life?" I asked. "Are you truly ready to die to cause them an hour's delay for dinner?"

"Yes," he said without hesitation. My husband nodded, too. Gia looked at me with hollow eyes – it was my choice.

"I don't want to hide anyone. I'm not sure Luca should train either; what if your untrained militants are captured and tortured? His name will surely come out."

"That may happen. We have grenades that every member of our group will wear while active. But capture is always possible."

"This seems disorganized, Marcello," I said.

"That's only because we are still organizing. I am satisfied with what you can give us and your training, Luca. But know I'm not the only person you know committed to fighting our oppressors. One of our nephews is involved, too."

"No! He can't be!" It could only be Imma's Niccolo with his limp. "He's not fast enough. You are setting him up to be a martyr! Tortured even!"

"He knows the risks, and he's chosen to help anyway. It's honorable."

"It's stupid!" Poor Niccolo, a man now but my youngest nephew always, was marked for death with his family leading him into the grave.

"It's time for a rest," Luca said. "You two must sleep here. You can't be out at night."

"Yes, thank you," Marcello said. The two men shook hands, and Gia and I went upstairs to make up the blue guest room.

"It's all right not to know, Franca," Gia whispered. "Not knowing means we still have a choice."

17

I saw the Leibstandarte soldiers tear down the highway toward the fork at the base of the lake that split the road in two directions toward Milano or Torino. Not all of them were leaving, but as many could be crammed in about ten vehicles – muscled arms were flopping out of every window – and the 1st Panzer Division's tank. I was watching from Enzo's old room, where Luca had set up a watchman's perch with a rifle loaded at the floor of the large window. We had taken to one of us sitting there and watching over the gate and road most of the time. We were only rewarded with jolts of breathtaking terror when we saw a pair of patrolmen walking the road or one of their vehicles breeze down the highway. Luca and I recorded every activity.

Two days later, our neighbor Massimo Boronnini came to tell us the resulting news from those southward-packed vehicles. Massimo's mother was half German; his appearance distilled the incongruent traits of German and Italian heritages. His head was blond and balding with age, though he had dark, long, combed-over arm hair. Massimo was tall, and his weight gain from age settled in the middle. He had one daughter from a marriage that ended a decade ago when his ex-wife moved back to her home country of Malta. She took the daughter Massimo saw once a year.

"Would you like some tea?" I offered. We sat in the dining room and sadly never used the table on the veranda for conversation anymore, even on beautiful days like this one.

"Si, si, grazie."

"Massimo, what happened? We heard the Leibstandarte massacred an entire town," Luca asked the huffing man.

"Well… you see… yes and no. There's a small town called Boves in the south of Piemonte. It's tiny. Near the French border and the Mediterranean coast. Can't be larger than Pallanza. It's very small–"

"All right, go on," Luca interrupted him. Massimo was given to excessive sweating.

"Survivors of the Italian Army have massed there. Our soldiers have mixed with armed resistance fighters committed to fighting the Nazi hold. There is word of a swelling resistance movement throughout Piemonte. I commend the partisans' tenacity, but it is foolish to think they can defeat the most organized military force ever if you ask me. It's trying to defeat an empire with fly bites. Now, those two groups have formed a small base in the mountains of Boves. It's very mountainous, you see, thickly wooded. The Reich would have to pursue them on foot, and at that point, they would be subject to traps. It's much harder when you don't know the terrain, and the Nazis don't, so of course, that gives our men at least one advantage—"

"Go on," Luca pressed.

"Well... where was I? The Leibstandarte has orders to disarm and neutralize anything left of the Italian Army. So, when word spread that our army was gathering near Boves, part of the Leibstandarte was dispatched there to find them. The partisans were in the mountains outside tiny Boves – the name even sounds French, so you can only imagine what it's like there. They were driven mad from starvation. They couldn't approach the residents of Boves because the Nazis had swarmed the town, not that the locals had plenty of food to give them anyways. Well, the partisans fired at the Nazi soldiers from the mountains. When the Nazis pursued them into the mountains, the Italians killed one and captured another two."

"How? Where did they hold them?"

"In the mountains somewhere. So the Leibstandarte try to rescue their two captured men. There's a shooting in the woods and one man dies on each side, but they fail to rescue the captured. The German soldiers drag the Italian fighter's body to the piazza of Boves and light the body on fire. Then, the leader of the Leibstandarte, Pieper was his name, begins negotiations for the captured men through Boves' priest. The one church there... the place is that small. The two men were released at Pieper's promise to spare the town." He looked at Luca, beginning to shrug until his hands rose and fell for shaking. "Can I smoke?"

Luca nodded. Massimo pulled out his carton of cigarettes and his lighter. After several lengthy inhales and exhales, he continued.

"But... they are liars. After they secured the two men, the Germans opened fire on the village. They say only about twenty or twenty-five people were killed. The fighters were in the hills, nowhere near the town. On their way out, the Germans set fire to the homes in Boves and other towns they came across. In total, over three hundred houses were burnt to nothing."

"The Leibstandarte did not find our forces in the mountains though?"

"No. They are still free to starve and freeze in the wilderness."

"They won't freeze for months yet," Luca said. "And the Leibstandarte?"

"They are regrouping in Lago Maggiore while the weather is nice."

"They can't be here for long. It seems they go where they are needed."

"I am sure you're right, Marinova. It's…" Massimo began to shake again. "It's devastating being…" The large man, sweating from lack of drink for two days, crossed his arms across his chest and gripped each shoulder as he shuddered.

"Surrounded? Exhausted?" Luca listed off, lighting a second cigarette for Massimo. He passed it to him.

"Thank you, thank you," he smoked for a minute or two before becoming still enough to speak again. The man was in terrible health and lived alone, though he had a sweetheart who stayed with him for weeks at a time. "It's devastating to be part German when my soul is Italian. I was educated in Berlin until I was twelve, you know. It feels like… or rather, I feel the shame of the predator and the unrest of the prey. I'm a live, fateless worm squirming in the dark belly of the bird, and I'm also the bird who can feel it moving around inside me. I'm perpetually nauseous. Maybe that doesn't make sense. Nothing makes sense anymore."

Luca patted Massimo on the back. I stood to fetch the bag of produce from the garden I gathered for him; he was one of about thirty people I was managing to help. I wondered if Luca was proud of being descended from the Soviets and the Americans. Did he feel like the worm or the cat spying the bird?

✺

The story of Boves traveled quickly, but the murders on our lake were slow to reach us. I barely left our property anymore. The local paper had become half-truthed and inconsistent. A couple of times a week, Luca went to Intra. He would be gone for an entire morning or afternoon and come back smiling, eager to be helpful around the house, and with more patience for Buffo than me.

Early in the occupation, the Leibstandarte arrested Jewish families, the old and young, and held fifty Jews in Hotel Meina on the western side of the lake. The imprisonment indicated to Luca that the Leibstandarte might have had unclear directions on how to handle Italian Jews. A choice, perhaps. We could not see Meina from the villa, but we often sailed there for lunch. The hotel was small with a windowless stucco front, though inside, there was a lush atrium, and in the back opened to a canopied restaurant overlooking the lake. The Italian Fascists, still loyal to the disappeared Mussolini, tipped off the Leibstandarte soldiers to the homes of local Jews. The eastern side of the lake only had my sister Arabella's Jewish banker, and the rumor was that he had fled into the hills on the dark morning of September 9, which meant Verbania did not have the same opportunity for duplicity as Stresa and the other western shore towns across the water.

Last week, the men, women, and children were removed one family at a time. They were taken a quarter mile into the woods and shot. The soldiers placed the bodies in sacks filled with stones, rowed the bodies out into the lake, and sunk them. The inhabitants of Isola Bella and Isola Pescatori, who had developed a watch and, while visited, had not been necessarily occupied, claimed that they saw people still alive with their hands and feet tied and thrown into the lake to drown.

❋

In October, Arabella's Jewish banker, Andrea Zappa, was found hiding in Pallanza with his wife and two children. His children were twelve and nine years old. The four of them were directed at gunpoint to the piazza outside of town hall in Intra and shot thirty-four times by three tall Leibstandarte soldiers. They left the bodies there on the cobblestones.

❋

Christmas and New Year passed. We had little news of what was happening on the war fronts—silence from our king and Prime Minister Badoglio, who were safe in the south. There was a delay in getting news of a German assault on the *Piemontese* and the sister towns dotting Lago Maggiore. Hope was difficult to hold; it seemed to pass back and forth between people. The infantry division that held three of Arabella's sons, Niccolo, Antonio, and Roberto, had disbanded into the mountains of Yugoslavia and likely fled to Bosnia after the armistice. Many had surrendered to imprisonment or German execution. There was always a rumor that our armies were regrouping. We could not know which fate Ara's sons met or were yet to meet. There were no letters from Paolo or Luigi either.

The massacres on the lake had slowed. There had only been a handful of Jews to find. And yet the Nazis stayed here for the winter, patrolling the streets in their long grey coats. Whenever I let myself look at them, I saw boys. *They are just boys.* Boys who behaved with precision in the streets but laughed loudly and drank deeply in our restaurants. They were pleased to be stationed here where there was no action, and the winter was mild. When I saw the light-haired boys gathered over a meal, telling their stories in German, they sat where my nephews and their friends should be.

18

Even in the wintertime, farmers and artisans brought their carts to Intra's piazza for a small market on Saturday afternoons. The piazza was a large, cobbled square with one side open to the lake that bore stone steps down to a minor bank, more incredible when the tide was low. The two parallel sides of the piazza were lined with nearly identical buildings, high and skinny, with various shops and restaurants beneath the residences above. The weekly market was our weekly chance to see family outside the home. The women whose husbands were away with the army could bring their children out of the apartment and into the crowd. Many children had stopped attending school, and the market was the time to see their friends. The vendors could make a little bit of money from their work in these times when people had little to spend.

Luca and I met Marcello, Gia, Lucia, Ginerva, Arabella, and a handful of her older grandchildren there on the second Saturday in February. The temperature wasn't terrible, but the wind made it an uncomfortable day. We strolled through every aisle and made a half-dozen purchases, including a pair of light blue cups and plenty of poultry for the week. We were not as wealthy as we once were, but we were still wealthier than most. Luca had been instilled with a princely view of spending: to benefit the laborers. He wanted to contribute to their homes and ensure that the effort of bringing and setting up their cart wasn't in vain.

"What else is there for you to buy?" Arabella yelled at Luca as Gia, Lucia, and Ginerva laughed each time Luca purchased something. It became a game for Marcello. Knowing Luca was likely to spend, Marcello presented items to him theatrically. Arabella's grandchildren chased one another and neighborhood children, crisscrossing the aisles in the space between carts.

"You could have a cart here, Franca," Gia repeated her usual encouragement to me. Lucia nodded.

"If I need to someday, maybe. For now, I enjoy giving it away. And anyway, I can't have Luca purchasing his produce."

As we turned toward the lake, we saw three Nazi soldiers sauntering toward us in the same aisle. The blonde boys left their long coats unbuttoned. The vendors denied them nothing but went silent as the boys weighed and examined each piece of produce.

They prodded one another to look at what they had found when a fruit or vegetable looked peculiar.

"The way they move is too precise," Luca whispered.

"They remind me of children," I spoke at an average volume. They were yards away and could not understand Italian anyway.

After strolling up and down the four aisles of carts twice, Lucia and Ginevra left us to meet their friends in a restaurant on the other side of the square. Marcello suggested the five of us move inside one of the restaurants to get out of the cold. We ordered several pizzas to share before Marcello and Luca went to the bar for espresso. Arabella finally felt she could speak about the politics of living with her five daughters-in-law.

"After Paolo was born, I always wanted a daughter. Every time I was pregnant, I prayed to the Virgin Mary for a daughter. *Just one, please, just one.* But I was not meant to be a mother to daughters. I don't know how Mama did it. I don't know how you do it, Gia. Girls always have something wrong! If everything is alright, then they have to be sad about something that happened long ago or worry that something terrible will happen in the future. My home is in constant drama!

"I'm starting to think the house would settle if I sent Carina back to her parents in Pallanza. But they don't have the money to feed her and those three little children. She always cries, shuts herself in her room alone, and misses meals, declaring that she knows Antonio will not come home. It's challenging to get her to do her share of the housework. She has already decided she is a widow, which sets the other ones off. It tears at their hope my boys will return.

"Rosmunda is cruel to Mia behind my back. I'm trying to catch her at it because poor Mia is a sweetheart. She was orphaned so young, you know, and has nowhere else to go. She and Roberto weren't married very long before the war started. Little Roberto only met his father for several months before he left with the army – and now the boy is four without a single memory of his father! Mia has done a lovely job with him, though. Rosmunda is jealous that I gave Mia and Little Roberto a bedroom to themselves when Rosmunda shares her room with her four children. I think Rosmunda goads Gabriella to be unkind toward Mia, too. I've found Mia washing their children's clothes more than once.

Gemma stays out of it but yells at Carina's children too much. They are by far the worst behaved – as I said, Carina doesn't watch them closely – but it feels like they can't do anything without Gemma screaming at them. Kicking any of them out would damn them to starvation, but just when I think it can't go on forever, they begin fighting again."

"At least it's a distraction from everything," Gia said. "Maybe you should insist they find jobs? Then they could save up some money, get out of the house each day, and be too tired to fight each other. There is plenty of work to be done with the men away. Lucia and Ginevra have worked at the post office for two years."

"Not all women are like Mama. Most girls want to marry and not work. This group has no interest in working for money. Or even in the home. I have them operating the stationery store downstairs, which is doing as well as anywhere since everyone wants to write letters to their men who don't write back."

We paused a moment. Her tone almost mocked the wives of the soldiers hoping for their husbands, yet her sons were five of those men. The pizzas were set on the table, and my husband and Marcello returned to their seats beside us. The *pizza sopressata* was warm and delectable. The crushed tomatoes sang of summer. The salty bites of thick salami had the edges toasted to crunchy perfection. I hadn't eaten a meal in a restaurant in months, at least not since the armistice. Everyone at the table must have felt the same pleasure, for our conversation dimmed.

There were three quick gunshots outside.

We looked at one another. A pause. A fourth piercing shot. Luca and Marcello, among other men in the restaurant, rushed toward the door. Arabella covered her ears and looked at me, her wide eyes multiplying her wrinkles. Her grandchildren were out there. Gia reached for Marcello but was already pushing for a view of the piazza.

Then, there were dozens more shots fired.

"Get under the table!" Luca shouted at us. We shuffled to the ground in a jumble. The men at the window covered each other as they sank below the window in a mound.

A bullet pierced straight through that window to find a portrait on the opposite wall. Arabella screamed inches from my ear. With the hole in the window, we could hear screaming, and with each new shot, my sisters and I squeezed each other tighter, willing for the safety of ours outside. Were Lucia and Ginevra slumped in a restaurant as well? We had left Arabella's grandchildren to scurry among the aisles with their friends.

The shooting stopped. I opened my eyes but dared not move. There was shouting in German.

"Please don't!" A man's voice quivered in Italian.

The answer was a single gunshot.

The restaurant door flew open. The barrels of guns entered before the German soldiers carrying them. We were commanded to exit with our hands above our shoulders. The cobblestones pressed the bones of my knees as I was forced to kneel between Luca and Marcello. My sisters were on the other side of Marcello. Ara's eyes searched for her grandchildren. Gia looked at the soldiers as Marcello watched the young men barking at each other, everyone trying to understand what had happened. All the buildings were emptied of people as the soldiers lined up the people at the edges of the piazza. It felt like all of Pallanza was in Intra today. A team of five searched buildings as about twenty soldiers found themselves overlooking one hundred people of all ages, though mostly women, kneeling. Was this the resistance putting Lucia, Ginevra, and Ara's young grandchildren in harm's way? I craned to see a body or blood, any indication that the bullets had found life, but my poor eyesight and the standing carts hid any answers held there. If any shot had found a Nazi soldier, they would begin executing.

I prayed that if executions were to happen, they begin with us: the old. *It can be me, God. Dear Christ, it can be me.*

The longer we knelt, the more it became clear how indecisive these German boys were without instructions. They might just kill us out of incertitude. The boy pacing nearest me shouted over to his comrade, huffed, and then yelled at the gentleman four places down from Luca for trying to close his coat. Down the block, one of the soldiers lifted men by the collars of their coats and screamed in their faces as a fellow soldier pointed a gun at their families to deter any acts of defiance. The language barrier made them angrier, and each time he threw a man to the ground, he would render a blow to the man's face, gun in hand.

The crowd was unarmed and feeble. The winds blew colder off of the lake. Questioning followed by beatings went on for a time. We waited for them to arrive at us. What would they do when all have been questioned? Everyone knew the legend of Boves. Then, one of the soldiers, a tall younger man with his coat buttoned high, called several others to him at the lake's edge. The tall man blew a whistle. *Here it is.* I looked at the boy pacing over us. He raised his handguns to us on the mercilessly cold and hard stones, fingers on the triggers, and motioned for us to leave. He said in Italian: "Go home." No one said goodbye. Arabella peeled off from us. Gia and Marcello ambled toward their home on the hill. Luca and I rose and left.

It was a long walk home. We didn't stop. My shoulders were perched at my ears, expecting gunshots to ring behind us, even to meet our backs. But no. There was only a terrifying silence around us and between us.

※

Marcello found out later that the initial three shots were fired into the piazza from upper-story windows of the buildings lining the square. The shots were aimed at the Germans. There were about eight shots fired by the Germans into the crowd, and another dozen were sent into the buildings. Not a single bullet found a person: Nazi or Italian. The German soldiers ducked behind carts. They were unable to identify definitively which buildings the shots came from. German reinforcements flooded the piazza in less than three minutes.

Luca returned the following day to pay for our pizzas, find the things he had bought that afternoon and left behind in the restaurant. There was a rumor that the Germans had detained a retired fisherman for questioning. A curfew was put in place: no one was out after dark. Our judgment had led us to that rule since the occupation began, and it was natural to be home given the winter cold, but we felt more enclosed than ever.

19

"Franca, come here."

Luca was sitting on Enzo's old room floor with all four guns. We had moved the bed so the two woven chairs could be positioned comfortably at the window facing the gate.

"What is it?"

"Hold this." He placed a handgun in my palm. I tried to pull my hand back, but he let go quickly, so I grabbed it to keep it from falling. "We are going to hide two of them around the house. But first, I have to teach you how to use it."

"I don't want to learn."

"Why? It scares you?"

"I don't want to make anyone feel the way I felt when those guns at the piazza were pointed at the people I love. These things are bad."

"It will keep you alive. They can create time when there wouldn't be any otherwise. What if having a gun could help Lucia or Ginevra escape something terrible?"

"You think you are going to defeat the Nazis with four guns? Luca, if you ever even lifted this where they could see, they would kill you and me without blinking!"

"Can I just show you how? I would feel better knowing you knew how to use it. Here, this is the chamber," he pointed to the long top, "where you load the bullets like this," he pulled to slide it up, revealing it to have six sleeping bullets inside. "The safety is here. You always keep it safe unless you're preparing to use it."

He stood behind me and wrapped my hands entirely around the grip. I hated its weight.

"You hold here for stability." He tightened my left fingers around the base. "It will jerk up when you shoot. I wish you could practice to feel the kickback... This finger," he lifted my right pointer finger and placed it on the trigger, "will be on the trigger. It's best not to touch the trigger unless you are sure about shooting."

"So never again then."

"I wish I could take you somewhere to practice, but we would be surrounded in minutes. I will keep my shotgun up here. I am placing this one behind the English dictionary on the bookshelf."

"Why did you choose that book?"

"It's large enough. And I pray Mama is watching over us. Maybe making it so we never use it, as I barely used that dictionary. I will move the other shotgun to the hallway by the front door. When I am here at home, I will keep the second handgun in my waistband."

"Do you think that's necessary?"

He looked at me. We heard a black German car flying north on the highway outside the window. It was like reaching your hands into the sink before seeing a roach lording over the basin.

June 1944

20

The sun returned to the lake. The daylight extended the curfew. My sisters and their families came to stay at our home more frequently. Arabella's grandchildren swam, and many would stay for a night or two. I felt awful for the children of Carina and Antonio. In the spring, we learned that Antonio had been killed in one of the German onslaughts following the armistice. Carina had received a letter from Torino written on the word of survivors who had managed to make it to the region's capital. Our family held a memorial for him after a Tuesday morning mass, followed by a large, sad meal at the Terracci residence. The time seemed less dedicated to my nephew and more to his wife's mourning and Arabella's rising fear that there could be more memorials coming. My husband said that the best thing we could do for them was to encourage them to go to our home so we could feed the families, let the children enjoy the water, and send the women on walks through the wild garden. We only had our home to give.

I loved it when Lucia visited. She said she could relax at our home, which is so far removed and more private than anywhere else. She would stay for five days at a time. It was easier not to worry about the curfew at all. My niece was going through similar things I had at her age but carried it all with far more grace than me. She was nearly forty and without a child. Her husband had been gone for over four years. She feared that she would lose him and never have a baby.

"I wish I just had one," Lucia said on the terrace over our lemonade. "Like Mia with her son. Mia walks around with this light even though no one has heard from Roberto in ten months."

"She's not allowed to wallow."

"Exactly. I think that's kind of nice. I'm so bored of myself! I want to take care of someone. I would take in a dog, but Papa would never let me keep one in his house."

"You can take Buffo," I offered.

"No, no, Auntie. I couldn't. I know how much you love him."

The stupid dog was tracking a butterfly. Rather than moving his eyes only, his gaze moved from the neck.

"He's an idiot," I laughed.

※

A couple of days later, Lucia was still staying with us. We were sunning ourselves on the dock, discussing how the Allies reached Roma yesterday. The Germans retreated from Southern Italy to hold the northern half of the country east to west, from the coasts of Emilia Romana to Tuscany.

"Zia Franca! Zio Luca!" Patricio Terracci, one of little Paolo's children, called loudly at our gate. I couldn't hear him from the other side of the villa. Finally, Luca spotted the boy trying to climb the gate from Enzo's window. Luca brought young Patricio to us on the dock. He looked at Lucia as he spoke.

"The Leibstandarte has arrested Zio Marcello. They say he is in the resistance."

I looked at Luca over the boy's shoulder.

"Where did they take him?" Lucia asked, pulling herself to stand over the lawn chair.

"*Intra stazione di polizia.*"

"We must go," she looked at me.

"Change first, Lucia. We can't be in our bathing suits."

She ran up the lawn and into the house. Luca helped me stand, and we followed her. I put on a summer dress and walking shoes. I tried to comb my hair back, but Lucia stormed into my bathroom and demanded we leave now—we were still a fair distance away.

"Patricio, you should stay here," Luca mumbled. He was leaning on the hallway console, waiting for Lucia and me.

The boy shook his head and turned to me for help.

"No, Auntie, my mother will want me home."

"Stay here, Patricio. Your grandmother will be happy you're in Suna today."

I did not want to witness it, and I didn't even want to hear about terrible things. No people were standing in the streets of Pallanza, only those who walked in the same direction as us. At the bend where the hospital gave way to the bridge between Pallanza and Intra, little Patrizio sprinted past us, shouting: "Sorry, Auntie!"

By the time we reached Intra, there was no need to go to the police headquarters. We could hear the unrest coming from the crowd gathered at the piazza. Lucia searched the crowd for her mother. My husband, a few inches taller than me, couldn't hold his head up when he saw forty-one men, too young, too old, and too infirm, and two women standing in a long line along the lake with signs tied around their necks.

We followed Lucia through the crowd, maybe sixty people staring anxiously. Neighbors pointed us in Gia's direction. Ginevra was not with her. My little sister was a silent flame, barely flickering. She had a bruise forming along the side of her face. She let us hug her but said nothing and would not break her gaze from her husband. My niece held her mother's hand. Luca placed one hand on Gia's shoulder and the other on my back.

Marcello was near the end on the left, with a sign tied around his neck that mockingly said, "Are these people the liberators of Italy or just bandits?"

Tears flooded my eyes as I looked from face to face. I recognized half of them, men older than Luca and adults who were ill children at the hospital when I worked there. Luca squeezed my shoulder. *Be strong for Gia and Lucia.* I felt that if I took a full breath, I would weep.

The crowd stood for an hour. I shifted the weight of me between each foot. The sun fell closer to kissing Stresa's skyline. What would happen if we were all still here at curfew?

The tension was unbearable. Knowing the tension would crack was worse. I wrapped my arms around Luca and plunged my face into his chest. After taking a few suppressed, heavy breaths against his chest, I became still enough to feel a handgun strapped to Luca's hip beneath his jacket.

I leaned sharply into the gun to show him I was aware of it. My eyes panicked into his.

"No." I mouthed.

He looked at me with a soldier's stare. I was too late. Decisions were already in motion.

His bearded face touched my ear, and he breathed, "I won't go on my knees again."

The sun dipped below the mountain line. Two soldiers, one from each end of the line of detainees, checked their handguns. Luca dropped his arms around me.

The silent and still crowd became hunched forward. Calling out to loved ones began. The line of the condemned naturally looked toward the officers. The crowd pleaded for their gaze back. Some couldn't hear.

"Marcello!" Gia called out.

"Papa! Papa! No!" Lucia began crying now.

Marcello looked at them and took a breath.

The two officers took long, single-handed aim at the two Italians on each end of the line. The first two shots went off at the exact moment. There was screaming all around us. Another twenty young Nazis aimed warningly at the crowd.

Marcello's eyes met Luca's over my shoulder.

Two more shots; two more bodies dropped.

Marcello's eyes met mine, and he smiled a little. My heart stole two beats when the following shots were fired. Then he looked at Gia and Lucia until the officer obscured their view and shot Marcello once in the head.

Luca knelt to be near us as the three of us crumpled to the ground. We stayed there until the dead could be collected. I was terrified to look upon Marcello's face, imagining it could only be mangled and gruesome. But it was not. The single wound in his forehead was narrow. It took all four of us to carry his body to Arabella's, the closest home and where Ginevra was. I went inside first to warn those in the living room who would not want to see. We stayed at Arabella's for the night.

※

The next morning, I awoke with tight muscles in my neck and lower back from sleeping poorly on Arabella's thinly cushioned couch. I couldn't turn my head to the left for the first couple of hours of the morning. I didn't complain about it to anyone.

Last night, Gia cleaned his forehead as best she could and changed him into a giant suit of Paolo Terracci's that Arabella had never had the chance to pass down to her sons. Gia insisted she performed this all herself and refused assistance, though she hadn't expected maneuvering around the rigor mortis. When Mama died, Arabella and my grandmothers changed her into her final resting clothes, and I knew about the stiffness of lifeless bodies through my work at the hospital.

Gia slept through the night with Arabella. She slept so long that Lucia and Ginevra eventually woke their mother so she could see Marcello's body moved from the long kitchen table to the casket Rosmunda's sons brought home. They were nervous Gia might be disoriented if she entered the living room to see him moved to the casket. She rose and watched the body be moved by Luca and little Paolo's oldest son.

"We need to call Father Caruso," Gia mumbled.

"Father Nicastro will be here this evening," Arabella answered. "He is visiting all of the families of the deceased today in Intra. Father Caruso is visiting the families in Pallanza."

"I want Father Caruso. Can he come tomorrow?" Gia asked. She looked hollow and old, exhausted and parched.

"I'll send someone to arrange it," Arabella consented softly. "What about the mourners? Many will come this afternoon. Imma and her family are coming now."

Gia looked at her dress.

"I need something else to wear."

"Mama," Ginevra said, "I can go home and fetch you a bag."

"Thank you, Ginevra," Arabella answered. "That would be great. And you will all stay here until the funeral the day after tomorrow. Gemma and Gabriella, would you go to stay at Gia and Marcello's home? There will be plenty of room for you there, and you can be sure she returns to a clean home."

"Anyone can stay at our villa, too," I added.

"Anyone who wants to walk back and forth from Suna can go with Zia Franca," Arabella announced derisively.

"I would like to rest a while longer," Gia said to no one.

"Little Antonio – close the casket," Arabella ordered.

"No!" Gia yelled at her great-nephew, who lurched toward the casket. "It stays open."

Arabella nodded and returned to the kitchen. Gabriella and Gemma left to pack and gather their children for Gia's house. I walked Gia back to bed.

She was lying under two quilts. When I looked at her, my eyes welled.

"I'm so very sorry, Gia."

"He was calm. It's what he chose." She patted my hand. Then she whispered: "They didn't get all of them."

I closed the bedroom door behind me. Imma and her daughters were weeping at the side of Marcello's body. All of the people in the house made me feel claustrophobic. It felt like we had been at Arabella's for a week. I couldn't believe Lucia and I were relaxing on the dock only yesterday.

Imma rushed to me, kissed my cheeks, and interrogated me.

"You were there? What happened? We heard the resistance members were executed at sunset."

I nodded. As I opened my mouth to answer her, I saw Luca sitting on the small terrace with Niccolo, hunched over.

21

In the days that followed, Luca crafted a small sailboat. He hadn't built one for a few years. Years ago, he told me that working in the boatshed in the summer was like surrendering oneself to the heat of hell. The structure only had a side entrance and a large door for boats to exit cleanly on the lake. While he cranked the door high, the summer breeze wasn't enough to keep him from sweating through his shirt by mid-morning. He needed frequent breaks to step outside, place his hands on his hips to hold his upper body high and slow his heart rate. Still, it was a way to hypnotize himself—the rich boy with a poor boy's work ethic.

I spent years annoyed when he would devour his lunch with as few words as possible and promptly leave me alone with Mary to return to the boatshed. However, seeing him revive his passion for his craftsmanship, I ached to prepare him a special lunch each day. I wanted to make him smile for a moment. He often sat shirtless for lunch on the terrace, his old skin sagging in sweeping ripples from his muscles. Luca walked up the yard to the table as tall as ever. But then I might see his hand shaking as it gripped the fork or a flinch of tooth pain while chewing. These sunny days of artful sandwiches on the terrace would not last forever.

*

We were sitting at each head of the old terrace table. Luca was whittling. I was reading by candlelight more and more as the sun, long behind the Stresa mountains, searched the western skies. Buffo lay on the cool tile with his front legs straight out to frame his face.

The British had taken Elba, Assisi, and Perugia in the past few days. We would be their last stop on their way northward to pierce the underbelly of the Reich, but they were coming.

"Once they liberate us, I will join them and help them to Germany," Luca said.

"The British and Americans don't want you."

"We'll see. They may need help. Once they get to Piemonte, our forces in the hills will accompany them in removing the Germans from Italy. The resistance will reinforce them where possible."

"The resistance won't be wanted either. The best thing they can do is to let the Nazis implode as they see their end coming."

"The mission of the resistance is relentless disruption. The best thing they can do is capitalize on the little mistakes the Nazis make during this time and weaken the Leibstandarte so the Allies may free more people quicker."

I looked at him, intent to argue. What did Gia, Lucia, and Ginevra achieve from Marcello's sacrifice? He tried to fight them, and now Gia would have to live another two decades without her husband. A rage burned in my chest over Luca's disregard for his own life. At least Gia had her daughters; I would have no one.

Luca held his right hand up to me and pointed to his left ear with his left hand.

The hum of the Nazi transport vehicles on the highway. They had been darting north to south and south to north more frequently than usual.

Luca looked at me, startled.

The trucks came closer. I felt it before I heard it—a gunshot from the hills. Before the first echoes finished singing, there was another. The trucks skidded, slamming on the brakes; there was the sound of a collision of metal on metal. Another shot. Every muscle and organ in my body recoiled. Luca's face fell. He was without breath; his mind had forgotten his body. Buffo stared in the direction of the noise but made no move. All three of us froze.

Then came the hellfire. Every German soldier on the transport must have unloaded twenty rounds into the forest above the highway. Luca lunged sideways and pulled me by the wrist under the table. I was clumsy and landed on my other hand and knees on the tile. Then, – the sound that could have been my belief breaking – the high scream of our gate's metal hinges tearing from the property walls. Buffo took off toward the garden.

Luca pulled my face to his and kissed my forehead, but I barely felt the touch.

"It will all be well, Franca."

I couldn't think.

Six soldiers, weapons raised, approached the terrace from the north side of the villa. I couldn't understand their shouting. One hand grabbed me by my hair and dragged me out from under the table.

Two soldiers ripped Luca from the ground and searched him as a third pointed his gun at Luca's head. The soldier pulled a handgun from Luca's waistband and placed it in his own. Luca twitched, and the ugly one holding him reflexively hit him with a clenched fist.

"No!"

They turned to me and shouted things I couldn't understand until I was turned around and pulled toward the front gate. I struggled meekly but fought less when I could see that Luca was being dragged behind me in the same direction. Luca's hands wiped his nose, where they were now covered in blood. They put us on our knees in the driveway. One of the armored vehicles had rammed through the front gate. Two of the trucks on the highway were still there, fishtailed on the road. There must have been a dozen men in the three trucks. There was one body of a young German soldier on the ground in the road. Then there was another boy, *so young*, carried within our gates where two soldiers tended to him; they were trying to stop the bleeding in his thigh by wrapping it. It was bleeding profusely. The bullet must have hit the boy's femoral vein. If the leg wasn't amputated and the vein singed, he would die in the next several minutes.

The boy was lightheaded and moaning through clenched teeth. Over his shoulder, a dozen Germans brought our ten closest neighbors through the gates. At the front of them was burly Massimo Boronnini and his slender lover, an amateur opera singer named Eva. Following him were the two families that lived south of us: the Marchetti family of three, a father, mother, and teenage daughter, and then five members of the Santoro family, the young mother, and her four children between the ages of six and eleven. Jiovanni Santoro had been reported killed in action three years ago. All were looking at the ground. The summer night chill saturated my body.

The German boy yelled frantically to his comrades for help. None were medics. Looking at him made me tremble. I studied and worked to alleviate suffering without discrimination. It never felt like a choice before.

The Santoro family was to Luca's left. Massimo knelt beside me, with Eva to his right and the Marchetti family on the other side of her. When all twelve Italians were on their knees, a young man with broad shoulders and a broken nose strode over to us.

"This is your house?" He pointed at us and said in imperfect Italian.

Luca nodded. By now, he had let his blood-stained hands fall to his sides.

"I've been desiring a tour for a long time."

Thirty years younger than us, the man knelt down to be inches from Luca's face.

"Are you hiding any rebels on this property?"

"No," my husband said.

"I believe our dogs are better than any Italian. In my experience, all Italians are swindlers. Our search dogs will tell us whether you are telling the truth. Will you give me a tour until they arrive?"

"No," my husband repeated calmly.

The soldier shouted a command over his shoulder and pointed to the villa. Four men walked up the driveway and entered our home. The injured boy yelled out again. I couldn't look at him for being mesmerized by the lights appearing from rooms in my house, for every possession to race through my mind.

Massimo's breathing was very labored. *I will die to the sound of his breath.* The soldier who ordered the men inside lit a cigarette and passed it to the injured boy, who was begging to be transported to someone who could save him. Massimo leaned in to try to inhale the smoke released.

They emerged from the villa carrying as much as they could: a box of dinner china, sculptures by Pasquale pinned between elbows and ribs, paintings by Pasquale's acquaintances, tall candelabras, silk pillows from the couch. Luca sat back on his heels. His chest collapsed over his solar plexus.

"Ah, yes, very nice, very nice," the man said in Italian. From the sitting room lights, I could make out the name on his uniform: Prinz.

Another dozen soldiers entered our house over and over to take more and more. They found the wine cellar. One lifted the trunk Pasquale's wife had sent by himself – had he even looked inside? The prince's chess set. Rugs, lamps, longcase clocks, tablecloths, books, art. Finally, the shimmering chandelier that was Luca's most treasured part of the dining room. Luca stared into his dirt-caked palms. He was overcome. *He's given himself to humiliation.* Tears came from my old, exhausted eyes. I wanted his attention, to speak comfort to his heartbreak, but he was elsewhere.

"Oh, little old wife," Prinz cooed to me. "Don't cry. Is there anything else we missed that you think we might like?" He was shown a box of the prince's crystal glasses. The injured boy had gone quiet, watching the parade of our home through an overpowering stupor. "I already have plenty of drinkware," he waved it away. The older man holding the box, perhaps the oldest of all, hoisted it to eye level before throwing it to the ground. He repeatedly kicked the box, shattering the glasses into thousands of glass particles.

At that moment, Buffo surfaced from the garden at a pleasant prance and walked up to our party. Prinz and the men shoving and packing the Marinova heirlooms into the transport vehicles stopped to look at the mut.

"Go!" I yelled to scare the stupid creature back into the forest.

"Hi there, friendly dog." Prinz knelt to pet the dog, who sat happily beside him, panting. *Betrayer.*

Then, the dog walked over to one of the trees to the left of the gate. Buffo proceeded to dig at the base of the tree. Luca continued to gaze into his hands; he didn't know. Prinz walked over. With only some light brushing of dirt, Prinz lifted the box of Anastasia's jewelry from the ground. He opened the bag, opened the box, and then lifted the ruby necklace from the box. His eyes, the sparkle in those rapacious slits, settled on mine.

He seemed pleased enough until a soldier disrupted his gratification by holding out the notebook we had been using to record Nazi movements along the highway. On the other hand, he held Luca's precious shotgun.

Prinz's face turned. He shouted an order at his men. Meier paused. Prinz repeated himself, gripping the box as he screamed louder.

Then Meier, the tallest of them all, came from behind one of the trucks with two large pales. He dutifully carried them past us toward the house. Gasoline.

"No," I croaked. "Don't! Please, don't!"

I could feel the gasoline splash on the marble floors in the foyer as if it were being poured on me. The smell was unnatural.

Luca stared at the mixture of blood and dirt on his hands. The tall man emptied the pales. Meier took a few strides back from the house and lit a cigarette. The cigarette ember rose a few inches behind the man's shoulder and flew gracefully beyond the heavy front door. The fire blossomed instantly, licking the line of gasoline at first breath.

Minutes later, the main floor rooms of the house were lit from the inside. The couch in the sitting room illuminated the shelves of books. The ship on the stained glass window above the front door shone with the glory of light. The fire swelled around the dining room table without the chandelier to play its final dance on the ceiling. The marble staircase did not crumble, but the wooden railing ferried the fire upstairs. The Santoro children made sounds of awe. The sight captured the moment. The fire's strength devoured the house's façade and the overpowering smoke within meant that our glimpses of the inside had concluded.

The dog trotted off into the garden. They let him. My eyes held the destruction of our home, of Luca's family home. *I have nothing else to take.* But that wasn't true; the Marchetti girl and young Eva were still there. There was still us.

A series of unexpected small explosions came from the other side of the house. Massimo gasped. The fire choked the life from the electrical outlets; multiple pilot lights of kitchen appliances were combusting. We could hear debris hit the lake. By now, the fire stood and stretched to the sky from the height of the roof. The smoke drifted continuously over the lake and caught the fire's light. These false clouds internalized and floated the light.

"Stand!" Prinz barked.

We all shuffled to our feet.

Prinz pointed to one of the Santoro boys, the six-year-old, and ordered, "Pick a number between one and four."

His mother spun to him, maybe to order him not to answer the officer or answer for him, but the boy quickly responded in a high tone as if there were a correct answer: "Three?"

Luca squeezed my hand. I looked at him.

"Thank you," he mouthed to me.

I opened my mouth to answer, but Prinz lifted his pistol and shot the eight-year-old Santoro girl in the head. She was the third in line. Her mother screamed. The Marchetti mother began screaming too. Massimo cried out. Eva started shaking in a stationed panic attack, wrapping her arms around her torso.

Prinz took a couple of steps toward us. Luca, sixth in line, let go of my hand and looked Prinz in the eye. Prinz pulled the trigger, and my husband's body fell to the ground. My knees forgot themselves, and I fell to the ground with him.

Another shot. Eva's body hit the ground. Three other soldiers had to pry the Marchettis off of their daughter before the fourth and final shot took the girl's life.

"One death for every shot fired by the rebels tonight."

The soldiers returned to their vehicles and left us there.

The Santoros took turns holding the little girl's body. The Marchettis wept over their only child. Massimo fell onto all fours and vomited inches from me. I stared at my left hand, illuminated by the pulsing light of the villa's fire, and wept for where the blood and dirt had passed from Luca's hand to mine.

22

The Pallanza volunteer firefighters, the old and fragile, put out the fire. They strung a hose from the lake to spray the house until they could collapse the roof to suppress the fire. Ash rained on the garden.

"We'll take good care of him." One of the firemen, Vincenzo Laudi, the husband of Sofia Esposito, assured me as they took Luca's body with the other three safely to the hospital morgue. They also took the body of the German boy left behind as a courtesy to me.

"Franca, you have to let me escort you to Imma's," insisted Vincenzo.

"I can't leave my home," I muttered.

"You have nowhere to sleep. Sofia would never let me leave you here."

"Go, Vincenzo," I sighed. "I have Luca's brother's art studio up the hill. My sisters will be here as soon as they hear. I will be alright for a couple of hours alone. Please escort the Santoros home instead."

I waited until everyone was gone before letting my feet lead me to the old studio.

I woke up on the floor of Pasquale's studio alone at sunrise. I slept on my back on the rug by the hearth. My heart remembered the night before my mind. There was a bruise on my right wrist from when Luca pulled me underneath the terrace table.

I descended the hill to see the wreckage in the light. The prince's office and library made it through the fire. From the long wall of windows facing west, I could see right into the pile of beams mixed with possessions disregarded by the Nazis. I let the firemen take Luca's body for now, but he would have to be returned to be buried in the Marinova gardens. This is where he belonged, at home and with me. Perhaps there would be a walk from the funeral mass in Pallanza to the burial in Suna, a reversal of our wedding procession.

With the way the house had caved into the middle, I entered the library through the lakeside window. I just needed to be in there for a moment. I needed to hurry before word spread, and my sisters came looking for me.

I dragged a step ladder from the boathouse to beneath the library window and pushed it open. From there, I leaned over the ledge and used my weight to tip forward into the room. Many books had been thrown on the floor. Covers had been torn off their binding. Pages flew about the back of the room from the lake's breeze. I looked to the bottom shelf, where there was an untouched row of dictionaries. Shifting the Marinova collectibles around, I felt the cool steel of the handgun Luca had hidden there. I threw it out the window before climbing out myself.

The weapon was heavier than I remembered. Spiritually, I was reconciled to the task, but I wasn't confident in the mechanics of whether I could do it. By the sun's position on the water, I could tell it was nearly six o'clock.

I walked the garden and forest by the studio back and forth. Then I searched around the other side of the villa near the wine cellar entrance, and there he was. The dog was sunbathing on the broken terracotta tile. When he heard me approach, he looked up. I aimed as he stayed exactly where he was. Pulling the trigger, I exhaled, *"Fire."*

Part 4

October 1945
Ontex, France

1
Petyr II

  The room my father lay dying in faced west. This evening, he was lying on his back with one lumpy pillow supporting his head and neck. His frail legs bent at the knees under the top sheet and thin quilted blanket. Papa's study, now converted into his first-floor bedroom, was the last room to be immersed in the dark. I watched the sunset without interruption until Papa motioned for me to draw the curtains closed.

  It became my habit to keep the electric lights off as long as possible to preserve his eyes from straining. The thought that this was his last sunset had crossed my mind too many times to strike much fear. His body operated at its lowest degrees: able to swallow (not chew), digest, and excrete. It seemed awful. His decline to this strengthless and hollowed state was slow. Abilities dissolved piecemeal but, once lost, were never recovered: walking, writing, reading, standing, feeding himself, coherent speech.

  I first discovered Papa was "old" when I entered grade school and saw the other parents were bustling about quickly, without sunspots, and commanding their children at every turn. Other kids told me Papa was old. Still, the word "old" didn't insult me until I could see his strength decide independently when it was available for his use. He began complaining about spending more time indoors once he could no longer withstand high summer heat. He struggled to stand after kneeling in the garden for ten minutes. Years later, I saw the truth that some of the classmates who used to tease me about whether my father was my grandfather had fathers at home who had been maimed in the Great War and required more caretaking over a greater length of time than my ailing ninety-six-year-old father. It pained me to think as a child that my father would not be present for the majority of my life or possibly not even into adulthood at all. I never asked for a little brother or sister, and I never got one. Mama was still beautiful enough to remarry when the time came. She was better suited to the role of wife than mother, which is unfortunate because she has proven herself a terrible wife repeatedly.

In the year since the Second World War concluded, Ontex has nurtured a communal glorification of predictability and a shared mission to reinstate it into daily life. Little causes for celebration are amplified. I wish I could say I am immune to the euphoria, but I have fallen for a woman and asked her to marry me. She is eager to build a family to replace the one she lost when the Nazis shelled homes as they moved through Ontex. When she speaks of her older brother Phillipe, her eyes fill as if time had no alchemical mastery over grief. I couldn't mirror a tenth of that torment when speaking of Luca's death if I tried. We had never met. It was a death comprehended but not felt. There was also the loss of the large house on Lago Maggiore. The villa fell under the precept of "mine," but Papa sent the title to Franca. He was granting his late third son a favor, but the decision cleaved me from the lion's share of any possible inheritance. I had assumed that Papa was not fond of Franca due to the absence of grandchildren, as he mumbled intermittently how it was a mathematical farce that three married sons could collectively produce zero heirs. He said that *maison* wasn't worth anything, omitting that the land undeniably was and that he would never have the capital to rebuild at this stage. In Franca's letter, confirmed by another lakeside neighbor who wrote Papa a condolence letter regarding Luca, the house was destroyed, a charred pile of rubble. For him, it was one more amputation to his whittling holdings.

As a child, I would tell Papa I would give him a grandson, but he would rebuke me: "You probably won't. And you have to be ok with that. Daughters are a blessing. They don't hold back with their affection. They show you how important you are to them. It is very serious, being the custodian of your daughters' happiness."

I was surprised by his unexpected generosity toward Franca when she had lost everything else. He barely spoke about his children by name and nearly never spoke of Franca singularly; usually, she was tightly wrapped in "they" and "them." Even my mother, who desired Italian property tremendously, would say, over the years, "Why do you let them live there?" Signing over the property to Franca betrayed the egoic prospect that I might someday build on it. The month following the gift, each time I was in the same room as Papa, I burned with the thought: *why wouldn't you give me every advantage you could?* With seventy-seven years between us, he has little time to square me away for a life worth living.

Unlike his other children, his daughters had him as their societal peak. His time with his sons coincided with his physical and financial prime. Only inheritance could balance the scales for me. Even then, I would always be on the losing side. Money is not a proper consolation for the child who buries a parent early in life, but without the Suna hectares and gardens, there was little to leave me. I was a prince by title but not in wealth, status, or opportunity.

His breathing tonight was not as resolute.

It's hard to remember that this feeble old man lying on the bed was once tenacious. Our neighbor lent us the thin top blanket. Madame Desmarais was an old widow who carried a kind affection for Papa for as long as I could remember. When I met my fiancé Celestine for dinner, she would sit by Papa's side and feed him or read the paper to him while Mama was flitting about. She told me nine members of her family died peacefully beneath that blanket. I thanked her, but anyone who knows him well would know that Papa's not a man to do anything peacefully. If he could, he would have me fetch him a glass of Cognac, and he would sip it twice, slowly, before swigging the remainder. Then he'd stand up, answer my mother's desertion with a divorce, find a fourth wife, and begin another family. He would be the patron deity of starting families in new places for eternity: the god of reckless creation.

"Var!" He croaked.

I put my book down and turned the lamp on. He didn't blink – the doctor had warned of the blindness fading in and out. I tipped a little water into his mouth, cooing to him.

"Varv! Var!" He yelled between partly swallowing and partly dribbling. His searching brown eyes were wide, and tears trailed down the corners of his eyes.

"It's me, Papa, Petyr. I'm here. Everything's okay," I said in French, but suddenly, I was concerned that he might be speaking Russian, of which I had nearly no knowledge.

"I'm sorry, Varv," he cried and mouthed in French unexpectedly. "I betrayed you... and we suffered for it."

Varvara, his first wife. I only knew her name because Mama told me it once.

"Oh! We suffered!"

I didn't think he was capable of being this loud. His crying intensified and required heavier breathing now, a consuming physical undertaking. I put my hand on his forearm to soothe him, which made him quiver.

"Don't touch me!" I leapt back. "Four dead children. Two children I don't speak to... in America! Have they ever been happy? Estrangement is a cancer, not an amputation. The thought of them doesn't go away."

"They know you did the best you can," I said pleadingly, my voice too high for a man my age.

I started tearing up, unable to resist mirroring his distress for which there was no more time for a cure. *He would rather use this time to talk about those who are not here than cherish the time left with me.* His mind was too exhausted to hold his thoughts any longer. His heaving made this a physical dislodging in his body and excavation of his spirit's sorrow.

"I didn't. I loved Pasquale... more than anyone... more than any of my wives. I poured my soul into him. And he became nothing. The son I wanted, the want beneath all wants, every intention... consumed himself. Then, the other boys were too old. We had no foundation. My first life found Pasq, and it destroyed him. I'm sorry, Varv. No one is more sorry than me."

He let out a long, loud sob. A wail that sent bumps down my arms and caused my face to contort in disbelief. He was inconsolable. The anatomy of his soul was disparaged.

"What if I write the living two letters from you? What would you say to them?"

He shook his head, and his whole body reverberated from the motion like a serpent. "I have nothing to say to them. You are forbidden from telling them where you bury me!"

"Papa, how can you say that? It is a miracle you have lived this long, and maybe this is why."

He shook his head, squeezing his blind eyes shut. "I have nothing to say."

"I don't accept that. Tell me one thing you would tell your daughter and one last note to your oldest living son. Go on, tell me."

He shook his head.

"One sentence, Papa. One sentence to share by the two of them."

I urged him, but he didn't speak French again. He only muttered in Russian and broken English, which was infuriating. This was his last opportunity to provide his children with a peace he would never have, and he refused.

I paced the dim room, boiling with accusations I would never say out loud. His atrophied arms became still, and he quieted down. The prevailing sound of the room was the rattling fluid strummed up in his lungs with each inhale. Based on the fullness of his breathing, I knew he was only pretending to fall asleep as he did most nights when he wanted to be left alone.

Fine then, die! I thought as I closed the door to the study behind me. He must see that he has a shred of borrowed time to apologize or reach out in kind, yet he chooses to refuse the gift unopened. *Do something about your pain or die.*

That night, I was too agitated to fall asleep. I couldn't eat, read, or dismiss my frustration with him. Mama never came home. I drifted off on the living room couch.

When I woke up, I washed my face and changed out of yesterday's clothes. I made myself a coffee and sipped it with the resolve that I would convince Papa to dictate letters to my half-siblings today. As his oatmeal warmed over the stove, I wandered the cottage for his stationary and a pen. When I brought his bowl into the study, I found that he had passed away overnight.

2
Petyr II

My fiancé, Celestine, organized a small funeral ceremony on Saturday at Hautecombe Abbey in Saint-Pierre-de-Curtille, Ontex's neighbor commune. I trusted Celestine's insistence that we have a ceremony, which I was unsure about, and Mama was decidedly against. Celestine had organized six funerals in the last four years by herself, and I left the organizing to her. As I wanted to untwine my mind and fill the cavernous time I felt I should have been feeding, cleaning, bathing, or checking on Papa, Mama questioned Celestine on every detail and debated the expenses with her. There was strictly no money for flowers, which I felt dishonored the horticulturalist he was. His demand to be buried in a plot beside the Protestant church in La Chapelle-du-Mont-du-Chat rather than being interred within the Catholic abbey walls would have cost five times more, so this was also denied. Celestine's aunt was an influential sister of Hautecombe who secured the forty-minute ceremony for us.

All of this contesting of minutiae felt inconsequential. I presumed the three of us and Madame Desmarais would be the only attendees. However, Celestine's best friend joined us – a sweet girl, freshly widowed, who wore a bright blue dress, pristine matching heels, and a yellow chiffon scarf. She said it was a tradition in her family to wear bright colors to the funerals of the very old; it was an ode to a long and plentiful life. She reminded me of an iris in bloom, which felt like a cheerful coincidence.

When we arrived at Hautecombe, my mother's lover was there. I had never seen him before. The shock of it suppressed my instinct to burn the place down with him in it. I held Celstine's hand as we walked into the chapel with our small party. Her flittering gaze conveyed her distress on my behalf; I avoided her eye. Mama sat in the front row on the left side of the overly painted chapel, holding hands with this man a few years older than her. I let go of Celestine's hand, revolted by any gesture that would equate the two relationships. The rest of us shuffled in on the right side with Celestine's aunt. I hardly listened to the priest or the short eulogy given by Madame Desmarais, who was dressed in a black fur stole and diamonds. I could only try not to allow my nostrils to be cloaked with the pungent cologne emanating from the left side and not feel her hands move on this violator's knee as if they were moving on me.

※

Four days after the service, Mama had only come home once to pack a small bag. We did not speak. I felt torn open by the loss of my father, injured by her indifference toward our loss, and offended by the existence of her funeral companion. Fortunately, the weather was more excellent than usual, so I spent more time outside by the lake. I was reading more poetry, which was conducive to my serrated attention span. After fourteen months of caretaking for Papa, I had to remember how to fill my time on my behalf. Celestine came over for dinner every night. I could breathe with the full capacity of my lungs again when it felt like I could only fill the top third for months.

"You seem to be bending something around in your head," Celestine observed.

"I've been considering something but am debating its ethics." Her head tipped sideways mid-chew. Her blonde hair, curled at the bottom, bounced. "That last night, Papa refused to let me write his other two children a letter from him. I have a half-sister from Russia who is in New York now. My only living brother from Italy is also in America. I don't know if they've ever met. He was adamant that I not write to them. He even demanded I never tell them where he is buried." Cel's brown eyes glimmered with blinks of disbelief directed at her plate. Her family had been uncomplicated. "Well… I'd like to write to them."

"Do you have their addresses?"

"I found them in his office."

"I think it is fair that they know their father has passed away."

"Yes." I paused. "My hesitation isn't necessarily around informing them of that. That last night, I tried to get him to say something that would give them peace. He didn't have a good relationship with either of them. I'm mulling over whether when I write them, I… elaborate."

"You mean give them last words from him?" My beauty balked. "I'm not sure that's right. If he didn't actually, then it would be a lie."

"I know, and that's where I'm between two thoughts. Could this be an instance where lying is permissible? I can't imagine composing letters to them without including a line that would speak to their emotions. I see this as a key moment to heal."

"But is it true? You are changing the truth. There can't be healing without truth."

"I think there could be. It's the only possibility at this point."

"Don't you think it's deceptive?" she asked. "You would be starting your relationship with your siblings on a lie."

"I'll be easing the ending of their relationship with him. What would you give for last words from your parents?"

Her eyes flashed, and she covered her nose and mouth. Her inhale beneath the cupped hands was the sound of sudden agony.

"I'm sorry, Cel," I said. "I didn't mean it like that. I'm very sorry I said that."

She nodded and wiped her eyes.

"I know what you meant," she cleared her throat. "But I will say that when you put it that way, I see your side better."

Then I walked her home, as I did each night after dinner.

✳

The letters to Tatiana and Enzo had to be in Papa's spirit, so I couldn't drip the letters in love or lean apologetic; a small sliver of closure would be enough. My little training as a law clerk hadn't prepared me to construct such language.

What would they want or need to hear from Papa? It seemed impossible to write to someone as if you know him, nevertheless, as his father, when you've never met him. Enzo may resent me out of loyalty to his mother, who decayed in his American home. Does Tatiana know I exist?

If they are half like me, they'll know Papa was at the center of his universe. We were all on the periphery, rotating in and out of focus. Tatiana must be in her seventies; she could have had a father for four decades more than me. She could have been his caretaker in her old age and his ancient age. He could have met her daughter, his only grandchild. He could have seen his granddaughter grow up and marry to be twice removed from his surname. Entire lives were discarded at the expense of bringing my brothers and then me into the world.

It was unbelievable that Papa had their addresses. Tatiana's was sent along by Luca years ago, who once received a letter from Tatiana's husband's lawyer notifying the Italian Marinovas of the Smolnek estate sale with a new contact address. The addresses were copied neatly onto the same loose sheet and left in a drawer of his desk, which had been pushed against the wall and laden with items when his study was converted over a year ago. The piece of paper had been folded once lengthwise, with Tatiana, Enzo, and Luca's information on the left side. On the right side, he wrote the addresses for the graves of Elena, Anastasia, and Pasquale.

The lamp's faulty bulb trembled with the desk's slightest movement. With every few words I penned, the light flickered like it had a heartbeat.

New York, New York
January 1946

3
Tatiana

Our – I thought, though my husband had died eleven years ago – *first great-grandchild*. A baby! Is there better news?

I glided, as close as a woman approaching eighty can glide, to the living room window of my Second Avenue apartment and watched my granddaughter nearly skipping as she turned the corner hand-in-hand with her husband. The newlyweds were off to tell Jackson's parents, the Joneses, the news of their first grandchild over dinner. They were jubilant when they told me. For a few minutes longer, I am the first in the family to know. Natalya tried to persuade me to come to dinner, but the damp cold compressed the joints in my wrists and ankles. Also, I was not confident someone would escort me home after dinner, and I was scared of the streets at night. I am always careful to close my curtains as it gets dark, lest any loon off the street sees into my home.

As I settled on the worn-down couch with my ankles elevated by a pillow, my cat stood on her hind legs to rub the flat top of her head against my resting feet. Natalya picked this white cat for me four years ago. We named her Sekhmet, after the Egyptian goddess, because of her lioness concentration and because she does not have a sensible fear of fire; she sniffs at the hearth too closely. I am constantly shooing her from setting herself alight from the stovetop. I can no longer light candles, but everything is electric now anyway. Across the room, the darkness moved. It was the fat tabby cat. She kept her distance unless she determined it was time for me to put her food out. I picked at the pages of the newspaper for a while. Sekhmet leaned against my foot at the pillow's incline. Within minutes, my left foot had completely ebbed beneath her warm fur.

When my daughter Katrina told Dmitri and me she was having a baby, I was pleased for her, but being a young grandmother disinterested me. I was forty and a new immigrant to the United States. Katrina had a boy. I adjusted from the immodesty of the Marinova manor to the low ceilings of my three-room home. Formerly a diplomat's wife with hostessing responsibilities, I was now a foreman's wife with abundant time. Even after Katrina announced her second pregnancy, I remained distant. My infrequent visits to her uptown consisted of one-way conversations, half-sipped refreshments, more observing than participating, and no assisting.

During one of my no-more-than-forty-minute visits, a three-year-old Viktor strode to where I sat perched on the chair and leaned in until our faces were an inch apart. Conversation between Dmitri, Katrina, and her husband Ivan stopped around us. He hadn't learned boundaries yet. I couldn't place his eyes' familiar shade of brown; could it have been my mother's? Katrina was poised, unsure whether to intervene. Everyone watched as the boy's palm gently cupped my cheekbone, and he whispered: "beautiful." It felt like he was speaking to my soul. The whole room emitted a soft sigh. I was reduced to a handful of warm, overflowing adoration. Then, he leaned in even closer and yelled into my face, "Only kidding – you're not!" He bolted from the room in laughter, and Katrina raced after him. Ivan apologized, but it was too late. It didn't matter what Viktor yelled. At the molecular level, I had already surrendered myself in the palm of his little hand.

Being a parent is difficult. It felt like I was always unsure and four steps behind, unable to see around each corner. Being a wife was difficult, too, for the woman constantly adapts to the needs of the man and the family. I responded to the unending demands of both roles with bitterness, resentment, indifference, and detachment. How unsuspecting I was when grandmotherhood cracked me wide open. Being a grandmother was the clean air of a higher altitude. The expectations I imposed upon Katrina seemed naked and untransferable to my grandchildren. This love doesn't require earning. Merely by being, they are deserving. And now, I'll get to feel what it's like from one more degree above as a great-grandmother. For a little while, anyway.

I upset Sekhmet when I pulled my foot from beneath her to put on the kettle for my nightly cup of hot water. After a minute I changed my mind, I turned off the gas stovetop, and even though it was 7:30, I slipped on my clogs, clutched my keys, and closed my front door just enough to prevent anyone walking down the hallway from seeing my kitchenette mess overflowing into the living room area. Crossing the beige and russet-tiled hallway quickly by my typical standards, I knocked on the door of 2D. Lightly at first. Then I rapped as firmly as I could, thinking maybe she was asleep.

"Coming... I'm coming... I' M-COMING-DAMN-IT!" she yelled, though I had stopped knocking at the first acknowledgment.

I wrinkled my face into its many smiles when Irina finally opened the door.

"We only saw each other two hours ago!" Irina mumbled in Russian. She was wearing a thick, brown flannel nightgown and the same blue floral robe from Macy's that her husband had given her years ago as a birthday present.

"Natalya is pregnant! I'm going to be a great-grandmother!"

"A second chance," Irina joked. "Though really, I'm happy for you. Congratulations to her and what -"

"Jackson. And if it's a girl, they will name Tatiana!"

"Probably going to be a boy then," she rubbed her eyes, slowly circling at the wrists due to the arthritis.

"No, the first grandchild tends to be a girl," I waved away her cynicism.

"Your first was a boy."

"He was an exception. Would you like to come over for tea? I can't sleep. I feel...bubbly."

"Bubbly! I haven't felt bubbly since... there's not much that makes one bubbly after forty...thirty-two... eh, twenty-five, more like. Yes, I'll come over. But, now that you have me up, I haven't gotten my mail downstairs in days. Let me check it, and then I'll be over. I can check yours, too?"

I handed my keys over and busied to start the stove again. A couple of minutes later, Irina shuffled into my apartment, sat at the table, and placed a small stack of mail on one of the seats. I hadn't gone further than Irina's door in a week or so. I brought the pot of black tea and a small tin of milk to the square, four-person table, the only surface I tried to keep unburied by clutter. My two hand-painted red hibiscus tea cups and their saucers were already arranged on the table. I felt grateful I still had nineteen unbroken pieces from the original set at the Smolnek manor from my grandmother Marinova.

"The child will certainly be a boy since you are so wound up over a little Tatiana." She saw the world like that. After spending hours a day with her for decades, I knew her words had no malice.

"None of my nine granddaughters are named after me. They all have American names. This generation wants their kids to be American... they don't care about heritage and history..."

Picking through my mail, I dropped a letter when a terror choked me. My eyes closed to keep the room from spinning. I clutched my heart, which felt like it had swollen into my neck.

Irina, alarmed, held my shoulder to keep me upright and repeated: *"Where is the pain? Where is the pain?"*

After multiple frantic gasps, one took. I seized the oxygen back. When I knew I wouldn't be dizzy, I opened my eyes. Irina returned to her seat and gave me time. My breath stabilized. My thoughts caught up to my feelings.

"Was it your heart?" Irina asked, releasing a long exhale herself.

"Yes." I gripped my teacup with both liver-spotted hands; I didn't trust either hand alone not to drop the cup. Drops of tea sloshed onto my lap as I sipped to calm my nerves. I permitted myself a few more breaths before addressing what had finally found its way to my table.

I lifted the ecru envelope to eye level to be sure I hadn't misread it. The letter was thin, though the paper was heavy. The personalized stationery had the name and address printed on the back: *P. I. Marinova*—my father.

"What is it, Tati?" Irina stirred milk into her tea, aiming for the exact shade of wet-sand beige she always tried to produce.

"These are my father's initials. This is a letter from him."

"Your father? He is still alive? That's impossible. How old is he?"

"He would be ninety-six. I have only heard from him once in seventy years. He's never met Katrina or my husband."

"He didn't come to your wedding to Dmitri?"

"No. He left my mother and Smolnek when I was seven. He got an American pregnant, and she had the son my mother never gave him. Mama always went on about how genders come in threes, and her fourth child would have been a boy. I'm not sure if I told you, but I had a sister, Elena, a few years younger than me, who passed away very young. That was shortly after Anastasia was born."

I rambled. Inside the cavity of my chest, there was a wound unfelt for decades. I could feel its weighty outline with serrated edges lodged within me.

"I think he's dead," the words fell out of my mouth as I stared at the black-and-white photos blotting the white walls. My life was one that my father only briefly touched—the entire, completed lives of my husband and grandson. I was resentful that Anastasia lived with him in the nineties. Mama transformed Anastasia's misfortune into the opportunity to eat with him, hear his stories, and make memories with his second family. My memories were a child's massaged version of reality.

"But if those are his initials, then maybe he is still alive and reaching out," Irina suggested in an unusually soft tone.

"No. I know it." My eyes filled with tears, and I shook my head.

"Well, allowing the anticipation to age won't help. You can't be sure until you read it."

"I am sure."

I took a deep breath, and when I let it go, I felt a sensation of unclenching inside me.

"I just never thought it would happen. It's always seemed like he was here before me and he would be here after me. What if my heart gives out when I read it? I can't die yet – there's a baby on the way!"

"That's why people die, to clear out and make room for the new. I'm going to rest," Irina walked over to the couch. "But I'll be here when you want to it."

I folded my arms and continued to stare at the letter.

It felt unbelievable that he should outlive two of his daughters by so many decades. Dmitri used to say he was happy that we had no sons because he was convinced we would have outlived them. Dmitri did not live to see Viktor die. Not that any of us truly saw him die, it was more that we saw him leave home in 1942 and then were told he would never return after he was captured from the USS *Endicott* at the Battle of La Ciotat. One hundred and seventy-four Americans became prisoners of war during that battle, and only a handful were executed, Viktor being one of them. Though my only grandson was born in America and had never left New York before the war, his East Slavic features did not serve him in the hands of the Nazis.

I turned off the two tasseled green lamps near Irina and then stood over the table bearing the letter. How could a piece of paper, folded to be tidy and unassuming, hold so much? I gently slipped my thumb under the seal flap.

Dear Tatiana,

I am heavy-hearted with grief to notify you that our father, Petyr Marinova, has been laid to rest at the age of 96. He passed peacefully on the morning of 7 October. He is now buried at La Chapelle-du-Mont-du-Chat in Saint-Pierre-de-Curtille.

He had a few last words for you that he dictated to me in his final days. He wanted you to know that his love for you never abated. He frequently thought of you fondly and spent decades unsure how to right a ship that was off course. You claimed his heart as his first child and, as his last daughter, your stake was never renounced.

He had several minor debts at the time of his death, and upon paying them, there remains no monetary inheritance for his surviving children: you, Enzo Marinova in New Haven, Virginia, and myself. Prior to his death, he gifted the Italian estate in Suna to the widow of our brother, Luca. His small estate in Ontex will become the possession of his wife, my mother, Claudia Marinova.

I regret that this is our first correspondence. I truly wish you well and would like to become your correspondent.

With sincerest condolences,
Petyr Ivanov Marinova II

Was Enzo the youngest of the three boys?

I read the letter three more times. The news of his passing hit like a dead weight cut loose.

Enzo is in America?

His penmanship was impeccable. All M's, H's, and O's bore a unique flourish.

Who is Claudia? Is Petyr not the oldest of Mary Harrison's sons?

I felt like a girl, filled with questions and unafraid to ask them.

Where is Ontex?

"Irina! Irina!" I shook Irina awake by her arm; her mouth was open in sleep, revealing grey and several missing teeth. "I have a brother!"

"Will you still have a brother in the morning?" She deigned only to open one eye while its pair remained shut. "Will you ever let me rest tonight?"

"I have two half-brothers. And one is in Virginia!"

"Your family is multiplying by the minute. Virginia is in the South?"

"Yes, somewhere there, I don't exactly know... but I have brothers!"

October 1946

4
Tatiana

There are no awkward situations, only awkward people, I thought as I met my two half-brothers for the first time, at age seventy-eight. The three of us could barely hold eye contact, with our very different eye shapes and colors. It seemed like one of us was always talking too much or too little. The age gaps, primarily Young Petyr being a decade younger than Natalya, did not help. I was terrified someone would ask if I was his grandmother.

We sat in the well-lit tearoom of Enzo's hotel, The Carlyle, beside one of the gallery room's expansive, floor-to-ceiling windows with a view of the idyllic atrium. The cerulean velvet chairs were enormous. Enzo had to push my heavily cushioned chair in for me when I took my seat; I would need assistance if I wished to leave. The room fell short of a modern take on the opulence of the Austro-Hungarian Empire. The room contrasted baby pink linens with bold furniture, overdone mirrors, wily flower arrangements, and golden table accents. At least the wallpaper was a simple print above the chair rail molding. Though, what does my opinion matter? My years of grandeur have been behind me for the entirety of Young Petyr's lifespan. When I did not prepare my food, I went on special occasions to Tommy's Diner with Irina or Mari Vanna with Katrina and Natalya.

Enzo resembled our father so undeniably. I had forgotten what our father looked like until seeing this apparition sitting straight and tall, strong for his age and lean, somehow evading the extra weight around the middle that was common in most men his age. The thinness of aging promulgated his bone definition and features. Only his coloring was off in the white of his hair wisps and light eyes. I imagined our father looked like this in his sixties, an age neither Young Petyr nor myself glimpsed.

On the other hand, I nearly laughed when I first saw Young Petyr. He looked like our father in miniature. He reminded me of the short Boris Marinova, a cousin despised by our shared grandmother. Cousin Boris attempted to move into the manor to "protect" us, and Mama's brothers had to "request" that he leave. Even Young Petyr's features were petite, which made for him to be a handsome boy. His mother must not have loved him enough to correct his abysmal posture. He shuffled in his chair a little too much for someone in his twenties and newly married. And yet, he was kind. It had taken him months to orchestrate our meeting, and I was grateful to him for crossing an ocean to be here.

"It was kind of you both to make the journey to New York," I said conversationally.

"There would have been plenty of space for you in Virginia. I live in my late wife's family home there. Josephine was a writer. Her first novel sold over two hundred thousand copies across the United States." He talked around the fact that her subsequent works were never quite as profitable, which Natalya had reported after researching Josephine Mark's work for me. "Josephine passed away two years this past June, but this meeting would have intrigued her. Furthermore, she lived in New York for four summers in her youth. Her first husband was a member of the wealthy Astor family. They divorced. After that, she returned to New Haven and wrote and traveled from there. We were introduced to each other in London by a mutual acquaintance. All that to say, I chose The Carlyle instead of the Waldorf-Astoria."

"I certainly understand why you made that choice," I said, somewhat struck by how plainly he spoke of his widow's divorce.

"Tatiana," Young Petyr began, "how long have you lived in New York City?"

"Nearly thirty-eight years now."

"Have you visited the Soviet Union since?"

"No. I haven't been there since before the revolution. Red Sunday disturbed my husband very much; he knew thirty or so demonstrators in St. Petersburg, and every single one was injured or killed in the massacre when the soldiers fired into the crowd. So much happened in a short time for us. In 1905, after losing Anastasia, my mother, and my husband's father, after the Russo-Japanese war and the first inklings of revolutionary stirrings, we sold the Marinova estate. My husband foresaw the turmoil, and I was a born imperialist, through my mother's blood, and because the Marinova rule of Smolnek was appointed in 1534 by Alexei Romanov. Dmitri moved us to Finland for a few months, where we decided to come to America, where he could use his English. We didn't intend for our move to be permanent. I didn't realize then that I would never go back. He had been a British liaison in Russia on behalf of the czar. Here, he worked eleven hours a day as a gas pipe foreman and ultimately died of lung cancer."

Enzo and Young Petyr could never know what it meant to sell the Smolnek property. Legally, they held no right to the manor or inheritance since Papa had left it to Mama so that she would agree to the divorce. Still, it suddenly felt wrong that I alone decided to release our ancestors' home and solely profit from its sale.

"Your mother died in the early 1900s?" Young Petyr asked.

"Yes, in 1901. It was Anastasia who predeceased my mother."

Young Petyr's eyes stared at the ceiling as his pointer finger arced over to Enzo like he was in the middle of a calculation. "Wasn't 1901 the same year Pasquale died?"

Enzo nodded.

"I didn't realize it was the same year," I sputtered.

Enzo nodded again. "In Paris, hit by a car in the street."

Our tea arrived at the table in a spectacularly large sterling silver kettle on a matching burner stand. The teacups and saucers were a hideous forest green. The room was drowning in its own glamour. The swirling steam rising from the thin-necked spout looked perfectly choreographed. Young Petyr poured the tea into our cups and proceeded to take his in the French way without adding any milk. Enzo opted for the British route, adding sugar and stirring in milk.

"How long have you lived in Virginia?" I asked Enzo. The tea needed a minute to come to a reasonable temperature.

"For thirty-three, or actually, thirty-four years… and two months." He answered with precision.

"Your wife is from there?"

"Yes. She grew up during Reconstruction. Her father was a colonel during the Civil War."

"For the South?" Young Petyr inquired unironically.

"Yes, for the Confederacy. In fact, Josephine's godfather was the Confederate General Robert E. Lee. An interesting fact I dare not say loudly in New York."

"I saw *Gone with the Wind* once," Young Petyr added as if he were no novice.

I took a small sip, carefully lifting the ugly teacup to my lips. My moment to ask the tough question had arrived.

"Petyr, could you tell us about how Papa died?"

"For the past few years, he had been more receptive to small ailments… he caught the coughing and sniveling that was going around. Though he was healthy and mobile for most of his nineties. I feared spending the majority of his time indoors during the war, and then the pain of Luca's death laid his defenses low for some illness to take him away."

"Did you fight in the war?" I interrupted him.

"No." He sent a hand through his hair. "I was born with a congenital heart defect. It's called ventricular septal defect. Essentially, there is a hole in my heart that can be heard as a murmur. I had a lot of breathing difficulties as a child."

I nodded, unsure what to say.

"Papa was on bed rest for a couple of months from bronchitis," Young Petyr continued. "He made it through the cough and fever, but his body couldn't flush the phlegm build-up and fluid from his lungs. He lasted months. I didn't even believe it would take him… that he was capable of dying. It was not excessively painful. He was able to speak until the end."

"What did he say?" Enzo asked.

"There wasn't much that came out clearly. It was muddled. He was mixing Russian, Italian, English, and some French, and I only knew certain phrases of the first two. I only caught some words and names. On the last night, the names were Pasquale and Varvara."

I could not believe he named my mother on his deathbed. The woman he discarded and humiliated, who would have had more of a right to name him on her deathbed and did not, who he hadn't seen in seventy years, and who has been dead herself for forty-six of them.

"Did he mention my name at all?" I asked shamelessly. I had to know. Enzo gestured to his chest to stretch my question to include him.

"You weren't named. But he was recounting his losses and referred to you both as the two children in America he doesn't speak with. He said that he never stopped thinking about either of you." Young Petyr's volume lowered hesitantly as if he was scared to incite an emotional reaction. "But no, he did not say your name explicitly. He also said 'she' and 'her' in a way that I took to indicate Anastasia. Papa once told me that she came to live in Suna and that

Pasquale followed her to Paris when she left, and Paris essentially undid him."

For different reasons, a shared sigh from Enzo and I filled the space. I needed a moment to let each of Young Petyr's sentences settle; every confirmation was a nail poised above my heart for years, finally coming home, shredding the barriers I'd made for myself.

"Was he resentful toward me at the end?" Enzo asked.

"No. Why would he be?" Young Petyr said genuinely.

"After Stasi passed away, it was clear Pasquale would stay in Paris anyway, and Pim's relationship with him was irreparable. There was a short time when he attempted to invest more of his time into me. I was young, and though I'm typically more… methodical than emotional, it felt too late for him to start taking an interest in me. That's when I went to London. I pulled away and never came back. My mother came to live with me years after they separated. She was an American, you know." Of course I knew, it was always an auxiliary insult to my mother. "So she enjoyed Virginia in her late years. I didn't attempt to stay in close correspondence with Pim. I've believed that he carried a torch of disappointment regarding me."

"I haven't seen him in seventy years," I said quietly, and their heads turned to me. "The time he left us was the last time I saw him. It was the eighth of May. Every year, that day is noted in my mind as much as any birthday or holiday."

"Did he ever write you letters?" Young Petyr asked.

"I received something for the first few birthdays in the beginning. Then, there was an attempt to comfort me when Anastasia died. I asked my husband to read it for me. But I never wrote back as a girl nor as a woman."

"To be honest," Young Petyr leaned back in his chair, and his voice became light. "He wasn't very good at being a father. That word was more of a title than a role to him."

The tension between us broke as our laughs, beginning as chuckles, grew and multiplied.

"I am glad he got a chance to try again, just to make sure!" Young Petyr pointed to himself, and we all laughed again.

"Did he ever talk about me?" I finally felt at ease to ask. "Sometimes I imagined that wherever he was, he was thinking about me and asking himself what my life was like. Or if he ever wanted to meet my daughter Katrina. She isn't as fiercely rebellious as him and Anastasia."

"He didn't speak about your part of the family until I was a teenager," Enzo began softly. "Once he did, it was with reverence and guilt. There was much unsaid about his past. Pasquale invented a story in which Pim murdered a life-long nemesis and took refuge in Italy, but we would eventually come face-to-face with that enemy's sons and have to defeat them ourselves. I believed that for years. Kids have a magical ability to make light of the visible pain of the adults around them. It takes time to understand harboring prolonged feelings."

"Were you close with your brothers?" Young Petyr asked.

"Luca and I wrote to each other occasionally after I left. Even as little kids before Luca was born, Pasquale and I seemed incongruous. Then, he was consumed by his work, which was worthy of his total focus. I was boring to him.

"Pasquale was closest to Stasi. They were similar – strikingly so. I was talking with this philosopher neighbor of mine a few weeks ago, and he said something that may not make sense to anyone else, but it helped explain a lot to me. He noted that inspiration plucks us from the masses; each idea is an intelligent, self-determining. An idea chooses who it wants to manifest it. Ideas are visitors of our minds, not born of them. Anyway, when Stasi came to live with us, it seemed like she and Pasq lived on a higher frequency than the rest of us, closer to where the ideas were. Pasquale had more advantages from youth than Stasi ever had, and she was aware of that."

"She never seemed to be of the here and now. Even as a little girl."

"Looking back, her death felt inevitable," Enzo continued over my comment. "If anything, I would've expected something more spectacular than falling ill. Luca said that Pasquale hadn't even known she was sick. None of us knew."

"Anastasia said he was also in Paris," I recalled aloud.

"I never knew you knew that," he paused in thought.

"I would have liked to meet her," Young Petyr said kindly.

"You would have liked her. Everyone did." I said, noticing a contrary twitch from Enzo, but before I could address it, Young Petyr asked more questions.

"And what about Pasquale? What was he like?"

"Erratic," Enzo said off-handedly, like that adjective had been marinating for years. Our expressions demanded more, and he continued. "At least he was in his final years. He was brilliant. He examined the world in great depth. His sculptures weren't renowned because they were aesthetically flawless, though they are lifelike, but they were famous because he captured character and intention in the eyes, intelligence around the mouth, and confidence in the way a head perched on the neck. He made the one taking in the piece feel. He had an obsessive nature."

There was a silence between us. The tea was gone and the dregs revealed. The topic of Pasquale is delicate because I never met him. I will never know him other than the child who stole my one father from me.

"His death broke our family," Enzo said, sounding as if he were my age. Young Petyr looked down at his empty cup. I looked straight at Enzo, understanding his sentiment but burning. *His birth broke mine.* "All of the signs had been there, screaming. Mother thought it was a chapter in some greater creative process, and he would emerge on the other side. Her end should have signaled his, for as much as he loved her."

"We all adored her," I quipped possessively over the loss of my little sister.

"No," Enzo shook his head slowly and locked his eyes on his liver-spotted hands. "Pasquale was in love with Anastasia. And Pim knew it."

5
Enzo

After the emotional content of each of the meals together, I was not necessarily eagerly looking forward to the visit's final dinner tonight. Petyr was exploring the city on his own—his pregnant wife did not accompany him across the ocean—and Tatiana requested she have the morning to rest. I resolved to visit the cemetery plot of my grandfather's family, the Harrisons.

There were still living Harrison relatives in New York and surrounding New Jersey suburbs. In Mother's declining years, she frequently talked about how she was the willfully forgotten rogue of the Harrison family. From what mother heard from her mother, she believes his wife knew about her existence, but there was never a divorce, an invitation to meet her four half-siblings, three brothers and a sister, or an inheritance. My grandmother suspected there were more Harrison bastards pocketed through the city as well. I wonder if Anthony William Harrison allowed them all to take his name. Mother said her father's obituary had been in the newspaper the day after the "intimate family service," otherwise Grandmother Florence likely would have insisted they attend, if only to see him one last time. I had no interest in kindling a relationship with those lost uncles, aunts, and cousins. Yet, it seemed like visiting the family grave plot, where Anthony was buried, might provide a sliver of closure.

Mother had described the location on Second Street to me. She emphasized that New York Marble Cemetery was not to be confused with New York City Marble Cemetery, though they happened to be across the street from each other. She lamented that there would be no "right" place for her body to be laid to rest: her mother was cremated, there was no place for her in the Harrison family plot, her only husband lived in France with his new wife, and her sons would be buried in three different countries. Ultimately, she was buried in New Haven, where she died, with the Mark family, where I would join her and Josephine someday.

The cemetery was a small, quarter-block of green with old oak trees that were as tall as the ones in Central Park yet stunted in width due to rowhouses towering over the square. I found the plot stone quickly, happening to begin my *passeggiata* clockwise. *Harrison, Vault N. 33*. The letters were not profoundly set into the wet stone;

it had sleeted through the night, and I had to read it several times. The dirt over Vault 33 did not appear recently touched, as the ground over several other plots was shoveled, piled, loose, or sparse of grass. I strolled around the rest of the cemetery, calculating lifespans and widow and widowerhoods. What could Mother's life have been like if these people had made a place for her?

✷

I arrived at Tatiana's apartment precisely five minutes after three in the afternoon to give the hostess an extra few minutes for last-minute adjustments; Josephine always had something emerge in the final preparatory minutes. The courtesy was in vain, as when I arrived, the living room was already brimming with her family members passing a fussing seven-month-old between them. Tatiana spun around her kitchenette, a maestro of whistling, steaming, and clanging.

"Hello, Uncle Enzo. I'm Katrina," said the woman, who was not all that much younger than me. "Please, sit on the couch and take a rest. I am very excited to meet you. Mother has been telling us about you ever since she sent you the first letter."

"Yes, it's been an unforeseen fortune," I said as I followed her direction to sit. The sinking couch demanded I work hard to keep my posture respectable.

"I'm Irina," the elderly woman on the other side of the couch said with a distinctly Russian accent. She had a sharp chin and thin eyebrows. "Quite an unlikely story, your family."

"Indeed. It's been informative to hear about Tatiana and Petyr's childhoods."

"Your father seems like an ass."

"Well..." I cleared my throat. Katrina tilted her head to receive my rebuttal politely. "There must have been reasons... I would not necessarily say that."

"I did. There's never been more of an ass than him. Did your wife get much money from her first husband, the Astor? Or was her family rich?" Katrina grabbed hold of her grandson and jumped up to help her mother.

"The Mark family has owned hundreds of acres outside of Charlottesville since before the Revolutionary War," I said proudly. "Josephine's great-grandfather was close to Thomas Jefferson. They own the Mark Hotel on the far side of the property, built on a quaint mountainside as a retreat for Washington politicians. The hotel has the finest private golf course and club in western Virginia. The Mark family vineyard is known, and its varietals win national awards."

"So they owned slaves. Do they still?"

"No! I mean, yes, regrettably, they did at the time. There are no slaves anymore." My perspiring palms glided along one other in my lap.

"Hello, I'm Petyr," Petyr extended his hand to Irina. I hadn't seen him enter. He held a bouquet of pink tulips for Tatiana. Did Petyr know Pim kept fifty-eight species of *tulipa*? I stood to shake Petyr's hand and used the opportunity to introduce myself to Natalya and Jackson.

"Uncle Enzo, would you like to hold Jimmy?"

Jackson lifted the baby to my chest before I could decline. The child had been crying on and off. Katrina hovered beside me, eager to snatch the infant back if he burst into tears, but his eyelid fluttered slowly, and he fell asleep. Once I properly adjusted his face to rest against my chest, I didn't mind his weight.

The apartment walls were painted light brown and covered in photographs and paintings with thick wooden frames, which made the space feel smaller and darker. Still holding sleeping Jimmy aslant, I examined one of the hand-painted images on the porcelain lamp beside me. It was a lush landscape of rolling fields with a boy and a dog. *I wish Luca were here.* The four-inch tassels trimming the lampshade suppressed the dark honey light of the lamps. Various clutter was piled in every corner and surface. *Like Pasquale's studio.*

The kitchen table could only hold four people, so when dinner was ready, Petyr, Natalya, and Jackson sat at the table and discussed Jackson's aerospace engineering studies, what Petyr's wife Claudia was like, and remarked how strange it was that Petyr's father was Natalya's great-grandfather. Tatiana and Katrina sat with me in the living room and ate their borscht perched on their knees, carefully lifting their spoons so as not to drip on their laps. By then, Irina had mercifully gone home. We three listened to the three youth talk and laugh. Jimmy slept on, and when the group moved on from the red soup to the lamb and potatoes, I declined Katrina's offer to take him from my arms, as my body had adjusted to the warmth and feeling of his little body breathing. He anchored me in the room I otherwise felt apart in.

"Enzo," Tatiana said my name in a low tone, "I think you are the only child of our father to meet every one of his other children."

"I never thought of that," I whispered.

"You may know Jimmy more than my sister ever knew Katrina."

Katrina stared into the space somewhere between my face and the baby's. Perhaps it was disguised by age, but I couldn't find any of Stasi's features on her face. Her coloring was much darker than Stasi's reddish-brown, though the whisps at her temples were graying. The photos showed that Tatiana had dark brown hair at one time, which was inherited from Pim.

"Katrina once saw your brother's sculptures in an exhibit on Italian artists at The Metropolitan Museum. The plaque read "Pasquale Marinova." A small summary of his life and work was below his birth and death dates. That's how I found out he was dead. That was more than twenty years after the fact."

"I don't know exactly how many of his works are still out there," I said. "Last year, Franca donated all of what he left behind in the studio to a local collection in Pallanza, the neighboring community on Lake Maggiore. When my mother moved to America to live with me, she only brought the one gift he made her, a set of sunflowers the size of my fingers that emerged from a rectangular, jagged base. Now I have it in my home. Perhaps Petyr has something in Ontex. Many of the works my parents left in the care of Luca and Franca on the lake were stripped or destroyed the night the Nazis gutted and then burned the house.

"It hurt to hear about it. I would rather have lost the home in New Haven. It is my mind's refuge. I only remember it with the sun's rays; I don't think of the cloudy days. The more complex the weather, the more beautiful the composition of the sky and mountains on the lake. My mind still holds Suna as an eternal place I can return to."

"Are the gardens intact?"

"After Pim left, Luca and his wife did not keep the garden. It was too expensive. Luca's wife gardened fruits, vegetables, and herbs; she was too practical to have poured her energy into manicuring acres of gratuitous flowers for aesthetic vanity. It would have been all-consuming to keep the flora alive. If any have survived the neglect, they surely have become overgrown, wild, or unrecognizable."

Petyr was listening to us, leaning back in his chair to see me over Natalya's shoulder, his eyes pensive and absorbing. Petyr's expression remained as smooth as glass, a compacted and more handsome rendition of Pim's. His hair was darker and more Marinova than mine or my brothers' had ever been.

"Your sister-in-law still lives there?" Katrina asked.

"Yes." I felt my first hunger pang, smelling the lamb from Katrina's plate. Yet to eat, I would have to release Jimmy.

"Papa gave Franca the house," Petyr said.

"But the house is gone?"

"She lives in my brother's old sculpting studio. It's a large single room about a hundred yards from where the villa stood. It doesn't have a washroom, an oven, a stove, or electricity. She will likely live there for the rest of her life. She wrote to tell me that she donated Pasquale's remaining work to a local museum. He has a few rooms dedicated to him there in perpetuity. She also petitioned to rename the main highway there, Via di Lago Maggiore, to Via di Pasquale Marinova."

"She sounds like an impressive woman."

"She is very resilient," Tatiana supplemented.

"She witnessed my brother's execution...."

"What was my great-grandfather like?" Natalya asked the room earnestly.

"He hugged me a lot," Tatiana began. "As a little girl, he would hug me in a tight grip, to discomfort, as if I was the only immovable object in the world. He was very tall and strong. We would go around Smolnek on one horse, with me in front of him in the saddle, and he would introduce every person we encountered to me. He was a young man with a large beard. It made his nose appear to be a normal size. He always left us behind when he went to Moscow, St. Petersburg, Bavaria, and Austria. He was researching churches; he made it sound like it was a divine pilgrimage. I tried to hug him goodbye the day he left us for good, but he only patted me on the head."

"He didn't have a beard when he died." Petyr began nostalgically. "Toward the end, shaving was the longest he could stand, but the focus was good for him. No one else could do it."

"Pim never hugged us," I whispered. "He was most interested in my older brother, Pasquale, whom he shaped into a famous sculptor when he was seventeen. When Pasquale was eighteen, he produced forty-one works, commissioned and noncommissioned, constituting the bulk of his remaining work. Pim didn't have much time for Luca and me. He spent most of his time in his study and the gardens, his corner of the world."

"It seems you had the most time with him," Natalya told me.

"I did. I hope he would be content with that."

"He loved all of his children," Petyr said flatly to the Bokhara rug beneath the table. "He didn't intend to cause any suffering." My old eyes blurred, and I looked up at the low ceiling.

"Suffering is conditional. Each person makes their own conditions under which to suffer." Tatiana said, stacking her fork and knife over the empty plate on her lap. "Katrina, will you bring the chocolate cake to the living room for us?"

6
Enzo

Tatiana had purchased a white crib and changing station for her second bedroom so Natalya and Jackson could come over with the baby as much as possible. When Jimmy woke up in my arms, Natalya went to feed him, and I relocated to the kitchen table with Petyr and Jackson to start my cold soup and finish my lamb. Tatiana and Katrina sat on the couch silently, whispering in Russian. I ate as the boys discussed New York and what Petyr should be sure to see and do before he left the day after tomorrow. Jackson invited Petyr to a dancing hall around the corner if Natalya could put Jimmy back to sleep in the next hour. The boys got along naturally, laughing and speaking of their work and passions grandly. Neither was embarrassed to declare what he wanted to achieve. Perhaps they were a generation of men unafraid of the abstract landscape. Both had been eager to be married after the war and begin families. Both were at the beginning stages of careers that would keep Jackson beneath fluorescent lights researching aeroelasticity, while Petyr would be in an office writing contracts at the local law practice. Jackson had served in the war. Petyr knew more who had not returned.

When Natalya emerged from the bedroom, sans Jimmy, the boys' eyes widened brightly, and they smiled at each other before scrambling to stand and flank her, whispering eagerly about their party going dancing. Natalya patted her stomach, which had subsumed its taut place in her slender waist, and consented to two hours away from the baby. Jackson nodded and quickly fetched their coats.

"Mama," Katrina yawned. "Would you mind if I rested in your room? I'll stay here until Natalya returns."

"Of course."

Katrina came over to the table and kissed me warmly on the cheek.

"It was nice to meet you, Uncle Enzo. I hope you will return soon." Katrina was the only other left-handed relative I knew. I found myself nodding, unsure what to say back.

"If you are not here when we return, it was lovely to meet you." Natalya also kissed my cheek goodbye.

"It was a pleasure," Jackson said, shaking my hand. Then he directed Natalya to the door, which they held ajar for Petyr.

I finally found my feet as I reached an outstretched hand to Petyr, but he moved it aside and hugged me.

"I'm so glad we've met, Enzo," my littlest brother said.

"Me too. I am very grateful to you for bringing us together."

"Promise you will keep in touch?" He pulled out of our hug but kept his hands clasped on my arms.

"I will."

He nodded, and the three merrymakers departed.

The door wheezed closed, separating the young from the old. Tatiana gestured for me to join her on the couch. A framed postcard on the wall caught my attention. Actually, it was the handwriting that caught my eye, small and curved into one line: "This is a postcard from Italy."

"Anastasia sent me that postcard during her time with your family. I had complained that I hadn't received one, and she sent that. She had sent me letters, too."

"I don't have a single relic in my home to remind me of her."

"I don't have anything in acknowledgment to you, your brothers, or Young Petyr."

"We have been untangling a series of knots we didn't tie."

"And some we did. I wasn't very nice to Anastasia. When she was little, she became enamored with fairy tales about mermaids. So I told her that foam at the sea's edge comes from dead mermaid bodies."

"Pasquale would have told me the same thing if he had considered it. Some things can't be fixed." I took my seat on the couch, where I had held Jimmy. This time, I allowed my posture to slacken.

"I think the three of us meeting now is how we fix it."

"I'm not so sure," I said, trying to remain courteous while being honest that I did not reciprocate the sentiment. "What results of our meeting? Are we meeting for its own sake? Petyr will go back to France. Petyr may remain in touch with Natalya and Jackson, but I don't have any children to continue the bonds established this week."

"Enzo," Tatiana stopped me softly. "This is like magic. I can't believe you can't see it. It can all be for healing's sake. Why shouldn't it be? Somehow, we have all come together and been able to puzzle together the missing pieces of our shared history. We are healing our preconceptions of each other and learning more about him and the ones we've outlived. I didn't even know Young Petyr existed, yet he was the one to unite us. Until now, seeing this generation through to the end has been painful. Our coming together is beyond anything Papa was willing to imagine. The last time I saw him, I was seven. I have goosebumps thinking about it. Family transcends time."

"Not my family. There were no children from me or my brothers. Pasquale's sculptures will last, but what else? Not even the house still stands."

"I am your family. Petyr is your family. Baby Jimmy on the other side of that wall is your family. I don't think you're seeing the gift of this situation. You are helping me understand my father. You could be the brother Petyr never had. He lost the male role model in his life. It's up to you what you want to make of all this. What does it mean to you?"

"It always felt like there was never any point to all the pain. What comes of a mind like Pasquale's? Or like Stasi's? The impersonality from Pim... when he tried to take an interest in me after Pasquale left for Paris. When I packed my bags for London, I was overwhelmed by the feeling that I would not be returning; I knew I wouldn't. I thought *what should I take with me?* I panicked. Then there was a voice that came into my head... I've never told anyone this, not even Josephine... well, it said, clear as the Lake Maggiore sky: *I will give you one thousand times what you leave behind tonight.* And I packed the small bag as best as I could. Pim could turn his ability to monetize talent onto Luca. I had to leave to succeed or fall short on my own. My writing had potential, but there was no room for Pim to nurture more than one person at a time. Pim only cared about his legacy, not people. A part of me always knew that but kept it secret from my conscious thoughts. Sometimes, the heart knows before the mind.

"By the time she married me, Josephine was too old to have a baby. She was six years older than me. And I was ok with that. It felt like a relief. It meant I didn't need to worry about unintentionally passing the hurts of my life on. Pim completely failed to bury his pain and poisoned each of us."

"Parents are people too. I wasn't a particularly great mother. I'm not making excuses for him, but I think you are being too hard on him."

Tatiana leaned against the armrest and rested her chin on her open palm, her long, wrinkled fingers enclosing her right cheek.

I exhaled slowly. "I think I judge him fairly."

"We can't judge him, Enzo. We are a family of overthinkers. It doesn't serve you not to forgive him. If he had been different, you would never have met Josephine. Maybe you never would have met me or even been born."

"What if it is too late for me to see it differently?"

"That is up to you," she leaned back, shoulders shrugging. "They say life is short, and for some, it is. But in my experience, life is long and offers frequent opportunities for change. My memory has been becoming slightly blurred. I've started thinking of time as yesterday and everything before yesterday in one merged block. It's allowed me to enjoy, rather than relive every detail about everything all the time."

I nodded, knowing the feeling. Tatiana and I were not raised together, but our minds seem to scrutinize the world similarly. Unlike the others, Tatiana listened to me… she wanted to help me. Her genuine interest in me made me feel seen in a way I hadn't felt since Josephine died.

"We can discuss more in the morning," she said. "You must come here before you leave for Virginia in the morning. Do you promise?" I nodded. "Good. Will you do me a favor? Will you check on Jimmy and make sure he is still sleeping? Think about how you would like him to know you." My older sister asked. I nodded again. I brought the cup of water left on the table with me.

The small guest room held only the crib, changing station, a second-hand rocking chair, and a twin bed pushed up against the opposite wall. I could only see the outline of each piece of furniture from the light of the single rectangular window. I slid the door mostly closed to stifle the reach of the living room's lamplight but did not close the door all the way.

In the crib, I could hear the baby breathing. Jimmy was lying on his back, hands resting by his ears, with his head tilted toward me. He was sleeping as soundly now as he was in my arms earlier. *Life replaces life.*

The index finger of my left hand lightly shaved the water's brim in my glass. My finger ferried a few droplets from the cup to the top of the baby's head. It wasn't truly water from the lake, but this I pretended. The drops of water rolled from his wispy down-feather hair to bedew the sheet. He did not stir. The baby was unaware and unmoved, but I was.

Epilogue

September 1966
Verbania, Italy

    He received directions from an Englishman on holiday. After an espresso taken standing at the bar, he picked up his leather traveler's bag, swung it over his shoulder, and walked north on the highway, Via di Pasquale Marinova. The two-lane road ran along a stretch of the western side of Lago Maggiore. The highway did not have space for a car to pull over; nevertheless, there was a sidewalk, only two feet between the guardrail and the painted white line. In this tiny sliver of space, he walked and walked. The cars came inches from his free arm, tightly held against his body. By the second mile, he was sweating at the bends in the road for fear that oncoming automobiles might not see him and drift dangerously close to the white line. One bend required him to clutch an iron gate to keep his balance and inch like a crab for several yards. At the third mile, he felt confident again and stared fondly at the lake, shining under the sun and reflecting the mountains. He looked for the white stucco house, hoping to see it jut out into the lake at each turn.

    It was smaller than he imagined and shaped differently from his great uncle's description. Where the garden must have stood, there were now several grand homes pearled around a divot in the road for a bus stop. Through the gate, he could see where the old, grayish foundation met the bright, newer leveling. There was a bronze plaque on the wall beside the steel gate. He couldn't read much Italian, but by the date and names provided, he knew it described the night in 1943 when the original house was burned down. The plaque decreed the house's name to be Casa di Luca Marinova.

    He raised his fist slowly, disbelieving that he was here, and knocked on the gate. Softly at first, but then hard, long hammering. He called out, "*Hello!*"

    Finally, the gate opened. It glided to the left smoothly, and he faced a driveway. Beyond the driveway was the sparkling lake where two teenage girls were swimming, laughing, and rolling around in the water. The blonde girl and the brunette girl splashed each other as a figure beside the shining lake sat in a rocking chair on the veranda, watching the girls play.

A stylish, older woman emerged from the house and walked up to him. "*Ciao! Posso aiutarla?*"

He expected to find ruins here—a burial site. Catastrophe paved over by a new housing development. But here it stood: renewed and spectacular. Half a dozen citrus fruits were growing from potted trees and bushes. Pink bougainvillea flowers blossomed on vines clinging to the house. Tiny birds fluttered in a bird bath. One word came to his mind, and it was not the word he would have predicted: *Life*.

The woman who approached wore a loose white blouse tucked into bright blue pants. Her wild, curly hair bounced with her gait. She called out again, asking if she could help him. He nodded and handed her a pre-translated note for the property owner. The note stated that he was a historian visiting the home of his great-great-grandfather and was here to see where his great-uncle Enzo grew up. The woman's head snapped up. Her eyes, friendly and open, examined his face.

"Lucia," she smiled wide and reached out her hand. The air was fresh. The sunlight warmed his face. "Please, come in."

"Jimmy Jones, nice to meet you. I'm here to learn about Luca Marinova, whose father built the original property. Did you know him?"

"*Si, certo*. He was my uncle."

"Really? I was just in France, meeting his half-brother. I know very little about Luca. Would you mind if I asked you some questions about him?"

"Why don't you ask his wife? Zia Franca is with my daughters. Here, this way."

Acknowledgments

When Bone Melts has been nine years in the making. There are so many family members, friends, and coffee shops to thank for helping this project of the heart arrive into the world.

Eternal thanks to my mom, Catherine "Citsi" Conway Castro, for sharing your love for reading and encouraging me to walk hand in hand with my dreams. Thank you to Jerry Castro for inspiring me to think bigger and reach higher.

Thank you to my siblings for your support and love: Meghan and Michael Houston, Marley and David, Elizabeth Catherine Wood and Tyler Wood, Jerry Castro Jr., Carolyn Elise Castro, and Jett Castro. Thank you Jack for the help from heaven. Thank you Aunt Teresa and Uncle Mark for sharing your love for living life.

I am indebted to the readers of my earliest drafts for their thoughts, support, and wisdom: Katy Dozier Fox, Lynn Carroll Looney, and Nathan O. Stringer.

Thank you for the endless fountain of encouragement, laughter, and friendship from Brett B., Savannah Jean Callies, Claire Gilbert, Andrea Kerns, Mark L., Meighan Middleton, Becca Murdock, Grace Paulino, Samantha Leigh Pirro, and Morgan Schmidtendorff. A special thank you for the love always from Karen Shea, Elizabeth Shea, and Hilary Shea.

For Maeve my daughter, I love you. May you hear the call inside you and trust it to guide your way.

To my husband, Danny Harlow, I love you and am grateful to share this life with you. Your constant support and partnership is the foundation of everything.

About the Author

Elise Keitz Harlow is a graduate of Pepperdine University where she earned her bachelor's and the University of Southern California where she completed her master's in Communication Management. *When Bone Melts* is her debut novel and was inspired by her time teaching English in Italy. She loves yoga, reading, the beach, and traveling. A Maryland native, she currently lives in Florida with her husband and their daughter.

Made in the USA
Middletown, DE
24 July 2024